VIRTUE AND VENGEANCE

Empire of Cinders Book 1

M.A. LIGUORI

Hydra
Publications

Hydra Publications LLC
Goshen, Kentucky 40026
www.hydrapublications.com

To Toni, my love and my light. Without your support, I would've accomplished nothing.

Also to Stuart Thaman, for his guidance and enthusiasm, and for giving my story a chance to be read.

VAUL TRIBE   SERKUT TRIBE   TIRAKULTAN TRIBE

NIDRAK TRIBE   **THE GRAY PLAINS**   VASKULTAN TRIBE
(THE GRAVELANDS)

HOWLER PASS

CYAN MOUNTAINS

SKYDEEP   BLACK GATE PASS

CRAGSPAWN

SNOWFLOWER   ÁMARANTH POINT

SILVERLEAF   ANIR MOUNTAINS

WHITECROW

THE STAR OF THE HOLLOW

COBALT   WINTERSUN   BLUE WOLF HILLS   ASTER FALLS
RIVER   HILLS

THORNBERRY   INDIGO COVE   GRAYLING RIVER

AMBER RIVER

FORESTYN   HORNS OF
VERMILLION   **STORMHAVEN**

PEARL RIVER   **RIVERWIND**

LAKEWOOD   SPARROC
MOUNTAINS

**CERULEAN
SEA**

THE AZURE

DEADMOON
VALE

WILLOWSEA

BARROWSTONE   BLACK SANDS
(THE REDLANDS)

ZIRCE   **SIJIA**

PROLOGUE

The hour was late, and the sun was a wash of blood on the horizon.

"It was you who broke the enemy," the bondsman said. "Your strategy that won this war."

"I told you it was luck," Anseth replied. "Nothing more."

Kirik pursed his lips as he guided his mare along the Gray Plains. He was a young man, a boy still in Anseth's eyes, but at twenty and three he was already considered a veteran of the tribe. In fourteen out of the twenty-six raids he had fought in the forward army. He'd lost half an ear at Ice Lake, and two fingers at Red Goat Hill. At the causeway of Iron River, he'd been stabbed so hard in the gut he had puked black blood for days.

"Luck or not, the vanguard is yours now," the bondsman said.

"I don't want it," Anseth told him.

"Why not? You know you deserve it. We're here now. This is it."

Anseth dismounted before the hill and tethered his gray roan among the ranks of juniper and pine. Kirik did the same. The bondsman stood half a head taller than Anseth but was only of middling height for a Vaskultan, and like many of the northern tribespeople, he was built broad and thick, with a head of long, knotted hair and a face as dark as beaten oxhide. The growing wind forced him to hold tight the top clasp of his overcoat. Well, Anseth *called* it an overcoat, but in truth, there was no Anirian word for the knee-length heavy wool garment the Vaskultans wore.

The air grew chillier as they climbed. It wasn't a difficult ascent, but Anseth was terribly cold and terribly tired, and beneath the layers of fur and boiled leather and wool, a nagging ache from the earlier battle continued to prod at his lower ribs. *A man's death is the only honest thing you will ever see in this life,* the Vaskultan chieftain had once told him. *The more you see it the less it becomes, until one day it is no more than a sunset, or the rolling of gentle clouds.* Anseth had only recently come to learn the grim truth of those words. The battle of Snake Tail Ridge had been the most violent affair of his life, and yet he bore it stoically, laboriously, like a butcher at his block. He didn't remember when, but at some point Anseth had no longer feared even his own death. Strangely enough, *that* scared him.

Near the summit the biting wind left Anseth grimacing despite the generous coating of mutton grease applied to his face. Little flora thrived here save some lowly sagebrush and needle grass, and the few trees he did see were stunted and gnarled. Anseth went to the nearest overlook, gazing out over the vast stretch of gray tablelands . . . his bleak and unforgiving home for the past eight years.

His eyes followed the undulating hills to the east, where bodies lay scattered along the base of the slopes, bodies of slain men from both the Vaskultan and Serkut tribes. Even now, after all these years, Anseth still had the urge to have his men buried, as customs to the south— Anseth's customs—dictated. But then he would remember: *the flesh descends to the Landforger, the spirit rises to the Skybringer.* It was a Vaskultan prayer and a Vaskultan tradition. The tribes of the north didn't retrieve their dead; no, here the deceased were to remain wherever their last breath was taken. There were no interments, no obsequies, no amnesties between warring tribes. Nothing. It was a simple yet undeniable truth of the north, and one of the many that Anseth had come to accept.

He moved alone through a stand of wild thicket, drawn by the call of a brook. The gentle waters glistened beneath the last touches of the setting sun. Anseth knelt on a lichened slab of stone, pulling off his worn wool gloves and pushing back the sable-trimmed hood of his overcoat. The water was cold and briny but refreshing on his face, and working quickly he washed and scrubbed at the caked blood on his wool sleeves. When he pulled on his gloves, he paused midway, watching as the wavelets reformed and rendered clear the contours of his reflection. *By the gods*, Anseth thought. The face in the water was unrecognizable.

Gone were the smooth features of his youth, leaving Anseth with those as hard as the land around him. A sloped and bony nose protruded between a pair of drawn cheekbones, while sunken eyes lay hidden beneath a brow of deep creases. His long, clumping nest of black hair looked as filthy as it felt, but now he could see where it was beginning to recede at the sides of the forehead. He was only thirty-six, and yet the face in the water looked a decade older.

It was true then: life on the Gray Plains—or the Gravelands, as it was known to outsiders—did age you twice what you were. The weather here was as austere as it was unpredictable, with summer temperatures shifting from raw heat to a harsh chill within minutes. And in winter, snowbanks were known to rise so high they could bury the tallest horse to its withers. For eight years Anseth had endured here, arriving first as a captive under the cruel fist of the Serkut tribe, and rising over time to become a celebrated commander of the rival Vaskultan tribe. How had Anseth, a small and unassuming southerner, attained such high rank among these northern barbarians? Certainly it was through his shrewdness in military strategy, but he couldn't deny a modicum of divine fortune.

He returned to Kirik at the overlook. His bondsman was a handsome man as far as Vaskultans go, though Anseth always thought he had a strange, almost reptilian look to him, surely because of his protruding lower jaw. "We should be celebrating this victory with our brothers, not freezing our goddamn pricks off up here," Kirik went on. "We have scouts for this, you know. Not that it matters, there's nothing out there. See? Not a single soul. The war's over, the Serkuts have surrendered. We have their chieftain clapped in a cangue. The survivors have long fled. You still think they'll somehow muster the strength to reform and strike back? I tell you I don't see it happening. You *broke* them. You broke their spirits and for that you deserve the van. Why would you refuse it? And don't you dare talk to me about impure blood. You are a Vaskultan through and through."

Anseth looked down. Kirik was right; he did break the Serkut tribe, and he did deserve to command the vanguard, certainly more than any other Vaskultan, including the chieftain's own son. Right now, because of Anseth, the victorious Vaskultans were raiding the Serkut encampment below, rounding up the surrendered and distributing the spoils and claiming the women and doing all the things that hardworking men did in triumph. It was a triumph that Anseth wanted to share, but couldn't. "I'm leaving, Kirik," he confessed at last.

"Don't do that. Don't jest with me, not now."

"It's no jest, my friend. I'm leaving the north, the tribe. I'm going home."

"This is your goddamn home," the bondsman said, frowning. When Anseth offered no reply to that, Kirik said, "The chieftain knows of this?"

"Not yet."

Silence spread between them for a time. *I'm going home,* Anseth repeated to himself. So strange, how he'd longed for this moment for years and years, and now that it had finally come, it wasn't so grand a feeling after all. Still, he missed his home, now more than ever. He missed the halls and walls and all the amenities afforded to a privileged son of aristocratic stock. He missed his wife and daughter and father and mother and brothers and even his sister, Nyvia. For the past eight years, everyone in the south had thought Anseth dead, killed at the battle of Black Gate Pass. Only his brother Alarin knew the truth. For years the two men communicated through secret letters couriered by secret riders, and for years Anseth had stood by his promise to return only when vengeance against the Serkut tribe freed him of his shame.

And now it had.

Overhead, twilight gave way to dusk, a radiant dusk, with the full moon gazing down like a great orange eye. Anseth brought out his leather skin and took a long gulp of Vaskultan blackmilk. The kumis was bitter on his tongue, but warm in his belly. He took another drink before stoppering it, then allowed his gaze to drift skyward once more. The moon was so large here on the Gray Plains, so dominant. *It's the autumn equinox, the harvest moon.* To the southern people, the moon on this day was a gift from the gods. It lent more light, which meant more time on the fields.

But Kirik, like all northmen, would never truly understand. How could he? The Vaskultans were nomads, hunters and raiders, not field hands and husbandmen. They were men of meat not grain. Men who lived without art or song or even a written word. Men whose only treasures were those obtained through theft or plunder, and men whose only banquets belonged to the wretched scavengers that dined on their fallen brothers-in-arms.

Not so back home. *Today is a day of celebration,* he thought, *a grand feast in a grand hall.* The Autumn Moon Festival showcased the finest in entertainment, from singers to jugglers to acrobats to funambulists and sword dancers and countless other talents. The memories rushed back at Anseth now, like morning sunshine pouring through opened shutters. There was wine—good Anirian wine, not this fermented black piss. Wine carefully aged in casks and barrels, then heated and spiced and served in ornate vessels. Anseth would spend the entire day in the company of his brothers and the highest-ranking civil and military officials, while cooks, carvers, servers, and waiters would shuffle busily around him, offering course after extravagant course. So many favorites: whitebait poached in wine and herbs, roasted pig and venison, parboiled sea cucumbers served in a salty broth. Each dish would be complemented by servings of spinach, sword beans, amaranths, hyacinth beans, and of course the radishes grown in the imperial hothouse. And the desserts! Certainly he couldn't forget about the cakes: steamed wheat, broomcorn, cakes in the shapes of leaves, hickory and oak and—

"That's strange," Kirik said. He was peering through a stranglehold of thicket, toward the woods nestled along the hills. "Look at that."

Anseth turned. Birds. Dozens of them, pheasants and grouse and snowcocks of various sizes and plumage, all emerging from the woods and either taking to the sky or gliding down the open slopes. Anseth motioned for Kirik to blast his horn and alert the others. His bondsman only smiled at that—until Anseth shot him a glare that killed his mirth. "They're just birds," the bondsman said, "what's the matter with you?"

"Not just birds," Anseth told the young man. "You think such a sudden flight is without meaning? No, those birds were startled by something in those woods, something large. Now blast the horn."

Kirik nodded but still seemed hesitant to obey. *Damn you for doubting me,* Anseth thought. He meant to grab the horn from the bondsman's belt, but then, just as he raised a hand, his eyes caught a dark mass of mounted men emerging from the shadows of the hillside trees. Serkuts.

"Blast the *goddamn* horn," Anseth shouted. "Do it, *damn it.*" He took off at once, racing back down the hill. He heard the horn come alive, a deep blast that resonated across the land like a spirit's mournful cry. Anseth mounted his roan and whipped the beast into a run. The wind screamed in his face, shrieking above the thunder of hooves. Bramble and bushes passed in blurs. It seemed like hours before his view finally opened up, and another before he could see the mounted Vaskultans under the lee of the mountain, struggling against the Serkut ambush. The low rumble in the distance became the sound of horsemen in battle. Bowstrings twanged and arrows flew like locusts on the wing, piercing and puncturing bodies and leaving them like tamped sprigs to blacken and die. Anseth could see the path blazed by the enemy's desperate charge, could see what could only have been the rescued Serkut leader galloping off to freedom.

No. It can't be, by all the gods in the goddamn heavens, this isn't happening. It was but an instant, and now everything was gone, ripped away like a doll from a child's hands. His plan of returning home, of seeing his wife and his brothers . . . all of it gone. There was only a dull ache inside him now. Above, the moon loomed over him, watchful and bright and enormously commanding. Anseth couldn't bear to look at it. *I was supposed to leave this wretched place,* he thought. *It was the end . . . it was supposed to be the end.*

BOOK I: MACHINATIONS

CHAPTER ONE

G rand Commandant Demien Mordall had a terrible headache. He stood on the upper story of the auditorium, in full imperial battledress, his gauntleted hands resting on the carved sandalwood balustrade. His eyes were drawn below, to the assembly of civil and military officials seated in the curved rows of lacquered trestle benches.

It was the annual Shadow Play of the Autumn Moon Festival, and the Imperial Theater was ripe with drunken energy. The vaulted ceiling extended three bays across, with streamers of dark silk racing across the exposed rafter tails of the pitched roof. Paintings and scrolls adorned the walls, floral masterworks all, and affixed to each of the four pillars were the gray-black banners of the Anirian dynasty, each emblazoned with the horned and bestial creatures called Sadralen. At the far end of the auditorium was the performance stage, a tall frame-work of stained elmwood fitted by a wide mulberry screen.

A few more hours, Demien told himself. The sweltering heat had long persuaded him to remove his halfhelm and undercap, letting loose a disheveled crop of chestnut hair. Beads of sweat dripped down his body, clinging to his silks and leathers and of course the heavy plates of his irritatingly cumbersome armor.

Still, it was a fine battledress: a blackened steel cuirass of imbricated scales, matching spaulders and vambraces and gauntlets, and a waist protector of lacquered lamellar. Lower, a pair of cuisses protected his thighs while greaves and boots secured his legs and feet. His officer's cloak was a flowing garment of distressed gray, not rich but rather homespun in appearance, with black trimmings and serrated hem edges that gave it a slightly ragged look. Such was the Anirian way.

Demien turned at the sound of the upper postern door opening. The Minister of Ceremony emerged, a portly man in loose gray robes that trailed in lengths behind him. To be fair, calling this man portly was a bit of an understatement, and yet Minister Thomen never once seemed hindered by his weight, always moving with a touch of zest in each step. He stopped at the balcony's overhang to address the crowd, his great belly pressed against the balustrade, his jowls jiggling with every trumpeting word: "I am honored to introduce our gracious host and most worthy lord and protector, Zantherei Athera, the Storm of the North, the Tamer of the West, and Lord Regent of the Anir."

Zantherei made his way inside, surrounded by his usual swarm of guardsmen and ministers and endless hangers-on. He threw a brief wave to the crowd before turning back to sit on an ornate, thronelike chair. He was a compact and muscular man, with an austere face and slightly wandering eye that made him look one part annoyed and another part angry. Beside him, and in blatant contrast to the regent's less-than-regal air and attire, stood the Lady Regent. Miriana Athera was like a stately foxglove in the springtime breeze, a beautiful woman in a fantailed gown of fine blue silk.

"The ample virtue of our courageous Lord Regent has awarded us yet another year of prosperity," Minister Thomen went on. Gifts were carried in and placed before the regent, gifts of fine agate goblets and blue-green obsidian bowls and small sharkskin boxes. The regent accepted them the same way a full man might accept another serving of mutton, but that mattered little to Demien. It was the gifts themselves that spoke clearly enough; they said it was Regent Zantherei Athera who ruled here, while the realm's true emperor remained voiceless in the dark.

I should go to him, Demien thought. He turned and walked down the aisleway, moving along the auditorium's high outer wing and down a narrow stairway that brought him behind stage. The energy was thick back here, a tense cacophony of voices and strings and random drum cracks. Attendants shuffled to and from their duties, fluttering like little moths beneath Demien's towering frame. In adjacent rooms, masked dancers rehearsed their techniques, artisans adjusted the steel rods of their donkey-skin puppets, and musicians pursed their lips and nodded as they made their final tuning adjustments.

Demien found Emperor Thavian Siven behind a five-panel sateen screen, standing before a pair of young retainers, his handsome consort Dahlia at his side and a dozen of his blue-cloaked imperial guardsmen lingering nearby. The emperor was a boy of sixteen, fair-haired and wiry and rather tall for his age. He stared absently as the retainers adjusted the lacing of his cord-and-plaque armor, archaic pieces now, but the standard protection of some four centuries ago. And while the thick plates did well to bulk the boy's frame, they did nothing to hide his face, which was unmistakably young and unceremoniously sullen, and deeply flushed with wine.

"We have long honored Lord Zantherei's valor and exceptional military prowess," Minister Thomen went on, his voice audible despite the commotion backstage.

The emperor frowned at what he heard. He snatched his goblet from a side table and took a long gulp. When he brought it down, Demien approached and placed a hand over the boy's wrist. "No more, Your Majesty."

The boy looked startled for a moment, but when he saw who it was he wrenched his hand free and scowled. "I'll do as I please, Lord Demien."

"A dram to calm his nerves," said a soft voice nearby. "No harm in that, is there, my lord?"

Demien turned his eyes upon Privy Counselor Vylas Voren. *Miriana's little watchdog,* he thought. *What is he doing here?* Vylas was a small man dressed in gray imperial robes just a hair too large for his frame. A black halfmask covered his left eye, further hidden by the long hanks of his soot-black hair. Demien disliked the man, but in all fairness he disliked any man who skulked in the shadows for scraps of information. Truly, such scavengers were the detritus of the realm, and Demien was about to tell him that, but then the Lord Regent's deep voice, from the upper auditorium, stole his attention. "Without my illustrious generals, I am without merit. It is only through them that I am able to succeed."

The audience cheered. The emperor's frown deepened. Beside him, the affectionate touch of his consort went ignored. His attention instead went to Demien. "Do you see how they love him?"

"He is the regent, Your Majesty."

The boy's bitterness was palpable. "And I am the *emperor.*" He gave a sigh and looked away. "By the gods he aggrieves me so."

Demien couldn't have the boy becoming so agitated—not here, not now, and not with Miriana's little counselor lurking about. Besides, it was too goddamn hot and his head ached too goddamn much. He just wanted to get through the rest of this evening as smoothly as possible. "Later, Your Majesty. We'll discuss this later."

That only seemed to fuel the emperor's hostility. "If the emperor cannot speak freely in his own hall, where then can he speak?"

Demien said nothing to that. He turned to Vylas, who was doing a fine job pretending not to take interest. "Counselor, spare us a moment." The one-eyed man hesitated, but withdrew.

Demien turned back to address the boy, but it was the boy who spoke first. "Let him tell the Lord Regent," he said. "I don't care. My indignities *must* be made clear."

"And they will be," Demien said. "The sacred throne will avail itself to you when the time is right, Your Majesty."

"*Tonight,*" the boy said at once. "After my performance, after I cast down the villain and rise as the hero, they will all see—"

"It's just a show, boy," Demien cut in. "A play. No more than that."

The boy gave no reply. He turned and gestured for his helm, a domed and damascened piece fitted with two ridged horns that corkscrewed up like those of a Sadralen. "You're wrong," he said at last. "You'll see. Don't give me that goddamn look. You'll see soon enough."

"See what?"

"The *truth*," the boy shot back. "The truth of my performance, and what it will reveal to the court. You'll see. When I emerge victorious from behind that screen, the audience will acknowledge the true and rightful ruler of the Anir. They'll rise and demand the Lord Regent to abdicate the—"

BOOOOOOM BOOM BO-BOOOOOOM. Drums snatched the words right from the boy's lips. The helm slipped from his hands, crashing soundlessly to the floor. *BOOOOOOM BOOM BO-BOOOOOOM.* Shelves and furnishings shook, bowls and vases and fine vessels trembled. *BOOOOOOM BOOM BO-BOOOOOOM.* Over and over again, a loud, pounding rhythm that could only mean the Shadow Play was soon to begin.

It seemed an eternity before the drums died away, and when they finally did, Demien was left with a hammering in his head twice as painful as before. Still, he couldn't complain about the dulcet melodies of the pan flutes and fiddles and zithers and bronze bells that all filled the hall now. He unfastened his winegourd from his belt and took a gulp, then turned his eyes back on the emperor. The boy had just slipped the helm over his cloth undercap. It looked rather impressive on him, but Demien Mordall was a seasoned man, a general, and the empire's Grand Commandant, and as such he saw the helmet for the garish and useless thing it truly was. In actual combat, a foeman's weapon could easily get tangled in those spiraling horns, and a single pull was all that was needed to send its wearer off his footing. Still, this was no battle but simply a staged event meant only to entertain, and for that, it should serve well enough.

The emperor stared at Demien while one retainer fastened the helm's leather straps and the other adjusted the bevor at his chin. "You still see me as a boy," he said.

"I see you only as you are, Your Majesty. The last of your name, the last scion of the Anir."

"Of age and meant to rule," he said. "You'll see, I'll be the greatest ruler the realm will ever know, greater than my father, greater than Thalastor even!"

"You *foolish* boy," Demien snapped. "Only a fool talks of greatness before actual accomplishment."

The look the emperor gave him was a mix of incredulity and abashment. It took him a while to react, and when he did, it was only to clang down the black faceplate of his helm. Instantly, the boyish face became that of a Sadralen, a bestial, leonine thing forged in a perpetual metallic snarl. "It's my time," he said, his voice hollow beneath the mask.

Demien sighed. *When did that boy begin to hate me so much?* "I will cheer for you, Your Majesty," he said, and with that, he withdrew.

Vylas was still milling about in the nearby corridor. Demien grabbed his robed shoulder and spun him about. "No more wine for His Majesty, is that clear, Counselor?" The little man nodded swiftly, his single eye wide with fear. Demien left him there and exited through the door curtain, moving with anger and with purpose. Attendants and guardsmen wisely stepped aside. Returning to the upper auditorium, he saw the Lord Regent's chair was empty. *Strange*, he thought, but said nothing of it as he took his seat among the other high ministers and councilmen.

Below, the soft glow of a single lamplight threw a handful of shadows onto the screen, shadows of masked figures in flowing garb who swayed and danced in rhythm with the soft music. Demien's eyes lost their focus. He'd seen all this before, many times, as he'd personally prepared the young emperor for his upcoming performance. He couldn't help but worry about the boy. Emperor Thavian was growing more and more restless each day, which meant he was putting himself in greater and greater danger. *Why can't the boy just be patient?* Yes, he had the rightful claim to the throne, but what did it matter if he wasn't alive to claim it?

It had always been Demien's duty to protect him, ever since the boy's father had lost his life in a plot of murderous intrigue. The traitorous group of officials had meant to murder the boy, too, but Demien single-handedly slayed them all, barefoot and in bedclothes and groggy from sleep. Well, not all . . . one man had managed to escape, a general by the name of Raas Dragath. The traitor had fled to the southern Redlands where he used his wealth and standing to gather the support of the populace and raise an army. To this day, Raas Dragath remained a threat to the imperial bloodline, but young Thavian didn't seem to care about that. His only concern was the goddamn throne, and the regent who refused to give it up.

A shadowed pair of Sadralen appeared on the screen. Hulking and powerful things they were, easily larger than the largest tiger, and probably three times as long. Not fur but scales covered their elongated bodies, scales like plates of armor, and when their maws opened they revealed fangs longer than a sabercat's. The two shadows crept and prowled with the music, their unseen puppeteers controlling them in a way that only a lifetime of practice could allow.

Soon, the pounding of the drums returned, guiding both the bowed and plucked instruments in an ominous direction. From the center of the stage rose the Villain. This was no puppet but the shadow of a man, a massive man, and in his massive hands he clutched a massive halberd. The Sadralen lowered their horned heads and began stalking him, their growls given to life by the low droning of two-stringed fiddles. Around and around and around the beasts moved—until, *BOOM,* they charged. The Villain's halberd cut an arc through the air. *SNNNICKKKK.* The Sadralen flopped to the ground and immediately fled, their frightened cries sounded by the skirl of reed pipes.

The display cowed the crowd into silence. Who could stop this man? A second shadow appeared behind the stage, spear in hand and adorned in cord-and-plaque armor and a horned Sadralen helm. Cheers and applause lifted the theater. "The Hero!" a man cried. "Our emperor the savior!" another shouted.

The two shadows, Hero and Villain, faced each other, poised and still. Demien's heart thumped in his chest. He knew how much this performance meant to the boy. Thavian had rehearsed these maneuvers for weeks and weeks, through soreness and pain and repeated bouts of self-doubt and failure. Demien wondered if it was enough. *Did he perfect his three-even stance and single hand parry and thrust? What about his lower sweeps, did he practice each and every step to mastery?*

All doubts vanished from Demien's heart the moment the Hero and Villain clashed. It was a beautiful exchange, two silhouettes crossing polearms in complete harmony with the driving music. It was a show of skill but it was also a dance, a warrior's dance, a dance of rhythmic beauty. *Clash. Clang. Clash.* The crossing of their arms was brought to life by the precise timing of chime and bell. Demien took note of the boy's technique. Both stance and step were sound. Every strike and every parry executed to near perfection, even as the two shadows started moving faster, propelled by the hastening tempo. Faster and faster they went, louder and louder, until the drums roared with powerful urgency, the strings wailing with dire necessity. At the height of all this excitement, tendrils of mist began creeping down the screen, slowly, growing thicker and thicker and thicker until at last . . . the shadows were gone.

The clashing ceased. The drums died and the music stopped. No wait, not the strings. Soft and mournful, the strings played on.

The mist broke apart like sunlight through a morning fog. The Villain was on his knees, a spear lodged in his belly. Nearby, the Hero unsheathed a shadowed saber with a gentle ring of cymbals. Wooden clappers accented his footfalls as he walked over to his fallen foe. The saber came up. The mist thickened once more. It was hard to see. Down the weapon went. The Villain fell but the mist took him at once, like a man wrapped in a funeral shroud. He was gone.

The crowd erupted. Wild cheers and drunken cries shattered the quiet like a steel hammer on glass. Attendants moved quickly to light the silver vermeil sconces along the walls of the theater. The Hero stepped out from behind the screen. No more a shadow, he stood gloriously before the crowd, his features hidden beneath that fierce Sadralen faceplate. Demien nearly forgot it was Emperor Thavian Siven under all that armor. *He looks as an emperor should. As the realm's very first emperor undoubtedly looked, some four centuries ago.*

The crowd began to chant. *"LONG LIVE THE ANIR! LONG LIVE THE EMPEROR!"*

Demien was on his feet now, along with the others around him, an act he didn't remember doing. *You were right, Thavian*, he thought. *I see it now . . . it is just as you said.*

"LONG LIVE THE ANIR! LONG LIVE THE EMPEROR!"

The emperor's hands went to his helm, his fingers working the leather straps. *Show them,* Demien thought. *Show them the true and rightful emperor of the Anir. They will demand the Lord Regent's abdication.* The straps came free. A deafening frenzy of cheers followed. Slowly, ever so slowly, the helm came up . . .

"LONG LIVE THE ANIR! LONG LIVE THE EMPEROR!"

The chant blazed on, but the face beneath wasn't the emperor's at all. It was the regent himself, Zantherei Athera.

CHAPTER TWO

When dawn broke, Alarin Athera was still seated at his writing desk, brushpen in hand, observing the dying murmurs of an oil lamp. He could hear the palace grounds bustle to life just as the morning drum tapered off into quiet. He shifted his weight to set the pen back onto its holder, wincing mid-turn at the sharp pain in his lower leg. A hand reached down—an instinctual response—though he only cursed when it met the familiar shank and socket of his carved wooden leg.

From an adjoining chamber, Kalen entered, one hand wiping the sleep off his pox-scarred face. He seemed to sense the discomfort in his master's bearing, as the young retainer always did, and he scurried off to a nearby house cupboard, its lacquered doors creaking as they opened. Just then a knock came from the main chamber door. Alarin turned to the sound of his guardsman's familiar voice, announcing the presence of the Minister Steward.

"My lord," the dour Minister Sydrian Rane said when Alarin

permitted entry. "Lady Nyvia requests your presence at the morning banquet."

Kind sister, never giving up on me, Alarin thought. "I must decline. I'll have it here, as usual."

The old minister bowed and left. Kalen returned to Alarin's side, a balm of warming oils in hand. He set it down to loosen the cords and straps of his master's limb. He was a good lad, small and diffident, and at twenty or so years he seemed more than content with a life of servitude. "You haven't slept, my lord," he said, his hand massaging the rounded stump that was once Alarin's right leg.

It had been eight years since the limb was taken from him . . . eight years and still he could hear the awful *snap* of bone, still feel the immense weight of his own horse crashing down upon him. Alarin had never forgotten what he saw when the others had dragged the beast off him. It was an unresponsive, alien thing—all twisted and misshapen and just . . . wrong.

Alarin sighed. Eight years and still the phantom limb ached. It had become an unpredictable pain, distal and pathless. On some days it was a stabbing, others it was a grinding, but on rare days like today, after a shift in the clime or a season's turn, it was a deep ache that pierced the very core of his being. His only relief came with sleep—and often in his dreams he could still walk, still ride, still command. Sometimes they were so vivid that upon his wake he would forget that he was a lamed man. But only for a moment or two.

Kalen wiped his hands on an old rag, then reattached the wooden limb to his master's stump, fastening a series of leather straps into interlocking bronze catches. Secured, Alarin stood, leaning on his carved blackthorn cane. The young retainer helped adorn his lord in his usual array of ministerial silks: an embroidered inner robe of muted black, a scrollwork sash and matching cuffs, and a wide-sleeved silk outer robe in distressed gray. His mark of office was a black jade seal worn about the neck, embossed and carved in the likeness of a horned Sadralen. The seal of the Imperial Advisor.

Kalen moved away to tend his own dress, quiet as a marmot. Alarin turned his attention back to the pile of silk letters stacked upon his writing table. His life revolved around these letters now, as his informants constantly relayed information from all corners of the realm. Especially troubling were the Zhoul people who continued to ravage their western-most borders, leaving an embittered provincial governor desperate for relief. Exacerbating the issue was that Governor Tavarin's petitions, along with those of his surrounding districts, had all gone ignored by Alarin's brother Zantherei Athera, the capital's ever-so-delightful Lord Regent. Alarin planned to speak with Zantherei about this matter, and soon.

He rose, shaking his head. *But not today.* He limped across the chamber, stopping below a curved archway to unbolt the door. The stairway beyond rose in a gentle incline. His residence was the old clock tower that once oversaw the imperial district; it'd been aban-doned when the newer tower was built to the north. Since taking occu-pancy, Alarin had all the machinery removed, the gear-wheels and rotating manikins, the time-keeping shafts and bearings, the spokes and scoops, the chain drive and clepsydra tank. In place he'd built private alcoves and stairways, and now used the top level as a private observa-tory, with a bronze armillary sphere to gauge heaven's celestial entities.

He emerged onto the rooftop now, inhaling the crisp autumn air. Rising sunlight flooded the sky in a radiance of pastel hues, oranges and pinks and touches of gold that lined the big bloated clouds. Gusts of wind wreathed him as he stepped closer to the terraced edge. From here, he had a grand view of a grand capital. The Star of the Hollow, or simply, the Hollow.

Walls upon walls made up the wards upon wards of the city; walls of stone outer shells and tamped, earthen underbellies. They protected —and segregated—the crisscrossing avenues that ran in north-south axes, broken occasionally by canal or streamlet. In the market squares, commerce was already stirring, as citizens moved to and from the various inns, smithies, merchant stalls, brothels, and gambling dens. Farther out rose the city's outer walls, an impressive perimeter of battlements, sentry pavilions, gates, and watchtowers, encased all by a protective moat. The north-south walls ran impeccably straight, while those east and west meandered down in curves. The latter was dictated by the course of the Cobalt River, a lesser arm of the Grayling, with the former constructed to mirror the pattern. As pleasing as the symmetry appeared, the western length was in fact shorter in height, as it stood on a depression that allowed for the drainage of rainwater and sewage.

Alarin's eyes wandered beyond the outer walls, at the newer suburban developments, the roadside inns and thatched-roofed farmhouses and the endless rows of threshing fields. The bisecting highways were staggered by checkpoints, most already dotted with oxcarts and porters. Farther in the distance the waterways widened—and it was just clear enough today to see the distant merchant junks bobbing in the trough of the rough autumn swell.

Alarin observed it all absently. In truth, a strange feeling of dread pulled at him today. It wasn't the usual affairs that troubled him . . . no, it was the Shadow Play, and that despicable little act Zantherei had put on. Alarin knew he wasn't the only man displeased by what had happened that day.

He returned to the inner chamber of his private quarters. A handful of attendants were moving about inside, some cleaning his washbasin, others sweeping and replacing the rushes. Servers entered bearing trays and dishes. Minister Sydrian appeared in the entranceway, offering a solemn smile. "Forgive me, my lord, but the lady insisted." Behind him, in the dimness there, stood Alarin's sister.

Nyvia was a small woman, dark of hair, plump of figure, and born with a face that could only be considered comely because of her highborn status. She wore a high-collared blouse of black silk, a gray pleated skirt, doeskin heels, and a wide-sleeved outer jacket embroidered in the puffy white petals of cloudfalls, mystical flowers known to have magical healing properties. If only those cloudfalls still existed today . . .

Despite her lovely garb, Nyvia looked rather awful. Her face was sapped of color, her eyes red and swollen as though from crying. Such was expected, with Father's death so imminent. Alarin meant to address her, but his attention was diverted by his breakfast of cullers and dried scallop porridge, which was served with a glazed celadon vessel of wine. His stomach groaned at the very sight of it all.

He'd already swallowed a few bites before she finally approached. She moved slowly, her eyes stealing quick glances of her surroundings, like a cautious tomcat in an unfamiliar place.

"You come bearing news," he said, chewing. "Of Father, is it?"

Nyvia's nod was slow and sorrowful. "Master Lorian can do no more. The Minister of Faith is with him now."

Alarin swallowed and took a long drink. The wine had an ideal taste, fully formed and tannic, yet abundantly fruity. "His tomb waits beneath the northern mountain," he said. "The coffins are decorated, tunnels prepared, instruments arranged, weapons—"

"He asks for you, Alarin."

Alarin paused. He had not spoken to Lasarin Athera since he'd given Zantherei the regency. How could his father have been so heartless? Alarin was the eldest son—to reject the elder in favor of the younger was to plant the very seeds of strife. Still, Alarin never faulted his brother for his father's ruling, though his father he would never forgive. *I am the heir apparent,* Alarin thought. *The regency belongs to me by right.*

"A brief audience," she said. "Please, Elder Brother."

Alarin chewed on the golden-brown cruller, ignoring her for a time. "Old bones," he said at last. "Pointless to rattle."

"Not to him," she told him.

He took another bite, swallowing before he continued. "Zantherei's the Lord Regent, and I have nothing to say about it."

She seemed insulted by the way he said that. "Why would you? Your brother has done well to keep our realm safe."

Alarin scoffed. "He's done better to keep it in his own hands." He paused to sigh. "My dear sister, the Athera clan has held name for five generations, gaining allies and followers in all areas of the realm. Everything Father has done was to better serve the House of Anir. Everything our brother does is to better serve himself."

"Zantherei serves the Anir," she said. "What are you trying to say? He will abdicate."

"When? When will he?" He shook his head and stopped her before hearing her trite answer. "I once thought the same, but no more. Not since his little charade at the Shadow Play." His voice was cold, colder than he'd meant it to be, but he was too prickled with irritation to care.

She shrugged. "Your brother did what he thought was best. His Majesty had too much wine. He was ill."

"He was *plied*," he said at once. "It was all planned. Don't you see? Our brother has done a terrible disservice to the Anir."

"Disservice? The emperor is still a boy," she argued.

"A boy of age to rule," he said. "Sister, don't be so blind. At sixteen I was already serving in the Black Pine regiment." It was a shock unit of cavalry, the most experienced soldiers of the empire. Alarin Athera later became the youngest man to ever take its command, leading veterans thrice his age.

"I remember," she said. "As I remember the man you were then." A frown found her face.

Her words stung, but only because there was truth to them. He was looking down now, looking anywhere except at her. The silence was unusually awkward. Appetite gone, he signaled to his attendants and absently watched them remove the tableware.

Nyvia turned to leave but instead seemed to think twice of it. She looked back at him, her voice pleading. "Grant your father this request, Alarin. I beg you, while he still draws breath."

Alarin scowled at her. "I've too much to do," he said. There was something about Nyvia . . . he was colder to her than anyone else, despite her tenderness. He wasn't sure why.

She crossed her arms. "He is your father, Alarin. All other obligations can wait."

"Can they? Funeral expenses, labor designation, logistics—"

"Alarin—"

He slammed his fist on the table. "*WHAT* do you want from me?"

Nyvia stiffened at his temper.

"What do you think will happen, if I go to him?" he went on. "Do you think he'll suddenly recover—or that I'll somehow grow back my leg? Do you think he and I will go frolicking through the imperial wood, perhaps procure some mulberries and bake a pie?" His hands were trembling. *Stop it. You were once a greater man than this.* He turned away from her. "Just go, Nyvia. Please."

Silence hung between them like a cold fog. She turned, her skirts swirling about her. Defiant footfalls stomped to the door. As he watched her go, Alarin suddenly felt guilty. "Nyvia . . ."

She spun, her eyes near tears. "I'm your *sister*, Alarin. I'm as much as your blood as your brothers. I want only to help you." She remained there for a moment, as if expecting some reply. But then the moment passed, and she turned and withdrew.

Alarin let her go. At length he went to rise, only to stagger from the sudden pain. He groaned. There was a rustle from nearby, and within moments Kalen stood beside him. "Here, let me help you into bed, my lord. You should rest now. You need to rest."

"I'm fine," Alarin said, but accepted the help all the same. The featherbed was warm and soft and Alarin sank into it, exhaling in relief. His eyes were heavy—he must've been more tired than he thought. Kalen draped the silk coverlets over him. "You are a good man," Alarin said. "Too good for an old goat like me."

"You're not a goat, my lord," Kalen said, polite as ever. Alarin smiled at that, though it faded quickly as more pressing matters came to mind. "I'm expecting word from the north. Anything at all and you wake me, understand?"

"Of course, my lord."

"Will you be at the academy today?" The boy studied as an apprentice physician.

"Yes, my lord," Kalen answered.

Alarin felt himself beginning to slip away. "Before you go . . . my petition to Zantherei, please send it."

"Already have," the young man replied. "Yesterday, just before first watch. It was your request, my lord."

"Oh it was? Oh, very good then." Alarin yawned and mumbled to himself for a bit, before saying no more. And as the gentle light of morning filtered in through the surrounding windows, he slowly drifted off into the darkness of sleep.

CHAPTER THREE

T he riders returned before daybreak.

Anseth Athera had been among the first to hear the reports, but among the last to respond to the chieftain's verbal summons. He was moving through the encampment now, Kirik at his side, their sheepskin boots crunching across stubbly gray grasses whose tips glistened with hoarfrost. All around, the Vaskultans were stirring to tend the duties of a new day; it was a collective process, like a crew of shipmates churning to life some great seagoing junk.

The predawn wind was furious. Hooded, faceless figures passed him, men and women huddled beneath layers of heavy felt and worsted wool. It was one of those rare days, so cold that your hair might freeze to the ground while you slept, or if you looked carefully enough, you could see tiny diamonds of ice forming in the air. Even in his thick oxhide gloves, heavy layers of fur and lambswool and more fur, Anseth was *still* so goddamn cold.

He was exhausted, too. He'd spent half the night riding with men still wounded and weary from the recent days of battle. They'd ridden on and on until they could ride no longer, and even then they were forced to press on. Only after a man had died on his saddle did the Vaskultan chieftain relent. And despite Anseth's exhaustion, sleep did not come that night. Instead he'd lain awake in his private yurt, cold and tired and wholly dispirited. And while Kirik had wakened the next morning grumbling about his aches, Anseth would've gladly traded that for a few hours of uninterrupted rest.

He spotted the Vaskultan chieftain standing on the outskirts of the encampment, overseeing the amassing ranks. Lord Volduk was a man blessed with both frame and height, but it was his prized and luxurious desert bear hide that made his presence unmistakable. The golden fur covered him to his knees, concealing the boiled leather armor and layers of wool beneath.

The chieftain's son stood beside him. Both men shared the same build, but where Lord Volduk's face was broad and fierce, Dariok's looked strangely withered, like the puffy-eyed face of an old man—or as Kirik once put it, the face of a shrew, starving and shriveled and plagued with mange. Yes, Kirik was an amusing fellow at times.

The chieftain and his son were arguing as usual. Anseth was so focused on the two men that he nearly collided into a stray buckling. *Stay alert*, he told himself, watching a ragged urchin of no more than ten blindly scamper for the goat's halter. Anseth heard Kirik say something from behind, but the wind was too strong so he simply continued on.

Lord Volduk spotted Anseth and approached. He draped a massive arm around Anseth's shoulders, drawing him close and walking in step. "The Serkuts are holding up in the White Throat Mountains." Close as they were, the chieftain had to yell over the gale.

"How many?" Anseth asked.

"No more than three hundred." His beard poked at Anseth's face. It was wiry and black and strong like the bristles of a boar.

Dariok approached, looking as bothered as he always did whenever Anseth was near. "Best to surround them," he told his father. "Give no chance of escape."

The chieftain's eyes narrowed beneath the thick fur of his hood. "No, like I said, we must draw them out and take them in the lower passes." He turned his head back to Anseth, removing his arm. "You understand, Revek?"

The name Anseth didn't exist in the north. He was called Revek, a name given after Lord Volduk's raid had freed him from the Serkuts, six or seven years ago. If such a word had any special meaning to it, Anseth didn't know it.

Dariok said, "Father, they're only a few hundred men, weak and half-starved. A stratagem is not needed to take the Serkut chieftain's head."

"A stratagem is *always* needed," Lord Volduk said. Dariok scowled at that, and tempers flared as another altercation arose. Anseth turned away to study the Vaskultan ranks. It was a regiment of about fifteen hundred men, divided into center and wings and rearguard, followed by the women and children and remounts and standard bearers. They had no supply train.

Behind them, dawn broke, and Anseth had to shade his eyes to discern the face of General Severak standing at the foreranks. They called him Severak the Bonesplitter, and not because he was good at knitting footwear or telling charming little stories to children. Still, despite his name, and despite his powerful build and angry, hawkish face, Severak was a rather placid man, levelheaded and likeable. He reminded Anseth of some of the northmen that had settled along the Anirians borderlands, those that became peaceful from years of sedentary life. Anseth's father used to refer to these types as 'clean' men, because they weren't nearly as violent and savage as the barbarians farther north. But make no mistake, Severak was as unclean as the rest of these Vaskultans.

"You take the left wing," he heard Lord Volduk tell his son. "Severak takes the right."

Dariok looked puzzled. "What of the van?"

Volduk's gaze fell on Anseth.

Dariok's fury came at once. "You're giving him *MY* soldiers—"

"Your soldiers?" Lord Volduk's face darkened. He looked his son up and down, his eyes narrowing as the wind tossed about the snarled braids that hung past his shoulders. "I thought *I* still ruled this tribe." From beneath the parting of fur and wool, he brought out a talisman, which was nothing more than a leather thong attached to a round, palm-sized stone, soft blue on one side, earthy brown on the other. There were no thrones and no crowns here in the north. The entire tribe was ruled only by this crude little thing called the Earthstone.

A Vaskultan could win the Earthstone by declaring a blood challenge. Chieftain and challenger would fight to the death in what was called a cage of bones. Anseth had never seen this cage erected, as no one was foolish enough to challenge Volduk's might. And even though time seemed to be catching up to the great chieftain, Volduk was obviously still a formidable opponent, so it was no surprise when Dariok backed down. And yet the chieftain's son just couldn't accede to his father's command. "You cannot give the supreme command to southern blood, Father," Dariok said.

"He is a Vaskultan, same as you," Volduk said.

"No, he's not. Look at him, the runt's smaller than most women. What do you think the Serkuts will do to him?"

Now Anseth's own pride was pricked. He stepped forward to object, but Lord Volduk's upraised hand stopped him. The chieftain said, "Revek, tell my son why I don't want to take the enemy in the mountains."

The question caught him unaware, and in his hesitation Dariok sprang forward to argue. "I don't care what—"

Volduk cut him off. "Please, Revek, tell him."

Anseth said, "It's hemmed-in ground, difficult terrain. It matters not how outnumbered they are. In such conditions, a small force can overcome a much larger body."

"Yes," Volduk said, nodding. He turned back to his son, his voice edged in cold steel. "Even on the run, the Serkuts are still dangerous. We must draw them down to more accessible terrain. Revek will lead."

Dariok's glare took a stab at Anseth before he turned it back on his father. "But I am your son."

"I treat men based on merit, not blood."

"You treat him as the prized fucking colt!" He spat at his father, but it was stolen by the wind. "You bring shame upon your own blood, to go against your own son."

Lord Volduk clenched his jaw, goaded to anger as only Dariok knew how to goad him. More words were exchanged and before long the two went back to arguing, their breath steaming in the frosty air. Anseth went to intervene but Volduk shrugged him off. Severak and a few others managed to finally break them apart. The shouting went on, though Dariok soon ran out of things to say, and so he kept repeating, "The van is mine, the van is mine." Over and over again.

"*I don't want it,*" Anseth shouted. No one seemed to hear him, so he shouted it again and again until finally Lord Volduk stopped struggling and turned about, his face red as bloodroot sap. "You don't want the van, Revek?"

"Lord, I am honored but—"

"*Spare* your false humility," he boomed, his wrath both sudden and terrifying. "Do you not accept?"

"He said no," Dariok blurted.

"Be silent," Volduk told his son. Then to Anseth: "Speak."

Anseth had to be careful here. He didn't want to insult the chieftain any further than he already had. For all his strengths, Lord Volduk was a volatile man, not the sort you'd want to bring to anger. "I want to lead, lord," Anseth told him. "But I must not act with self-seeking ambitions. I must consider what is best for the tribe. Your son is right. He's better suited for the task."

Lord Volduk looked deeply disappointed. Dariok put his hand on his father's shoulder, to gentle him. "He speaks the truth."

"I said *be silent,*" Volduk snapped, shoving him off.

"I am the only man worthy of such command," his son shot back. "You know it, the others know it, too."

"Only if by right of birth," his father said with a scowl. "But every man here knows what you truly are, Dariok."

"And what is that?" he questioned. When Volduk didn't answer Dariok paused and seemed to rethink his words. Finally, he said, "I will prove my worth. Allow this of me, Father. Give me the van. If I fail, I offer my own head in reply."

"Do not make a jest out of so bold an oath."

"It is no jest." Something sharp appeared in his hand, a glint of steel there. The dagger ran down his palm, his face betraying no hint of discomfort as the flesh sliced open. He raised his open hand for his father to see. Droplets of bright blood splashed onto the earth. "As the Landforger devours my very essence, so too does it attest to my oath."

Volduk studied the wound, his eyes small and shadowed beneath the windswept fur of his hood. Finally, he nodded. "Revek, take the left," he said. Then he turned to his ranks, addressing the soldiers while holding up Dariok's bloody palm. "My son has made an oath, and his blood shall stand as his word. He will return with the traitor's head, or forfeit his own."

CHAPTER FOUR

Two miles from the capital, the Anirian army drilled on a gentle slope before the steep headwall of a cirque, surrounded by hills and valleys and earth-eaten gulches. Perfect terrain for training soldiers, but horrible going for a lamed man like Alarin Athera. Still, he had no choice; again and again his requests for a private audience with Zantherei had gone ignored.

In summer, the pathway's bisecting meadows brightened with radiant wildflowers, but right now it was the warm autumn hues that ruled the land: the reds and yellows of maple and larch, the greens and greys of the subalpine cone-bearers. The small and stunted hills were forested at the western trailhead, but grew more and more bare as they climbed toward the white-crowned chain of the formidable Anir Mountains. It was from these very mountains the first men had descended. Four centuries later and still the Anirian people flourished, spreading north as far as the Gravelands, east as far as the Black Sands of Sijia.

Kalen walked steadily beside his master. The young physician had insisted on a litter, but Alarin of course refused that. *Infirm or not, I'd rather not greet my brother in such a vulgar way,* he thought. Still, it was a decision he was beginning to regret. His phantom pain grew more intense after each step; it mattered not how lightly he moved or how much weight he placed on his cane.

A covey of grouse drew his eye, passing just over the timberline. He could hear the clangor of steel now, that and the low rumble of voices, and just over the next rise Alarin could see the ranks of conscripts. These were not fighting men at heart, but men who, from the moment they took up arms, counted down each day of their two years of service before finally being sent home. Most were simple farmers, men whose only concern was returning to their lands without disabling injuries. Agrarian life was taxing enough on a man's body— for a cripple, well, he would be all but worthless. Sadly, it was better for such a man to die on the battlefield. At least then his surviving clan might receive a bit of monetary compensation, usually a small amount but still undoubtedly better than what a disabled farmer could provide.

A detachment of crack soldiers drilled on a higher plateau to his left, strapped in leather masks that allowed only the tiniest breathing hole in the center of the mouth. The higher altitude and lower oxygen intake was said to strengthen a man's endurance and harden his spirit, but Alarin, who'd endured such agonizing training more times than he cared to recall, never noticed any benefit. In fact, he thought it rather harmful to deprive any man's lungs of precious air. *We don't form our ranks like we once did, and we certainly don't bear the same weapons or equip the same armor. Why then, do we still suffer the same antiquated training exercises?*

Alarin observed the familiar switches brandished by the arms instructors, remembering back when he himself stared at the very end of those weapons. By the gods, that was a lifetime ago. A time when the prodigious young Alarin stood as the rightful heir to his father's legacy. Certainly no one thought he would one day become a cripple, and certainly no one thought this cripple would one day lose his right to the regency to his younger brother.

He found Zantherei Athera standing amid the flutter of banners.

The hulking man was clad in black-scaled lamellar armor, his gray military cloak both ragged and worn and made to look that way. He was not so tall as Alarin but built thick as a gaur, with a deep-set skull, powerful jaw, and angry brown eyes. Father had often said Zantherei resembled more his late uncle in appearance, but Alarin never saw the likeness. Probably because he only remembered his uncle during the man's declining years, when he was fat and suffering from gout.

Alarin came to stand at Zantherei's side, but only after a long moment did his younger brother acknowledge him, and when he did it was with a look that seemed to beg the question: *what are you doing in my yard, my crippled brother?*

"Ignore my petitions all you want," Alarin said to him. He did his best to sound as firm as a tired old cripple could sound. "But I'll not give up so easily."

Zantherei gave no reply. Alarin eyed the Lord Regent's prized saber sheathed at his hip. Sunburst was once his father's sword, and once meant for Alarin's hands. It was a fine weapon, an eight-surfaced blade plated in chromium and set into an amber hilt with matching pommel. It was both longer and lighter than the average saber, which of course spoke of the skill of the smith who had forged it. Often it was the smallest details that provided such a perfect balance in a weapon— knowing precisely when to cool the tip, or how much carbon to infuse in the steel.

"I come here to avoid the endless prattle of the court," Zantherei said.

"Is that how you see your Imperial Advisor?"

"No, Elder Brother." He crossed his arms and said no more, obviously in no mood for idle chat.

Alarin wasn't either. "There are growing concerns that must be addressed," he told him. "For one, Lord Tavarin's petitions—how long will you ignore our good provincial governor?"

Something on the field caught Zantherei's eye, and he turned to shout an order to the appropriate instructor, who quickly heeded it. Afterward he said, "Until fealty is paid."

"You know his treasury runs empty."

"Empty because he gave it away," he snapped. "The man's a fool to think the Zhouls wouldn't return after a taste of such riches."

Alarin sighed. Yes, Lord Tavarin had erred in thinking he could bribe the raiding Zhoul people into peace. But that was in the past now. "Brother, our western borders are buckling; soon they will breach."

"I've already sent reinforcing regiments," Zantherei replied.

"That was last summer, over a year ago," Alarin said.

"Yes, and last summer the Zhouls were but a rabble of undisciplined men, ripe for submission." His voice was hoarse and hard, and his irritation was plain to see. "But Tavarin's done nothing but fail. The man's a sheep. A sheep cannot lead a pack of wolves."

"Then shepherd him, Brother. He is still your vassal."

Zantherei cursed, but not at Alarin. He sprang forward at something he saw on the drilling grounds. Alarin followed with his eyes. A weapons spar between two young soldiers had ended with the loser on his knees, grimacing as blood poured down his nose, which, by the way both eyes had swelled and empurpled, was obviously broken.

Zantherei ordered him punished. Not because the young man had been beaten, but because he'd failed to execute a basic defensive technique with the long-handled saber—the scooping and parrying of a strike, a core technique learned during the first months of drilling. Such a poor display had obviously infuriated Zantherei, and so the boy stood to face a terrible flogging. And when it was done and the poor soldier carried off, Zantherei offered a stern reproach to the others. "The next offender will have his bones peering through his skin," he promised.

"You are too harsh, Brother," Alarin said when Zantherei returned to his side.

"Harsh? These men will be filling the ranks of our most elite divisions. Do you think we have room for impetuous fools who falter on basic techniques?"

"They are still young—give them time."

Zantherei's eyes narrowed. "Tell me, Elder Brother, would you feel confident heading into battle with that soldier at your side? Would you trust him with your life? I know it's been a while, but surely you must remember what it's like to take the field."

Alarin gritted his teeth at that little jab.

"Are we finished?"

"No," Alarin said. "There's something else. Something you should know."

Zantherei nodded impatiently. "Go on then."

Alarin went to speak, but found it difficult to get the right words out. "I tried to remain silent. But I can't. Not anymore. Not after what you did."

"What are you talking about?"

"The Shadow Play," he said at last. "I heard all about your little farce." He shook his head in disappointment. "A warning, Brother. For every hundred or so men who cheered for you that night, do not doubt there were two or three who stood with hatred in his heart."

Zantherei took a quick step back, as if Alarin were an enemy. "Elder Brother, your warning sounds more like a threat."

Alarin sighed at that. His brother's intransigence was always expected, and always tiresome. "It is but a warning. You would do well to heed it as such."

Zantherei studied Alarin silently. At length he said, "You are my brother, and I will not punish you for your words, however treasonous they may sound." A shadow passed across his face. "Perhaps in time you will learn to accept me as the rightful heir."

Rage filled Alarin's heart. "This isn't about the *goddamn regency*." He was trembling so much he thought Zantherei might notice. "You know, Brother, I pity you. Funny—the lame man pitying the able. But I do. I pity you because you are blind to the darkness that is stretching over this city." He turned and stormed off—or tried to storm off rather, but as a cripple he simply hobbled off. When Kalen rushed to his side, Alarin pushed him away, hard, harder than he meant to. "I don't need your help," he scolded. "Just go. Leave me alone." The young retainer looked confused for a moment, but disappeared as ordered. Alarin could feel the eyes of the onlookers—conscripts and veterans and arms instructors all watching curiously as Alarin limped by. *That's it, get a good look at the goddamn cripple*, he thought. *I don't care anymore.*

The walk back to his quarters was long and painful. He hoped

Kalen might be waiting with some warming oils and perhaps a flagon of wine, but no, the young physician was nowhere to be found. Alarin removed his cloak but missed its hanging peg. He left the garment on the floor and settled onto his featherbed, removing his wooden limb and taking comfort in the swell of relief that suffused him. But even as his physical aches began to ebb, the torments of his mind only rose in their place. He lay there for some time, sleepless and drowning in the roaring riptide of his own insufferable thoughts. And when nightfall flooded the empty chamber, Alarin leaned over and lit a bedside taper, then watched the hours slowly melt it away.

CHAPTER FIVE

At dawn, they found horses.

Dappled and dun mares milling about the flat of the pass, still saddled and bridled, grazing at the sparse bunch-grasses. They were not startled by the presence of men, as was expected. "Bring them in," Dariok ordered at once.

Ansetheral Athera observed with his head lowered against the wind. The Vaskultans had reached the foothills of the White Throat Mountains. Here, the Serkuts had abandoned their mounts for the higher slopes, where the terrain grew narrow and difficult. When Dariok heard this he'd only gloated over their desperation, but Anseth wasn't so confident.

Scouts spent the morning hours detailing the surrounding uplands. Dariok decided they were to follow and take the enemy on foot. Upon hearing that, Anseth couldn't hold his tongue any longer. "Lord, I suggest you take caution. They have a considerable advantage in this terrain."

Dariok's sneer made him look uglier than usual. "Their claws are dulled, it's best to strike before they find a way out."

Anseth shook his head. "Remember your father's words."

"His words aren't worth the wipe of my bunghole," he retorted. "The man's getting old, he's obviously losing his thirst for battle."

"Lord Volduk is still the chieftain of this tribe," Anseth reminded him, rather coldly.

Dariok paused and pointedly turned his puffy eyes on Anseth. The hatred in them was downright palpable, but Anseth dared not look away. It was Severak Bonesplitter who finally broke the silence. "Revek's right, lord. Besides, you looked about ready to piss yourself when the old man challenged you." He added a snicker for good measure.

"Eat my prick," was all Dariok said to him. It was amazing how Severak could get away with such blatant disrespect, even if it were in jest. They were like brothers, these two, always bickering and yet fiercely loyal in the face of an outside threat. "I let my father have his day," he added. "The Skybringer knows he hasn't many left."

"Still, I think it best if we draw the enemy to us," Anseth told him.

"I don't give a goat's bleating arse what you think," Dariok said. His gloved finger jabbed at the distant standards of the waiting ranks. "You see those yak tails? Those are *mine*. My standards. You understand that, runt? And I say the best way to catch a wounded snake is to invade its den." His eyes flashed darkly, and his cracked lips spread in cruel satisfaction. "Kaigon, take the right. I am relieving the runt of his wing." When the robust General Kaigon nodded, Dariok's eyes fell back on Anseth. "You will hold the rear and protect the remounts, understand, runt?"

The insult was egregious. "How dare you—I am one of Lord Volduk's most esteemed generals. I broke the entire Serkut army at Snake Tail Ridge!"

"I don't care," he said. "When I am chieftain no pale-skinned pissant will *ever* hold rank over one of our own. Now get out of my sight."

Anseth spent the remaining daylight hours perched alone on a hillcrest, his discontent alleviated somewhat by the humbling view. Snow-helmed peaks shouldered one another like the scales of an open pinecone, their great stone spurs stretching out in all directions. Streams and tarns pierced their flanks and shimmered in the light. Anseth watched it all while absently sucking out the milk curd that had churned in his leather skin. Afterward he picked at the nearby sage-brush and watched the occasional goshawk or upland falcon soar over-head. More than once he heard the echo of male mountain sheep as they clashed horns in the distant ranges.

Severak came to him at dusk. He wore his usual black wolf fur over his coat and armor, his hawkish face concealed beneath the dark trimming of his hood. "Dariok's a snot-dragging fool, I know," he muttered.

Anseth shook his head disappointedly. "He's putting our men in unnecessary danger. Is he that arrogant or just stupid?"

Severak gave a shrug of indifference. "The Serkuts are huddled along the high eastern ridge, no more than a few hundred by the count of their cookfires. Dariok plans to strike from the front, while I am to lead a detachment from the west." He studied the orange sky for a long moment. "We're moving tonight."

"Tonight?" Anseth questioned. "The terrain is treacherous enough in the day—is he mad?"

Severak shrugged again. "Probably," he simply said.

The night was still and cold, and the moon was a wildcat's eye peering through a scrim of blue-black clouds. Anseth watched the Vaskultan regiment vanish along the sloping ridges below the snow line. He wished he didn't care for these men so much—he really shouldn't care, in truth. It was only a matter a time before he freed himself of this goddamn place anyhow. Still, most of these men had become brothers to him, treating him as a fellow Vaskultan even when he didn't feel like one. And Lord Volduk . . . well, in some ways the chieftain had become a second father to Anseth.

The initial reports were encouraging. The ranks had covered more ground than expected, as the upland paths proved not nearly as treacherous as anticipated. Not a single injury was reported. *It's more than what could be said of the rearguard*, Anseth mused. During the idle hours a soldier had broken an ankle after a fall from a crag that housed a raptor's nest. Another man nearly tumbled off a cliff chasing a fox. Anseth had shaken his head and ignored the urge to discipline his men. He knew they were simply bored and cold and restless. Soon enough they would drink their fill of blackmilk and curl cozily in the warmth of their yurts, dreaming of conquest.

A distant rustle interrupted his thoughts. He turned about, eyeing the hills to the southwest. A dark mist had settled over the landscape, obscuring all but the closest pathways. He felt something there, something in the semidarkness. "Stay here," he told Kirik, rising.

"Now what?"

Anseth motioned for a torch. "It's nothing. Stay with the rearguard."

The path twisted and turned down the hill, leading him to a narrow passage. He stopped here, waited. Nothing. The area was as still as the night. *My mind's toying with me.* He waited a bit longer, making sure of the silence, then turned and headed back.

He got only a few yards before someone appeared on the path—a tall figure, though a bit hunched from the cold. "Kirik," Anseth said, groaning, "I told you to stay there—what is the matter with you?"

No reply. Anseth stepped forward and extended the torch. Warm light washed over a man in a tattered coat and mismatched clothes. Their eyes met. Cold eyes, hollow and unfamiliar. *Do I know you?* Anseth felt something tickle at the back of his neck, a chill beneath his many layers. His heart hammered to life. "You're not—"

The man lunged at him.

Anseth threw up his hands, but the attacker's weight punched the breath from his lungs. The torch fell. He couldn't see. Anseth clawed at the man's arms but couldn't pry the bastard off. He reached inside his coat for the dagger sheathed on his belt. He came out stabbing, again and again, a blind fool in the dark. Finally the blade bit into something soft, but then Anseth lost his footing and the attacker fell atop him.

Scrambling, Anseth turned and stabbed again. He struck something hard, a stone perhaps, something that shot bolts of pain through his fingers. The blade fell from his hand. His attacker rose over him. All Anseth could think to do was shout, and shout he did. The man quailed, hesitating, and Anseth scrabbled off into the darkness.

Serkut—that was a Serkut. But how? He forced errant thoughts aside so he could visualize an overhead of the area. *There's a path, it's close now, I think. Yes, this is it. If I can get around this ridge I can get back to camp.* But just as he turned he saw a strange glow up ahead, a soft buoy of light, flickering and bobbing, visible one moment, gone the next. *What am I looking at?* Another light flashed. Then another. More brightened as they rose over the hillcrest. Dozens of them now, torches too many to count, their bright orange tongues licking the dark sky. *They're flanking us. By the gods the Serkuts are flanking us.*

Anseth threw himself out of sight, wedging his body inside a tall cleft of icy rock. The rubble at his feet began to tremble. He thought he heard the sound of rushing water, but no, it wasn't water, it was men. Scores and scores of men, roaring past, torchlight flashing. Anseth turned to stone and held his breath.

When the clangor finally died, he edged himself just enough to peer out. He heard a handful of voices, Serkut voices, alarmed and searching. Getting closer. Anseth moved back inside the cleft. He was trapped. No, he could squeeze farther in. *Keep going, keep going.* There. A cavern opened before him, the darkness so thick he could barely see his own hand just inches from his face. He lit a torch using a piece of dry wood, some strips of cloth, and the steel and tinder fungus that took an eternity to find in his pack, then he moved deeper inside.

Something flitted past his ear; he swatted at empty air. Another whir; he swatted at that, too. He could hear chittering from somewhere above. He raised the light. Bats, all along the cavern ceiling. Most were just beginning to twitch as they woke from their torpor, though some had already taken flight while others simply crawled across the cracks in the ceiling like monkeys up a tree. *I need to move. Now.* Anseth dashed through the cavern, his boots splashing and sliding across a carpet of slippery bat guano.

He had to weave around jutting columns and duck under bony stalactites that reached for his head like spindly fingers. Easy enough to do, except he had to constantly look down to watch for the drop-off of shelfstone. Fortunately, the chamber widened again soon after. Still, his resolve began to weaken. He knew nothing of this cavern. It could end after a few more feet, or after a few miles. Hell, there might be no way out at all. Anseth hesitated. He needed to turn back. But then, just as he was about to, the faintest hint of cool air brushed his face. A way out, at last.

He followed it around a narrow bend and almost wept when he saw the sliver of moonlight in the distance. His legs pumped harder, harder and harder until he was at a full run. He could feel the cold air pushing against his face now, could taste the moistness of the night on his lips . . .

Then the ground vanished.

There was a brief moment when, in midair, Anseth tried to shift his momentum, as if to somehow redirect himself back to safety. But it was too late. His torch flashed in his face, blinding him, then the cavern spun and spun and the ground reared up like a massive fist of stone.

CHAPTER SIX

L etter in hand, Demien Mordall stood in the palace's western wing, silent and motionless. The instructions had been clear enough, but the tower had already drummed fourth watch—about an hour after midnight—and still Demien remained alone. *This is a mistake,* he thought. *I should never have come here.*

A muffled noise made him turn. There, from the nearby alcove, a dark figure emerged in long robes. Ministerial robes, Demien realized, just as Sydrian Rane revealed himself in the dim moonlight that poured through the open window. The old Minister Steward looked wan and tired, his receding mop of white hair uncommonly tousled. He used a single finger to beckon to Demien before dissolving back into the darkness. Footfalls carried him away as softly as a fleeing wildcat.

Demien stuffed away the letter but was hesitant to follow. *What am I doing here?* He was not a man made for skulking. No, Demien was a large man, a man whose broad and powerful legs were accustomed to taking broad and powerful steps. He had no experience in sneaking around like this, and even if he were to try, his heavy armor would undoubtedly make such movement impossible. Still, he didn't expect to be met with so prominent an official as Minister Sydrian Rane, and perhaps it was that reason alone that persuaded him to follow.

Strange, how a corridor he'd walked countless times before could suddenly appear so unfamiliar. He found himself taking notice of the tiniest of details: the hairline cracks in the black pillars, the slight imperfections in the decorative tilework, the silver vermeil sconces and of course the cast-iron sentinels that stood in the shadows of the adjoining alcoves. From stout plinths these armed statues stared down at Demien, wearing long cloaks and those archaic suits of cord-and-plaque armor. Demien was so lost in them that he nearly passed Sydrian, who had come to a halt before one.

The minister quietly slipped behind the sentinel. The silence gave way to a muffled grating, the sound of metal against stone. It wasn't loud, but the longer it went on the more Demien wanted to simply walk away. But then it stopped, and Demien moved for a closer look. An open slab of featureless stone revealed a narrow stairway coiling down into the swallowing darkness. Sydrian urged him down with a hand caked in soot. *Again, what am I doing?* Demien questioned as he went.

Each step was narrow and misshapen and rather precarious underfoot, and Demien had to duck to get under the lintel at the very bottom. It was so hot and congested down here that Demien could feel his body tighten, and he silently prayed not to develop another headache like the one he'd had during the Shadow Play. Sydrian moved past him, oil lamp in hand, its glow so weak it barely revealed the narrow tunnel stretching out before them. Demien followed with cautious steps. He was looking around, his fingers exploring the cracks in the wooden shoring and the crannies in the tamped earth walls. Loose dirt occasionally crumbled at his touch. He passed a few small nooks before the old minister disappeared inside a room to the left. Demien stopped. *I shouldn't be doing this. I should go back.*

The minister's face appeared from the open door. "Please," he urged. "The Lord Regent has ears in all places. Only here can we speak freely."

With a sigh, Demien entered. It was a surprisingly large room, maybe five or six paces across, the walls dark and mortared with variegated stone. The only furnishings were simple mats of chaff. Sydrian sat down on one, but Demien refused. "I've obliged you enough, Minister," he said. "Now tell me what this is about."

Sydrian looked down, as if searching for the right words. When he seemed to have found them he looked back up and said, "I was there, beside you, at the Shadow Play. I saw your face, plain as summer rain, Lord Demien."

I'm being deceived. Demien stepped back, fearing a host of guards would rush out from the dark and seize him. His hand raced to the hilt of the short sword he kept sheathed at his hip. "Do not be alarmed, Lord Commandant," Sydrian said calmly, reassuringly. "I share your sentiments toward the usurper that is Zantherei Athera."

"I have no sentiments," Demien told him. "Nor would I ever hold such a thought against our very own Lord Regent. His Majesty's illness was sudden. Zantherei should be praised for taking the boy's place, so the Shadow Play could go on."

Sydrian frowned. "I come to you because you are the Savior of the Anir. More than that, you are a surrogate father to His Majesty. I come to you with an undraped heart and yet you play me false, Lord Commandant." He flicked an embroidered sleeve and a scroll appeared in his hand. "The emperor has come of age, and the regent is sworn to give him the right of the throne. But we both know that Zantherei Athera has no such plans."

Demien took the scroll and unrolled it in the light. He read:

"With the growing power of the regent, we the empire's representatives fear the inevitable usurpation of the throne. Breaking the faith laid by the honorable Lasarin Athera, the seditious son Zantherei has abused and taken all imperial power into his own jurisdiction, centralizing all military and civil affairs from taxation to land grants to holdings. He continues to enforce his authority by unjustly drawing support and influence from the feudal barons.

We, the honorable subjects of the sole remaining scion of the realm, have forged this union with the aim for change. Our unimpeachable loyalty will scourge the realm of the regent's wrongdoings, and together we will restore the holy shrines that have guided us since our ancestors descended the very mountains of the Anir. There will be no rest until the rightful sovereign ascends the throne. It is through our hands, as sanctioned by Emperor Thavian Siven himself, during the tenth month, fall, year 442 of the dynasty of the Anir."

Below the text were close to a dozen signatures, ranging from court officials, counselors, imperial inspectors, and of course Sydrian Rane's. At the very bottom was the imprint of the Sadralen—the emperor's official mark. The sight of it stole Demien's speech; his chest became heavy, as if pressed by some unseen weight. He went back and reread the mandate, then, with sudden anger, he looked up and said, "He's just a boy."

"He is the *emperor*," Sydrian said. "And for too long our emperor has been without a voice."

Demien wanted to choke him. He wanted to crush the minister's skinny neck—or better yet, slit his throat and watch him die in agony. His fingers twitched thirstily for his dagger. Rage and hatred washed over him, fast, like a floodtide through a sluice gate. It would be so easy, ending the minister's life. But no, by the gods Demien wasn't some impetuous young fool. "You conniving old wretch," he scolded. "Do you have any idea what you've done?"

The minister took a step back, but the conviction in his voice held. "The public's response to the play has only emboldened Zantherei's resolve. How long can we avert our eyes while he climbs higher on the throne?" His voice went lower, more subdued. "I know how you felt at the Shadow Play, Lord Demien. I know because I felt the same. The same betrayal. The same anger and injustice—"

"*Enough*," Demien snapped. "I felt none of that—do you hear me? Only *concern*. Concern for the boy's goddamn safety." It wasn't a lie, not entirely.

"Fine—but then what? What did you feel when you found the boy safe in his chambers? When you were left with the truth of what you'd just witnessed." Sydrian scoffed. "Do you not recall the official statement? 'His Majesty had consumed an excess of wine and had fallen too ill to participate.' Come on, Lord Demien, you knew it was a stinking heap of rot the moment you heard it."

Demien's teeth ached from clenching his jaw. His eyes wandered downward, to the mandate crumpled in his fist. Demien wanted to tear it up, and he would've too, were he a less honorable man. "You're speaking of regicide, Minister," Demien said, handing it back.

The scroll disappeared in the sleeve of the minister's robe. "I speak of heaven's will," he said. "The only offender here is the man who remains idle. I'll not turn my back on heaven. Will you?"

Damn Sydrian for being so persuasive. The minister was certainly correct in his own right: instead of slowly stepping away to allow the emperor his rule, Zantherei was only gripping his power tighter. *But why do I mistrust Sydrian so?* Demien should've been privy to all this *before* the mandate was signed—before this whole plot was set in motion. Still, it didn't take a cunning mind to know why he wasn't. *I would've stamped out this little coup long before it grew to this,* he thought. But now the edict was written and signed, and now the conspiracy was given irrefutable life. *Only now when it's too late am I informed. Very shrewd, Minister.*

But how Sydrian meant to carry out this task was another—and far more difficult—matter entirely. "You are a fool if you think you can succeed in this. Between the regent and his wife, they have eyes and ears in all places."

Sydrian sighed. "Not all, Lord Commandant," he said, gesturing to their surroundings. "Every city has its secrets, especially the Hollow. These tunnels run like unseen fingers beneath the entire imperial district. It once served as a secret tomb for the second emperor, and later used as an escape route for another. Do you know what I speak of, Lord Demien? During the siege of the Mas—"

"The Masgals, yes," Demien finished. He'd spent years studying the Annals of the Anir, so of course he knew the tale of the Masgal barbarians who laid siege to the Hollow for nearly a year. When they'd finally broken through the North Gate, the ensuing destruction was something the Anirians had never experienced before. Men were slaughtered and women raped, treasuries were ransacked and mounds of coin and countless bolts of silk and satin greedily plundered. The wealthy were tortured for their hidden caches, and even the tombs of high-ranking officials were desecrated for their jewels.

But through it all, the emperor himself was never found. Story-tellers whispered of a great ivory cloud that had whisked him over the walls to safety, but as time passed and the seasons turned so too did the stories begin to fade. It was nearly two years later, during the spring thaw, when Emperor Tharain had reappeared outside the North Gate, armed, ahorse, and backed by the grim ranks of his reinforcements. The reclaiming of the capital was swift and brutal, and before summer's end the rightful emperor had once again returned to his throne, which he held until his death, nearly two score years later.

Demien tore himself from his thoughts. These tunnels did give Sydrian an advantage of secrecy and stealth. But was it enough? Likely not. "Even if you do succeed, you are forgetting about our Imperial Advisor. The moment one of your little cronies makes a mistake Alarin will have the whole goddamn coup unraveled within a moon's turn."

"That he would," the old man replied. "Which is why Alarin will be made to serve our needs. The growing enmity between the brothers is too ripe for the plucking."

"A scapegoat? Alarin Athera is an innocent man."

His face soured. "Innocent?" He shook his head. "There is nothing innocent about a man who does nothing while his own brother corrupts the realm. He's broken, I tell you, broken and filled with bitterness and jealousy and resentment." He shook his head. "No, there is nothing innocent about that man."

"I would be careful with my words, Minister," Demien warned. "Lord Alarin still has powerful allies in his command. My own brother for one, in case you misremember."

Sydrian frowned at that, as if he hadn't thought about it. But then his face softened. "Szathan Mordall is a worthy man, but with all respect, he still serves the man Alarin once was, not the man he's become."

Demien paused. He took a long moment to consider everything, then said, "So tell me, Minister, what is it you're after?"

Sydrian's dark eyes narrowed at that. "I am only a simple functionary. I seek only for the great dynasty to live on, like the great Lasarin Athera had once envisioned, like heaven longs to see."

"Yes, as all men of honor would say. But surely you must feel entitled to some measure of compensation, however small it may be."

He glanced away but nodded the point. "If the emperor and his council should deem my actions worthy and righteous, then perhaps I would not decline my services as prime minister," he said.

Demien scowled. *I knew it, you goddamn snake.* He turned and headed back to the stairs.

"Lord Commandant," Sydrian called after him. "That day you saved the boy, did you not accept a rather generous advancement yourself?"

Demien kept going. "That was very different, Minister."

"Why? Was the former emperor's blood still warm on your hands when you took the seal and cord of Grand Commandant?"

That made him halt. Slowly he turned to the old minister. "You know nothing of that. I had no such intentions."

"Yet you are guilty of them all the same," Sydrian replied. Before Demien could rebuke him, the old minister went on, "You have all the love of the court and the people. Only with your support will the realm be safe once again."

"I'll not serve as one of your minions," he said. "And I'll never forgive you for exposing His Majesty to such danger."

"The danger was already there," Sydrian told him. "Perhaps you can't see it because it bears not a sword. Listen, the Shadow Play was only the beginning. Zantherei's actions are like a tincture of mercury spreading silently through the empire's blood. He must be removed . . . you know he must be removed."

Demien hesitated. "I swore an oath to do whatever was necessary to protect the boy and preserve the ruling house . . . but regicide, under any circumstance, is not something a man of my standing could ever take part in."

"I know," Sydrian said, "and that is exactly why you *must*."

CHAPTER SEVEN

Anseth awoke in silence, his body stiff and cold. His eyes searched for the center firepit, but there was no firepit, because he was in no yurt. He groaned then, remembering. He tried to get up but couldn't find his balance. He tried again. No luck. Panic seized him. *Get up, get up, damn you. No one will ever find you here, you must get up!* He clawed at the nearby wall for help, clawing and clawing until his hand lodged itself in one of the crevices of the scalloped flowstones. He gave a pull but the stone only tightened around his fingers. Anseth had to reposition himself and give a second, harder yank to finally free himself. He cradled the hand, his ungloved fingers slick with blood. *When did I lose that glove?* Anseth wondered. *I don't remember losing that glove.*

It took a little while before he managed to shake off his dizziness and get back to his feet. Thank the gods he could still see the glow of the exit. He found his torch but this time it took even longer to light the goddamn thing. He raised it up and surveyed the chasm. The rimstone shelf dropped off once, then again, and after a third time, there was only darkness. By the gods he'd been lucky.

The only way across was a thin ledge that abutted the lip of the limestone wall, no wider than an arm was long. Anseth took a deep breath. One small misstep and the chasm would gobble him up. Worse, he was still on wobbly legs. But it was either that or head back the way he came. No, he couldn't go back. That would take too long. He had to get across this goddamn hole.

The first few steps were the most precarious. Never in his life had he moved with more caution. For the past eight years he had been a man of the Gray Plains, a man used to the vast open land, not the dark and narrow confines of a cavern. His injured fingers ached in protest when given the torch, but he needed the grip of his good hand. *Almost there now, almost there.* He spotted a cave spider scurrying off, a huge thing, its spindly legs longer than any spider's legs had a right to be. How lovely.

A few more steps and at last the chasm was behind him. Anseth lowered his head and thanked the gods, all the gods, the numerous Anirian deities as well as the Vaskultan Landforger and Skybringer. Then he made his way out. The night still owned the sky, showing no sign of dawn. He moved around a screen of gray thicket and headed up a rocky incline, using the stars to guide him northeast. He was tired, aching, and covered in bat shit and grime, but all he could think about was getting back to alert the Vaskultan soldiers, even though he was surely too late.

A body lay twisted in the snow. Anseth knelt and lifted the man's felt earflap. He saw a lifeless face, distorted and frostbitten yet unmistakably Vaskultan. He found others farther along, cleaved men, cold and dead; some he didn't recognize, others he knew as friends. He left them there, all of them, moving on and on until he eventually regrouped with the Vaskultan rearguard.

The fighting was over, but the soldiers were moving this way and that, frantic of pace but strangely quiet—except of course for the wounded. Anseth saw a Vaskultan soldier standing over a fallen Serkut, trying to pull his spear free from the man's breast. The poor impaled victim was still alive and tugging at the soldier's overcoat. The frustrated Vaskultan finally knelt and stabbed the man with a dagger until he died. Casually he rose and wiped the blood from the blade—a comical gesture considering how much blood he himself was matted in. At last he grabbed the haft of the spear and heaved the weapon free, but it was with such force that he tumbled back and disappeared into the shadows of the surrounding outcroppings.

Anseth turned at the sound of his own name. Severak emerged from a haze of dust, recurve bow in hand. The general's overcoat was torn and filthy and smeared in dark blood at the shoulder. "Lord Revek—"

"I'm fine," Anseth answered at once.

"The Serkuts, they flanked us, the bastards outwitted us again."

"Where's Dariok, where are the others?"

"They're here, they've just returned."

They found Dariok by the sound of his voice—that ugly, strident rasp of his. His helmet was missing and his long hair was scattered in greasy knots. He was scolding his soldiers and generals, stamping his feet and shouting and placing the blame on anyone and everyone but himself.

Damn him, Anseth thought. *I've had enough of this.* "They baited you," he said, and loudly. There was a sudden lull, as if every sound had simultaneously died at once. Dariok turned slowly. "It was all a ruse," Anseth went on. "The cookfires were a decoy. The abandoned horses and checkpoints—all of it planned."

Dariok remained still for so long that Anseth wasn't sure if he even heard him. Then he burst into motion, advancing upon Anseth, his eyes full of hatred and violence. He shoved aside any man in his way, knocking down wounded allies without a shred of concern. Anseth could feel his heart pounding, but he refused to back down. *I'll not give this wretched brute the satisfaction.*

Kirik appeared, stepping in the way. Dariok tried to push past him, but the young bondsman held strong. Severak and Kaigon and a few others moved to intervene, leaving Dariok with no choice but to draw back. He turned away from Anseth and took long strides in one direction, before quickly deciding upon another. "We can still catch him," he said to no one in particular. "We can still catch that Serkut bastard."

"It's over," Severak said. Dariok yelled at him for that. Then he went back to murmuring to himself. "Think, Dariok, think." He continued pacing for a time, then halted abruptly to look up. "Somebody shut that miserable pissant up."

Only then did Anseth hear it. A man, wounded, wailing in agony. He lay propped against a mound of dirt and granite, a spear plugged in his breast, so deep its horsetail tassel was barely visible.

"Shut him up," Dariok said. "Somebody shut him up."

A pair of soldiers rushed over to quiet him, but had no success. Dariok yelled again, causing the soldiers to become anxious and forceful, which in turn made the wounded man's wails grow louder and more desperate. Dariok stomped toward the soldiers and shoved them aside. His backsword came free of its sheath. A shadow passed over the wounded man, then his throat smiled red. The poor Vaskultan clamped his hands over the wound, but he couldn't stop the blood from pouring out. He died like that, fingers around his neck, a position he held even after his body slumped over and gave that final, sickening rattle of death.

Anseth couldn't believe it. The man wasn't some servant or auxiliary—he was a veteran warrior. And yet, no one said a word. No, Anseth couldn't let this go. "You killed him," he said. "You just killed a Vaskultan."

Dariok simply shrugged. "I told you to shut him up."

Silence ruled the journey back to camp. Anseth's head pounded, his foot ached, and his left hand was a stiff, bloody claw he kept cradled to his breast. The nail of his middle finger had been ripped clean off, leaving a bright pink slab of flesh that blackened around the cuticle. Still, he was one of the lucky ones. The rearguard had lost nearly a hundred men, with thrice that in wounded. A good number of those would never make it home. Some died upright in their saddles, but most gave that dreadful *thump* as their corpses hit the earth. Startling at first, but after about the ninth or tenth time, Anseth no longer bothered to look back.

His heart was consumed by anger. Anger over Dariok's recklessness, his blatant stupidity. *I should've stopped him, by the gods I should've stopped the wretch from charging up that goddamn ridge.* His only comfort was that Dariok had sworn an oath, an oath he'd now have to fulfill with his head. The tribe was better off without him, wasn't it? The thought made Anseth wonder. With the chieftain's son gone, surely Anseth would be forced to stay and take command of the vanguard. He didn't want that. No, he wanted to go home. It was a selfish desire, but he didn't care. He'd been here long enough.

When at last the Vaskultans returned to the encampment, the exhausted men walked and staggered and limped back to their yurts, while their wives and children and relatives all rushed out to greet them. Bonesetters and shamans began tending the wounded, grumbling about the long workdays ahead. Dariok, alone, headed into the chieftain's pavilion.

"A fate deserved," Kirik said, watching him go.

Anseth nodded, but after a pause he said, "Maybe not." He left his bondsman and followed the doomed man into the pavilion.

He found Dariok on his knees, head down before his father. Volduk looked up at the disturbance, his broad face highlighted by the center fire. "Revek, I didn't summon you."

Anseth knelt beside Dariok. "I came to plead for your son's life, lord."

"I don't need your pity," Dariok snapped. His tone was cold and hateful as usual, but Anseth sensed a bit of anxiousness in it as well, a rarity for the brute.

Volduk looked at Anseth. "It is not my choice. He has sworn an oath. The Landforger and Skybringer hold the fate of every man, from birth to death."

Anseth frowned at that. "Lord, it is my failure just as it was his. He assigned me the rearguard, but I failed to repel the ambush just as he failed to take the enemy chieftain's head. If you take his life, then I must ask that you do the same with mine."

Volduk looked at him as though Anseth were mad. "Revek, you gave no such oath." He squinted his heavy eyes. "What are you up to?"

"Please, lord. This man's as reckless as he is savage, and surely he deserves to be punished for his actions, but I can't allow him to stand entirely at fault here."

Volduk's mouth hung open, but he seemed too incredulous to reply. There was a long moment of silence, then the chieftain rubbed the bridge of his nose and let out a deep sigh. "Fine," he said. "My son's foolish head is spared. Now get the hell out of here, both of you."

CHAPTER EIGHT

Miriana Athera was raised in brothels, had spent her youth traveling the breadth of the realm and beyond. From the quiet pleasure houses of Amaranth Point to the loud and congested brothels of coastal Willowsea, she'd served men of all sizes and shapes and colors. She would never be like the highborn women here, and she knew it.

When she'd met Zantherei, she was one of the many courtesans employed in his entourage. By fate she had caught the renowned general's eye, and was later summoned for a private audience in his pavilion. She pleased him well that night, and continued to do so when next he'd called upon her, and again as their meetings became more and more frequent. Then one evening he'd told her he wished to take her as his wife. She'd only laughed, but after returning to the capital, Zantherei did just that.

Well, it took some time, in truth. Zantherei's father Lasarin was regent then, and naturally the conservative man was opposed to such a union. But when illness had left him bedridden, Lasarin resigned the throne in favor of Zantherei, who immediately abrogated the law so he and Miriana could wed. Criticisms still abounded even to this day, nearly three years later. And Lasarin Athera had always looked upon her as though she were a weed in his garden of peonies, even down to his final days.

But not anymore, she thought. Outside the gates of the imperial district, the populace gathered to mourn the death of the former regent. Miriana mourned as well, but of course that was a facade. In truth, she was glad to see Lasarin dead.

She watched her servants dress her husband, amused by the puzzled look on his face. Never was there a greater proponent for the modesty of Anirian customs than Zantherei Athera. Like many "true" Anirians, the man detested excessive pomp and finery, instead choosing a day-to-day dress that made him look more like a ragged commoner than a regent, something he seemed rather proud of.

Miriana had always served him more than she loved him. Her husband was a distant soul, slow to smile, rare to laugh. A lifetime of persisting injuries often did that to a man. Zantherei's left foot had endured a break that never healed properly, causing him to lean a bit when he walked. His left hand couldn't form a solid fist because of damaged nerves, and more often as of late, he struggled with chronic pain in both his lower back and right shoulder. The man was yet to reach his fortieth year, but by the gods his body seemed far older. Injuries that would've once gone forgotten in days now lingered for months or even years.

His mourning robes were an array of tasteful white silks so unlike his usual plainwoven garb. He lifted a boot to examine the white leather, his expression like a farmer's after losing his crops to a swarm of locusts. Still, for once he looked how a regent should look, and she told him that. "I feel like a fool," he replied.

Miriana turned her eyes to view her own reflection in the look mirror. She saw a handsome woman of twenty-four years, her complexion pale and smooth even before the touches of makeup. She wore a white overskirt over an embroidered floral dress and a white outer jacket laced with gray. She was a tall woman, and in her heeled leather shoes she stood almost as tall as her husband.

She adjusted the hairpin of snowflake obsidian that bound the black hair atop her head. She usually preferred wearing her hair down, but the cut of her dress begged her to show off her neck and shoulders and of course her lovely face. Her eyes, upturned and shapely and long of lash, shone like blue roundels of lapis lazuli. "More beautiful than the blue discs of coral that grace the southern coastal reefs," a wealthy fisherman had once told her. Most men admired her for her looks, but it was Miriana's inner strength that she treasured most. After all, it was her strength that allowed her to endure abandonment, loss, poverty, illness, abuse, and the countless other hardships that defined her life as a young courtesan. Miriana was strong, and she persevered. She always persevered.

Her husband moved to the window, pulling aside the wall curtain to open the scrollwork shutters. Morning light bathed him in an aura of crystalline white, showering the room with sunbeams that made visible the dust in the air. He seemed distant today, as he usually did, but there was something else about him . . . something other than grief. He seemed troubled. She wanted to ask, but lately Miriana had a difficult time talking to her husband. It was no secret how disappointed he was in his wife. Three years and she still hadn't given him a son.

"Master Arden Lorian saw it in the stars," she'd told him earlier. "He predicts that soon the seed will grow." It was mostly to appease him, as she'd long given up hope that the Grand Physician's promises would fare any differently from the promises of all the others. She'd already spent a small fortune on stargazers whose divinations had promised fertility but never delivered, and another on alchemists whose tonics and salves did little but upset her stomach or yellow her urine. No matter how bold the promises or how much coin she'd spent, only apologies and disappointment came back in return.

She looked down at her dress. She didn't care for the streaks of gray on her outer jacket. The color was too bold, too contrasting. "This doesn't work," she told the attendant, a shapely young woman that looked capable of producing three or more sons herself. Miriana hated her for that, and hated her more when the girl's clumsy hands kept pawing at her like a cat. She ended up pushing the attendant away and reaching back to undo the garment herself. *What cruel gods would give a woman such beauty, only to make her barren?* she wondered.

She replaced her jacket with one more suitable, but now her over-skirt felt too tight. *I can't go back to a courtesan's life. Not now, not after standing as the Lady Regent.* The attendant tried to help, but again she kept getting her annoying little fingers in the way. She was useless. Miriana wanted to rip this goddamn skirt altogether. *Why can't I just give him a goddamn son?*

Something pinched her hip, and Miriana lashed out. She shoved the girl, hard, dropping her to the floor with a loud *thud* that echoed throughout the chamber. All movement died at once. The girl lay there, dumbstruck, her plump cheeks reddening, her doelike eyes watering. Miriana sighed and sent her away. She could feel her husband's disappointed eyes on her even though she refused to look up.

The carriage ride to the temple was a tedious affair. Miriana endured it beside her husband, gazing out through the parting of silk curtains, observing the distant mountain ridges and colorful autumn trees. The constant din of the surrounding wagons muddled her thoughts. Wheel and axle groaned in strained movement, oxen and horses lowed and whinnied, imperial carters cracked their whips and bawled commands. *Better this than silence*, she mused. Her husband's demeanor hadn't changed a bit. He was just sitting there, all in white and wearing the same troubled look as before.

The main road narrowed to welcome the oncoming rows of marble statues. Most were carved as men, though some were given wings and others had heads of black-scaled Sadralen. A few looked more bizarre than menacing, but all were captivating to the eye, especially now in autumn, when the fallen red leaves of the surrounding maples lodged themselves in the crooks and crannies of their limbs, like open wounds on whitewashed skin.

The imperial procession came to a halt before the temple gate. The stone guardian here was Azrial, the Protector God. He stood twice the height of the others, having a man's muscular frame but with four arms. It was said Azrial the Protector used those arms to draw and loose arrow after arrow, without pause and with uncanny accuracy.

Miriana averted her gaze as attendants helped her from the carriage. Her Captain of the Imperial Guard, Cyrille Vileron, came to her side. He was a tall but ungainly man, wearing heavy black plates of armor and—like all imperial guardsmen—a ragged outer cloak dyed in mottled shades of blue. Black strips of leather swathed his forearms, like the strange burial wrappings of the kingdoms far across the Cerulean Sea. An open-faced helm was in his hand, revealing a bald, pink head and the nasty scars that crisscrossed it. He was not a comely man by any means, but he was certainly among her most loyal. Cyrille Vileron had been at her side since her days at the brothels. She trusted no other man's steel at her back.

Inside the temple, she took her spot in the nave, while her generals, ministers, and lesser officials all found places around her. Her half brother, Vylas, stood nearby, biting his nails as usual. Drums pounded as the monks entered, dressed in simple muslin cassocks and holding small iron censers whose smoke clouded the air around them. Pallbearers followed, sandaled and expressionless as they carried the white-lacquered coffin. Even before they lowered the bier onto the dais, she could already hear plenty of sobbing.

Zantherei was the first to ascend the platform. He knelt before the coffin, praying for a time, then lowering his hand to overturn a flagon of wine. Miriana watched the stream of dark liquid run down the cracks of the stone. Her husband quietly asked his father's spirit to accept his libation. Then he rose to face the audience. He looked tired. "I could speak for hours and hours about Lasarin Athera's military triumphs. I could explain in detail how he repelled the Sijian Empire, how he decimated the Redlands' naval forces on the banks of the Pearl River, how he repeatedly outwitted his enemies with far fewer men in his ranks. I could tell you all this, but I won't. I will say only this: the glory he attained on the field was matched only by the humility he showed as regent."

Zantherei paused before going on. "I see your tears now, I hear how you weep. I wept too once, years ago, at my grandfather's funeral. I was twelve or thirteen. I wept when I saw his face, how withered and frail death had made it. It was then my father leaned down and told me not to weep. I asked him why and he said"—he cleared his throat—"he said, 'Never weep for a man who dies aged and at peace, with capable sons to carry his name and loved ones to sing of his accomplishments.' " It was a bit before Zantherei spoke again. "Now I may be the only son here at my father's funeral, and me without a son of my own, but I stand here now, before all of you, to implore you not to weep. I know in my heart that Lasarin Athera died just as his own father had died, aged and at peace."

He stepped down. No one made a sound. Shame filled Miriana's heart, the familiar shame of not bearing him a son. *Oh, how Zantherei loves to salt my wounds.* So what if he was the only son to attend his father's funeral? Alarin had pleaded illness, Anseth of course was dead, and the youngest Merio was too busy governing the eastern city of Stormhaven to care. She knew her husband wasn't offended by Merio's absence. Zantherei thought him foolish and indecisive and blinded by his unhealthy love of finery and excessive pomp.

After the final prayers, the pallbearers returned to their places beside the biers. The dirge of the drums led the mourning procession out through the rear hall, down a flagstone walkway and toward the altar proper, a two-level circular terrace of marble stone. In its center a burnished bowl gilded with stars sat atop a stone pedestal about the height of a child. Miriana took her place around it, awaiting the sacrificial offerings.

Handlers brought first the goat. A healthy buck—it was placed on its belly over a slab of wood, legs left to dangle off. The Chief of Sacrifice came forward, a massive, jewel-encrusted cleaver in hand. The deliverance of steel was loud and jarring; the goat's head fell away, its body still bucking and kicking even as it was dragged off. A horse was offered up next, and lastly came the boar. Now this boar seemed to know something was amiss, as Miriana could hear its bloodcurdling squeals just as it appeared over the lip of the altar terrace. It fought against its handler, pulling and jerking and jerking and pulling until *snap*, the tether broke, and the beast went barreling into the crowd. Panic threatened. Women shrieked and men shoved one another. The bowl flew off the pedestal, blood spilling everywhere. A handful of guards formed a wall at the exit, but in the confusion the swine slipped through and went racing down the stairs.

Zantherei snapped a command, and Demien Mordall sprang forward, nocking an arrow in his bow. He drew and took aim down the stairway, loosing with a *twang*. He drew again but didn't fire the second shot. Instead, his hands relaxed, he turned about, and gave a nod to Zantherei. The boar was dead, but it mattered little. The blood had been spilled, the offerings tarnished, the portent grave.

When Miriana finally mustered the strength to speak about the incident, it was long after they'd exited the carved tomb deep in the mountainside, and sometime during the carriage ride home. The sky had deepened into dusk, and the growing northern wind howled and beat against the noisy procession. Zantherei didn't answer, not until she repeated herself. "It matters not," he replied with a scowl. "Don't speak of this any longer. Not another word. Do you understand?"

"I didn't mean—" She closed her mouth and turned her head away.

A long while had passed before Zantherei spoke again. "Forgive me." He was looking off at something—the trees, the mountains, maybe the moon. She saw it too, a silvery crescent cutting the night sky. She looked back when she heard him sigh. "Alarin fears I moved too hastily at the Shadow Play," he confessed.

So this is what's been troubling him, she thought. She hated how much influence Zantherei's elder brother still had on him, hated more how she couldn't speak her mind about it. She wanted to tell him that he was a fool to put his faith in anything his elder brother said. By the gods Alarin lacked the decency to even attend the funeral of his own goddamn father. "You saw what happened," Miriana said. "They loved you. The entire audience, courtiers and ministers and generals—they all loved you. The time has never been better to depose the boy and rise as emperor yourself."

"Still, I don't want to be seen as a man who is too eager to rule."

"You won't," she told him. "You've waited long enough. Too long even. The boy is growing restless. He is coming of age, do not forget."

He waved the notion off. "He's just a boy." He looked down, rubbing at his thick brows for a long moment. Then he sighed.

———

Alarin Athera struggled down the stairway of his rooftop observatory. No matter how slowly he moved, or how much weight he displaced with his cane, the result was always the same: bolts of jarring agony up a limb that wasn't even there any longer. Halfway down he stopped to rest against the baluster railing. The narrow window to his right revealed the evening sky, dark as the plumage of a blackbird. He watched absently for a while, before moving on.

Inside his bedchamber, Alarin limped over to his writing desk, collapsing into the chair with a tired groan. He was so wrapped in his own thoughts that it took a moment before he noticed his sister, Nyvia, standing in the room.

She wore a long white gown that did little but accentuate the dumpiness of her build. Her hair was tousled despite the adornment of silk purple threads, threads that matched the brocade lining of her garb. An amethyst-studded necklace hung around her neck.

She began to approach; Alarin turned away from her. *Not now, Sister. I don't need your wretched consolation.* It took a moment before he realized she was moving rather quickly and rather loudly, and looking up he was so stunned by the terrible scowl she wore that he barely saw the hand that came down and struck him in the face.

"You *slapped* me." It was all he could think to say. It startled him more than it hurt, but he pressed his hand against his cheek anyway. *I can't believe it. She just slapped me.* The scowl remained on his sister's face. She was a small woman, and yet she looked no less fierce than any of her brothers right now. In fact, standing there, half hidden in shadows, her face resembled Anseth's—especially in the deep-set eyes and high cheekbones.

"May the gods forgive you for your callous heart," she said.

What? Oh, the funeral, of course. His hand came off his cheek. He could feel the sting now. "I was too ill to attend. In case you forgot."

She scoffed at that. "Oh please, Alarin. Your brother should throw you in a cangue, that you learn some humility."

"Zantherei's done enough, I fear."

"And what about you?" she retorted. "You've become a shadow of yourself, Alarin." She scattered the papers on his desk. He watched them fall to the floor. "You think a few words scrawled on some scraps give you power? What happened to you? The Alarin I once knew would've been at his father's dying side, offering all the filial support a son could offer, chosen heir or not. The Alarin I knew would never lie to cover his beaten sense of self-righteousness. The Alarin I knew would never spend his days hiding in this dreadful—"

"That's *enough*," Alarin cut in.

"No, it's not. You think the people would want a broken man as their Lord Regent? That is what you are, Alarin. A broken man. And you know what, nothing's more pitiful than a broken man who does nothing but *covet who he once was*." She turned away; Alarin could hear her sobbing now. He moved to console her, but she pushed him away.

"Father was right to choose Zantherei over you," she went on, her eyes still angry despite her tears. "By the gods, you didn't even attend your own father's funeral. What is wrong with you?" Not waiting for an answer, she turned and headed for the door. Alarin remained there, speechless. He could only watch her go.

Silence returned, grim and familiar. Alarin Athera sat on the edge of the featherbed and watched the droning flicker of an oil lamp. He couldn't think of a time in which he'd felt more ashamed than at this very moment. He'd failed in his duties, offended his sister, and sullied his character. *Once a famed general . . . once at the helm of thousands of men. And now?* He sighed. *When did everything become so difficult? When did I become so lost?*

Nyvia was right; he was a broken man. But he wanted to mend himself—he just didn't know how. Every time he tried he only became more lost and more bitter. He was tired of it all. Tired of trying to mend himself . . . tired of trying to become the man he once was. It was like the Alarin of old had somehow become a separate entity, this pinnacle of loyalty and manliness and all that piss his father used to go on about. *That* Alarin was meant to serve as regent.

He eased himself back onto the soft silks. He could never be that man, not now, not again. That man was gone. Alarin let out a moan of despair. *I am broken now, as I will be for the rest of my life.* He knew it as truth and yet he also couldn't accept it. It didn't make sense, no more than a limb that still ached eight years after it was removed from his body made sense. He wanted more than anything to have his old life back—to be bold and strong and feared and admired and just be everything he once was . . . everything before he lost his leg and before all this sadness took up permanent residency in his heart.

CHAPTER NINE

The Imperial Garden was a stunning landscape of curved walkways, tiered flowerbeds, shaded arcades, sculpted arbors, and carved flagstone bridges. On clement days like today Miriana Athera enjoyed relaxing in the square pavilions of river rock and cedar, or sitting at the edge of the lotus pond to watch the carp jostle for feed. During the summer months, both the pond's edgings and the surrounding walkways would bloom with creeping thyme and pink hydrangea, with occasional rows of wisteria twining gracefully overhead.

The warm midmorning sun was a welcome respite from the recent chill that swept the capital. Oversized clouds, like billowy cushions of white down, drifted leisurely across a soft azure sky. Sometimes they would swallow the sun, but the cover was always brief and the sun would always emerge more radiant than before. "The gods are at peace," Vylas had remarked of it earlier. Right now he was peeling the skin of a persimmon he took from a gilt silver bowl. He offered a cut to

Miriana. It was perfectly sweet, almost creamy in her mouth. "As pleasing as the day, my good brother," she told him.

Vylas thanked her and went back to his peeling. He was, in fact, only her half brother, as he often pointed out, though Miriana wasn't so keen on making such distinctions. To her Vylas was simply her brother, but more than that, he was the only family she'd ever known. And as such he was everything a dutiful younger brother was expected to be: loyal and honest, deferential, and not without the occasional bout of overprotectiveness. And much like Captain Cyrille Vileron, Vylas's ennoblement had been the direct result of Miriana's own rise in status. No better way to win a man's lifelong fidelity, she knew.

She watched him part a hank of his dark hair, exposing the half-mask that covered the left side of his face. It was black as unpolished jet and decorated in subtle wisps of smoky filigree around both the eyehole and the outermost edging. Miriana was among the rare few to see the horrible scar beneath. She remembered every detail of that haunting day—the blood, the gore, the way he screamed when the outlaw's knife went into his eye. By the gods she remembered it all.

He offered her another cut of the persimmon and she thanked him. Her mind drifted off to its usual concerns. Miriana knew her time as the Lady Regent was coming to an end. What purpose did a wife serve if she could not give her husband a son? Perhaps there was another way. A boy was a boy, was it not? From her belly or some whore's, it mattered not. She could deceive him of course; there were concoctions she could ingest, concoctions to make her menstruation grow absent, to make her breasts grow tender, even concoctions to stimulate a woman's quickening. Yes, she could make her body do all the things it was meant to do when with child, except of course, give actual birth. And so she could deceive her husband and watch him raise the boy as his own, and perhaps even she might grow to love the child as well, should she choose to. It sounded simple enough, did it not? Oh, she was a goddamn fool to even consider this. No, only the gods could save her . . . only a goddamn miracle by the same goddamn gods that made her barren in the first place.

The sound of her name broke her from her reverie. Vylas was

standing farther along the walkway, his attention focused on the outer gate. "Soldiers," he called to her. "From the Pit."

Miriana moved closer for a better view. A throng of armed and armored men gathered before the garden's entrance. *Why are there soldiers here? And why so many.* She ordered Cyrille to see to it at once. The tall man returned quickly, so quickly it made Miriana's heart speed up. *He never moves that fast,* she thought. *Something's wrong.*

"My lady, it's your husband. He's taken ill at the Pit."

Taken ill? Zantherei? That didn't sound right. "What are you talking about, what do you mean?"

He didn't meet her gaze. "They're taking him to the palace. Arden Lorian's been summoned. Come."

The avenues beyond were choked with dust and crowded with soldiers of every rank and size. Court officials appeared as well, some curious of the tumult, others crestfallen by what was being told to them. A few began to weep. One man, she saw, was lying prostrate, slamming his forehead repeatedly against the earth. A robed fellow ran around him, flailing his arms and wailing in grief. Sorrow clutched the scene like a terrible pall. Only the billowy clouds and the radiant sun seemed impervious to it all.

Cyrille and his fellow guardsmen did their best to clear her a path, but the congestion only thickened as they went. A cloud of dust swept into her eyes and left her briefly without sight. Bodies loomed all around her, thick, armored bodies of confused Anirian soldiers. Miriana struggled to breathe, and what little air she found reeked of sweat and unwashed feet and other things better left unsaid. And just when she thought it couldn't get any worse, a mass of puffy clouds decided then to conveniently settle over the sun, and all light around her suddenly died. It felt like an ominous plunge into a murky, subterranean pit.

Then Cyrille Vileron appeared, taking her hand and barking orders to the soldiers, sending men this way and that. And finally, through the endless side roads and darkened alleyways, he brought her to the forecourt of the palace. She saw soldiers, eight at least, carrying Zantherei up the stairs, shouting as they went. Her husband was stripped of his chest plate, wearing only a simple tunic and trousers, and oddly enough a single greave. Imperial guardsmen hurried to open the doors and allow the Lord Regent inside. Miriana followed, making her way down the left wing to enter the imperial sickchamber. Cyrille barked an order and moments later the heavy, double doors groaned to a close.

All was quiet.

Attendants hastened to light the braziers and wall sconces, the growing light illuminating the robed physicians huddled around the featherbed. Between their movements, Miriana saw glimpses of her husband. One moment he was lying motionless, the next he was jerking like a bird with a broken wing. She could hear him retching from the herbal emetic he was given. When he turned on his side, she saw a face as blue as a dayflower. Sweat dampened his short brown hair, trickling down to disappear in the stubble of his close-trimmed beard. Blood oozed from the corner of his mouth and inner ear, staining the silk coverlets and eventually finding its way down to the tiled floor, where it dripped and dripped and continued to drip.

She turned away and fought the urge to weep—not for her husband, but for what his death might mean for her. Would this be the end of her pretty little life of aristocracy? The very thought made her knees buckle, made her legs threaten to falter and give. She had to fight to keep that from happening.

"Hurry now, he's weakening by the moment," Master Arden Lorian was saying. She saw him only by the wrinkled, hairless head bobbing beneath the taller figures. And old and frail though he was, Lorian seemed to move now with strength and with purpose, somehow managing his own complicated duties while simultaneously instructing each of his assistants to theirs. He even paused to urge the host of inquisitive soldiers to stand back. His wishes were obeyed but only for a short while, forcing the old physician to repeat his request.

One of Lorian's assistants uncorked Zantherei's winegourd and began sniffing and sniffing while furrowing his brow. When Lorian saw this he reached over and snatched the gourd from the young man's hands. The old physician scolded his assistant for smelling it, but then took a whiff himself. Afterward he said, "Some poisons don't have a scent, the good ones at least."

Poison. The word came to Miriana like a blow to the stomach. *My husband was poisoned.* It was so obvious to her now. How did she not realize it? *Poisoned . . . but alive. He's still alive.* The very thought rejuvenated her senses. Gave her purpose. And purpose gave her strength. *I must find out who did this.* "Captain, bring me that winegourd."

Cyrille Vileron approached the featherbed; Lorian spun angrily at the disturbance, but shrank back the moment he saw who it was. Cyrille took the vessel and brought it back to Miriana. She uncorked it. Indeed, no odor. She looked back at Cyrille. "Bring me a hound from the kennel. An older sire, but one still in good health. Be quick now."

Cyrille took a handful of guards and exited. Before the door closed, Nyvia made her way inside. The small plump woman was in tears even before she got to her brother's side. Master Lorian tried to ease her back, but Nyvia fought him, weeping and shoving, until finally she went limp in the old man's arms.

Miriana turned at the sound of her name. The Minister Steward Sydrian Rane approached to stand in the light. The man looked ever somber in his distressed gray outer robes, his eyes black against his thin white hair and matching whiskers. There was a figure at his side, an equally diminutive but younger man dressed in a field tunic and simple breeches of drab olive. Sydrian introduced him as an assistant to the head of the commissariat or something near to that. Miriana studied the assistant's nervous eyes and mousy face and didn't like what she saw. Nevertheless she beckoned him forward. The young man bowed his head more than once, then stated his name, Oladd or Oledd or whatever it was. She ordered him to speak.

"I-I saw to a guest in the Lord Regent's quarters," he said. "It was just after the midday drill sessions. The Lord Regent spoke to him briefly, but after he left, that was when the Lord Regent . . ." The young man stopped, and his nervous eyes wandered to where Zantherei lay.

"Tell me who it was you saw, soldier," she ordered.

"Him," Oledd said, pointing. He singled out a youth who was working alongside Lorian, back turned and draped in the long robes of an apprentice physician. Miriana ordered a pair of guardsmen to retrieve the accused. In the interim, she asked the young assistant, "You are certain of this?"

"Yes, my lady," Oledd said, nodding more than once. "I wouldn't forget a face, especially one like *that*."

She was about to ask him to explain but then the guards returned and she saw the face for herself, saw the craterous scars that ruined his complexion. It took her a moment to recognize the owner of that face, but when she did her chest tightened. *Kalen. By the gods . . . it's Alarin's young retainer.*

The door groaned open, startling her. Cyrille Vileron entered with the kennel master, a squat, portly man who was clearly out of breath. He bowed his head in greeting then yanked the leash of a frightened brown sire. Behind him, the crowd in the antechamber threatened to spill inside. Miriana needed to quell this commotion. She turned and picked out ten or so guardsmen from her surrounding host. "Clear the halls. Now. I want them all gone." The blue-cloaked men hustled to obey. Only Cyrille Vileron and a handful of others remained.

The kennel master held the dog between his thighs while Miriana grabbed the beast's foreface and brought the poison to its flat, wrinkled muzzle. It was a clumsy effort, and the hound more than once managed to either squirm away or turn its head from her. When she finally forced a good amount down its throat, the poor beast recoiled and licked and licked at whatever it tasted, then slunk away to lick some more. It wasn't long before the dog sank to the floor, hocks twitching and blue-black tongue lolling as it struggled with each painful breath. It was a pitiful sight, watching the dog die. "Take it and be gone," Miriana said afterward. The kennel master and an attendant hauled the carcass out in silence.

Miriana turned her glare on Kalen. The ugly youth's face paled and his pockmarks seemed to pulse with fear. Beads of sweat gathered on his brow, moistening the tips of his hair. "By the gods I had no part in this. My lady, I—"

"*Look* at him," she said, motioning to her husband. Kalen looked like he wanted to obey but was too afraid to move. "My husband still draws breath," she told him. "You've failed, you know. You've failed and now look at you—a true coward in the face of the truth." The stubborn fool began pleading his innocence once more, but she put an end to that with a stern command. Then she said, "As deplorable as you are, I know this vile scheme is not yours alone. Name the conspirator and you shall be given mercy."

Tears were glassing his eyes. "I—I had no—"

"I said *name the conspirator*," she seethed. "Or be assured you will face a most unforgiving punishment."

A pool of urine darkened the young man's trousers. Miriana stared at it but her thoughts went elsewhere. *How could I have not foreseen this?* Zantherei had been given a title long meant for Alarin. The younger was chosen over the elder—how could she not have foreseen the hatred that could only have filled Alarin's heart? In truth, she never imagined he would go so far as to conspire to kill his own brother. She'd misjudged him—a single oversight that may very well cause the end of her privileged life. That thought enraged her. "You *poisoned* the Lord Regent of the Anir," she snapped. Her hands balled into fists, her nails digging into her palms. *Be strong, Mir,* she told herself. *Strong as silk, strong in body and mind.* Her eyes moved to find Cyrille Vileron's. "I want his confession."

The first blow was the loudest, an awful *crack* of knuckled steel that crumpled the young physician to the floor. There was an immediate cry from behind—Nyvia. The small woman tried to interfere, but Miriana placed a pair of guardsmen in her way. More blows followed, rendering Kalen prone and begging for mercy. *Be strong, Mir. A strong ruler offers no quarter to the traitors of the empire.* She repeated those words to herself, again and again, as each terrible blow further broke and bloodied the young retainer.

It soon became hard to watch. Kalen's begging was reduced to an indecipherable whimpering, his face a mask of blood, his skin bursting open like the ripe persimmon she'd eaten yesterday. *Yesterday? No, that was today, mere hours ago.* By the gods she would've done anything to go back to that time and prevent this nightmare from happening.

Nyvia shrieked, begging for mercy on the boy. Cyrille Vileron ignored her, pummeling and pummeling the young retainer, though the blows had grown weaker and weaker, and he seemed more and more exhausted after each. Miriana had seen enough. She ordered him off. Cyrille bent over and rested his hands on his thighs, taking heavy, heavy breaths. Blood from his armored knuckles dribbled down to the floor.

Arden Lorian came forward to check the young man's pulse. When he shook his head, Nyvia sank to her knees and wept. Miriana had the guards haul the body out. Attendants cleared the stained rushes and began scrubbing at the trail of blood. *Kalen deserved this,* Miriana told herself. *He deserves to die just as Alarin deserves to die.* But she knew she couldn't just take Alarin's life—certainly not publicly like this. No, the Imperial Advisor was obviously too powerful a man, with too much protection and political sway.

Miriana turned and went to the nearest desk, lifting the writing brush from its holder and unrolling a scroll. No one moved. She wrote fast and she wrote recklessly, and when she was done she rolled up the scroll and haphazardly pressed the regent's seal. "I am the Lady Regent," she said, rising. "And until my husband departs from the realm of the living, my imperial decree stands as heaven's will." She handed the edict to Captain Cyrille Vileron. "I want Alarin Athera bound and arrested."

CHAPTER TEN

A sudden clamor yanked him from sleep. Alarin Athera pulled aside the silk curtains to see Captain Cyrille Vileron standing in his bedchamber, hulking in his full captain's attire. An oil lamp carved as a leaping wolf was in his left hand; the other clutched a scroll. Around him, fellow guardsmen were ransacking the furnishings. Attendants, frightened, fled.

Alarin rose and reached for his cane, then retrieved the heavy wool robe from its peg. Throwing it on over his nightshirt, he said, "You have not the slightest shred of authority to enter my private quarters, Captain." He called for his own guards, but they were nowhere to be seen. Kalen, too, was missing.

Cyrille's vulturine face managed a look of smugness. In his throaty voice he said, "I bear an edict sealed by Lady Regent Miriana Athera." He set the lamp down on a nearby stand, using both hands to break open the seal. Unrolling, he read:

"Alarin Athera, Imperial Advisor of the Anir, is hereby ordered bound and detained for the crime of conspiring against Zantherei Athera, Storm of the North, Guardian of the West, and Lord Regent of the Anir, by way of poison. He is to be stripped of his rank and his quarters shall be given to full search by the Imperial Guard."

Vileron lowered the edict just enough to show his thin, falcate eyes. "Bind him."

Before Alarin could protest, a swarm of blue-mottled cloaks shoved him to the floor and pressed his face against the tiles. It was cold and the rushes poked at him and his jaw ached from the pressure. Another guard came over, snapping a length of cord. He turned Alarin over with the toe of his boot and lifted him enough to bind both hands at the wrists. "Is my brother alive?" Alarin demanded to know. "Vileron, is my brother—"

A punch to the gut pushed the air from his lungs. Alarin coughed and wheezed, powerless and winded. Blurrily he watched Cyrille's black boots approach. "You meant to take the throne," the captain said.

Alarin couldn't crane his neck to meet Vileron's gaze. "That is a lie," he said. "I demand to speak with him. At once, Vileron." Cyrille laughed his cruel, grating laugh. Alarin tried to squirm free, a vain gesture. *Even if I do, what then? Run? I'm a goddamn cripple.*

Strong hands hoisted him to his feet. "Listen to me," Alarin said. "I would *never* harm Zantherei. He is my blood, Vileron. My *brother.*"

"And fortunate for you that he is," the captain remarked. "Otherwise your head would already be on the North Gate." He motioned to his guardsmen. "The lower cells will suffice for now."

They dragged him across the floor. It was a showing of profound indignity, but Alarin didn't care; he thought only of his brother. *Poisoned?* He tried to convince Vileron again of his innocence—what else could he do? If he could just get the man talking, he might be able to influence him.

Suddenly Vileron stopped. For a moment Alarin thought his words had gotten through, but then he looked up and saw his sister standing beneath the door lintel. She looked as cross as the day she'd slapped him. Alarin called to her. "Nyvia, by the gods, is Zantherei all right? Is our brother all right?"

She ignored him and spoke only to Vileron. "Not the cells. He'll not be taken there." Though dwarfed by the armored guards, she looked unusually formidable, like a wildcat protecting her young.

Vileron flashed the edict. "My lady, these orders are from Lady Miriana herself. You bore witness yourself to the pressing of the seal."

"I bore witness only to an edict that condemns a man without fair judgment."

Vileron's expression was vacant. "It is not within my authority to question the ruling of the Lady Regent."

"Don't be a fool," she snapped. "You know my brother is innocent of these charges, and soon it will be proven. Without Zantherei, the Hollow will stand as vulnerable as an abandoned sheepfold. You know our advisors are incapable in military affairs. How long will it be before the court pushes for Alarin's reinstatement? And he will certainly get it. And then . . . after he's finished beating back our enemies, he will turn to the Hollow, to those who have wronged him. Now where do you think that'll leave our good Lady Regent? She'll be lucky to keep that pretty little head of hers. Do you understand what I'm telling you, Captain?"

Vileron looked nonplussed. "I cannot ignore a direct command," he said at length, though his voice was now stripped of its cruel edge.

"I didn't ask you to. Fulfill your duty and arrest him. But let him remain here, in his own chamber, at least until Minister Korval sees him properly judged. A few weeks ago this man was your Imperial Advisor—treat him with the respect he still deserves."

Vileron took a step forward. "My lady, please stand aside."

Nyvia didn't move. "Only when a blade pierces my heart."

Alarin said, "Sister, I beg you, stay out of this."

Nyvia ignored that. "Remove his bonds," she ordered the guardsmen. They looked to Vileron for help. The captain hesitated; he could do nothing. He simply shook his head and sighed, then gave the command.

The guards unhanded him, and the bonds of Alarin's wrists fell away.

"Lady Miriana will hear of this," Vileron said, motioning his men out.

Nyvia stood aside to let them pass. "I would expect no less from so loyal a minion, Captain."

When Vileron was gone, Nyvia immediately went to Alarin, helping him to his bed. "I thought you were angry with me," Alarin told her. She unfolded the silk coverlets to ease him into it. She seemed no longer formidable, but the same demure and tender sister he'd grown up with. "Does it hurt?" she asked when she saw his wrists. He told her no. Then he said, "Listen, Nyvia, I am grateful for what you've done . . . but you shouldn't have interfered. Lady Miriana will not take kindly when she learns of this."

"I don't care. You are entitled to the fair laws of judgment." She paused for a long moment, then lowered her eyes as she spoke again. "Alarin . . . I need to know. The truth, Alarin."

"I would *NEVER* conspire against Zantherei," he snapped, wounded by the accusation. "He is our brother, Nyvia—he is our *blood*. You should understand that . . . you most of all."

She looked relieved. "I do," she said, nodding. Then she began to weep. He embraced her, letting her weep, and when she was done he brushed the dark curls from her eyes and wiped the tears from her plump cheeks. "He's alive," she said, her voice choked with grief. "Master Lorian's doing all he can, but . . ." She fell silent for a moment, then said, "I will arrange a private meeting with the Minister of Judgment, maybe Korval—"

"No," Alarin said at once. "Korval's a venal old man. Miriana will tighten his lips by fattening his purse. I must persuade the court myself, and soon, before judgment is cast."

Her hand squeezed his own. "How can I help," she said.

"You've done enough, Sister. More than I deserve."

"Stop it. Just tell me."

He fastened his eyes on her and thought for a long, quiet moment. "The poison. I need the poison."

"Lorian has it," she said. "I can get it."

"Good. If we can strip it down we may be able to trace each component to a definite origin. The truth will be found there, in the commonalities."

She nodded. "Is there anything else?"

Alarin was silent again, thinking further. Truth was, he had little more use of her. His next moves required using informants to comb the capital for word of the true conspirators, as well as sending letters to all his sworn military officials to reassure them of his innocence in the face of these accusations. But no, first he needed to send a letter north. He needed to warn Anseth, to make sure his young brother knew the truth. He looked at his writing desk. It lay upended and smashed, its contents ransacked by Vileron's guardsmen. Papers were strewn, brushpens broken, his seal of office gone. Black ink oozed from a cracked inkwell, staining all it touched. Alarin hoped he had enough to write what he needed to write. He couldn't wait—he needed to send Kalen out with the letter tonight, no later than third watch. *Poor lad will not be happy about this.* That reminded him . . .

"Kalen," he blurted. "I need to speak with Kalen. Where is he? I need you to bring him here at once."

Her expression wilted. "I can't," she said, in her softest, quietest voice. She eased herself away from him. "Oh, Alarin . . ."

She thinks I will put him in danger. "Listen to me, Kalen won't be involved, not in any of this." He wanted to tell her why he needed the boy. He wanted to tell her about Anseth, that her brother was still alive. But he couldn't betray his oath. "I would never place him in harm's way," he insisted. "Kalen's like a son to me. I have to speak with him. He's likely at the academy, no wait, he must be with Master Lorian, yes he's—"

"*I can't,*" she cried. She looked down, sobbing now. Her outburst bewildered Alarin. *What's the matter with you? It's a simple request—why are you being so difficult?* When she finally lifted her head, he saw a face twisted with anguish and blanched of color. "She *killed* him, Alarin. He's dead. I'm *so* sorry—Lady Miriana had him killed."

CHAPTER ELEVEN

"A n innocent man is *dead*," Demien growled, shoving the minister against the wall. Tilework crackled in response, dust and debris sputtered beneath the light of a nearby wall sconce. Demien pressed the steel of his vambrace hard into Sydrian's neck. "Your coup is a failure."

"I b-beg . . ." Sydrian's words became a wheeze through such constricted breath. Sweat glistened along his receding crown of gray hair, and his dark eyes, usually calm and solemn, were now pools of fear.

Something crunched from down the corridor; Demien turned but saw nothing. Just an empty stretch of tile and the fading glow of the retreating wall sconces. "Please . . . we cannot speak freely here," Sydrian whispered. Demien shushed him, his eyes still watchful of his surroundings.

The minister gave fight then—a disarming burst of strength that nearly broke Demien's hold. Still, it didn't take much effort for

Demien to regain control, and for that little outburst he decided to tighten his grip. The minister's hands clawed for freedom, his lungs begging for air. Demien wanted nothing more than to choke him into an endless sleep. *I'd make sure no one finds you*, he thought, *the same with all the other schemers from your little conclave. You're all snakes seeking to defile the sacred shrines.* The minister's face was turning red as a pomegranate. Veins bulged from places that normally didn't bulge. *It would be a favor to you. I'm saving your neck from the axeman.* The old man's eyes glazed over. Demien could see the darkness overtaking him, that gentle hand of comforting, painless sleep.

He let go. The old minister collapsed with a heavy *thud* that echoed down the corridor. He gulped and gulped mouthfuls of precious air, a loud and painful effort. It took some time before he was able to speak again, and when he did his voice was hoarse and weak. "The traitor will not . . . live long," he said. "Alarin is immured in his tower . . . it is all as planned."

"The young physician was *innocent*."

The old man braced himself against the tilework and rose. His long, tapered face slowly found its natural color, but there remained a deep weal on his neck where the steel roundels of Demien's vambrace had dug into it. "When lightning strikes the tree, only the foolish bird blames the bough."

"What?"

Sydrian shook his head. "It matters not. Listen, Zantherei will soon breathe his last. The sacred bloodline of the Anir will be preserved." His confidence seemed to quickly return. "My hands may be soiled, but His Majesty's remain clean. It is as I intended."

"Zantherei may yet live."

"And if he does, then I accept my fate. I accept that I am not to succeed in restoring the Anir. It was my sole purpose. The Anir must survive. Look at me. The Anir *must* survive."

Demien turned and left the minister there, storming off into the darkness.

The midday sun blinded him as he exited the interior palace. He shaded his eyes as he made his way across forecourt, then again as he reached the double-arched gateway of the Imperial Garden. A pair of sentries, one tall, one short, bowed their heads, but only the taller showed any deference—the short one just stared with contempt in his eyes.

Just a hateful little man, Demien told himself. *Nothing to be concerned about.*

The white cobblestone walkways carried him along the twists and turns of the garden, around colorful saplings of cherry and winter plum. Usually a dozen or so civil officials could be seen by the pond or seated on the benches of the waterside pavilions. But today he saw no one. The place was as empty as it was in midwinter.

He found the young emperor in a small clearing whose entrance was a trellised archway half hidden by the surrounding flora. The boy was standing beside a rockery, adorned in his midnight-blue imperial silks. He held something in his hands—a bow, Demien saw, and not just any but the imperial bow, a dynastic heirloom. The boy raised the weapon, aiming at a small bale of straw, which for some reason, he had set here, away from his usual practice yard.

The boy drew on the thumb ring. His feet weren't the correct distance apart, his elbows weren't aligned properly, and his posture wasn't straight enough. When he loosed, the arrow struck just along the lower edge of the target. The boy stood there for a long moment, then he reached down into his quiver. He drew again and loosed. That one missed entirely. A third attempt, another miss. He flung the bow into the grass, then sank to his knees, holding his head in his hands.

Demien retrieved the bow. Encrusted jewels studded the length of the carved horn base, each shimmering under the sun's glare. The catgut was taut but with acceptable pull.

"Such relics shouldn't be discarded so heedlessly," Demien said, offering it back to him. "This bow served your father well for many of his days."

The emperor rose and took it. "Where have you been? I summoned you an hour ago."

"Forgive me, Your Majesty."

The boy frowned. "How long have you been watching? No matter, I don't care." He ran a finger along the bowstring. "A fine weapon, but only as effective as the hands that use it."

"It takes a lifetime to master, Your Majesty."

"Enough with that. No one's around." Alone, there were no courtesies between them, no lord and vassal—only man and boy, or, as Demien liked to think, father and son. Thavian looked back and frowned at the target. "The Spring Festival, four years past. The entire assembly was watching me." He made a sound like a bowstring's twang, once and then again. "Both my shots hit their mark. You remember, don't you?"

Demien nodded.

"Of course you do," the boy went on. "Such adulation I received. Many said it was heaven itself guiding my fingers." He gave a pause. "I don't understand. How could I have been a better shot at twelve than I am now at sixteen?" He didn't wait for Demien's response. "Wait, I know the answer. I wasn't any better, isn't that right, Demien?"

It took a moment before Demien nodded.

The boy moved a dozen or so paces east. He stopped and looked at the target, then back at Demien. "This looks about right. Tell me then, was it here?" He took a few more steps. "Here, Demien?"

Demien watched him absently. "I don't remember."

The emperor scoffed. "I don't believe you. Tell me where you stood when you loosed. I *command* it." He took another step, south this time, toward the spreading branches of a golden crabapple tree. "Was it here?"

Demien crossed his arms. *Must I play this game?* He gestured a ways to the left.

The boy studied the spot, and then again the straw target. He seemed unsure.

"The creeper trellises used to extend farther, to about there," Demien pointed out. "I stood behind them."

The boy stared off for some time, and when he looked back his eyes were glassy. "Why, Demien?"

"I was ordered."

"I *know* you were ordered. Don't antagonize me. I want to know *why*. Why was the order given?"

He sighed. "Because the future sovereign of the ruling house needs to have all the confidence of the realm."

The boy frowned at that. "Confidence even in deceit? How honorable of you, Demien."

"I told you, I had no choice."

"You *did* have a choice," the boy snapped. He turned and walked off, back toward the arched entranceway. Demien stood there a moment, then followed.

The emperor stopped under the walkway arbor, staring at the shimmering autumn foliage, fingers clutching the latticework. He no longer looked angry, but sullen and meek. "You're displeased with me," he said when Demien drew near.

Demien sighed. "I'm concerned for your safety."

"Don't be. Zantherei won't live long, that's what Master Lorian said."

"He may not."

"Do you think he will be mourned?"

Demien nodded. "He provided protection to the city folk and modest taxes to the husbandmen."

The boy was hurt by that; Demien could see it in his face. They may not have been of blood relation, but Demien had raised him since he was but a babe, and was closer to him than to his own son, although in truth, that wasn't saying much. Silas Mordall was a small and sickly babe that had grown into a small and sickly boy. And worse, he'd never gained the ability to speak. He was such a disappointment that after Demien's wife had died, he simply left Silas in the care of his wet nurse and palace orderlies.

"Sydrian promised nothing would go awry," Thavian said.

"You should've told me."

"You would've stopped me." He tugged at a small vine wrapped around the woodwork. "You think she'll find the mandate?"

He nodded. "Lady Miriana is shrewd."

"Then do something about it. Protect me. Do *something*. Anything. Wasn't there a time in which a noble's death forced his wife to lie beside him? Can I not propose that same ruling? When Zantherei dies, the lady must die with him."

"Lady Miriana would never sanction such an antiquated—" Demien stopped, not even bothering to finish. He shook his head. "You think too much like a boy."

"I don't understand. She shouldn't even hold power. By the gods she's just a lowborn *whore*."

"She *was* a whore," Demien corrected. "Now she is the wife of the regent. And she will do whatever it takes to remain as such. Listen boy, Lady Miriana is full of wiles. She knows how to make men crook the knee or bloody their hands at her request."

Thavian began pacing back and forth. "I don't fear her," he said, though his voice sounded quite the opposite. "Let her find out, I don't care. Let the wretched whore find out!"

Demien grabbed him by the wrist. "You'd better pray she doesn't."

Thavian wrenched himself free. He opened his mouth to reply, but only paused for a long moment. "Why are you bleeding?"

Demien looked down. The cuff of his tunic was drawn up, revealing deep gouges in the flesh along the underside of the vambrace. "It's nothing," he said, pulling down the sleeve.

"It doesn't look like noth—"

"I said it's nothing."

Thavian narrowed his eyes but spoke no more of it. Instead he moved off, now heading down the footpath toward the lotus pond and skirting pavilions. Demien brushed aside a hank of brown hair from his eyes and joined him. Birds sang hidden in nearby boughs, the shy bunting, the gentle thrush.

"You hurt him, didn't you? Sydrian, I mean. Is he . . .?"

"He's fine."

The boy seemed relieved. "Sydrian told me things. Things you never told me. My father—I never knew my father was so bold a man. Sydrian said I am meant to be bold as well, but you are keeping me meek."

"I am keeping you safe."

The boy looked down. "Yes, your oath. That was a long time ago, Demien. My father's been dead a long time. Fourteen summers. His son is a man grown. An emperor can't stay hidden forever."

"He will remain safe until his mind is keen and his judgment wise," Demien said. He let out a sigh, and when next he spoke his tone softened. "You must be patient. Your father was indeed bold, but it was such boldness that led to his untimely death. Your bloodline has to spread to ensure the survival of the Anir."

"I didn't ask for this," Thavian said. "I didn't ask for any of this."

"It is heaven's will."

"I knew you'd say that. Stupid words. Sydrian offers real counsel. He listens to me, he wishes to see me enthroned."

"Sydrian desires only to see himself on the prime minister's seat."

"That's a lie."

"Power drives men to dark places. I've seen it all too much. Sydrian might even do worse to you than Zantherei has."

"That's *a lie* and you know it. Sydrian wants me on the Imperial Throne. He signed the mandate, he is devoted to my will—"

"You *stupid,* stubborn boy," Demien snapped. "A man's words on a sheet of paper bear no more meaning than those on his tongue. It is a man's actions alone that reveal the truth of his heart. Don't you dare forget that."

The boy was silent for a long moment, then he spun and hurled the jeweled bow into the air, sending it crashing into a cluster of branches. A group of sparrows took flight. The garden fell into quiet. The boy looked close to tears. "You think I'm weak. I can see it in your eyes— the way you look at me."

"I don't think you're weak, Thavian, I think you're afraid. The difference is sun and moon. A weak man has already given up, a man who's afraid still has a choice. There is no shame in the latter. I'm afraid too, you know, the same as you."

The boy scoffed at that. "You? Please, you are the Savior of the Anir, your very name is legend. At my age you already mastered over eighteen weapons—you could kill a man in over a hundred different ways."

Demien shook his head. "Yes, but that is the path of a soldier. His enemies are always obvious, his objectives always clear. But you . . . you are the last remaining scion of the ruling house. Your path will never be simple, your battlefield always underfoot. Foemen come at you not with steel but with smiles and gifts and years of bowed heads. You are never safe, not while you sleep, not while surrounded by guardsmen or protected by walls." He placed a hand on the boy's shoulder. "If I seem overbearing that is because I am afraid this plot has exposed you to all the vile creatures of the Hollow. These men are hungry, Thavian, they're hungry to devour every last morsel of power in the dynasty."

CHAPTER TWELVE

Seric Dyre was ready to move against the capital. Since Lasarin's resignation he had quickly grown resentful of Zantherei Athera. *The Storm of the North*, he thought with scorn. The regent was nothing more than a cruel wretch who commanded with a thirst for his own rule. Nothing pleased Seric more than to know that now the fool lay dying.

Inside the rear hall of his stunted, single-story home, Seric adjusted the clasp of his tattered cloak. The garment was so old that the black brocade embellishments and fancy lining had dulled to match the cheerless gray of the fabric. Not that it mattered, as Anirian customs long favored homespun over flashy. Still, it was one thing to *choose* to adhere to such customs, and entirely another to have no choice in the matter.

He lived in a communal abode, his old and filthy private quarters tended by an old and filthy servant who seemed to stay more out of indolence than duty. The veranda and courtyard were neglected, the outer framework in disrepair; even the shuttered windows looked terribly worn. He gazed out of one now, observing the afternoon sun as it hovered over the western ridgeline. It was a soft and shimmering light, but Seric found no beauty in it. Not anymore. Everything now was so stale, so insipid. How come? *Because I'm a worthless, miserable wretch.*

Hard to believe now, but there once was a time in which Seric stood as one of the greatest military talents of the realm. Many years ago, when Seric was a boy first arriving to the Hollow, he was taken in and adopted by a military officer named Nethan Dyre. Nethan took young Seric on every campaign, where Seric committed to memory every move of every battle, from the smaller skirmishes to the large-scale sieges. During times of amnesty Seric had buried himself in the military texts of former dynasties, some so old he had to have them transcribed from the oracle bones on which they were carved. Sure, at times he'd neglected his studies, sometimes for weeks or more, but he always, always returned. And why was that? Because he was damn good at it.

Years later Seric had been married to Nyvia Athera. From her loins she'd given him a son, and from her highborn house she'd given him coin and fiefs and titles and high status. Lesser men had obeyed him without question, bowing their heads and calling him "Lord". It was a wonderful time, but like all good things in his life, it didn't last. When Nethan had died his surviving sons conspired against Seric, tarnishing his name through slander and deceit and eventually stripping him of all military standing. Denied of his ambitions, Seric had become lost and purposeless.

For a time he'd earned his share as a moneylender and merchant, dealing mostly in silk, jute, and occasionally mustard seed. It was tedious and thankless work, and he hated it, and before long usury and fraud had become common practice to him. Such dealings had gone unnoticed for a time, until a nosy aristocrat publicly denounced his ways, stealing every ounce of Seric's credibility and leaving him neck-deep in a morass of financial ruin.

It was around then he'd begun to resent his wife. That highborn bitch swam in her finery while Seric drowned in his debts. Their intimacy had ceased, so naturally Seric's eye roved elsewhere, mostly to the young courtesans of the pleasure houses. They adored his dimpled chin and boyish smile, the same of his long nut-brown hair and big summer pine eyes. He was of good stature as well, tall and slender and tinged with the olive skin tone his half-Zhoulish blood had given him.

But soon even the brothels had begun to grow stale, so Seric moved onto greater prizes of interest—the highborn women. Women like Perilia Valayne, who served now as governess of Silverleaf. Seric had once shared a tryst with her in her guest chambers while her fat husband Tavarin was off with his advisors. She was a fiery little thing, passionate and minxish and strong. A shame the affair didn't last. Somehow Zantherei had found out, and in one swift stroke he not only annulled Seric's marriage to Nyvia, but also had Seric shunted to this ramshackle hovel, leaving him to fester with the rest of the city's trash.

He'd lost everything.

It wasn't fair. It wasn't fair that Nethan Dyre had died, and it wasn't fair that his jealous sons conspired against Seric. And it certainly wasn't fair when Zantherei ended his marriage and sent him away. *I deserve more than this, I know I deserve more,* he thought. *How can a man of my talent be reduced to this?*

Seric was thirty-seven. It seemed just yesterday he was a decade younger, but no, here he was now, standing at the doorstep of his middling years. His heart felt both empty and heavy. *How can it be both empty and heavy?* He didn't know, but it was. Yes, this last, lonesome year had truly buried his heart.

But things are going to change, Seric thought, *and soon.*

The warm light of the late afternoon sun bathed him as he exited the household gate. The stench of the surrounding ward made his nose twitch, but his eyes remained alert for cutpurses who lurked in dark alleyways or toughs who waited in shadows beneath the overhang of building eaves. When he spotted a gaunt and hard-eyed fellow watching him from under a tavern awning, Seric mingled with the nearby crowds until he felt safe.

A trestle bridge led over the western canal, bringing him to the avenues of the more affluent districts. Once he'd walked these streets fanned by an imperial escort. It amazed him how quickly people seemed to forget that, how quickly they returned to treating him as a guttersnipe or cur. Of course Seric hated them for it, hated them all, especially the wealthy and the highborn. By the gods he hated those bastards most of all.

The avenue widened upon reaching the crowded market square. Despite the waning of the day, people remained huddled together like scales on a fish. Stallholders loudly rattled their wares, dogs barked, horses clopped, and jugglers and acrobats vied for space to showcase their talents. The axles of oxcarts groaned, churning an endless sheet of dust across the roadways. From inside shop windows, geese and ducks wriggled and honked, hanging from bound feet. The crowd grew so thick Seric had to push his way through, and when he finally got out he was so disoriented he nearly collided into the shoulder pole of a burly porter.

The Red Mimosa stood two blocks away, down a side road in a quieter nook of substandard housing. The brothel was a two-story, timbered structure, warped and old and gray, with broken roof tiles and a windswept façade locked together by horizontal beams of dovetail mortise and tenon joints. Inside, an acrid haze stifled the length of the common room, thickening most near the gambling dens. Seric weaved around benches and tables and screens and serving girls, halting when some drunken fool fell from his seat, and shielding his face when a man blew smoke his way. He climbed the staircase two rickety planks at a time, listening to the aged wood groan underfoot.

He rounded the upper story, guided by a railing that overlooked the bottom floor. To his right were the private rooms, most still vacant at this hour. Seric stopped at a particular one, announcing himself before the door curtain. A courtesan emerging from a nearby room drew his eye—a pretty young girl, barefoot and clothed in a sleeveless blouse just tight enough to keep her plump breasts from spilling out.

The doorkeeper's voice beckoned Seric inside, and he gave one last look to the girl before heading in. He found Ravathyr Aeryn in the small chamber, sitting on a mismatched bench of old cypress. The

Redlander emissary was a slim man who always wore robes too short for his tall frame. His face was narrow and plain, features mousy and forgettable, eyes old and tired and perpetually ringed in dark circles. Hard to believe Ravathyr was only two years Seric's elder. *Either he looks old beyond his years, or I don't look as young as I think.*

Seric found a seat across from him. An oil lamp illuminated the sparseness of the room: a broken cupboard, some old, slanted shelves, little else. An attendant poured two flagons of wine from a vessel that appeared dull and plain, but upon closer look Seric saw a faint texture of gold dust over the russet finish. "It's vintage elderberry," Ravathyr told him. "Sure to suit your palate, my friend." His voice was youthful and energetic, quite the opposite of his tired visage.

In all their meetings, Seric had rarely shared a drink with Ravathyr. He found the emissary difficult enough to read even without wine dulling his senses. In all honestly, Seric didn't like the man much, and he always had a sense that he wasn't liked either. But that mattered little. It wasn't the emissary to whom Seric's faith was sworn. It was to his lord, Raas Dragath, the ruler of the Redlands.

"I called you here to say goodbye," Ravathyr told him. "I am to depart tomorrow at dawn. Lord Dragath fears for my safety, with all that has recently befallen the Hollow."

"A prudent move," Seric told him.

He nodded. "It seems the great Athera clan is not immune to battles of the hearth after all. I never thought brother would betray brother."

"Neither did I."

"It matters not," the emissary said. "Such news is providential. My informants tell me that Zantherei Athera is alive but bedridden, and the Lady Regent has since taken the Imperial Throne."

Seric nodded. "The Lady Regent bears no lack of ambition."

"And in military matters, how does she fare?"

Seric scoffed at the question. "Like the finest steel in the hands of a child . . . utterly incompetent."

Ravathyr's smile was crooked, his teeth the color of bone. He took another gulp of wine. Seric decided to try a sip after all, since this would be their last meeting. It tasted fine. The vintages of the subtropical south were known to be far more pleasing than those of the north, as their fruits were sweeter and more abundant. *Such pleasures I will indulge in soon enough*, Seric thought.

"Lord Dragath moves by night marches into the heart of the province," Ravathyr said. "Thornberry stands no more than two days away. The defector will open the gates, and His Lordship will storm the city." He took another drink. "Dragath will send for you once the city is his."

Seric nodded. "Remember, I am to be appointed director general. Anything less is an unforgivable offense." With that, Seric rose from his seat.

"Of course," Ravathyr said. "It was an honor to have shared such pleasantries with you these past few months, Seric Dyre."

"The honor is mine." He turned and made his exit, heading down the stairs and exiting the brothel.

Outside, a dull gray sky shrouded the earlier radiance of the sun. A light drizzle persuaded Seric to pull up the hood of his cloak. He spotted a clattering of jackdaws perched on the crossbeam of a gate, their gray-black heads cocking and jerking. At Seric's advance they took flight, filling the sky with a chorus of screeches and caws. He watched until they became splotches of ink that eventually faded into the gray.

It means nothing, he decided.

Seric returned to his own household, cold and wet but filled with hope. *Soon I will be free*, he told himself. *Free of all this misery*. He crossed the center courtyard and entered the rear chamber, his heart burning in anticipation of the events to come. If all held true, Seric Dyre would return to power soon enough.

CHAPTER THIRTEEN

Ansetheral Athera had always been short of build, most noticeable when standing beside his eldest brother or his father, who were both men of impressive stature. Brothers Merio and Zantherei were of lesser height, but while Merio was slender and handsome, Zantherei was wide and robust. Anseth was neither handsome nor robust, and he was shorter than both. Truth be told, he was not much taller than his sister, Nyvia.

Now the Vaskultans, like all the Gravelands tribes, were tall men of stern and rugged features, thick of bone and with strong white teeth. Their diet consisted primarily of meat and dairy, while the Anirians relied on grains of millet and wheat, or rice in the far south. And given the average Vaskultan was taller than the average Anirian, many of these men simply towered over Anseth, some uncomfortably so.

He slunk past a pair now, huge guardsmen with massive hands and massive skulls. Their pikes alone must've weighed sixty pounds each, with wooden hafts as thick as the bough of a tree. Anseth felt like a child beneath them—and yet, despite that, he couldn't deny the empowerment he felt whenever he witnessed such large men bowing their heads and standing aside.

The inside of the chieftain's felt-covered pavilion was dim despite the glowing firepit of thorns and sheep dung. Furnishings were scant: stools and animal hides and cushions on the floor, tools and weapons and ladles and pots hanging on the walls. The place was enveloped by the ever-present stench of fish glue and felt and sweat—a stench that used to make Anseth gag, though now he barely noticed.

Lord Volduk was slumped on a bone-carved chair that seemed to serve as his throne. His desert bear hide was draped over him like a blanket, the tips of its golden fur shimmering in the firelight. His grandson of nine was playing at knucklebones by his booted feet, while the lad's elder sister sat braiding horsehair, her close-set eyes and equine features resembling more her uncle Dariok. Volduk's wife stood in the rear of the pavilion, lining felt for embroidery.

Drinking skin in hand, Volduk gestured to the boy. "Here," he said, chuckling. "Give it here." The chieftain shook the knucklebones before tossing them, smiling as he watched the boy snatch them up. Volduk took the bones and played again.

Anseth observed in silence. His injuries had nearly healed—his ankle no longer ached, and his finger had mended without complication. And yet, his physical recovery did little to stanch the anguish of defeat at the hills.

The boy tried to get his grandfather to continue playing, but now the chieftain simply shooed him away. Then he sat back and exhaled. He looked old; Anseth wasn't sure how many springs he'd seen, close to three score, perhaps, but he never looked older than he did at this moment. His eyes were red and strained, his gray-streaked hair twisted in knots, his beard bristly and unwashed. He didn't bother to wipe the snot that seeped from his nostril. "His father," Volduk said, gesturing the boy, "was among the worthiest of men."

It was no secret that the chieftain still grieved over the death of his eldest son, also named Volduk. He had died several years ago, by a salt-tipped arrow that pierced his breast. "Your son's spirit will always live in his child," Anseth told him.

Volduk gazed at him, looking half drunk and rather amused. "You always offer such tripe to those who grieve?"

"It's the truth, lord. When the boy becomes a man, he will make you proud, the same as Volduk."

The chieftain sighed, long and deep. "He may," he said. "Or I may die before then, and the tribe will pass to my remaining heir." He pulled at the golden fur at his shoulder. "Long have I prayed on this matter. Nights I've begged the Skybringer to prevent the passing of the tribe to my unworthy son. Months passed, seasons, before I was finally given an answer." He shook his head and laughed. "And then you went and ruined it."

"Lord?" Anseth was taken aback.

Volduk nibbled on a finger-length stick of milk curd. "Why did you plead for Dariok's life?"

"To honor my own fault, lord."

The chieftain shot to the edge of his chair, fingers grasping bone. "Don't lie to me," he said, grimacing. His grandson, nearby, cowered. "Haven't I always done right by you?"

Anseth looked down, like an abashed child before his elder. "Lord, of course . . ."

Muttering, he slumped down again. Dirt-crusted fingernails tapped the skeletal armrests. "Not all men of the north are slow-witted brutes." He paused, only slightly. "You are planning to leave, am I right, Revek?"

Anseth found it difficult to meet the man's eye. "I . . . well, lord—"

"Just answer the question," he snapped.

"Yes."

Volduk offered him a cut of the curd. Anseth declined. The chieftain leaned back and tugged again at the golden hide at his shoulder. "The subjugation of the Serkuts will place four tribes under my rule. Four, Revek. Only one will remain unconquered. Do you know how long it has been since such the northland has seen such dominion?"

Anseth looked down. "I don't know."

The chieftain was quiet for a time. "I'm getting old," he said at last. "The years, they ravage my body. Dariok is eager to take my place. Utterly incapable, but eager."

Anseth didn't know how to reply, but it seemed the great chieftain didn't want one. He spat into the fire and then stuffed more milk curd into his mouth. Swallowing, he said, "You are much like young Volduk, you know. The day I first saw you . . . was the same day my son breathed his very last. His body was still warm when the guards brought you over. You were in a cangue but you looked just like him— smaller, and not so dark as our kind, but there was that same fire in your eyes, that same cunning and strength. I thought the Landforger had returned to me Volduk's spirit . . . I thought you were him, a ghost returned, a revek."

Anseth stuttered to reply. "My lord, I—"

"But if you leave the north I'll know that I was wrong."

That angered him. "Lord, I am grateful for all you've done. But I no longer owe you a debt. It was paid when I smashed the Serkut army at Snake Tail Ridge and gave you Lord Yugarak on a salver. And were it not for his general's ambush, I would be home right now, not forced to winter another year in this wretched place."

Anseth immediately regretted his temper. Not only that but he'd said too much, revealed too much of the frustration in his heart. Lord Volduk remained impassive, unmoving. "You might not have to," he said calmly. "Lord Yugarak will soon face betrayal."

Anseth only looked at him, stunned and without speech.

"I've arranged a meeting with the first general, the one who led the ambush that kept you in this 'wretched place', as you say. General Guriyek has offered to deliver his lord's head in exchange for the salvation of his tribespeople." He took another chew of the curd. "You need not stay any longer, Revek. I am freeing you of your burden." He took another long swig, belched, and signaled to the door of the yurt. "You can go now."

Outside, the dull pink of twilight was swiftly descending into darkness.

It looked much like the very day Anseth had returned from the White Throat Hills, the day he'd saved Dariok's life. He remembered emerging from the pavilion, turning when he'd felt the chieftain's son grasp his arm. "I didn't ask for your mercy," Dariok had said. "And I won't be your suckling because of it."

"I didn't do it for you," Anseth had told him.

Anseth tore himself from the memory, his eyes drifting up to the waxing moon. *Haven't I always done right by you?* The chieftain's words weighed heavily on his heart. Dariok's death was best for the future of the tribe, and yet he had prevented that. *I've wounded Volduk with my deceit. How could I commit to such selfishness? This man has done nothing but carry me. I shouldn't be allowed to keep my head, never mind return home.*

But he was free now, free to leave without fear of reprisal. Still, even as his heart enlivened with the thought of returning home, guilt and shame quickly pulled him back. Anseth knew he couldn't leave, not yet, not like this. Not until he could make peace with Volduk, if that was at all possible. *I must be patient a little longer.*

That night he tried not to think of his family, yet his thoughts betrayed him. He wanted to look upon Alarin as he was now, the man with only one leg. And what of everyone else? Brothers, sisters, uncles and cousins. *What will they think when they see me?*

A week later the drone of the horn pulled Anseth from sleep. He rose at once, groggily adjusting the fit of his armor. He threw on his heavy coat, fastening it beneath the left underarm, and over that he put on a thick fur. He applied a layer of insulating grease to his face rather desultorily before heading out. It was the dead of night. The wind bellowed and the snow blasted with uncanny strength, blanketing the area in a haze of white.

Kirik was preparing the horses. The bondsman's mare was so unsettled he had to give her flank a good drub or two before he could tighten the saddle straps and mount. "Too cold for this shit," he grumbled. A gloved hand came up to shield his eyes from the gale.

Ahorse, they trudged through snow already several inches high, and likely to double by the hour. Along the outskirts of the encampment the Vaskultan ranks were forming. Volduk stood at its head, his guards and generals around him. Dariok was wrapped in his wools, brooding, while beside him stood Severak Bonesplitter and the powerful General Kaigon.

Anseth dismounted and handed off the reins to a groom, then joined the foreranks to silently observe the dark smudges in the distant white. It was a company of Vaskultan outriders leading a disjointed column of Serkut survivors. The poor wretches looked half dead as they fought through the gale and the snowpack. Leading the miserable lot was General Guriyek.

The general came before Volduk and fell to a knee. He offered up something to the chieftain—it was a head, the head of Yugarak, Lord of the Serkuts. Volduk held it up and the surrounding Vaskultans cheered and shouted and blew their horns. The lifeless face stared back at them, its ears and nose already blackened by frostbite. Volduk roared and flung it into the snow. Strings of hair were left waving above the snowline, like the tentacles of a sea anemone.

Volduk turned to the captives, observing the mass of hollowed eyes and shrunken, defeated faces. "Submit to me and be spared of your transgressions."

The Serkuts fell to their knees, almost all at once.

Volduk nodded. "Your soldiers will serve as bondsman, your old and infirm will serve in the yurts. Your women will be ours to claim, and any offspring will be left to the discretion of the promised suitor. Honor me and be honored in return. Cross me and suffer a traitor's death." Volduk turned and gestured to his generals. "As you can see, rank is gained through merit and worth, not by name or blood. All Vaskultans are brothers."

Volduk ordered his soldiers to escort them to the waiting yurts—all except General Guriyek, who remained kneeling in the snow. Volduk stood over the Serkut, blowing a wad of snot from his nose. "Rise," he commanded. Guriyek was not a small man, but right now he looked puny before Volduk.

"They say you were born with a bow in your hands, general," Volduk said. "You would've slayed me at Red Goat Hill, had your arrow struck an inch lower on my helm."

General Guriyek nodded humbly. "I was honoring my duty, lord."

Volduk nodded at that. "Yes, and now, no more?" There was a pause. "How long have you served Yugarak?"

"Twenty-one years, lord."

"And now you wish to serve me as you did him?"

"Yes, lord. If I am deserving of such an honor, yes."

Volduk thought about it for a moment. "Death is all you deserve." He motioned to his guardsmen.

The general said nothing, brave in the face of his fate. Dariok, however, spun furiously on his father. "What is wrong with you? He gave us the head of the Serkut chieftain. You gave him your word. How could you break faith?"

Volduk turned. His eyes first went to Anseth, a knowing gaze, as if to say, *this is why he cannot rule*. Then he turned to his son. "Any man who betrays his lord will do the very same to you," he said.

CHAPTER FOURTEEN

He wore his finest tunic and trousers, boots of sheared lambskin, and an outer jacket trimmed in fox fur dyed a deep green to complement his eyes. His cloak was the only plain garment in his ensemble, worn in reverence to the drab Anirian customs. That aside, Seric looked more than proper enough to fancy an audience with Lady Miriana Athera.

And yet, as the armed escort led him down the imperial avenues, Seric couldn't help but feel as though he were walking to his own execution. *Why would the Lady Regent summon me? Was she somehow apprised of my alliance with the Redlands? I don't see how.* Images of what she'd done to that boy Kalen flashed in his mind. *I'll not beg as he did. My life may be of little worth, but I will not beg.*

The Lady Regent's imperial bedchamber stood in the eastern wing of the palace. Inside, scents of fresh lavender touched his nose, that and the subtle nuances of hyacinth and perhaps lily. The room was furnished with a curtained bed, couch and desk and washstands, rosewood table screens, and a number of curio cabinets. Luxurious wall carpets hung between the pair of large scrollwork windows, and lighting the chamber were braziers and sconces finely detailed in black and gray floral lace.

Lady Miriana was standing at the foot of the bed, her servants and guardsmen around her. She was a tall woman who looked taller with her adorned feather-and-pearl headdress. Lower, she wore a gray brocade dress with a long fantailed skirt, tight and pleasing. When she saw Seric she casually motioned for him to sit on the couch. He obeyed at once, his attention falling to the exquisite details in the furniture's woodwork. Feather-carved armrests joined with the back slats to form the wingspan of a roc, a bird so large it was known to haul oxen into the sky.

Miriana's handmaiden offered Seric a goblet of wine. She was a young thing—no more than twenty, with curly dark hair and smooth dark skin and eyes that were like two chestnut fruits buried in clear white snow. It was no mystery why Miriana seemed to favor her above the others. She was a pretty little lady, especially in those gossamer silks.

"Yana, you may go now," Miriana said. The young woman bowed and withdrew. Seric said, "Yana? I was expecting something a bit more difficult to pronounce, my lady." It was commonly known that most Sijian names were lost on the Anirian tongue.

Miriana chuckled as she came closer. "Her name's Yanha'ashtu . . . but Yana suits her well enough." She took a moment to adjust the fall of her silks before taking a seat nearby. "She was my gift after the Sijian subjugation. An eastern courtesan trained in western etiquette."

Seric went to reply, but his eyes were drawn to the surrounding blue cloaks of her imperial guardsmen. "Leave us, all of you," Miriana suddenly said, dismissing even Cyrille Vileron. Soon, they were alone —or it seemed they were alone, as Seric remained wary of the wall curtains and recessive alcoves—anywhere a guard might lie in wait. He dared not trust her. "Tell me why I'm here, my lady."

Miriana quietly observed him for a moment, then her hands came up to remove her headdress. Black tresses cascaded down past her shoulders. She nudged the loose strands away from her face; she was beautiful. "Your candor is uplifting, Seric." She looked down and was silent for another moment, as if considering her thoughts. "Three nights ago Raas Dragath stormed Thornberry and routed the Anirian garrison. Action must be taken, now, before he moves on the Hollow. The court seeks the counsel of my husband, they believe he is still within his faculties . . ." She hesitated. "I lied to them. I lied to maintain my standing. Truth is, my husband remains unconscious, the same as the day he fell."

Seric didn't know how to reply. He wasn't surprised by her words but her choosing to confide in him.

"If I seek counsel from inner strategists it will arouse suspicion," she went on. "Vylas offers his hand in support, but I have no faith in my brother's strategies. But you, Seric, my husband has always spoken highly of you, in regards to military matters, that is."

Seric paused. "My lady, are you asking for my counsel?"

"Listen, Seric, I know well the animosity between you and Zantherei. I never condoned how he treated you. But I—"

"My lady," he interrupted, angry. "I will sit here and drink wine from your fancy goblet and play to your courtesies, but I will never believe you have ever given a rat's prick about me. The fact that I am here right now shows only the depths of your desperation. Your husband is two shades from being a corpse and you have no strategy in you. Soon the truth will come out and the court will cast you from your high seat."

She glared at him quietly, long and hard. Seric didn't wilt under that glare, didn't regret what he said—it was the truth, after all.

"You're right, Seric," she said at last. "All I can do is plead for your aid . . . in my greatest time of need, and without public acknowledgment."

"My lady, you cannot ask this of me."

"But I am asking this of you. Would you deny your Lady Regent because of past grievances? If so, then perhaps you're not the man I thought you were."

"Oh but I am, my lady." Seric knew she was goading him but

didn't care. "I'm no armchair strategist. My knowledge was gained on campaigns—on the field and in the messes, the tents, around the cook-fires. I've come to learn our generals well, was taught to use their strengths while avoiding their weaknesses. General Pentagath is brave but reckless and vainglorious. General Sabriel Soffin is disciplined and strong but only under a clear objective. I have *real* experience, my lady. I am no petty bookworm or scholar."

"Impressive, Seric," she said. "Now prove it."

Seric paused. If he agreed to offer counsel it would be a direct breach of faith with Raas Dragath. All that planning, all the letters and promises, all the private audiences with that irritable emissary—it would all be severed. *And for what? What do I hope to gain in this?*

Her hand reached for his, her fingers soft and smooth and slightly darker about the knuckles. Every rational thought told him to get out of this, told him that the webs were tightening . . . and yet, he couldn't deny her. Their eyes met. Stunningly blue, they were. Seric sighed. "You must not allow Demien Mordall to take command of this campaign."

"Lord Demien Mordall is our most paramount hero," she said firmly. "Not only that but the defeated general is his brother. I don't understand—how could I not allow him to go?"

"Because that is what Raas Dragath expects. In fact, he is strategizing for it, planning on playing against Demien's emotions, his clouded judgment. Trust me, my lady, do not send him."

Miriana seemed unwilling to accept his request. "No one else can stand against Raas Dragath."

"Not in a direct clash of steel," Seric said, "but any military strategist of worth would avoid facing Dragath in such a way anyhow. He would always look to use his weaknesses against him. What are his weaknesses, you're going to ask. Well, the man is arrogant for one, quick to temper and overzealous at the first hint of victory. Do you understand?"

She told him she did.

"In knowing this, I would advise you to mobilize the reinforcing army and engage Dragath's troops just east of the Horns of Vermillion.

But instead of pushing the advance, draw the enemy into the western valley between the twin Horns. Dragath will follow, knowing the slope of the surrounding ridges offers no chance for concealment. Understood?"

Again, she told him yes.

"Now, during the midnight hours, divide the army. Send a regiment of bowmen to the southern ridge, on foot, since the terrain will be difficult. The north is far more passable, so send a mounted force of the empire's crack soldiers. Come morning, have the center host resume battle. By signal, both regiments will assail the enemy from above. It'll be over quickly, in minutes."

She leaned back, her face darkening in disappointment. "Seric, you just said there's no place of concealment on those ridges. Raas Dragath will spot the flanking regiments clear as day."

Without reply Seric stood and walked over to the window and opened the wooden shutters. A soft pinkish twilight glowed above the mountaintops to the west.

"What are you doing?"

"Won't you come here, my lady?"

Miriana was frowning. He could tell she wasn't in the mood for such a seemingly inane request. Still, she did as he asked.

"The greatest military strategist is he who is aware of more than just strengths and weaknesses, or simple advantages of terrain," Seric told her. "He is receptive to all signs from the heavens—climatic as well as prognostic." He pointed to the sky. "Look, my lady. The clouds are shallow and clustered like fish scales. The birds fly low, and the leaves of the trees are slowly baring their undersides. Soon, heavy rains will sweep down from the west, bringing with it a great blanketing fog down from the highlands." He turned to her. "Now, what happens here on the third day will fall upon the Horns of Vermillion on the fifth. And not only is the fog thicker in the valley, but this time of year it will take longer to die away, because of the weakening sun. There will be no better concealment for the soldiers on the ridges."

She was still looking off in the distance. When she spoke she spoke quietly, reflectively. "Raas Dragath will never suspect . . ."

He nodded. "Again, his arrogance, my lady."

She was silent for another moment, before suddenly turning on him. "And who would you appoint as commander of this campaign?"

"General Sabriel Soffin will not deviate from his orders," he replied. "He alone is fit to lead."

She seemed comforted by his words. It was nice, standing there with her, watching the twilight deepen into dusk. Finally, in a near whisper, she said, "Bring me victory and I will be most generous in return, Seric."

"I have debts," he said.

"All will be paid, plus an additional five thousand strings, and not a single coin less."

"You are kind, my lady."

Seric took his leave soon after. Conflict ruled his thoughts. A part of him was elated by Miriana's warmth and excited to please her, and yet, he couldn't help but fear the consequences. *What am I doing? I shouldn't have counseled her—I've been offering intelligence to Raas Dragath this whole time.* He almost laughed at his situation, having severed his faith to the Redlands and abandoned his lofty ambitions of director general. *And for what? A private offering of wealth?* But it was more than that, he knew, it was for a chance to serve her again, to climb the rungs of Anirian power. Still, everything was growing too complicated, too blurred. It was as if he had been handed the executioner's axe, and he was sharpening the steel himself.

CHAPTER FIFTEEN

The Hall of Obsidian Light was large enough to comfortably seat a small army, with rows of fluted columns dividing the bays and massive pilasters, gilded sconces, and ornate relics embellishing the deep interior. The ceiling itself was a round coffer carved in a large bas-relief of clouds and stars and multi-headed beasts of various shapes and sizes. On the dais below stood the empire's most privileged seat, the Imperial Throne, a massive carving of black pine, with armrests shaped like the heads of howling Sadralen, and a high splat centered by twin, spiraling horns. It was an empowering feeling to sit here, even though aside from her usual host of guardsmen and attendants, Miriana Athera sat alone.

She watched absently as her attendants removed the tableware. It had been a less than pleasing meal; the honeyed calf liver was over-seasoned, the mushrooms flavorless, the shaddock too sour. She had downed it all with a few goblets of wine, but even that tasted blander than usual. Thoughts of Seric Dyre kept her in good spirits, however.

He was the unpolished gem in her arsenal. If his stratagems proved as effective as he claimed, then her seat on the throne was secure. And just by giving this man such an unlikely opportunity meant she would always have his loyalty.

The double-doors at the far end opened with a tired lurch. Miriana saw the Minister of Finance enter. Garlan was a small pear-shaped man who walked with an awkward waddle. When the minister took his seat opposite her, he unslung a haversack from his robed shoulder and placed it on the table, smiling nervously. He stood again when he realized that he'd forgotten his bows and courtesies, but Miriana held out a hand and motioned him back down. He apologized fervently, sat, and scratched at the gray stubble that clung to his chubby jowls. "M-my lady," he said, stammering as he always did. "I am grateful, very grateful for your audience." His nasally voice was as awkward as his gait.

"I am available to all honorable ministers of the realm," she replied, though not hiding her impatience.

He smiled, retracted it, then smiled again. "I humbly petitioned for your audience because I . . ." He stopped to unbind the leather thong of the haversack.

"Go on, Minister," she urged, although her attention was diverted by the letters he'd pulled out. They were sheets of old mulberry, wrinkled and discolored with age. He said, "I was given the Imperial Advisor's private accounts, as you know, after his . . . detainment."

"Yes," she said, her fingers drumming the tabletop.

He placed the letters before her. "Well, while I was sorting through . . . I happened upon these strange correspondences, my lady."

She read the words but the context meant little to her, so they were forgotten a moment or two later. She looked back up to regard Minister Garlan. "I've no time for pettiness. I wished only to be informed if anything of note was found."

Minister Garlan jumbled his words before finally getting them out properly. "My lady, but . . . these are of note, please—"

"Just tell me then, and do it quickly," she snapped.

He swallowed. "They are of note because you see, well, my lady, they appear to have been written by Ansetheral Athera."

It took a moment or two before the name sank in—and even when it did, she still wasn't sure she heard it right. Anseth Athera had died at the hands of the northern tribesmen, at the battle of Black Gate Pass, and she told him that, adding, "Are you are trying to make a fool of me?"

He shook his head vehemently. "No—never, my lady. But they *are* from Anseth. The earliest are dated two years after Black Gate. The exchanges go on and on until"—he was rifling through the pages now—"Here, this one. This seems to be the most recent. A lunar month, if that."

Miriana skimmed it, focusing mainly on the last lines. *The Serkuts are tired and their mettle is dulled. Tomorrow I will face them at Snake Tail Ridge. The hour is at hand. My faith will soon be fulfilled. I will send again with word of victory. Wait for it, my brother.*

Her heart thumped faster. The minister began speaking again but Miriana wasn't listening. *How could I have not known of this?* she wondered. *How did he keep this a secret for so long?* Not even Zantherei knew. Miriana's head became heavy, her eyes dull and tired. *Another blockade in my path.* She rested her chin in her hands, lowering her gaze. "Minister," she said. "Have you shared your findings with anyone?"

His eyes remained downward. "Not a soul, my lady . . . a loyal vassal comes to his lord—his lady, first. Always."

She believed him. The man was a garrulous old fool, but he wasn't dishonest. "Good," she told him. "You must keep it this way. Can you do that for me, Minister? No need to unleash the rumormongers before I confirm the truths."

He told her yes and she thanked and dismissed him, watching as he tottered down the length of the hall in small ungainly steps. Miriana then shoved the letters back into the haversack and headed back to her bedchamber without so much as a glance at anyone around her. Once inside, she dismissed her attendants and went to her writing desk.

Her hands trembled as she pulled the letters from the haversack.

She studied the most faded of the stack, likely the earliest of the correspondences. She stopped at one and used a finger to guide her through
the worn and smudgy print as she read. *These men are naught but
savages and nomads, forever at war with competing tribes. Raiding
and looting and stealing women are no more to them than sleeping or
eating. These past two years I have suffered untold hardships. I am
only able to write you now because of a raid from a rival tribe had
freed me from my captors. I'm now in a strange sort of solidarity with
my saviors, these Vaskultans, they are called. Their chieftain seems to
have taken a liking to me. His soldiers display no ill-will toward my
foreign blood.*

Miriana couldn't read the next few lines, so she skipped down a bit.
*I implore you, as my brother, who has fought beside me, who has
suffered the humiliation of defeat just as I have, I implore you to let me
remain here, in the north. I plan to ride with these men, these Vaskultans, until I've avenged our defeat at Black Gate Pass. This is my
word, my proclamation, and be assured if I see a single Anirian standard I will not halt the Vaskultan attack, nor will I be cajoled, and if
force is attempted in my retrieval I will slit my throat or bash my head
on the nearest stone. I know you will honor my wishes, my brother. You
are a man of integrity.* Again, the next lines were illegible, so she
skipped farther down. *I will return after the Serkuts are vanquished.
For now, let the news of my death keep over the Hollow. No one can
know the truth, not our brothers, not our father, not even my wife and
child.* Miriana gave pause at that. In grief, Anseth's wife had killed
both her daughter and herself after word of Anseth's death had reached
the Hollow. She read on. *I know my return can only come through
redemption, and redemption can only come through vengeance. It is
not a selfish act, but my duty to the realm, and to the House of Anir. If I
die here it is without regret, but be assured that I plan to return with
the enemy chieftain's head upon—*

A voice at the door startled her. Miriana shot to her feet, her arm
bumping the table and sending the letters to the floor. She cursed.
Cyrille's raspy voice called again. She snapped back, "What is it? I
ordered not be to disturbed."

"My lady, it's Vylas. He humbly begs your audience. It's of great importance, he says."

She sighed. From the nearby bedrail, she threw on a silk robe. "Let him in."

The door opened. Vylas was frowning as he stepped into the light of the braziers, his halfmask and face both highlighted orange-red. His good eye drifted to pile of the fallen letters. "My apologies, Sister, but this cannot wait." The flame of the nearby brazier crackled, sending a spark to the floor. Vylas glimpsed there briefly, then his pale hand went to the sleeve of his robe, emerging with a scroll. Miriana took it at once. Opening, she read:

With the growing power of the regent, we the empire's representatives fear the inevitable usurpation of the throne. Breaking the faith laid by the honorable Lasarin Athera, the seditious son Zantherei has abused and taken all imperial power into his own jurisdiction, centralizing all military and civil affairs from taxation to land grants to holdings. He continues to enforce his authority by unjustly drawing support and influence from the feudal barons.

We, the honorable subjects of the sole remaining scion of the realm, have forged this union with the aim for change. Our unimpeachable loyalty will scourge the realm of the regent's wrongdoings, and together we will restore the holy shrines that have guided us since our ancestors descended the very mountains of the Anir. There will be no rest until the rightful sovereign ascends the throne. It is through our hands, as sanctioned by Emperor Thavian Siven himself, during the tenth month, fall, year 442 of the dynasty of the Anir.

She observed the mark of the emperor's official seal and the signatures beneath it. Signatures of high-ranking officials—men of purported good faith, men who smiled and bowed when they saw her. One name in particular stuck out like a dagger in her heart: Sydrian Rane. She read the name again, as though her eyes were deceiving her. "Our very own Minister Steward," she muttered. The man had been loyal to the Anir longer than she'd been alive, and had served as a high minister since before the capital had moved north to the Star of the Hollow. Never would she have suspected such treason in him.

A sudden memory hit her. The day her husband lay poisoned on the featherbed. Miriana had killed the young retainer Kalen that day, and had ordered Alarin stripped of rank and arrested. But this . . . this mandate proved both innocent. She brushed back her hair, her fingers warm and clammy. "I have done a terrible injustice," she confessed. "I killed an innocent man. It is I who deserves death."

"No, Sister," he said. "You were goaded by duplicitous men. It's not your fault."

Kind words, but she found little relief in them. *He understands, but the court will not.*

That night Miriana lay awake beneath her silk coverlets. Yana snored softly beside her, the dark curls of her hair draped across Miriana's chest. She caressed the young woman gently enough, though her mind was awhirl with disquiet. She focused on what needed to be done, now, first and foremost. To expose that wretched Sydrian and his fellow conspirators would exonerate Alarin, and in turn, subject herself to his recrimination. That damn cripple would never let Kalen's death go unpunished.

She would have to remove him. There was no other way. She would have to eliminate him. And to deflect any suspicion from the court, the death must be seen as natural, as though from illness. A certain poison could do that, and rather effectively, but Nyvia had her personal sentries posted all over his tower, making it nearly impossible to get a man like Cyrille Vileron inside, nor any nameless hired hand for that matter. No, she needed the right person. Someone she could trust, yet also someone of good faith with Alarin. Someone like Seric Dyre. Only Seric could get past Nyvia's guards, and only Seric could coax Alarin into lowering his guard. Still, to commit an act so heinous, the price would not be so simple this time. She had to offer something more.

That left her with her one final snag; well, two: the first being that portly little minister whose silence she wasn't completely assured of. The second was much more disconcerting—the snag of Ansetheral Athera. To remove Anseth she needed a loyal man with limited ties to the Athera clan. Her mind eventually settled on Lord Duren Lygrest, the provincial governor of Cragspawn. He liked Zantherei little, and Alarin even less. Yes, Lygrest could carry out her wishes in secret—of course for the right price. She would find out that price, and arrange it. *You can do this, Mir,* she thought to herself. *You are strong, strong as silk. Strong as any man.*

Content at last, Miriana's eyes began to close. She drifted off to thoughts of how she would expose the conspirators, of how they would die. And the very next day, she stood on the balconied terrace, engulfed by the morning light as she watched the courier ride out of the gates, bearing a sealed letter addressed to Governor Lygrest. Two days after that, Miriana was busy organizing the funeral of Minister Garlan, who had died suddenly in the comfort of his own bedchamber.

CHAPTER SIXTEEN

H is milkname was Little Beast, a name given by his aunt not in jest but in bitter cruelty. She would call him that and she would call him other nasty things, and when she was truly angry, she would send him into the dark of the nearby wood, where the ugly bugbear creatures preyed on little children. For years Szathan Mordall had believed this, for years he had thought himself a cursed little bantling who never should've been born. It wasn't until much later that he learned the truth: his aunt wasn't his aunt at all, but in fact his mother, a mother so shamed by her son that she had denied ever giving him life.

She died when Szathan was twelve, and at fifteen he left the life of a farmhand to follow his elder brother, Demien, and enlist in the imperial academy. He'd already been an ugly young man, but when he began to grow and grow and grow, he only became uglier and uglier and uglier, which led to mockery from his peers and ridicule from his arms instructors. Why? To this day he couldn't say, though he'd never been among the smartest of men.

His unnatural growth spurt had left him a disproportionate thing. His head was long and misshapen and fitted by tiny blackberry eyes that looked even tinier beneath his overextended brow. He suffered throbbing headaches and terrible cramping in his oversized hands and feet, but a worse pain came from seeing the complete opposite features in his brother. Demien Mordall stood among the tallest heads of the academy, but unlike Szathan, he was a well-proportioned individual, with a powerful build to match his chiseled features.

Still, ugly as he was, Szathan had excelled as a fighting man, and at twenty-four, he found himself in the foreranks of one of the empire's most prominent military regiments. But his head was too large to fit the helm of standard issue, and his purse too light to afford his own. His rankmates had of course jeered him for this, too, calling him Szathan the Unhelmed or Ogre Mordall. It was around then he met a newly appointed squad commander, a paunchy, two-fisted sort by the name of Gilberon Brehems. Privately, Brehems had said, "Prove your mettle, my friend, and I'll have them fools ante up enough coin to forge you a proper helm."

Well, Szathan did prove his mettle, in the first skirmish and the next, and many more battles after that. Now, at thirty-four, he was not only an esteemed military commander of the city of Thornberry, but one of the empire's most illustrious generals. Gilberon Brehems now served proudly as his second, and he, like all the soldiers here, had come to deeply respect and admire the big man.

Well, they used to, Szathan thought bitterly. *Not so much now. Not since I'd been driven out of Thornberry.* He shifted his weight in the saddle, steadying the massive black charger beneath him. When the beast calmed, Szathan's eyes turned upon his serried ranks of heavy cavalry. Thick morning fog swaddled the men like a blanket of snowy fleece, obscuring the raised ensigns and reducing the depth of the ranks. It was a welcome fog, a fog that would provide the cover needed to ambush the enemy below. Since dawn, the Redlander army had swarmed upon the Anirian soldiers in the lowland valley, with none other than the abominable Raas Dragath himself leading the assault.

It'd only been a few weeks since Dragath had taken the city of Thornberry, and the defeat still plagued Szathan's heart. If he were more cunning perhaps he would've foreseen his own officer's defection, but no, in the end that traitor Hiriam Thraves had opened the city gates and allowed Raas Dragath to storm inside.

Half of Szathan's garrison had been slaughtered that day, with many more wounded. Szathan himself had only escaped after a dangerous leap from the wall parados to the outer stairs. Raas Dragath had pursued him doggedly, calling for his oversized head. He nearly had it when Szathan and the remnants of his men became trapped in a defile. Only a flanking charge by his old friend Gilberon Brehems had saved him, miraculously pushing the enemy back and bottlenecking them in a narrow bridgehead. Eventually Dragath withdrew, but little did Szathan know, the true ordeal had only just begun.

The regiments, bloody and beaten, had limped across the countryside for weeks, exhausting what little sustenance the surrounding villages could provide. For Szathan, as it probably was for any commander, it was more painful not to see his men die bravely in battle, but to see them die alone and scared and succumbing to some terrible affliction, be it dysentery, pneumonia, ague . . . whichever decided to take them first.

Gilberon Brehems had lost two brothers. One died honorably in battle, but the other succumbed to a single gash of the thigh. It was one of those goddamn wounds that just wouldn't stop bleeding, no matter how much you'd staunch and suture and dress it. After four days the poor man could no longer walk, so Brehems had to carry him, and carry him he did, for two days and over some harsh terrain at that. And he would've kept on carrying him had someone not pointed out that the man was dead. Even then, Brehems still didn't stop, not at first, not until Szathan talked a bit of sense into his head. They buried his brother that night, and poor Brehems hadn't been the same since.

Reinforcements from the Hollow had arrived a week later, but strangely enough, Szathan didn't find Demien at the van, no, it was

General Sabriel Soffin. What? That made little sense. Demien was the Grand Commandant of the Hollow, the realm's highest ranked military commander. The decision to take up arms was his to make. How could he not rush to the aid of his own goddamn brother?

A flash lit the sky, yanking Szathan from his thoughts. A moment later the signal bomb burst. With a shout Szathan set the mounted ranks into motion. The ground shuddered beneath the boom of horse hooves. Thick fog parted like soft white silk. Szathan stole a glance at his men. Grim-faced veterans they were, all clad in imbricated scale armor and steel halfhelms, with spears or halberds or long-handled sabers sitting in the saddle rings of their caparisoned horses. This was the Black Pine regiment, a handpicked force of the empire's most elite soldiers. Szathan had no less than his complete faith in every one of his rankmates.

He estimated the enemy's distance. *Two hundred yards. One-fifty.* To the east, misty shapes began to form into aspens and oaks and maples, colorless and nearly bare yet somehow still elegant, like graceful strokes of ink on soft vellum. The trees began to part, allowing a view of the battleground. *One hundred yards now,* Szathan thought. *Ninety, eighty.* The remainder of the fog gave way to a darker, dustier cloud of churned earth. Shadowy forms rose to reveal a column of Redlander infantrymen. Oblivious they appeared to the oncoming threat, like chaff waiting to be husked.

Fifty yards. Forty. The impetus of the charge was unstoppable now, a great wave of steel and iron and flesh. Szathan could see clearly his enemies' weapons, the spears and sabers and broadaxes, along with the protection of lamellar plates and open-faced helms and the occasional shield. *Thirty, twenty.* He pulled his figured halberd Nightwing from its saddle ring. Enemy banners waved frantically now, signaling the Redlander soldiers to turn and face the oncoming charge. And they did, the soldiers did eventually turn . . . but it was too late.

CRACK. A tremendous sound, like a hundred trees snapping at the bole. The Redlander wing bowed and buckled but somehow held, even as men were smashed and crushed and sent flying through the air. Szathan barreled through the enemy ranks, his thoughts moving faster than the world around him. It was strange, how differently time moves when a man enters battle. It slows to a sluggard's pace, yet a man's thoughts were as swift as ever, so Szathan had planned out three or four different maneuvers in the time it took for him to execute but one. A difficult concept to explain to those who'd never soldiered.

Szathan cut down the first foeman he saw, some poor wretch who didn't even see him coming. The steel blade of his figured halberd sliced through the base of the foeman's neck, tearing through gorget and flesh and bone. Szathan retracted his weapon to parry the thrust of another man's spear. *Clang.* Nightwing juddered in his hands. A sweeping counter struck the enemy in the face, sending ribbons of blood through the air, some splashing into Szathan's eyes, blinding his left. He pawed at it once, but that only made things worse. He fought on until he could spare a moment to give it another wipe. Got it. The eye reopened. A spearhead came screaming at his face. Szathan parried the thrust and whirled to retaliate, but the enemy was gone, hacked down by a nearby rankmate.

Forward, forward he pushed his men. Forward into that dark gulch of hot, sweaty death. Szathan used the top spike of his halberd to stab a foeman's throat, and when he yanked it out, cartilage and windpipe came with it. Szathan flung the gory pink tentacle at another Redlander before cleaving him down through the forehead. He heard a terrible shriek from one of his own men, some two or three bodies to his left. It stopped suddenly, like a corked bottle, and so it went forgotten, as Szathan continued to cut down foeman after foeman. Blood and gore painted the land around him. Forward, he pushed. Forward, forward, forward.

Soon, the dark began to give way. Dust broke apart. The enemy was fleeing now. A chaotic rout, with men running every which way, trampling one another, stabbing one another, anything to get through the wall of steel and horseflesh. The Black Pine regiment chased them down, slicing their backs and skewering the disgraceful cowards as they fled. Swords and shields and discarded pieces of armor littered the ground. Szathan searched for Raas Dragath's personal ensign. There it was, the two-headed serpent of the Red Terror. The bastard was his at last.

He never saw the axe. It cut through his stallion's forelegs, throwing Szathan off the saddle. The ground rose up. *Boom.* Pain shot through his body, pain that Szathan was trained to ignore. Experience told him at once that he needed to move, and move he did. The axe thrummed down, splitting the earth. Szathan lunged at its owner, tackling the smaller soldier like a man overpowering a child. He rammed the steel brow ridge of his helmet into the foeman's face, once, twice, three times before the bastard finally went limp.

He could hear Brehems calling for him. Szathan lurched to his feet and motioned for him to go on. "Bring back Dragath's head," he shouted. Brehems gave a fierce nod and galloped off with a host of men. Szathan staggered over to his wounded charger. One leg was sliced clean off, just above the forehoof, the other left dangling by ribbons of pink tissue. Szathan unsheathed his saber and ended the beast's suffering. Then he turned his eyes back on the battle. The clash of steel was fading now, the thunder of horse hooves no longer deafening. Soon, all that remained were the anguished wails and dying moans of those left behind.

Hours had passed before Gilberon Brehems finally returned. The stocky general wore a disappointed frown as he explained in detail how Raas Dragath had gotten away. Still, Szathan didn't care, and not because he'd already drunk enough wine to sooth his aches and drive away the demons of his mind. No, he didn't care because today was a day of victory, and a day of vengeance. The city of Thornberry was his once again.

CHAPTER SEVENTEEN

"I felicitate you, my lady," Seric told her. "They call you the Lady of Divine Whispers now."

Miriana smiled at that. "Such praise is meant for you, Seric."

They were alone in her chambers, seated on the wooden couch before the licking flames of the braziers. Seric was sure the excess of wine had gotten to him, but he couldn't help but ogle her, and now without any sense of discreetness. She seemed not to notice, or maybe she did and simply ignored it. Either way the woman looked especially stunning today, from the smoothness of her high-cheeked face to every lock of her bound, dark hair. Her eyes were most engaging of all—upturned and blue and deeply alluring. There was a certain mystique about a woman whose beauty was almost too dazzling to be that of a mortal. *Settle yourself, Seric,* he thought. *You've had far too much to drink.*

"It is enough to know I have helped secure your standing, my lady," he told her. "Enough to know that you've chosen me in your time of need." He stopped himself from speaking further, for fear of saying too much. She offered no reply and only moved to fuss with the cap sleeve of her silk blouse, a beautiful, high-collared garment embroidered in rich cherry blossoms. When she was done she said, "Master Arden Lorian informs me that my husband moves closer to death. I fear it will be soon. Tell me, Seric, does that please you?"

Yes, he thought. *And more so if the wretch is suffering*. But aloud he said, "My lady, only a small-minded wretch would take pleasure from an honorable man's misfortune."

She looked down, nodding. "Yes, and you are no such man. But I . . . I wish I could say the same of myself." She sighed deeply. "I've recently learned the names of the conspirators involved in the plot against my husband. The evidence proves Alarin innocent of collusion —in fact, he was made to serve as scapegoat."

Seric nodded. He had suspected as such. For generations the House of Athera raised itself on pacts stronger than earth and steel. The devotion of their kin was indissoluble.

"My husband once told me that a worthy ruler never acts out of anger, or through clouded judgment, or without assurance of proof," she went on. "I have acted out of all three." Her next words hung in the air like a grim portent. "Kalen was like a son to him. To exonerate Alarin is to surrender my neck to the axeman."

Seric wasn't sure if he should offer consolation or counsel. And despite how glum and pitiable she looked, he couldn't deny the feeling that it was but a ruse—that she was simply plying him. *But why?* He would have to wait and see.

"My fate stands then," she went on. "No matter my decision, my head will be impaled on the North Gate."

"Not true, my lady," he told her. He reached for her hand. It was warm and smooth and noticeably paler than his own. She didn't remove it. "Don't absolve him, and don't condemn him."

She looked displeased. "So, do nothing? I can't just do nothing."

"Publicly, it is the only thing you *can* do. The court doesn't know the truth—make sure to keep it that way."

She asked him how, and Seric paused to take another sip of wine from what was probably the most expensive goblet he'd ever held. *By the devil's arse she is making me say what she doesn't want to say herself.* Still, there was something desirable about a woman whose guile almost matched his own. *Almost,* he thought, *but not quite.* He decided then to end this little charade. "My lady, if you truly wish retain your hold of the throne, which I believe you do, then you do not need me to tell you that you must do. Heaven knows you have already thought of it, are perhaps already working toward it. I'm sure you know how easy it is to silence a man."

Her eyes flashed at him, but her calmness held. "Alarin is an innocent man," she said. "To do such a thing . . . what kind of a ruler would I be?"

"One who still rules. Isn't that all that matters?" Seric paused for a moment. "Please, no more wiles," he went on, removing his hand from hers. "The wine may have freed my heart, but it has not made me blind. The real question here is what do you want of me?"

She stared at him, seeming genuinely surprised. "Like I said before, Seric, your candor is uplifting." She took another sip from her goblet, the enchased garnets sparkling in the firelight. "Alarin is guarded by your wife's appointed guards, day and night. No hired hand or any of my own vassals could ever get inside. It has to be someone she'd not expect—"

"Nyvia bears no fondness for me," he cut in. "She is my *former* wife, my lady."

"You've shared your pillow with her," Miriana said. "Surely you know how to make her receptive."

"You mean, know how to cozen her."

She paused abruptly at that. "She trusts you, just as Alarin trusts you."

"Yes, and Alarin is one of the few who showed me any measure of kindness after your husband sent me to a life of poverty," he told her. "He is a good man."

"Yes," she said, "but it matters not. Do not let your sentiment dissuade you, Seric. You will be well compensated for this."

He shook his head. "My lady, with respect, neither coin nor enfeoffment would ever make me consider such an offer. I cannot do this for you."

She leaned close to him now, so close he could smell the fragrance she wore, the pleasing aroma of rose hips and fresh currant, with perhaps a hint of sandalwood musk. A licentious smile had formed on her face. "That was not what I meant to offer." Then she stood, pulling free the gilt spray of berries that twined her hair. Black tresses cascaded down to her bosom like the flowing of dark silk. Reaching up, she untied the clasp of her blouse, letting the garment fall to the floor, followed moments later by her outer skirt, then her tight inner skirt, and finally leaving her with only a simple undergarment beneath.

It was a diamond-shaped camisole that looked to be of fine silk crepe, soft gray in color and tied by a thong in the back and around the neck. The fit was snug against her belly and hips, the brocade edging running down in an outcurve that just covered her sex. Seric, flush with wine, could only goggle at her, his eyes combing every inch of her—so astonished that he couldn't even speak or move. Well, that wasn't *entirely* true. His manhood certainly moved, pushing against the inner fabric of his trousers.

"I see how you look at me, Seric," she purred.

Seric could restrain himself no longer. He went to kiss her, but she only lifted her chin, rebuffing him. His lips brushed against her milky white neck instead, inhaling the momentary sweetness of her flesh. He tried to once more to kiss her lips, and again was rejected. But it was a gentle rejection, a playful one.

Her intent was obvious. To manipulate him through seduction. He knew all this, knew it plain as rain and yet he didn't care. She was the Lady Regent, the most powerful woman in the Hollow—but more than that, she was Miriana Athera. Men would happily give their lives just to glimpse her without her outer garments. Seric himself had more than once fantasized pillowing her, this woman whose beauty had brought the eyes of men from as far as the south-reaching Deadmoon Vale. And now, here she was, alone and nearly naked before him.

He went forward again, firmly now, and suddenly he was on her, kissing her lips and her neck, his hands groping at her camisole, at the soft flesh beneath. She raised her head and emitted a soft moan that made his heart pulse. It was so intense and yet he knew she would soon pull away, and when she did she simply said to him, "That's enough for now."

But Seric wasn't ready to cork his gourd—and not only because of his primal urges. "Not enough," he told her. "Not enough for what you want of me."

She studied him for a long moment, then rose to stand directly before him. Her blue eyes stared down into his. "So be it," she said, reaching back and undoing the thongs of her camisole. Like the gentlest feather, the silk fell away. Bare breasts tumbled free, not the largest he'd seen but certainly smooth and of fine shape, with nipples small and pink. He studied them for some time, before his eyes drifted down to the softness of her stomach, then lower, to the dark curls of her sex. He went to touch her there, but she turned away from him and padded barefoot to the featherbed. Seric watched her go, observing her firm buttocks and long, muscled legs. She lay back on the silk cover-lets, naked and waiting. "Do you accept my offer, Lord Seric?"

Seric was already halfway over to her, his every rational thought overcome by stark impulse. Never had his urge been so fundamentally consuming, an urge that gnawed and gnawed and would continue to gnaw until it was sated with deep, carnal pleasure. He climbed the bed and bridged himself on hands and knees over her. Miriana's eyes were wide with desire; he stared deeply into them. "Yes," he whispered, spreading her legs.

CHAPTER EIGHTEEN

After Seric left, Miriana remained in bed, her loins aching from the girth of his manhood. Her head was still swimming from all the wine, as she had not planned to drink so much, no more than she'd planned to enjoy his touch so. Seric Dyre was of different stock than Zantherei—a comelier man, with his soft green eyes and boyish smile. Not only that, there was compassion in him, a kindness in his caress. Truth be told, he'd stirred a passion that had long been dormant in her, one that she thought might never resurface. But now the very thought of bedding him again made it stir. She couldn't help but smile, although she berated herself for it. *Now is not the time for foolish woolgathering,* she thought. *There are pressing matters at hand.*

And yet, she was still smiling as she swung herself off the bed and stood, suddenly aware of the stickiness between her legs. She listened to it *squish* as she padded barefoot to the scrollwork window, and again as she reached up for the wall hook to pull aside the curtain. Opening the shutters, she closed her eyes and let the crisp evening breeze engulf her. She couldn't help but think again of Seric. He had indelibly proven himself a rare talent, as attested by the victory at the Horns of Vermilion, a victory that had solidified the faith of her subjects. He had further gained her favor by agreeing to the task of removing Alarin Athera. Surely he was proving himself anything but the faithless wretch her husband once denounced him as.

When the cold had worn its welcome, Miriana closed the shutters and had her handmaiden heat a cup of white chrysanthemum tisane with wolfberries, as her head was still throbbing from the excess of wine. Then she had servants prepare her bath, and once ready she entered the grottolike alcove, her bare feet warmed by the underfloor heating. She disrobed beside a gray pillar and waded into the lotus-petaled pool, the effervescent mineral waters soothing her skin. Afterward she lay on a padded table while Yana massaged her body with a mix of fractionated oils and salts. The Sijian girl's touch turned from dutiful to sensual, and Miriana, still infused with wine, felt herself grow aroused. She closed her eyes and thought of Seric Dyre while the young woman pleasured her dutifully with her fingers.

Over the subsequent days, the Hall of Obsidian Light bustled with celebration. Military men and civil officials crammed the rows of benches, shoulder-to-shoulder as they laughed and dined and jeered and jostled. Wine was hauled in no quicker than the empty casks were hauled out, and servants struggled to move through the throng, sidling past large military men too drunk to walk, and likely to remain that way for days to come.

Miriana attended—not to share in the festivities—but simply to observe. From the overhang of a private balcony, she gauged the faces of her conspirators, their jaunty spirits leaving her disgusted and angry and wishing to exact retribution right away. But Vylas managed to conciliate her, as only her brother knew how to do, and under his gentle urgings she left the celebrations entirely.

She found contentment in time spent with Seric, either dining in private or, should the evening be comfortable enough, sharing a peaceful saunter through the Imperial Garden. She was candid about her former life as a courtesan, about her hardships and dejections, but in return Seric only offered glimpses of his life as the baseborn son of a Zhoulish chieftain. She came to the understanding that the abuse he'd faced as a child was deeper than he could articulate, and sometimes he would try, only to stumble and stammer and finally fall into silence. When that happened, she would remedy the mood by either distracting him with playful banter or, when appropriate, a soft caress. On clear nights they would sit and study the stars, sometimes in silence, other times with him rattling off the names of constellations and asterisms, sometimes using his finger to draw their paths and boundaries. More often than not they would return to her private chamber and bed each other, and soon days passed in this manner, days of neglected duties and idle dalliance.

When at last the celebrations ended and the buzz of the capital slipped back into normalcy, Miriana returned to her preparations against the conspirators. But she was suddenly blindsided by countless issues that needed her attention, and she lost the following days tending the whims of the court, as all principal concerns, military and civil, were thrust in her hands. There were piles of petitions and pledges to be scrutinized, government officials to be appointed and demoted, judgments, amercements, anything and everything. She delegated what she could but still her hands would cramp and her energy would be squandered before the end of the day. Worst of all, the treasury was floundering under the new Minister of Finance. Still, incapable as he was, Miriana was loath to remove him. She eventually gave in to the urgings of her administration, replacing him with their championed bureaucrat, who was quick to prove himself no more competent than his predecessor. More than once Miriana found herself wishing Minister Garlan hadn't been so damn curious, so that he'd still be alive today.

Her imperial obligations went on and on until, one day, as if the sudden cessation of a great tempest, they stopped. At last, she was left to make her move.

The hour was late when Miriana entered the dim hall. She wore a plain gown dyed an inky blue that looked black in the gloom. Over it she wore a silk gauze scarf, gray and embroidered by thin, wispy filigree that ran to the tasseled ends. Her hair was styled in ropelike side braids, accentuated by a simple fillet of polished silver.

The rows of waiting guardsmen were stern and silent, offering only the occasional cough or clink of armor. She passed them to ascend the dais, where both Vylas and Cyrille Vileron waited. Both men followed her to her seat on the throne. She took a long moment to adjust her silks, an action that hid what she was truly doing—gathering the courage needed to raise her eyes and look upon the bound and kneeling line of conspirators.

Some faces were familiar and others not so much. She recognized the young assistant Oledd—the one who deceived her by naming Kalen—but only after a long moment, since his face was so twisted by distress. In fact, all of them shared a similar look, their visages either remorseful or meek or utterly defeated. All of them, she realized, except the Minister Steward Sydrian Rane.

The old minister looked angry—no, rabid even, his face flush and twitching like some feral beast ready to strike. There was no fear in him, only an unrestrained hatred, as though it were Miriana who was at fault, as if it was *she* who had conspired against him.

Without realizing it her hands went to the pommel of her husband's prized and jeweled saber, Sunburst, which lay sheathed and concealed beneath the loose folds of her gown. She honestly didn't know why she'd brought it—she had no intention of using it, but perhaps it was something that Zantherei had once told her, some time ago: *a coward orders a traitor's death, while a man of character sends him off himself.*

Miriana rose and stepped to the edge of the raised platform, her leather heels clacking across the glossy gray-and-black tiles. "Such a craven lot," she said. "Together again, as you once were." She pulled the mandate from her sleeve. Its very sight seemed to further sap the strength of the conspirators, as if their last breath of freedom had just been yanked away. A balding man with a beard of fine down staggered forward on his knees, hands bound and raised, declaiming his innocence. When the guards shoved him back, he crawled again forward. They did it again, more forcefully, and finally Cyrille had one of his guards strike him so hard in the gut that Miriana felt it in her own belly. The man crumpled, spewing thick yellow chunks all over the floor. A nearby guardsman groaned when he saw it all over his leather boots.

Miriana's stomach had already been in knots, but the sight of the man's vomit only made it worse. While servants tended the mess, she stood over the man and scowled. "You sicken me." Then, louder to the rest: "All of you. To think such a sorry lot nearly ruined the empire." She made a few *tsk tsk* sounds, then motioned to Cyrille Vileron, who came to her side in a blue-mottled flash of his cloak. The vulturine captain cleared his throat with a raspy huff, then began to read aloud the mandate. His words condemned all the conspirators to death, and their deaths would be carried out tomorrow at dawn, before the main gates of the city. A few began to moan and even weep at this, and continued to do so after Cyrille was finished. And then a shout cut through:

"It is *NOT* possible for a man to betray a usurper of the Imperial Throne!"

Miriana turned her eyes on the speaker. It was none other than Sydrian Rane. "Tell me, Minister," she said. "For how long did you act as my husband's loyal vassal, while behind closed doors you were mixing your poisons? You betrayed not only your Lord Regent, but your own peers and loyal vassals. You deserve a heinous death, but out of kindness to your long years of service, I will give you a merciful one."

"I do *NOT* want mercy from one undeserving of the imperial seat," he spat.

"Insolent old fool," Vylas cut in. "The lady offers clemency and you fling insults in return?"

Sydrian didn't even spare the one-eyed man a glance. "The realm will rejoice once the traitor breathes his very last. And again when the whore is stripped of her power."

The insult bludgeoned her like a fist. A man like Zantherei would never allow others to speak to him in such a way. But she wasn't Zantherei—she was only a woman. Still, something must be done. As the Lady Regent, she could not allow this to go unpunished. She gripped the hilt of her concealed weapon, so tight she felt the ridging of the hilt dig into her palms. "Bring him to me," she ordered. Guards hauled the minister forward. Despite his hoary old face, his eyes never looked clearer. He seemed nothing like the gentle minister who had once welcomed her to the Hollow. "You've made a grave mistake," she told him.

"The only mistake I made was not poisoning you along with your husband," he said.

Enraged, she yanked aside the fold of her robe, unsheathing the saber with a metallic hiss. "Put his hands on the table."

Sydrian was shoved forward, both hands slamming palm-down on the black lacquered table. He struggled only briefly, surely realizing he was no match the strength of his captors. She ordered the guard to hike up the wide sleeves of his ministerial robe, revealing his pale and mottled arms. *You are strong, Mir*, she told herself. *Strong as silk, in body and heart.* "I would have given you an honorable death," she said. "But you chose this instead, you chose the punishment of those who pen false words." His eyes looked away when she brought the blade closer, to hover over his wrist.

"My lady, if I may," Cyrille Vileron interjected. Miriana turned and saw the captain motioning to the nearest guard. "Bind it," he ordered. A length of cord was wrapped around the Minister Steward's wrist. Sydrian offered no protest. Satisfied, Cyrille bowed his head to Miriana. She reaffirmed her grip on the weapon, her hands clammy now. In truth, she wasn't sure if she still had the strength to go through with this, but she was committed now—she couldn't go back. She had to either show these men that she was as strong and capable as any ruling man, or retreat like a cowardly woman she was. *You are strong, Mir. Strong as your husband. Do it . . . do it now—NOW you stupid bawd!*

The saber came down, biting through the flesh and bone of Sydrian's wrist. But for all her strength—or perhaps her lack of it—she didn't cut all the way through. To finish she had to chop down not once but two more times. It was awful, like slicing through a stubborn scrag of mutton, and when it was done the severed hand was left lying on the table, blood spurting and fingers twitching. Sydrian mewled and moaned and his body began to thrash. Three guards rushed to restrain him, and in the scuffle the severed hand was knocked off the table.

Miriana watched in horror. "Now the other," she ordered, her voice weak. Sydrian was howling in pain now, a howling so loud it rattled her focus and blunted her mettle. It was unlike anything she'd ever heard—more animal than man; even the guardsmen holding him averted their eyes. Finally, Cyrille Vileron, perhaps the only man with sense in his head, used a ragged scrap of linen to stopper the minister's mouth. Then, at last, she was able to raise again the bloody weapon, though her arms struggled with the weight of it. *Once more, Miriana, once more and it's over.* Her eyes closed. Again, the steel came down . .
.

Clang. Her hands jolted from striking something hard—the table, she realized, just as the blade fell from her grip. She winced when she saw she'd missed the wrist entirely, severing the minister's fingers. They were rolling every which way now, like bloody little sticks of bean curd. Chaos broke. Sydrian's howling returned, somehow, and the guardsmen fumbled for the scrap of linen to stifle him. Blood from the minister's flailing arms splashed into one's eyes and he winced. Cyrille chastised the guard's efforts while trying to retrieve the cloth himself. Vylas was yelling too, at what Miriana couldn't say. Another guardsman was shooing away a pair of hounds that were fighting over something on the floor—the minister's fingers, she saw in horror.

Miriana's legs buckled, her lungs gasping for breath. All she wanted to do was run, to be somewhere other than here. She nearly gave in, so so nearly, but before she could turn a guardsman came to her proffering the weapon she had dropped. She stared at it as though it were a live adder. Then she pushed his hands away, getting that blade out of her sight. "Just get him out of here," she shouted. "Take them *all* away. *Now!*"

The guards clanked and clinked as they hauled off the rest of the captives. Cyrille gave specific instructions: "Have Master Lorian dress the wounds. He will die with his wits about him." Finally, the noise began to recede, and Miriana could feel the tension of the room begin to dissipate. But no sooner came Sydrian's voice from afar.

"I am ready to die," he shouted. She barely had the resolve to face him. "To die not as a traitor—but as a loyal servant *OF THE ANIR!*" A guard yanked him through the double-leaf doors, and he was gone, his voice left to reverberate throughout the hall, a voice more powerful than what should've been allowed of that old man's lungs.

Miriana lowered her eyes in the haunting stillness. She could hear the thrum of her own heart, so loud the others must've heard it, too. But no, there was another sound—an incessant lapping. Lapping and licking. At first she thought it was only in her mind, but then she spotted the hounds hunkered on the floor. There was blood everywhere —around the lapping dogs and running off the table, in the crevices of the tilework and spattered on the dais. Her hands too, were slick and red—and now trembling so much she had to hide them in the folds of her robe. "Forgive me," she blurted, to someone, anyone . . . perhaps to herself or perhaps to no one at all. And with that, she left.

She returned to her private chambers with Sydrian's howls still in her head. She barely saw Yana until the dark-skinned handmaiden began peeling off Miriana's bloodstained gown and scarf. Miriana felt wetness along her inner thighs, and after touching it, she sniffed and wondered if she had loosed her bladder. Then Yana took hold of her hands and began scrubbing the blood from them, under her nails and between the crevices of each finger. When the handmaiden finished and went off to do something else, Miriana was left staring at the water in the washbasin, which had turned a bottomless black.

It all felt so surreal—and yet, she had only taken a man's hands, not his head. She had killed before, once, but not with steel. It was too hard to end a man's life that way. *Maybe I'm not so strong after all, maybe I'm no different from any other woman.* Still, as quickly as those thoughts came to her, she stamped them, or tried to, at least. *You are strong, Mir. Strong as silk.*

Yana returned in a rush, her hands full of clothing and her mouth full of words. What was she saying? *Do you prefer this one, the silk with embroidered diamonds . . . or the stitched filigree . . . maybe the heavier . . . perhaps this?* Yes, yes, whichever is fine. *Is this hairpin comfortable? Do you want the look mirror?* No, no that is all right. Maybe later.

Yana guided her to the featherbed, but Miriana stopped midway, turning instead for her desk. She lifted the brushpen, thinking, her eyes absently examining the celadon holder and all its intricate details. Then she wrote fast and she wrote fiercely, and when she was done, she sealed the edict and forced back the urge to weep.

She summoned Vylas before the day's end, and upon entering he rested her husband's saber in its place on the wall, polished and pristine, as if the weapon had not seen blood this day. Her brother's embrace was as affectionate as ever, but the gaze from his single eye was enigmatic. *You did well,* it might have said, or perhaps, *you did well before you lost heart.* She handed him the edict and quickly retracted her hands, since they still bore a slight tremble. "Take this to Minister Korval," she told him. "Make sure it is carried out tomorrow. At dawn, no later."

He nodded but said nothing.

"I want the families of those who conspired against me," she went on. "I want every bloodline snuffed out . . . every brother, sister, mother—I want them *all* executed. And I want their heads placed at all four gates." *And with them, any future conspiracies against me.*

Vylas clasped the scroll. She heard him turn to leave. But he didn't leave. Instead, he simply asked, "And of His Majesty?"

She looked long and hard at her brother. "I will deal with him soon enough."

CHAPTER NINETEEN

There was no warning.

The heavy door burst open, thundered as if from a cavalry charge. Imperial guardsmen swarmed inside, shattering the quiet of the private hall with the menacing clangor of scale and steel. Lady Miriana was the last to enter, her leather heels clacking across the floor tiles. She stopped several yards before Emperor Thavian Siven, who sat frozen at his desk, his hand still raised even though the writing brush had fallen from his fingers.

Demien Mordall had long expected this day. The treasonous plot had been uncovered, Minister Sydrian and his fellow conspirators all executed, and now Lady Miriana had come for her final revenge. She looked elegant today as always, wearing a gray and ivory robe that resembled the plumage of a junco bird. Her hair was pinned up, allowing a clear view of her high cheekbones and blue eyes.

She gazed suspiciously at Demien—at his prized short sword, Dreadfang, clasped tightly in his hands. Realizing his offense, Demien

knelt and placed the weapon on the floor, bowing his head apologeti-
cally. When he looked back up, Lady Miriana's focus had already
returned to the boy.

"Under heaven's imperial decree," she declared. "I am bestowed
with the duty of purging the realm of all traitors." She took a few steps
closer, *clack, clack, clack.* "Was His Majesty aware of such treason
against our realm's illustrious Lord Regent?"

Any attempt Thavian made at appearing brave vanished the instant
he spoke. "I-I had no such knowledge," he squeaked.

"Then perhaps you've forgotten about the mandate bearing your
very mark?"

Thavian's face went white. It pained Demien to see the boy so
cowed and afraid. He wanted nothing more than to step before this
cruel woman and denounce her ways. But that would in turn condemn
himself, and he wasn't ready to die so foolishly, and certainly not
without knowing Miriana's intentions. Cold as she was, she must've
weighed the ramifications of publicly eliminating the last scion of the
ruling house. Surely she knew that the realm would be plunged into
chaos, that countless pretenders would vie for power, that the land
would inevitably become torn by war and famine and death. Surely
Miriana knew all this.

Still, her words seemed driven only by wrath now. "Abdication is
too kind a punishment for you. You should be made to suffer as my
husband has suffered."

The boy finally lowered his hand, and slowly he rose to his feet. He
was not short of stature by any measure, but neither was Miriana, and
in her heels, she stood nearly the young emperor's height. "You c-
cannot harm me," he stammered. "For the sake of the empire. For the
realm to carry on, and for the dynasty to flourish. I am h-heaven's last
son . . . the last of the Anir."

Miriana seemed to regard him with as much amusement as one would
a small child. "As foolish as you sound, Your Majesty, there is truth in
what you say. To end your pitiful existence would cause an internal rift
that even I cannot think to bear." She shook her head scathingly, and her

next words came out in a scornful rasp. "But I will still make you *suffer.*" She snapped an order to Cyrille Vileron, who immediately went to the door, calling a pair of guardsmen inside. Between them was the emperor's handsome young consort Dahlia. The poor girl looked awful; her face was in tears, her hair tousled, her pretty silk gown and all its furbelows dirtied.

The very sight of her broke the emperor. "Let her be!" he cried. *"Please,* she holds no fault in this. Do not harm her. *Let her be."*

Demien shook his head. *Do not beg*, he thought. *Do not beg for her life*. But beg the boy did; he sank to his knees and begged and begged until his words turned to gibbering sobs, until tears streamed down his cheeks and rimmed red his eyes.

Miriana grabbed a fistful of the consort's flaxen hair, then turned back to Thavian. "You want me to let her be?" She gave a yank, and the poor girl squealed in pain. "Why? So you can continue to share your wretched pillow with her? So you can bed her while I sit here, the hapless victim of your treachery? Perhaps she will bear you a child, perhaps a son. Tell me, will you instill the same treason in your own son's heart as well?"

"Please . . . Dahlia's done nothing," he whimpered.

Miriana's face turned to ice. "No, but she will suffer the cord all the same." She shoved the girl into the hands of the guards. Dahlia shrieked as she crashed headlong into steel and scale and leather. When they hoisted her upright, Demien saw blood trailing from her nose.

With an angry shout, Emperor Thavian rushed at the Lady Regent, fists upraised. And for the tiniest, briefest of moments, Miriana's blue eyes widened and her mouth twisted open and she looked downright afraid. But then Cyrille Vileron appeared, a huge blockade of leather and steel that deflected the flailing boy and sent him tumbling to the floor. Demien took a step forward; Vileron reacted to the movement. Their eyes locked.

The Grand Commandant's fingers twitched. His short sword, the jewel-encrusted Dreadfang, lay sideways at his feet. Demien knew it would take but a moment to snatch it up and but another to strike down this scar-headed fool. His body tensed, legs ready to launch, fingers ready to grasp . . . but no, he stopped himself. He stopped himself and simply stood there, in silence, listening to Dahlia's anguished cries as she was hauled out of the chamber.

The Lady Regent was left glaring at Thavian. "Do not weep for her life, but weep with the comfort that you still have *yours*." She turned to leave, but not before looking Demien's way. "Anyone who seeks the boy's audience without my consent is to be brought to me at once. *No exceptions.*"

"Yes, my lady."

Her eyes strayed once more to the boy before she finally left. Her armored entourage followed, and at last the doors slammed shut, leaving Demien with the sobbing heap of blue silks that was the emperor. "That's enough," he told the boy. "You are an emperor. Act as one."

"To hell with you," the boy growled, his face crimson with anger. Snot stretched floorward like a skein of wet thread; he didn't seem to notice. "You gutless wretch—how could you let that *whore* do this to me?"

Dahlia had to die, Demien wanted to say, but it was a sour thought, and so it remained unspoken. Yes, the poor girl was an unfortunate pawn. Yes, her death would be tragic. But it would allow Thavian to live. *The dynasty is all that matters. The dynasty is all that has ever mattered.* In his heart he knew it was the truth, and yet, why did he feel so ashamed?

Perhaps the boy was right—perhaps Demien was gutless. Perhaps he'd been idle for too long. Idleness weakened a man. It had precluded Demien from marching to his brother's aid when his aid was sorely needed. By the gods, Szathan had been driven from Thornberry and nearly slain—and Demien didn't do a goddamn thing about it. Under Miriana's orders, he'd simply remained at the capital. How could he be so foolishly subservient? The Demien of old would've scoffed at her orders and smashed anyone who tried to stop him.

And now? He'd done nothing except remain meek and obsequious while the fires of discord and unrest rose higher and higher around him. *I'm no more than an imperial lapdog—no different from men like Vylas, men I despise.*

Anger rose in him, swift and urgent, like a river's swell under a storm, and when his mind flashed to the image of poor Dahlia being hauled out to die by strangulation, his gauntleted fists smashed through the wall. Again and again, breaking tile and brick and spewing dust and debris into his eyes. Half blind, he staggered back and collapsed against a nearby pillar, burying his face in his hands.

Two weeks later, Demien exited the emperor's chamber alone and unarmored. All was soundless and still at so late an hour, his own shadow but a fleeting wisp under the dimly lit sconces. He stopped near the far end of the palace wing, the same place where Minister Sydrian had once taken him. Behind the sentinel, Demien pried open the floor slab, and by lamplight he headed down the stairs into the dark maw of the subterranean passage.

Demien's thoughts drifted back to the days after Dahlia's death. He'd met privately with Nyvia, while the young emperor was still grieving in his chamber, and while the Lady Regent and her courtiers were busy attending a sword-dancing spectacle at the Imperial Theater. Demien had offered to move Alarin into safe hiding, and the plump woman agreed at once. "No one must know of this," he'd warned. "Miriana has too many eyes and ears in her retinue—some you may even mistake as confidants."

He'd told her he needed a day or two to map the way to the tower, but in truth it took nearly a week. He'd spent three goddamn nights alone just finding the secret entranceway again. At one point Demien had almost given up on the plan entirely, even thinking that perhaps the entrance had somehow been sealed, but driven by Nyvia's relentless urgings, he continued to search and search until finally he found it.

Demien hastened his pace through the tunnels now, as the earthen floor softened underfoot and the air thickened with the stench of sewage—a stench driven by the adjacent waste line that emptied out into the outlying river. He found the privy chute here, an open hole rimmed with broken stone and wooden shoring. A thick hempen rope dangled in wait, just as Nyvia assured him it would. And yet, tall as he was, he couldn't quite reach it.

He backtracked through the tunnels in search of any cabinetwork or wreckage. In what looked like an old storeroom, he found a table of hardwearing rosewood, its doweling still intact and its mitered corners still strong. Cobwebs broke and wood protested as he hauled it through the narrow tunnels. He needed two hands to carry it yet he needed the light as well, so he had to drag the table for a distance before going back to retrieve his lamp, again and again. It was a tedious process, but Demien had plenty of time, and soon enough he set the table down beneath the dark hole of the privy chute.

The old hardwood creaked under his weight. Demien reached up and grabbed the frayed end of the rope. He pulled himself up, hand over hand, using the knots in the hemp for support. Soon, the chute itself became tight and bumpy and knobbed with enough earthen hand-holds for him to shinny up, and up and up he went until he clambered over the wooden support lip and hauled himself out of the foulness and into the quiet of the privy chamber.

He found Alarin in the adjoining room, seated and patient, dressed in heavy wool garb and holding his blackthorn cane. He gave a nod but said not a word, and with Demien's support, in the late hours of the night, the two men retreated down the chute and into the dark of the underground.

CHAPTER TWENTY

Seric brushed at her nipples with his fingers, watching as they firmed. Lady Miriana gave a soft purr in response, her own fingers running softly down his bare chest. Seric gently retracted his hips to allow her a brief stroke of his manhood. Though his seed had already been spent, he felt himself quickly hardening again.

There was no greater reward than to be here, beside the Lady Regent, now and after all he'd been through. All the lingering doubts that had burdened him, all his concerns over broken faith with the southern warlord—it was all inconsequential now. Nothing mattered except the beautiful woman in his arms.

Then Miriana whispered, "The day grows late."

He glanced out the window, observing the warm hues of the late afternoon sun. He knew he could delay no longer. He had a promise to fulfill, a promise to pay a visit to Alarin Athera.

It wasn't the task itself that concerned him, but what would happen *after* the task was completed. Would Lady Miriana continue to share her pillow with him? Or would she send him back to the city, fattened of purse but still the same lowly cur as before? Seric couldn't live with the latter; he was a man who desired status and recognition above all. But what could he do? If he made plain such desires she might become doubtful of his virtue, perhaps decide it was only cold ambition that drove Seric. He certainly did not want her to think that his affections for her were anything less than sincere.

So for now he said nothing, and lowering his head he kissed her breasts and licked and tongued her nipples, while she replied with soft moans of pleasure. She seemed a bit distracted as of late, but Seric forgave her for that. After all, no more than a fortnight had passed since she ordered the execution of over two hundred citizens. The families of all the conspirators, entire clans, some many generations deep, had been utterly eradicated. It was a day of terrible grief; even some of the most hardened soldiers had wept.

Seric remembered when Lady Miriana appeared atop the North Gate, addressing the populace, composed and with aplomb. Such strength lay inside her, and yet, right now, in his arms, she was as tender as any woman could be tender. "My lady, I know I should be on my way," he said, caressing her long tresses of black hair, which smelled sweetly of jasmine. "But I'm not quite ready to let you go."

"Nor am I," she replied softly. "But a man's faith should come before reward and pleasure. Not the opposite."

"True, but after a man's faith is fulfilled, what then is left?"

"More reward and pleasure, of course. What else is there?"

Her question wasn't meant to be answered, but Seric did anyway, and only after a long moment of thought. "With Alarin's passing, the Star of the Hollow will be left without an Imperial Advisor. If I may say, my lady, there is no one in the six provinces better suited for the position than I am."

She looked at him as though he were making a jest. "Seric, it has not been long since Zantherei stripped you of your status."

"I know," he said curtly. "But you are the Lady Regent, are you not? Abrogation is certainly within your scope of authority."

"Yes, but going against Zantherei's ruling will surely raise a few brows in the court, don't you think?"

"To hell with the court," he said.

"I don't wish to endanger my standing," she said.

"It was my victory at the Horns. I deserve the recognition."

She seemed at a loss for words. "Earlier, you said . . . you said it was enough."

"That was earlier," he said, rising to dress. "Before I grew tired of hearing the highborn fools praise a half-dead wretch." He had spoken that in a low mutter, and when she asked him to repeat it, he didn't. Still, it was the truth; such praise was indeed meant to be his. Just as Miriana was meant to be his. But knowing his luck, Zantherei would awake and recover and abruptly ruin all that. *Even dead to the world, the bastard still has his claws in me.*

He was no longer content to remain removed from his accomplishments; it was only a matter of time before spies revealed the truth of his betrayal to Raas Dragath anyhow. And so what? It was the very nature of a great man to have enemies. His birth father once told him that, and he was right, the cruel old prick.

"You speak the truth, Seric," Miriana suddenly said. "To deprive an ambitious man of glory is no different from depriving a bird of its wings. Forgive me for not seeing that."

Hearing those words made him go to her, and he brushed tenderly the hair that curtained her face and covered her bare breasts—breasts that he'd come to know so intimately. He said not a word but gently guided her onto her back, his hands holding hers flat against the bed. They stared at each other for a time, then she pushed playfully against his weight, giggling when he nudged her back. Soon the two lovers were pushing back and forth, rumpling the silk blankets and rollicking like children. After a time, her body relaxed and she submitted herself meekly to him. He caressed her cheeks, staring deep into her eyes. "I would be your husband," he said.

"Of course you would," she replied. "To have the Lady Regent under the Dyre banner would be a most fortunate move—"

"No." *She doesn't understand.* "I would be your husband because I love you."

She looked at him blankly for a moment, then burst out laughing. "Only a fool would marry for love," she said.

He shied away from that, hiding the hurt as best he could. "Yes, well, perhaps you think me a fool, and perhaps you are right to think that. My lady, have you heard a tale called A Fool and his Lute? Well, there once was a famed musician who went from tavern to tavern wagering he could make any woman swoon with the pluck of his lute. At every challenge he would succeed, no matter how noble or wealthy or chaste the woman. One day he was challenged to woo the heart of a wealthy iron-shop owner's daughter, and since she was a rather plain woman, it seemed an easy enough challenge. But no matter how long or how passionately the lutenist played, his music had no effect. The man was so devastated he ended up throwing himself off a bridge."

"An amusing little anecdote," she said. "So are you saying that I share the same qualities as that woman?"

"No, I'm saying after I first heard it I immediately sought the most expensive luthier in the city."

She laughed at that, an endearing laugh.

Seric said, "Turns out it was a cruel joke, as the woman was deaf."

Miriana nodded and was thoughtful for a time. At length she said, "You used to play your lute at the Autumn Moon Festival. I met you for the first time there. Two years, yes, two years ago we exchanged our very first words. You said something that I'll never forget, do you remember what it was? You told me I was strong and beautiful, a dangerous combination."

Seric nodded. "Everyone was talking about how beautiful Zantherei's new consort was, about this woman whose face could collapse the heavens, or persuade the very gods themselves to do battle. But I saw something more than just your pretty face—I saw strength in you." Seric laughed. "Nyvia did not like you at all."

Miriana nodded. "Few women did."

"Ah, they're just highborn broads with nothing but their name. Jealous crows and such—Nyvia was one of them." He paused at the memory. It seemed so long ago. "My lady, the others may frown upon your past, but it is because of your former life of adversity that I am most drawn to you. In a palace of highborn fools, it is a rare comfort to share the pillow with a kindred spirit. No one else could ever understand you. Not like I do."

She seemed to like what she heard. "You are a wise man, Seric Dyre."

"A capable ruler needs a wise man at her side," he said.

She softened at that. "I still have a husband—"

He put a finger to her lips. "A husband soon to pass."

A knock at the chamber door interrupted them. It was her brother, Vylas. He sounded a bit vexed when Miriana sent him off. Afterward, Seric, in a somewhat playful tone, remarked, "As if your brother doesn't loathe me enough already . . ."

That made her smile. "Don't fret, Vylas loathes any man that catches my eye."

"Lord Zantherei, as well?"

"Not really. He always held this belief that I was never truly fond of my husband." She paused. "Either that or Zantherei scared him witless."

Seric chuckled, and a brief moment of silence passed between them. "Is there any truth . . . to that belief?"

She looked mournfully off, staring at something he couldn't see. "When I saw my husband, lying there, so weak and full of poison, I felt more concern for my own standing than Zantherei's life. I never shared that with anyone."

Seric propped himself up on his elbows, studying the smooth contours of her naked body. He caressed her shoulder, brushing the faint spray of freckles there, then down her arm and hip and along the soft curve of her backside. When his fingers turned in toward her folded legs, she opened them, allowing him a caress of her inner thighs, and eventually the soft sex in between. She exhaled at his touch. Seric undressed himself and the two lovers shared each other for a second time.

Afterward, they lay together in silence, with Seric listening to the gentle rise and fall of her chest. The chamber was so quiet, so serene; his eyes closed and he began drifting off. Then, somewhere off, the drum tower sounded first watch of the evening. "Seric . . . the hour grows late," Miriana said, stirring. "Your promise, do not forget."

Seric rose and dressed himself once more, then bent down to retrieve a winegourd from a trunk at the foot of the bed. She watched him, coverlets drawn to her chest. "You know what to say, how to gain his confidence?" she asked.

"Yes, my lady," Seric said, in a tone that he hoped would set her at ease. His fingers ran along the grooves of the winegourd, ordinary as any other, but this vessel had a hollow slit in the cork where the poison was secretly kept. He opened it now to examine briefly the dark powder. "I do hope it is as you say. It would be a great misfortune for him to feel its effects while I'm still in the chamber."

"Trust me, the concoction is insidious. His health will deteriorate over time, several days, weeks even. By the time he dies your visit will be all but forgotten. A natural death by all accounts. No one will suspect."

"Poison can be traced. Black spots on the bones."

"This isn't some alchemist's petty trituration," she told him. "The Mists of Midnight leaves no traces."

He studied her. "You've used it before."

"Once."

"I'd like to hear of it."

She clothed herself in a silk robe, then went to him. They shared a kiss, long and deep and markedly passionate. "Later, when you return."

Seric nodded. "I like not having to bend down to kiss you." He ran his hand down her back, squeezing her buttocks beneath the thin layer of silk. They embraced for a while longer, before holding each other at arm's length. Solemnly, he said, "I'll return soon, my lady. Think about what I said earlier."

Alarin's tower was already a long walk from the palace, but in the cold it seemed twice as far. Seric endured it with a strange mixture of hope and dread. Winning the man's confidence shouldn't be a difficult task, but cajoling him into drinking the winegourd may require a bit of finesse. Wait, forget all that—did he even have the heart to do this? Unlike Zantherei, Alarin had never been cruel to Seric. Still, at the same time, Alarin had done nothing to help Seric when he needed it most. Nothing at all.

He passed through the outer gate, flashing the Lady Regent's edict to the sentries of the main forecourt of the tower. Once inside, he found the waiting antechamber small and musty and dark, but at least it was warm. A stairway brought him to a wider room guarded by a handful of imperial sentries—not dressed in the typical blue and gray of the empire, but in mismatched, drab-colored raiment. They were hired hands stationed here under Nyvia's authority. Two were chatting in front of the massive door, another four or five were crouched on the floor drawing lots. One rose to confront the visitor.

"You have no business here, friend." He was a gruff fellow, with black pits for eyes and a belly that revealed too clearly his penchant for wine. He seemed the head of this paltry band, so Seric flashed the edict his way. "I am to speak privately with Alarin Athera."

The gruff captain took the scroll, his deep-set eyes moving back and forth. When he finished he gave Seric a long look. "Search him."

They found only the winegourd, of course, and when questioned, Seric took a swig to satisfy them. The portly captain then went to the door, rapping two times and announcing his guest.

No reply.

"He's asleep," one suggested.

"This cannot wait," Seric urged. "Open it."

The captain narrowed his eyes but conceded. Seric went in.

It was so dark Seric had go back out and ask for a lamp. Someone handed him one that was spiral-shaped like the horns of a Sadralen, and heading back inside, Seric saw a chamber that looked odd in its bareness. Most of the furniture had been removed when Vileron and his men ransacked the place. Seric walked to the bed and pulled aside the drapery. Nothing. He turned about and passed the light across the entire room. Nothing, nothing at all. The adjoining chambers and vestibules were also vacant, the privy chamber too. He searched every alcove, nook, and crevice. He checked them twice and then again, and combed the outside terrace. *He's gone. Oh wretched hell, he's gone.* Sweat dripped from his brow; his mind began to whirl. *I waited too long and now he's gone.* Panic seized him by the throat. *He's gone. By all the gods in the goddamn heavens, he's fucking gone.*

Seric stumbled out of the chamber to raise the hue and cry.

CHAPTER TWENTY-ONE

The growing thud of heavy footfalls sent verminous shadows scampering into the dark.

Oil lamp in hand, Demien Mordall entered the underground chamber, unslinging his haversack and kneeling to distribute its contents. It was of the typical fare—foxtail millet, dried cuts of beef, blood cakes and dumplings, spices of star anise and cinnamon. And this time, however, he had something more with him. "An unguent, for your ache," he said.

Alarin Athera ignored the offering. "The letter—did you send the letter?"

The Grand Commandant's sigh was answer enough even before he placed the small pouch at his feet. Alarin stared at it, his eyes drawn to the pyrography of the kidskin: the simple lines and swirls of filigree, the familiar horned head and eyes of the Sadralen. The letter he'd written to Anseth was still inside, still unsent. "You have to go back. He's there, my courier is there. Did you ask the proprietor, not the son but the older fellow, the graybeard—did you ask him?"

Demien Mordall was not a man of soft words, and certainly he wasn't soft right now. "I asked him, I asked the son—I asked every pair of ears from patron to pander to bawd. Word of Kalen's death has silenced them all."

"You have to try again," Alarin said. "If you can't find my courier, then hire another. By the gods, you must know of at least one man trustworthy enough to take a simple letter to the north. He won't have to cross into the Gravelands—Amaranth Point is as far as he will go."

"My lord," Demien said, clearly exasperated. "There are imperial soldiers scouring every inch of the city, along every road, at every checkpoint and picket line. Anyone without proper credentials is being hauled to the palace for questioning. Not only that, Lady Miriana has placed a high price on your capture. You know there's no loyalty among men when coin is concerned."

Alarin did know that of course, but he let out a curse anyway. He *had* to find a way to warn his brother. Since Captain Cyrille Vileron had ransacked his chambers, he was sure Lady Miriana had all their correspondences. *She knows about Anseth . . . about the north, the Vaskultans, everything. By the gods, she will have him killed.*

Demien asked, "Have who killed?"

Alarin looked up—he must've been rambling aloud. *Be quiet, you old fool.* "Lord Commandant, please, I urge you to try again." He handed him back the pouch and began yet again to describe his contact, but before he got to finish Demien rose and left.

The former Imperial Advisor leaned back against the tamped earth wall. *By the gods, Anseth, stay in the north, stay until I can reach you.* Either he would find his courier or he'd hire another, and if he couldn't do that he'd ride to the north himself. Yes, he could ride himself . . . but a month-long journey for someone who hadn't ridden a horse in nearly a decade? *Your mind must be crippled as well, idiot.*

Still, Alarin had to get out of here—he couldn't bear it any longer. His phantom limb ached so much in this hellish place, ached to the very core of his being. At times all he could do was lie on his side and imagine he was somewhere else, somewhere but the dark and muddy bowels of the underground. It was hard not to let yourself get disoriented. It was not like a cave—no, these man-made places had a different sort of darkness, far denser and far more sinister. Down here, days passed like weeks, a fortnight easily a year, and he had only Demien's footsteps to break the insufferably monotony, and always had he come with that same haversack of food, and that same empty promise of escape.

Alarin fished through the fare now, eating his fill and then downing a gourd of wine. Then, after relieving himself, he carried the chamberpot down to a small ordure room, the one he called the 'shit pit.' The pot was heavy and close to overflowing from his previous days of indolence, and he nearly spilled it when he tripped on some strewn potsherds. Fortunately, his cane kept him upright.

He could hear them before he got back, creeping about, scavenging for scattered morsels. They were becoming braver each day, the rats. Last time Alarin had dozed off he awoke to find his finger covered in blood. Little beasts must've smelled the greasy mutton jerk still on his fingers. He'd been surprised to see such a deep gouge from so little a creature.

Since then they'd been going about their business more and more in plain sight. Alarin didn't mind; in fact, it served as a fair distraction from his ailments. Under lamplight he'd observe them either sneaking about or grooming one another as lovingly as a mother coddling her babe. Sometimes they would fight, and when they did it was brutal. Two males—obvious by their bulbous testes—would engage in a frenzy of incisors and fur and angry little rasps. Often the loser, in his wounded state, would be killed by the others in the clan. How cruel, Alarin thought, even if it were necessary to keep the pack strong. Still, as a cripple himself, he couldn't help but feel indignant at that.

Alarin would find the unfortunate carcass imprinted in the earth, usually near the walls or sometimes buried in the rushes, scraggly and desiccated, as if it had been molded there over years, not hours or days. Repulsed by the rank smell, he'd toss the poor thing into the chamberpot, to be hauled off to the shit pit.

They were all he seemed to think about lately, the rats. Even his dreams were filled with them. He would dream he was back at Black Gate Pass, lying wounded in the tents, helpless as the physician pared away the rotting flesh of his leg. He would hear the rats scurrying about, darting here and there, over the physician's boots and across the tables. Sometimes the physician himself had a ratlike tail, sometimes he had beady little eyes, and once, Alarin's own leg was a rat's leg. Those were not even the strangest dreams, either. Once, he'd dreamed of bedding a woman who bore him a ratlike son that grew into a rat man. And then that rat man would die, and Alarin would drag him by his tail and fling him into the shit pit with the rest of the vermin.

He tried to tell Demien about his dreams once, but the Grand Commandant looked at him as though he were mad. *Perhaps I have gone a little mad. Who wouldn't in this place?* It was a silly question. *Emperor Tharrais Siven, you idiot, that's who.* The Annals of the Anir told of the sovereign spending the entire winter down here before escaping through the West Gate, and later raising an army from the surrounding districts to retake the besieged city. It was quite a tale, but was it true? Alarin had been here maybe a month and already his mind had long slipped away—how did Emperor Tharrais sustain such mental fortitude for thrice the length of time? It must have been a lie, an exaggeration perhaps. Or maybe it wasn't, maybe Emperor Tharrais was a far stronger man than Alarin could ever hope to be. *Maybe he wasn't wasting his time wallowing in self-pity and dreaming of rodents.*

Alarin gave a derisive snort at that, then turned on his side to stare at the dying candlelight. He closed his eyes, but tired though he was, it still took some time before his world finally faded into the deep recesses of sleep.

His eyes opened. He was no longer in the dark, no longer underground at all. He felt a breeze, crisp and invigorating, and there were trees and ramparts around him now—no, beneath him. He was floating up, somehow floating skyward on a puffy ivory cloud. Battlements came so close he could see the details in both crenel and merlon. Watch-

towers with eaves he could touch, and he would've touched—but then
he saw the sentries. They took no notice of him, moving only to shiver
or adjust their thick woolen garb. Alarin was so close . . . so close he
expected to see rats running along the woodwork. But strangely
enough, he saw none. Soon the watchtower was gone, and soon Alarin
floated higher and higher until he was enwreathed by a measureless sea
of night. The stars were too bright to describe, their pathways in
greater detail than any star map he'd seen. He saw the planets, Jupiter,
Mars, but it was Venus that drew his eye. She was in retrograde,
moving into the first section of the northern quadrant. There were
streaks of light fluttering there, into the horns of the constellation of
Sadralen.

The whole constellation began to flicker, once, twice, and then in
rapid succession. Faster and faster it went, brighter and brighter, until it
became a wild, amorphous swirl of white light, a vortex that spun and
spun until it climaxed in a single, gigantic flash, so bright and blinding
that Alarin had to shield his eyes. When it was over, when his sight
returned, the constellation was gone. Every trace of light, every junc-
ture and every path—utterly gone. It was as if an array of torches had
all been stamped out at once.

And now he was falling. The wind screamed in his ears, frost-cold
against his face. His stomach twisted. Watchtowers and sentries and
battlements all whipped past. He couldn't stop, couldn't do anything
but fall. He knew it was a dream and yet he still couldn't jerk himself
awake. All he could do was fall, fall and fall and watch the ground
grow larger and larger, and when it finally rose to meet him it simply
vanished, and Alarin was left to plummet down a gigantic, yawning
chasm, boundless and bare and full of never-ending blackness . . .

He awoke.

His lungs heaved for breath, again and again, while his eyes darted
around the room. His heart hammered in his chest, even when his mind
told him it was safe. Thumbing away the sheen of sweat on his balding
pate, Alarin lay back and stared at the ceiling. Images of the dream
swirled in his mind, intrusive and constant. *Stop it, Alarin, it was just
another dream. As senseless as the others.*

But no, the longer he ruminated on it, the more his heart told him otherwise. The details were so vivid and so precise: the sheets of snow and rime that layered the battlements, the sentries in their thick wool and fur. It was winter . . . yes, it was winter when the constellation vanished. Alarin felt a pang of dread in his heart. It was the same feeling from his dream, the same dread as when he was falling. He sat up to break free. A heavy breath lurched from his lips. *It's not a sense-less dream*, he thought. *It's something more. Something terrible. A terrible omen.*

BOOK II: COLLAPSE

CHAPTER TWENTY-TWO

Anseth awoke to the sound of the felt door flap opening. Kirik hastened inside, hunched and cold, the gale howling behind him like a wrathful demon. He knelt before Anseth and said, "Rangers brought in a stranded, he's chilled to the bone but alive. Under Volduk's orders he was taken to a guest yurt."

"Yes, there are plenty available," Anseth said, groggy and annoyed. "Kirik, why are you telling me this? I'm tired."

"He asked for you, lord."

Anseth turned. "What did you say?"

"He asked for you. He's one of your kind, a southerner."

"He spoke my name, are you sure?"

The bondsman nodded. "An-seth-eral Ath-era," he pronounced clumsily, then smiled.

"Take me to him."

The night was snowy and cold. The two men traveled beneath a dead sky, illuminated sharply by a silvery falcate moon. It was an arduous trip before they entered the commodious guest yurt, a bare place save a few cushions of felt and a center brazier given to life by dried dung—wolf, he reckoned, by the dark hue of its smoke. A handful of Vaskultan guards stood chatting inside, while a smaller figure was hunched over the fire, shivering. At the sound of Anseth's approach the man turned, revealing a pale and unfamiliar Anirian face. His garb was certainly from the south but not indicative of the Star of the Hollow—it looked more of eastern origin, the colors a touch brighter and the fur trimmings short and coarse. The man regarded Anseth with a worn, desultory gaze, probably since Anseth, in his heavy Vaskultan garb, looked every bit a northman as the others. But all that changed the moment Anseth spoke. "Who are you, friend."

The man's round, froglike eyes widened at hearing the Anirian tongue. "I'm a simple rustic, my lord, an envoy from the southern empire of the Anir. Jarreth Sorrel."

"An envoy, you say, yet you come with no horse, no company?"

"My horses . . . yes, well, one broke out in furuncles and another snapped his tether and ran off into the night. And the third . . . poor beast injured his foreleg and had to be put to rest." He shook his head. "As if I hadn't been subjected to all the goddamn misfortune a man could encounter . . . I ended up losing my entire host in this terrible blizzard. If your tribespeople hadn't taken me in, I wouldn't have lasted the night."

"Not all northmen are savages. Your saviors are Vaskultans. Remember that."

"I will, my lord."

"Good." Anseth found it odd hearing himself speak in his native tongue. Yet at the same time, it felt completely natural, as if it hadn't been eight years since he'd done so. "Your message must be of great worth, to carry on in the face of such grave omens."

He nodded. "I seek a man named Ansetheral Athera."

Anseth stared at him, at the way his thin lips had curled when he'd spoken that name. *How does he know of me?* He turned away sharply. "You are seeking a ghost, my friend."

"My lord, I was assured he is alive and well here in the north."

Anseth switched to the Vaskultan tongue and ordered Kirik to search him. When the bondsman put his hand inside the man's outer cloak, Jarreth knocked it away. The surrounding Vaskultans sprang to life, shoving spear tips and sword points in the envoy's face. Jarreth raised his hands in surrender, his fingertips patched in red and yellow from the onset of frostbite. Kirik found on him a pair of earthenware bowls, a winegourd, some twine, a talus bone, a small iron dagger, and finally a letter, which Anseth immediately motioned for. "It's meant for Lord Ansetheral only," the envoy urged.

"Where's the pouch?" Anseth demanded. "Was there a pouch with it?"

"I'm sorry, my lord, I don't understand . . ."

"Never mind. Whose seal is this? Who sent you?"

"Governor Duren Lygrest of Amaranth Point, my lord."

How does Lygrest know where I am? Anseth broke the seal and opened the letter. He read:

Lord Ansetheral Athera, my friend and ally, I write this message on behalf of your brother Alarin, who has recently been the victim of a vile plot against the capital. He lies ill but in my care in Amaranth Point. Between fever dreams he speaks of you, and only when I pressed him did he disclose the truth of your location. Now I am reaching out, asking you to come to his side. My advisor Jarreth will escort you, be assured he is among the finest of men. Do not delay. I implore you to come at once. This letter is only a fragment of what needs to be said. I await your speedy arrival. - Duren Lygrest, Lord of Amaranth Point and Provincial Governor of Cragspawn.

Anseth closed the letter. He sat in silence for a time, taking long gulps from his skin of blackmilk. The envoy was looking closely at him now, scrutinizing his face, as if he discerned something there, beneath all that grease and dirt and knotted hair. "Are you . . .?"

Anseth didn't reply. He placed a skin of blackmilk into the envoy's hand. When Jarreth took a drink, he grimaced and spat it out. The Vaskultans laughed. Anseth did too, but only briefly. Then he said, "You will stay here tonight. You'll have layers of felt to shield the wind, a fire to warm your bones, and hot food in your belly. Riders will comb the hills for the rest of your host." When the envoy agreed and bowed and thanked him, Anseth repeated the news to his men in Vaskulti, then left the yurt.

He trudged across the encampment, fighting the wind and the cold and the rising snowdrift. It'd been months since Anseth had heard any word from his elder brother—which was why he still remained in the north. He'd often contemplated riding back to the Hollow without Alarin's assent, but no, it wasn't safe. And now, this letter from Lygrest. It certainly seemed genuine enough, and it also corroborated the recent reports from his informants, regarding the turmoil in the Hollow and the arrest of the Imperial Advisor. Still, something didn't seem right. *Why would Alarin seek refuge with Lygrest?*

And why hadn't he sent the Sadralen pouch? All correspondences between him and his brother were hidden in a kidskin pouch, uniquely marked to prove the sender's authenticity. If Alarin had lost it, or if he was somehow unable to use it, he would've at least made mention of it —and certainly with this message coming from Lygrest. *Could he have forgotten?* No, Alarin was far too shrewd. Again, something just didn't seem right.

He entered the Vaskultan chieftain's pavilion and found Volduk seated beside a low brazier. The broad man was draped not in his usual golden hide, but in a long, cinnamon-hued fur of fox and fitch. Nearby, his wife and daughters and grandchildren were all asleep under blankets of sheep and goat wool. "The hour is late," Volduk grumbled, even as he beckoned Anseth closer. He looked tired, and not just because he probably was tired. He shifted his weight and muttered at something painful under his rump, then grabbed at what looked like a child's toy or bauble perhaps, and tossed it behind him. Then he gave a half-hearted motion for Anseth to join him on the nearest cushion.

"My brother has sent for me, lord," Anseth said, sitting. "He's taken refuge to the east. With your consent I'd like to go to him."

The chieftain was holding up his head with an open hand. His eyes were half lidded. Was he even listening? Finally, he gave a nod. "Then go. You shouldn't be here anyway, the Serkuts have fallen—you are free of your oath, remember?" He shoved a chewing stick of dogwood in his mouth, working his teeth. After a few minutes of this, he stopped and said, "I'll arrange the escort. Outposts will provide fresh mounts and tack every fifty miles. You can reach your lands in less than a month, barring any unforeseen issues. What's the matter with you?"

Anseth looked up. Volduk was studying him closely. "Is this man's word honorable or not?"

"He's sworn to the empire, lord," Anseth replied. "But . . ." He hesitated. "It's difficult to explain, you know."

"Difficult to an old savage like myself, is it?" He spat a string of Vaskultan curses, words that had no reasonable translation in the Anirian tongue.

"Lord Volduk, it's not that at all. The Anirian structure . . . it's not like the Vaskultans. You are the chieftain of the tribe, your might is undisputed, your power uncontested. It's not the same in the south. The Anir is built on the blood of its ruling family, generations upon generations that now rest with a single remaining scion. But the boy is too young to rule, and the Lord Regent—my own brother—lies near to death, and so the empire is left to suffer. Illicit men and pretenders to the throne influence the feudal barons and bend officials to their will."

"I understand," the old chieftain said. He grumbled something, then stroked his wiry, unkempt beard. "You have my consent. Is there anything else, Revek?"

Anseth lowered his gaze. "I cannot risk a small company, lord. I need two regiments, if you will."

The chieftain opened his mouth as if to speak, but dropped the chewing stick, so instead he glanced down, looking for it, grumbling until he found it. He shoved it back into his mouth and looked back at Anseth. "A large force will frighten the populace," he said at length. "Your kind doesn't know a Vaskultan from a Vaul. To them we are all savages . . . we are all—what do they call us?"

"*Barbarians*," Anseth pronounced in the Anirian tongue.

Volduk gave a snort. He repeated the word in the same language, and rather poorly. Then he said, "Your audacity amazes me, Revek. You know I won't deny your request." He paused to hawk and spit into small cuspidor. "Two regiments you shall have. Oh, and you're also taking my son, too."

Anseth went to protest that but Volduk silenced him. "You're taking Dariok and that's a goddamn order. General Kaigon will stay with me. We're moving north against the last unconquered tribe, the Nidraks. Soon enough I will stand as the Supreme Lord of the Gray Plains."

CHAPTER TWENTY-THREE

The chill of winter came early this year. Daylight dwindled and the nights grew long, nights that were dreary and lonesome and terribly cold. Seric Dyre had spent them sequestered in his abode, where he fell deeper and deeper into despair.

It had been two months since Alarin's disappearance, two months since Lady Miriana had denounced Seric as a man of broken faith. Sadly, the more he'd pleaded his ignorance, the more unconvinced she seemed, even going so far as to accuse him of using dilatory tactics to allow for Alarin's escape. What a goddamn joke.

That was the last time he'd seen her, as each subsequent petition for audience had been denied. And just like that, Seric had lost any foothold of power he'd accumulated over the past months, and just like that he had reverted back to the life of a commoner. It was all so difficult to accept, and yet . . . here he was.

He moved through the city avenues now, cold and bitter and clinging to the desperate hope that such a lengthy absence—the longest since their parting—might be enough to grant him an audience. *She can't deny me forever*, he thought. Something told him that she would someday need him, that she would apologize and seek his counsel. Unless of course Zantherei were to recover, but that was looking less and less likely by day.

If only I can speak to her in private, then she will listen to me. He knew Lady Miriana was not a woman to be won by compliments or praise; no, she was influenced by bold and confident words. Seric knew this because he had once used such words to win her affection. Now he planned to use them again to regain her trust.

He ascended the outer stairway of the palace grounds, making his way across the lengthy forecourt. A handful of sentries in winter garb regarded him beneath fur-trimmed hoods. Seric had gotten to know many of them well enough to know how to inveigle his way past, using either flattery or persuasion or feigning annoyance while flashing a false missive. Most of the sentries were too cold and too uncomfortable to protest anyway, so they just let him pass.

Once inside the palace, Seric moved with purpose, turning down certain corridors to avoid areas of greater vigilance. He made it all the way to the lady's wing, and just ahead now he could see the huge gilded inner door of her imperial bedchamber. Only two sentries were posted here. With confidence in his step Seric advanced—but then the great double-doors groaned opened and Privy Counselor Vylas Voren emerged, backed by several of the empire's blue-cloaked guardsmen.

The scrawny man stopped before Seric, crossing his arms. His good eye peered up while the other remained concealed by that stupid halfmask. "My sister doesn't wish to see you, Seric Dyre. You know this."

"Please, Vylas, the matter is of the utmost importance."

"Is it, now," he said in a mocking voice. Beside him, the guardsmen chuckled and shook their heads.

Seric took a step forward. "Either let me pass or turn about and inform Her Ladyship."

Vylas uncrossed his arms. "Your manhood is not a message," he said, waggling a bony finger. The guards chortled again, louder now.

"Had you kept it in your trousers, you might still have a room here in the palace."

"You are quite the man of wit, Vylas," Seric replied. "Is that why the Lady Regent keeps you around? All this time I thought it was to enjoy the company of lesser men."

His good eye flashed with anger. "You miserable, filthy, wretch of a—" He stopped midsentence, seeming to compose himself. His next words were spoken slowly and mechanically, as if Seric were a halfwit. "The Lady Regent does not wish to see you."

There was nothing he could do. *You little worm, I have done you no wrong.* Seric turned about. *I can't just leave, I am so close.* He took a step forward . . . then spun, shoving Vylas out of the way and slamming into the heavy, studded door. One, two, three solid raps landed, before he was seized and thrown onto the hard stone. A moment later, Miriana's voice called from the bedchamber. Vylas started to reply, but Seric cut him off. "A moment, Lady Miriana! I seek but a moment of your precious time."

One of the guards grabbed Seric. He resisted but soon there were too many hands on him, and now he felt like a rag doll being twisted and pulled and shoved. Finally, he gave in, and the guards hauled him down the corridor and tossed him out into the cold. He landed on his belly and hands, eating a mouthful of muddy snow. The guards muttered to one another for a brief moment, then the heavy palace door slammed shut.

Seric rolled onto his back, staring up at the gray sky. He watched the gentle white flakes drift and whirl and descend all around him, melting away like tiny specks of stardust. *I've nowhere to go*, he thought. His eyes turned to focus on the massive façade of the palace, from the tall stone colonnade to the projecting eaves. Between the high, enjoined roof panels rose glazed ceramic figures of mythical grotesques, each equipped with either fangs or wings or claws or scales or some aberrant combination of the four. The largest were perched on the edges of the tapered corners, monstrous things with tumid bellies and bulbous eyes that seemed to gaze warily down at him. Seric lay there marveling at the detail, until his ears and nose began to burn from the cold. *I'm a goddamn fool,* he thought, lifting himself to leave.

The heavy door groaned open. A pair of guardsmen emerged in motion, one nearly stumbling over Seric. Behind them, Vylas was shaking his head. "My sister will see you, Seric," he said, vanishing back inside. Seric followed, stopping in the entrance hall to warm himself by the nearest brazier—a brief stop, as not to keep her waiting.

The imperial bedchamber was as lovely as he remembered. Lady Miriana was seated on the wooden couch—the one he'd come to know so well—while all her usual attendants swarmed about her. She simply stared at Seric, or maybe past him; it was an empty stare, like that of a wildcat or pard. And despite her messy and unpinned hair, and despite the lack of safflower on her lips and cinnabar on her cheeks, she looked exceedingly handsome, but exceedingly cold at that.

Is she not the same woman who not long ago shared her pillow with me? The same woman with whom I laughed and bedded? It was hard to see it in her now. Now all he saw was the aloof Lady Regent that every other fool saw. "Forgive me, for my offense," Seric managed to say. "But attaining a moment of your time has been a difficult task for someone so meager as myself."

She said nothing to that, only giving a tired flick of her hand to dismiss her attendants. The room was empty now, save for the few imperial guards lingering by the chamber door, in sight but out of earshot. "You have a moment now, no more," she said, rising. She wore long fringed robes of ivory and black, simple but pleasing.

"For many days we shared each other's words, my lady, and for many nights we shared each other's caresses. Yet now you look upon me as though I am nothing but a faithless outlander."

"Because that is what you are to me," she said.

He advanced a step toward her. From behind, he could hear the guards rustle in reply. Miriana halted them with a raised hand. "My faith has *never* wavered," Seric told her. "You know that. In your heart, I know you do. It would be plain to see but for your brother's jealous whisperings. How do you not see that?"

Her pretty blue eyes narrowed. "Who were you meeting with at the Red Mimosa?"

"What?"

"The brothel in the east district. I have eyes everywhere, you know. You were meeting someone there, who was it?"

He suddenly feared for his life. *How could she know?* He needed to say something, and quickly. "I was seeing a courtesan—"

She scoffed at that. "Don't tell me you were importuned by some whore. I am no fool, Seric Dyre."

"I didn't betray you, my lady," he said quietly. It wasn't entirely untrue—he *had* intended to betray the empire, but then Miriana called upon him and altered his ambitions. "I proved as much when I charted the course of defense against the Redlands. It was I who defeated Raas Dragath at the Horns of Vermillion, remember? It was I who secured your hold on the throne. And I've done these services for nothing. I did them only in devotion to you. My heart bears no guilt."

She believed him, maybe. "And Alarin? A crippled man doesn't just vanish from his bedchamber."

"No, he doesn't," Seric said. "But I don't have an answer for that. Not right now. What I do know is that Alarin Athera is far more capable than he shows himself to be. There are only a few who can contend with his cunning." He took another step toward her. "You need me, my lady. You need me and you know it."

"Don't, Seric."

She wants to trust me. "You are but a woman, alone at the head of the empire. You cannot possibly hold the throne without me. You know it's true." He advanced another step.

"That's enough, Seric."

Seric ignored that and took another step—only to halt when he heard the armored guardsmen approaching from behind. A hand clamped down on his shoulder, but Seric didn't turn to acknowledge it, didn't let his eyes drift from Miriana. "I would've carved my own heart from my chest a thousand times had you asked it of me." He bowed an extravagant bow and left.

Outside, dusk was deepening. The snowfall had weakened, but the cold had only grown stronger, and now threatened to freeze all it touched. Seric's boots crunched across the snowpack. He didn't want to return to his communal home, but he had nowhere else, no one else. It was hard to accept that the Lady Regent might never call upon him again. The very idea of it made his chest twist with ache. In his stupid, prideful heart, he still believed he would one day again run his hand through her hair and caress her soft white skin. One day . . . but not today. Today there was only regret—regret and dejection and anger and frustration, sometimes assaulting him one at a time, other times all at once.

His desolate home looked more desolate than usual. No lights were to be seen. Usually there were at least a handful of oil lamps or braziers glowing in the common rooms, and another in Seric's quarters from that old, forgetful servant. *Where is that old fool?* Seric crunched across the courtyard, past the rime-glazed shrubbery and along the weathered veranda, and entered his private room, where he brought to life the center brazier.

It was strange how much he cared for Miriana. She'd roused a great passion in him, a passion that had lifted his spirits and carried him into some uncharted realm of ecstasy. When he had shared himself with the Lady Regent, he was no longer debilitated by that gaping pit of misery in his heart.

He had to get that back. He had to get *her* back.

The brazier's warmth lifted slightly his despair, and a few cups of wine softened his mind a bit. Strangely enough, his thoughts turned to Nyvia. One thing he learned over the course of his union with her was that she wasn't as diffident and demur as she seemed. If there was anyone who knew anything about Alarin's disappearance, it was Nyvia. And though she had undoubtedly parried a barrage of questions already, only Seric knew how to coax and cajole her in just the right ways to get what he wanted.

He opened a wooden trunk and pulled out his lute. The body was filmed over with dust and discolored from age and disuse, and when he plucked the catgut strings with his plectrum, it sounded awful. He tuned the instrument's conical pegs as best he could. He plucked again. Yes, that was better. *What was that piece I used to play?* Funny how he couldn't remember, yet the moment he plucked the first few notes, the entire sequence came back without a second thought. He played and played as the swirling, evocative melody whisked him off to better time. An earlier time, a time in which Seric Dyre was an up-and-coming man of the empire, his prestige bolstered by his adopted father Nethan Dyre, a man with extraordinary gifts of intellect and wisdom and wit. Seric was so passionate then, so thoroughly eager to devour everything Nethan could impart to him. Yes, that was quite a time. A younger, more exhilarating time.

Snap. The broken string vibrated and fell limp. *Stupid goddamn thing.* He threw the lute against the wall, something he'd never consider doing in the past. But what did it matter now? He yawned. It was too late to visit Nyvia tonight; he needed to rest anyway. Yes, he would retire early tonight, and visit Nyvia just after dawn. He didn't have much to go on, but at least he had a start. He stretched his tired limbs and slowly turned about—

There was someone by the door.

A tall figure, with a face hidden beneath a patched hood. The frame was undoubtedly a man's frame, too tall to be his old servant, too robust to be anyone from the resident communes. "Who are you?" Seric demanded.

The intruder took a single step forward.

"What do you want?" Again, no answer, just another step. Seric reached down for his dagger, but found nothing. *Fool.* He'd left it across the room, by the foot of the brazier. The intruder took another step, and another, swifter now. Seric's eyes turned to the exit, halfway between them. He bolted.

The exit was far, maybe too far. The intruder was running now, too. Steel flashed from inside the folds of his cloak. Seric wasn't going to make it. *Hurry, hurry goddamn it.* Too late. The man lunged at him. Seric sidestepped the attack, then turned and barreled into him, lifting the larger man off his feet, pushing him out of the doorway. They tumbled down into the snow-muddied courtyard. Steel twinkled as the blade flew from the man's hand, landing with its ridged hilt peering out from the snow. Seric scrabbled for it, clawing and scrabbling through snow and ice and mud. His fingers grazed the pommel . . . almost . . . almost . . . yes, he had it. He brought up the weapon and spun—but the assailant was already on him.

Fists rained down, one after another, knocking the blade from Seric's hand. All he could do was bury himself beneath his arms, bury his head and endure the pain, at least until he managed to grab the assailant's wrist. His other hand reached behind his attacker's neck to bring the man's head down against his own chest, removing both the distance to strike and the assailant's sight. His hood had fallen away, and hanks of ratty, unctuous hair fell into Seric's mouth, slimy like wet leaves.

The assailant snarled and flailed and bit Seric's breast, and when Seric cried out the man lifted his head and brought it smashing down on Seric's face. The world spun. Pain, white-hot, flooded through him. His left eye wouldn't open. *I can't see,* he thought. *I can't see goddamn it.* The assailant's fists struck down again, and Seric forgot all about his eye, forgot even where he was, until another blow knocked his senses right back.

The strikes kept coming, but soon they began to hurt less and less, until Seric felt no pain at all. Everything was drifting away—everything except his thoughts. It was so strange, how clear his thoughts were. They told him to defend himself, implored him, and he tried, but his body wouldn't respond. He gave up and resigned himself to the battering, but by then the blows had stopped, and the man's weight was no longer on him. Seric's one working eye slowly opened. He could see . . . could barely see . . . the man was looking off, distracted. *What is he looking at?* Then Seric saw it. Light, somewhere in the distance. Also footfalls—he heard footfalls now, and voices, yes, voices coming closer. *The nightwatch, it's the goddamn nightwatch.*

Seric tried to laugh, but gobs of blood came out instead. "You should run," he said. "They will kill you."

The man said nothing, and Seric wondered if he had even understood him. Then he pressed his weight down again, and Seric saw his greasy, ugly face. "Unlike yours," the foul man rasped, "my faith is sworn beyond death." One hand grabbed a fistful of Seric's hair; the other held a dagger. "Look at me, traitor. Raas Dragath wishes you a pleasant journey." Seric felt something cold across his throat. It took a moment for the blood to respond, but when it did, it came out in a terrible gush. He struggled and struggled for breath, and each time it came, it came less and less, until finally there was nothing left but a sickening wheeze, and it was then Seric knew he was going to die.

CHAPTER TWENTY-FOUR

Demien Mordall dragged himself out of bed and staggered into the privy chamber, clutching at his flaring abdomen. He leaned over the chute and spewed out everything inside him, colors and textures of every kind, even those he didn't remember taking in. And when it was over, when there was nothing solid left, he retched and coughed up spittle for a while, then collapsed on the floor, weak and dizzy and caked in sweat despite the chill. All he could do to deflect the pain was close his eyes and focus on taking deep, heavy breaths, in and out, in and out, in and out . . .

He must've fallen asleep, because next he knew, he was shivering and groggy and his gummy eyes were reluctant to open. The pain in his abdomen had relinquished itself to a dull, smoldering ache, and he was able to lift himself back to his feet. *By the gods, what have I eaten?* It had been a typical banquet of the typical fare, courses of roasted squab and chicken foot soup, spiced and seasoned with all the typical sprigs and herbs. No dish was out of the ordinary, though now he felt nauseated by the very thought of it all, and he leaned over to vomit once more, but nothing came out.

He emerged from the privy and staggered back across the bedchamber. He stopped only to throw on his cloak and grab an unlit oil lamp, careful not to disturb the sleeping emperor. He knew the hour was terribly late but this couldn't wait—he needed to see Master Lorian at once. Perhaps the Grand Physician could administer a tonic of chamomile or coltsfoot or some other demulcent. Anything at all to alleviate the disharmony in his gut.

The antechamber was dark and vacant. *Where are the damn night sentries?* Sometimes they would saunter down to the secondary post to chat at the intersecting left wing. By the gods if he found them there he'd have them flogged. But no, when he came upon the wing, he saw no one. *This isn't right*, he thought. He paused to light the oil lamp.

He could see them now, twisted and slumped against the far wall, in shadows beneath the tall arched windows. They were still as stone—dead? Demien went closer; the smell hit him in an awful gust, the unmistakable stench of a man's loosed bowels. He turned away at once. Yes, they were definitely dead.

Thavian.

He raced back to the bedchamber, his oil lamp flickering and flashing and throwing shadows in unusual places. He found the other sentries, four of them, crammed in the dark, the same as the others. All had suffered a single killing wound, quick and efficient and professional. Demien pried a saber from one of the dead sentry's hands, then went to the bedchamber door. He pushed it open.

The room looked no different from before, but he felt an odd uneasiness now, one that lifted the hairs on the back of his neck. He searched the room and its alcoves and found nothing, then he turned his eyes upon the emperor's canopied bed. It was a beautiful piece of furniture, from the detail in the openwork paneling and posts, to the elegant, floral-decorated valance and tasseled cords. Shafts of moonlight from the high arched windows bathed the closed bedcurtains of blue brocaded silk. It gave off such a picturesque glow that it took

Demien a moment to notice the stains of dark blood running down onto the tiled floor.

The saber fell from his hand. He heard a moan, then realized it came from himself. Rage welled up inside him, deep and terrible. He wanted to scream, wanted to smash the fancy shelving and daybed and the recessed-leg writing table that Emperor Thavian had so often practiced his poetry on. He wanted to shatter the decorative statues and tear down the fancy wall arras and topple the gilt-silver braziers and washbasin stand. His heart screamed at him to do it—screamed and screamed like a hateful banshee's wail. And yet, all he did, all he could do, was raise a trembling hand, and pull aside the bedcurtain.

He was still tucked in his coverlets, the boy. His eyes were closed and his expression one of peace, despite the bloody wound where the assassin's blade had pierced his heart. He died quickly, at least. Demien removed the bloodstained coverlets and tore a strip of curtain to cover the boy, then he lowered his head and murmured whatever prayer came to his mind.

He had failed. He'd failed the empire, his house, and most of all—he'd failed to protect the boy. The imperial cord was severed—the dynasty was lost. He glanced down to where the saber lay. He knew what he had to do. It was better to die in dignity than live in disgrace. But no . . . he had but one task left, one final deed before he could join the boy on his journey to heaven.

Demien removed his nightshirt and pulled on his winter garb—heavy trousers and undershirt and tunic and boots. He chose a simple gray cloak, fastening it about the neck. He paused when his fingers grazed his seal of office. He clutched it and yanked, snapping the cord and letting the object fall to the floor. He left it there and retrieved his haversack, stuffing it with clothes and gear and tinder and whatever else he thought to bring.

He grabbed an extra cloak, and lastly his short sword Dreadfang, which was resting on hooks beside his own bed. He had to pass the emperor's altar to get there, and as he did his eyes were drawn to the ornate, raised-pattern box that held the emperor's Imperial Seal. It was still inside. Five intertwining Sadralen with watchful eyes and long fangs and a complex spiraling of horns, all over a precise inlay of silver and black jade.

Demien reached for it—but stopped midway. His fingers instead closed into a fist, and then he spun and made for the door. He got only a few steps before he reconsidered. *It doesn't belong here, not anymore.* He went back and stuffed the box into his haversack, then went on his way.

A commotion grew outside the bedchamber—the movement and voices of imperial guardsmen. They advanced quickly, almost too quickly for Demien to extinguish the lamp and dart into a recess behind one of the stone sentinels. He saw Cyrille Vileron at its head, leading none other than the Lady Regent herself. He waited until the clangor died away. *Too close, Demien, much too close.*

He made his way to the secret entranceway, opening the slab and heading down the stairs. His walk turned to a sprint through the subterranean tunnels, his haversack rustling and his leather-soled boots churning the earth underfoot. He found Alarin in his usual room, asleep.

"We have to go," Demien said as he gave the man a firm shake.

It seemed an eternity before Alarin fully opened his eyes. And when he did he only flinched at the light. He looked thinner than usual, his eyes both sunken and rheumy. He was mumbling about something, but Demien didn't care to listen. "Lord Alarin, we have to go. Right now."

It took a moment before he seemed to understand. Demien helped him up. Alarin was a tall man, not so tall as Demien but certainly taller than most, and when Demien draped the extra imperial cloak about him, it fell just shy of concealing his artificial foot. *No one will notice,* he thought, drawing up the hood to conceal the man's face. Then he turned and led the way.

He wasn't entirely sure of his direction—which was strange considering Demien had not long ago committed every path to memory. But his mind was jumbled now, his thoughts hazy and uncertain. He only felt sure he was heading the right way when the tunnel began to climb in a steady incline. It wasn't steep, but it was enough to prove a laborious feat for the lamed man. At last they reached the exit, a small and unmarked wooden door that Demien had to pry free to open. Beyond that lay a narrow, lightless passageway. He turned to motion Alarin inside, but Alarin wasn't with him—he was a still a ways behind, turned toward the way they'd just come. He was just standing there. "Alarin." No response. Again he called, and again, nothing. *What is he doing?* Demien stomped over to him, placing a hand down on Alarin's shoulder. The man turned and said, "Someone's following us."

Demien froze. He moved only to raise the lamp, which illuminated the narrow tunnel from which they had come. He saw nothing. *Be patient*, Alarin's eyes seemed to say. Demien was, and then he heard something, a rustling, but it was so faint it could've been a rat or something even smaller. *Be patient.* Maybe Alarin's mind was fooling him. *How much longer must we wait?* Then it came—a scuffle of feet, undeniably louder, and from somewhere down the tunnel. Demien motioned for Alarin to stay, and, with lamplight in one hand, Dreadfang in the other, he headed toward the noise. His light startled something into a side alcove, something much bigger than vermin. Slowly now, he crept upon the entrance, inching forward, inch by inch, raising his sword . . .

It was a man, cowering and puny and—no, it was a boy. It was only a boy. Demien raised the light. "Silas?"

It was *his* boy, his very own son. Silas Mordall was all of ten or eleven, and small for his age, small and timid and weak—but most disappointingly, he was dumb. He was dumb and Demien knew he wouldn't receive an answer and yet he still rattled off question after question: What are you doing down here? Why did you follow me? This place isn't safe—where are your nursemaids, your caretakers?

The boy lowered his eyes, meek as always. He could hear well enough, he just couldn't speak. Never had, not once, not a single word, and no one knew why. Master Lorian once rambled on about certain damages to his speaking chords, but Demien never really cared to understand the extent of it. And after his wife Alana had died, he neglected Silas altogether, leaving him in the hands of the palace orderlies.

Right now the boy was doing that annoying thing he did: speaking in gestures with his hands, like how he communicated to his caretakers. But Demien never learned any of that. "Stop it. I don't understand you, boy."

"Bring him," Alarin's voice called.

"No," he said. But Alarin said there was no other choice, and by the goddamn gates of the netherworld, he was right. Demien sighed and his hand came down to raise the boy's head by his little chin. "When I speak, you obey. If you don't, we all die. Understood?"

The boy gave a pointedly slow nod, and Demien patted his head and mussed his chestnut hair and instructed him to stay close as he led the way.

They squeezed through the narrow passageway and moved into a dingy storeroom, then exited through a wooden door whose outer face was concealed by a heavy wall carpet. Soon they found themselves in the rear staging area of the Imperial Theater. It was not so long ago that Demien had watched the emperor perform here—or rather, he watched who he thought was the emperor, but in fact was the regent taking his place. Demien balled a fist. He should've done something then, before Minister Sydrian had ever come to him.

They exited the theater through the side door of the entry hall, moving down along the outer walkway and across the forecourt. It was a chilly night, starry and cloudless and bright. He could see the West Gate looming in the distance. Alarin's pace continued to slow, but fortunately, there were no sentries around. In fact, Demien saw no one at all. Not until they came upon the city avenues, but even then, nighttime curfew permitted only a small number of faces outside, and not one spared his ragged party a glance.

Somewhere down the avenue a company of riders stormed by, horse hooves thundering and steel clanging. Silas clamped his hands over his ears. Demien lowered his head and watched them pass. *Imperial riders . . . heading from the gate. I pray I'm not too late.* Just ahead Demien saw the massive auxiliary wall. He could see sentries atop the upper walkways, alert and wary and moving to and from the gatehouse. Demien turned to Alarin and bade him to stay behind him, the boy too, and he approached the large stone archway of the enclosed barbican. The sentries there regarded him with curt displeasure. Not unexpected, but when he declared his name and all his titles and demanded to speak with the gate warden at once, they moved quickly enough. Soon after, Demien watched his childhood friend coming down from the access ramp.

Briam Styrm was a robust figure with a stern jawline, stony eyes, and a head shaped perfectly for all its lack of hair. He was dressed in full imperial attire, though he somehow looked as though he had just woken up. He barely extended any form of greeting before saying, "I keep hearing reports of assassins, Redlander assassins—is it true, Lord Commandant? We saw nothing here."

"Briam, I need you to open the gate."

He seemed not to listen. "The people are already talking—is it the Redlands, my lord? Is it—"

"Yes," Demien said. "Now I need you to open the gate. Briam, I need you to open the gate and let me pass. Can you do that for me, old friend?"

He paused now, a long pause, before responding. "I've been instructed not to open the gate for any reason," he said. "An edict from the Lady Regent. The riders left not more than moments ago."

Too late, he thought. "Listen, Briam, look at me. I am your friend, am I not? I must leave the Hollow at once. Open this gate and let me pass."

Briam's eyes combed Demien's companions, the meek little boy and the hooded figure in the filthy cloak. When he looked back, his voice shifted from cordial to soldierly. "What is going on?"

Demien only blinked at him. *It's no use.* There was nothing he could do. So what if he and Briam were childhood friends, so what if they were raised in the same village—did he really expect the man would betray the ruling house over some boyhood camaraderie? He was a fool to think this would work.

He turned about and motioned to his companions to leave. He didn't get far before Briam's voice made him halt. Turning, Demien saw the gate warden standing there, his arms crossed, his face darkened by the night. He expected the warden would order them seized. But he didn't—instead he barked an order, an order to raise the portcullis and lower the drawbridge. One of his subaltern officers went to object, but Briam silenced him. Then he looked at Demien. "You are a dear friend, Lord Commandant," he said, "but more than that, you a man known throughout the realm for his honor and virtue and guileless heart. What you seek must only be for the good of the dynasty. I'd be a fool to suspect otherwise."

Demien went to thank him, but his words were soundless as the portcullis came to life with a groan. Briam nodded as if he'd heard anyway, and urged him to hurry. Demien and his companions headed across the enclosed barbican and out through the second archway. And as he made his way out of the city and onto the waiting roadway, Demien turned and glanced up at the archery tower where he knew his childhood friend was watching him. *He will die for this*, Demien thought.

CHAPTER TWENTY-FIVE

"Why was Demien Mordall granted safe passage?" Miriana demanded. "I gave orders that no man was to leave this city for *any* reason."

"My lady, he was—" Cyrille Vileron began to say, but Miriana cut him off. "The man still has his tongue, does he not? Let him talk."

Imperial Gate Warden Briam Styrm knelt before the Lady Regent in the rear chamber of the Hall of Obsidian Light. It was quiet here, but the neighboring throne room was alive with the thronging of courtiers and military officers and civic officials, all gathered in response to the sudden and tragic death of the emperor. Miriana didn't even know if she could muster the resolve to face them, never mind figure out how to mitigate their distress.

"The Lady Regent gave you an order," the Minister of Judgment Korval Syr snapped, standing beside her. He was an old, gaunt man who kept his thinning gray hair hidden beneath a black muslin cap.

The warden didn't reply, didn't twitch a single muscle of his stern face. It wasn't hard to see why his peers held the man in such high esteem. He was the perfect mold of an Anirian soldier, strapping and stoic and with a jaw chiseled from feldspar.

But admirable though he was, Miriana could not let his disobedience go unpunished. "I ask you once more. Did you give the order to raise the portcullis?"

"Yes, my lady," Briam answered quietly, though not without an underlying hint of strength.

"And his companions. Their names, if you will."

He gave the slightest shake of his head. "It was dark, my lady."

She sighed. *It's no use.* "You have betrayed not only your Lady Regent but the empire itself. Your head will serve to sit atop the very gate you commanded. Minister, the judgment, if you will."

Minister Korval's resounding voice took over for a while, dispensing the warden's fate without any notion of a fair hearing or trial. Briam accepted this without complaint, never once changing his stern demeanor. When it was time to take him away, the guards seemed rather disinclined to do so, and Minister Korval had to bark at them to obey. After that it was a smooth and quiet process—or it would've been, had all that wretched noise from the neighboring hall not made her tense.

When the condemned man was gone, Miriana turned to the massive General Aldebron Pentagath. The cold eyes of the bull-chested, bellicose man unnerved her. Nevertheless she said, "I want every roadway searched. Every hill and foothill, every roadside inn and every thatched cottage and outbuilding you see. I want all the village heads questioned. Any man suspected of granting Demien Mordall sanctuary is to be trussed and taken to the Hollow, along with his entire clan." The ferocious man bowed his shaggy head and turned to the exit. "Oh and General, make sure you return with Demien *and* his pair of wretched companions." The general acknowledged that with a single snort of his porcine nose, then he left.

Vylas came to her shortly after. Seeing the exhaustion on her brother's face only made her remember just how tired she was. How long had she been awake now? Her hair was a mess, her face greasy from not removing her makeup. Even her raiment, once silky smooth and in lovely tones of cobalt and slate blue, now felt uncomfortable and looked filthy. She could see the midday sun beaming in through the high scrollwork windows, but she couldn't say how many days it'd been since the emperor of the Anir was found murdered at the hands of Redlander assassins.

She needed to know Demien Mordall's involvement in this, and she hoped Vylas had answers for her, hoped he could in some way ease her mind, but he only maundered on about some vomit he'd found in the emperor's privy. She threw up her hands in exasperation and interrupted him. "The emperor was *murdered*, do you understand? He was murdered and our Grand Commandant has fled the Hollow with the Imperial Seal. Now I asked you for information and you dare return with some petty ramblings?"

"Sister, I—" He lowered his eyes, then went to biting his nails.

She pointed to the postern door of the adjacent hall. "Vylas, *listen* to that. To *them*. I have enough to deal with already. I need to know the Grand Commandant's involvement in this."

He stopped and shook his head. "We both know it is not within Demien Mordall's scope of integrity to ever betray the emperor."

"Conjecture is not enough," she scolded. "Not anymore. Vylas, I need proof."

"Well, as I was saying, in the privy chamber—"

She let out a grunt of frustration, and Vylas held out a placating hand. "Please listen, Sister. Lord Demien fell ill that night. He passed out on the privy chamber floor. I believe it was prearranged."

"You mean he was poisoned, are you certain of this? Did you question his taster?"

"Not yet," Vylas said. He looked down. "But someone so honorable as Lord Demien . . . I'd expect him to take his own life at the very sight of the slain boy. But he didn't, and I don't know why."

"Perhaps the man is guilty of some misconduct after all."

"Perhaps." He seemed unconvinced, his lone eye focusing on something she couldn't see. When next he spoke he spoke distantly, as if trying to repeat a passage of prose he'd been instructed to memorize. "What was important enough to persuade him to leave the city . . .?" He stopped and looked up at her. "I will find out what that is."

"Fine. When—when will you find out?"

"Soon."

"What does that mean—*how* soon?"

"Soon," he repeated. "I assure you, Sister, I will not rest until the truth finds me. Now don't fret yourself about the court, all they need from you is comfort and conciliation, and to be assured that the empire's high ministers are free of any malfeasance. A strong presence and firm voice will win their faith."

Miriana shook her head. "You're wrong, Brother. The court desires only to cast blame for this. And who better to blame than me? They'll say the fall of the dynasty wasn't caused by the schemes of Raas Dragath—no, it's a sign of heaven's displeasure, for having a woman on the throne. They will sooner punish me than face the true enemy to the south. Brother, I'm facing *exile*."

Vylas went to console her, and she let him, though his touch, while tender, did little to help. She loved her brother, and as a spy and a watcher he was adept, but he was not a man of strategy and intuition. Not like Seric. She wished Seric were here . . . no, she couldn't bear such a thought. *Not now. Don't you dare think about him right now.*

"I won't let that happen," Vylas said.

"If you truly mean that, then do as you're ordered and *return with the information I need.*" She turned away and went to the postern door. Cyrille Vileron went to open it. "Wait," she told him. Miriana stood there a long moment, one hand clutching the outer jamb, her lungs taking deep, calming breaths, one after another. *You are strong, Mir, strong as silk.* She closed her eyes. "Go on," she said.

The noise struck her like a giant fist. Before her stood a vast sea of faces, each laden with anger or sorrow or grief or something worse. Her heart rose in her throat, and she tottered forward as though her legs were gelatinous stumps. The entrance led right onto the dais itself, thankfully, so it was a brief walk to the Imperial Throne. But weak as she was, she didn't have the courage to sit, so she simply stood beside it.

Her presence soon quieted the assembly. It took a long moment before Miriana could speak, and when she finally did, she hated how weak her voice sounded. "I stand before you, all of you, never more fearful for the words that must be said." Someone shouted at her, startling her, making her forget her next words. More shouting. Shouting at her to get on with it, to discard the rhetoric and reveal plainly the truth. The more Miriana faltered the angrier they seemed to grow, like wolves gathering to take down a much larger prey. "It is true," she said over the ruckus. "It is true of His Majesty. By the will of fate he has begun his journey to heaven."

A wave of moans and cries unfurled like a great sailcloth over the hall. Miriana had to wait a while before continuing on. "Please, let me assure you, *all* of you, not just the faces before me now, but all the good people of the Anir, that this despicable act will not go unpunished. And since the emperor himself has left us, it is by heaven's will that I must serve in his place, as Empress Miriana Athera, Lady of Divine Whispers. And as your empress, I will do everything in my power to punish the traitor Raas Dragath and all those who have taken part of his evil machinations."

The assembly exploded with rage, man and woman and minister and official all shouting words of hatred and vitriol, some demanding that she be stripped and exiled, others screaming for her head.

Something whizzed by her ear. Miriana flinched, and her eyes searched for an exit—there, the small postern door. Another object flew past. She could feel the terrible wrath of the crowd, could feel its rancorous hate, and never before had she felt so much a lowborn woman—a lowborn woman and a bawd who had no business on the throne. She had to get away, had to escape this mob before her thin line of guards was overwhelmed.

A man vaulted on the dais. He was tackled at once by a guardsman, but another rose in his place, and next she knew he was upon her, his eyes red and murderous, his open hands reaching for her throat. But thank the gods for Cyrille Vileron. The tall captain threw the man clear off the dais. Miriana reached out and grasped her savior's arm, tugging on black strips of leather.

A great clamor of steel and armor arose from down the hall as Anirian soldiers rushed to her aid. At the fore was General Sabriel Soffin, in splendid blackened mail and matching officer's cloak. He moved with aplomb and purpose, subduing the crowd with the aid of his veteran soldiers. These men were big and mean and armed to the brow, undoubtedly among the empire's finest.

"Let me speak," Soffin shouted, over and over, until finally, the din diminished just enough for him to do so. He was an older general, surely past fifty or so, with a thick crop of badger-gray hair and a round, cherubic face fitted with a pair of close-set eyes. He was neither robust nor powerful of voice, but by the gods he was a man who knew how to command other men. "So you are angry," he said. "And when you are angry it is easy to cast blame, and it is easiest to blame the lady for what has happened."

"She's a curse upon the Anir," a voice shouted.

"The blight that ruptured the dynasty!" said another.

He listened and nodded, running a hand through his hair. "Or she is a gift sent by heaven to aid us in this dire hour." The crowd hissed at that. "Wait. Wait now. I must share something with you, something that I've learned over the course of my many years. It is really quite simple, you see. Heaven tests our mettle." He'd spoken those last four words slowly, emphasizing each, and when he was done he paused to gaze pointedly at the crowd. "You see, as all things begin, so too they must end. Life begets death, houses rise and fall, one dynasty eclipses another. It is not by chance that the Anir has drawn to a close. It is not by chance that the dawn of a new age is upon us. Heaven is testing our mettle. And how do you react? You seek to blame others for justification. You sit in the dark and blindly reach out to chastise anyone in arm's reach."

Miriana felt Minister Korval's skinny hand on her shoulder. "Are you hurt, my lady?" he whispered.

"I'm fine."

Sabriel Soffin was gesturing toward her with an open palm. "It is easy to blame this woman. Easy to point the finger and deem her the cause of the empire's misfortune. And yet this woman has done every-thing in her power to keep the capital safe. Did you forget about the victory at the Horns of Vermilion? Did you forget that it was she who uncovered the treachery behind the Lord Regent's poisoning? It is she who has the virtue to stand before you now and subject herself to your baseless anger. Lady Miriana did not fail the empire, *you* did. All of you—you have all disavowed your duties, bickering like jackals over a mouse when just beyond the ridge lies a herd of young antelope." He gave another pause to eye the crowd, as if to show he was in complete control of this meager lot of robed courtiers. After all, General Sabriel Soffin had spent his entire life squaring off against men armed not with words but with axe and sword.

"I know my life was spent on the field and not among the tomes and tables of privilege and academics," he went on. "But I assure you, there is much wisdom in this old heart." He took a few pacing steps on the dais; his soldiers stepped aside as he did. "And this heart knows how easy it is to renounce the will of heaven. I did, I did it for years. I blamed heaven for the death of my son. For years my heart was filled with resentment and indignation." He paused once more, pacing, and the assembly seemed to lean forward now, in rapt attention. "And the more the hatred and bitterness filled my breast, the weaker and weaker I grew, until one day I was so weak I became bedridden with illness. All the most expensive and notable physicians were brought to my side. None could help. They told me I was soon to die, that only the gods could help me. I balked at those gods, but as the days progressed the weaker I became, until I was in such terrible agony that I simply crawled to my altar and prayed and prayed, all day and the next, for days and days, never ceasing, no matter how terrible my pain. As the days progressed, the pain lessened, little by little, and before long I was able to ingest not just simple gruels but solid meats and hearty dishes. I grew strong again. I grew strong and I continued to pray, every day without fail, and still do to this very day. And as you can clearly see, the gods have answered my prayers.

"Heaven tests our mettle. All of us, the loyal and filial subjects of the Anir. You are tested not to blame or bicker, but to see the strength in Lady Miriana, to have faith that only she can guide us until the time of her husband's return. And I assure you, he is destined to return." His next words came out in a great shout, "Do you want the realm to be ruled by that scoundrel Raas Dragath?" The crowd gave an emphatic response of rejection. "Or do you wish to tender your allegiance to Lady Miriana Athera, who is ordained by heaven to ascend the throne as empress until Lord Zantherei's inevitable return?"

The crowd cheered and whistled and applauded, and soon the entire hall was awash with praise and joy. Even the eldest or most doubtful of the court became bright-eyed and hopeful. Sabriel carried the assembly to a rallying chant: "The Empire Lives On! The Empire Lives On!" He then turned toward Miriana, dropping to his knees and bowing his head in a grand display of adulation.

Miriana quickly helped him rise. A renewed cheer rippled through the crowd. She turned to the sea of faces. "Stand with me and I will make sure our enemies suffer. I will make sure Lord Raas Dragath suffers. The empire lives on!"

The chant still echoed in her head long after she'd returned to her bedchamber.

"I'll arrange for more guards at all times," Cyrille Vileron said. "That was much too close, my lady."

"I fear no danger with you near," she replied. She was sitting before the warmth of her braziers, still wearing the same outfit as earlier.

He nodded. "It is General Sabriel Soffin who deserves your praise, my lady, not me."

"Soffin's praise comes with a price, no doubt."

Cyrille seemed incredulous. "What could such a man want? Fiefs, coin, he has enough of all that."

"All men want something." She'd learned this lesson long ago, when she was a young girl of thirteen. It was a beautiful summer day when that handsome young man had given her a bouquet of nosegays.

She tried to hide it from her master, but of course he found them and tore them to shreds. She pleaded with him, tears in her eyes. "He is just a kind man, he doesn't want anything." A fist knocked her to the ground, and from somewhere above her master said, "Stupid *whore*. All men want something. Money, power, or in your case, your sweet little cunt."

She was too young to see it then, but the bastard was right. And now that she had much more than just her cunt to offer; it wasn't always as easy to decipher a man's intentions. But with a man as decorated and aged as General Sabriel Soffin, there wasn't much in this realm left to entice him. *Still, there must be something*, she thought.

Yana appeared to tend her dress, but Miriana stopped her and said, "I need you to inquire about Seric Dyre's condition."

"Yes, my lady," she said. She threw on a heavier robe and asked in broken Anirian speech, "If you sleep, I wake you?"

"No . . . not unless he is near death."

Yana bowed and departed. Miriana sent her other maidservants away as well, and when at last she was alone, she disrobed and slid into the warmth of her featherbed, too exhausted for any of her nightly ablutions. Her mind drifted to Seric. By some divine fortune he was still alive. For one the blade hadn't cut deep enough, and secondly, the nightwatch worked quickly to wrap the wound and rush him to the sickchamber of the palace, where Master Arden Lorian and his son treated his wounds. Miriana still hadn't gone to see Seric. She lacked the strength to go—or maybe the courage. Why? Did she fear she would grieve after seeing him? She didn't want to grieve. And she certainly didn't want anyone to see her grieve.

She fell asleep then, only to be roused sometime later, though it wasn't Yana's pretty face that had wakened her, it was her brother's. "I've found it," Vylas said. "The answers you seek. Come, Sister, you must come with me."

"What hour is it?" she said, exasperated. Outside the window, it was still dark. "Just tell me, and be quick."

He barely let her finish. "I urge you, Sister, this needs to be shown. It will be quick, I beg you." He looked at Yana, who was rising out of bed herself, her pretty little mouth opening in a great yawn. "Get the lady her robes," Vylas ordered. Then, to the sentries at the door: "You and you two, come. The lady will need an escort."

Miriana sat up, tired and annoyed and grumbling threats about how he'd better not be wasting her time. But then she saw the expression on her brother's face. He looked exhausted, sure, but he also had a strange, driven look about him, the twinkle of a man who'd just absconded with a king's ransom. And so she stood and allowed Yana to dress her, and with a heavy, reluctant sigh, she followed her brother out of her bedchamber.

CHAPTER TWENTY-SIX

R ows upon rows of citizens had lined the avenues of the city, men and women and young ones and seniors, all in praise of the return of Commander Szathan Mordall. He'd ascended the barbican and delivered a speech to ensure their safety during these trying times. Looking back, Szathan wished he had said more—but he wasn't very good with words, wasn't good at commiserating with these poor citizens after they'd lost so much. Threshing fields were trampled and burned and water wells were lost to poison; harvests were ruined and farmsteads lay abandoned. Many were left to suffer the oncoming wrath of winter, and when that wrath came, it drove the less fortunate to hunger and despair.

It was midwinter now, when the days were at their coldest, the sunlight at its dimmest, and misery at its highest.

Szathan didn't need to be a man of great intellect to sense the low morale of his soldiers. After the battle at the Horns, General Sabriel Soffin was commissioned to take all of the veteran reinforce-

ments back to the Hollow, leaving Szathan with a host of new
recruits, boys so young they were surely plucked from the Pit before
their training was complete. Others were conscripts forced into
extended contracts, and many of those men lacked the proper arms or
supplies, and had to acquire them by looting the bodies of their fallen
comrades.

Dusk darkened the sky to the east and glowed a dull orange to the
west. Szathan observed it from his private quarters in the barracks. His
eyes were drawn to the outer wall of Thornberry, a gray snake in the
misty gloom. Snow and hoarfrost glazed the merlons and crenels of the
battlements. The recent storm had been most unforgiving, blasting
down from the windward mountains and sealing everything in a coffin
of white.

"I'm doing all that I can," Szathan commented to Brehems, who
was seated nearby. "The soldiers ask for grain, so I petition the Hollow
and the Hollow sends, but when the river freezes and the supply boats
get stuck, no one wants to help break the ice. And when the boats
finally do come to port, the supply is only half the bushels I requested,
and of course I learn there was a mix-up with the commissariat. I try to
explain it to the men, but they don't care to hear it. I took no more
portion than any of them, but still they resent me. What else can I do? I
know it's cold and I know it's difficult, but there's little I can do until
winter breaks or another shipment arrives."

"Or those wretched outlaws raiding the roadways are eliminated,"
Brehems put in.

Szathan sighed at that. There had always been outlaws and brigands outside the city, mercantile leeches that survived off the bustling
highways to and from Thornberry. Most were no more than a nuisance,
easily driven off or made to submit. But the outlaws of Wintersun Lake
had grown numerous enough to pose a legitimate threat. And no longer
did they abide by the clandestine agreement once shared with the
commanders of Thornberry's militia: not to kill, not to rape or ransom,
not to waylay the principal highways and not to take more than half of
any merchant's goods. For years the outlaw leaders had remained
faithful to this, even sending gifts of silk and satin in return. But now

they seemed to forget the agreement altogether, as more and more poured down the hills to raid the major roadways, spreading fear and constricting the lungs of commerce. "Give me two divisions and I'll stomp this little insurrection," Brehems went on.

"I would, my friend, I would crush them all myself, but this is not some rabble of miscreants. Two hundred men won't be enough to ensure submission. No, I'd have to send nearly every fresh blood we have, and if I did that, we'd risk returning to find Redlander colors flying atop the walls of Thornberry. I sent a petition for aid to the capital, but it came back with a halfhearted response to continue holding the city. I don't know what to do. Every day I realize more and more just how much I need Hiriam."

"Bah," Brehems said. "I tire of hearing his name."

"And I tire of speaking it, my friend, but that doesn't make it any less true."

"To hell with the prick," the uncouth man said. "He's a traitor, a goddamn turncoat."

They ate in silence for a time. "The new bloods," Szathan said at last. "Lately when I pass them in the barracks, they fall into silence. Tell me that's not a sure sign of discontent if you've ever seen one."

"They belong to Sabriel Soffin's little nephew now. The wretch deserves to be stripped of his rank and sent to clean out the ordure pits."

Szathan nodded. It was true; many of the fresh faces here looked to Fenerus Soffin as their leader now. The young general had garnered quite a name for himself at the Horns of Vermilion, slaying two Redlander generals before nearly overtaking Raas Dragath himself. And since returning to Thornberry, his brash attitude had only grown, as did his influence over the young men. "I didn't . . . out of respect to his uncle," he said. "A decision I now regret."

Brehems handed his empty bowl of pottage to the waiting attendant. "So do it now."

"I can't, it's too late, Fenerus too powerful. The soldiers will mutiny." He shook his head. "I should've foreseen this—hell it was plain as day. Without a doubt Hiriam would've—"

"*Enough,*" Brehems growled. "Enough already. You speak of losing him like losing an arm or leg."

"So I do."

Days later, Szathan was roused by one of the young recruits. He'd come to him just after daybreak, a callow and awkward youth, surely no more than sixteen or seventeen years to his name. He seemed almost too eager to reveal that General Fenerus had mobilized half a regiment in a campaign to subdue the outlaws. Szathan spun so fast he startled the young messenger. "He mustered *my* soldiers? Under whose authority?"

"He . . . he s-said . . ." the youth faltered.

Szathan rose from his seat to his full height. "*Speak,*" he boomed.

"He said Ogre Mordall is too stupid to do what must be done."

Szathan turned to his attendants, ordering one to fetch his deputy general, the other to fetch his armor. When he glanced back the little messenger's freckled face had twisted into an expression of unbridled apprehension. But angry as Szathan was, it wasn't at the youth, and he tried to make sure the youth understood that. But it didn't seem to work, probably because Szathan was just a big ugly ogre.

The cold was merciless this morning, and yet when Gilberon Brehems sauntered in he was barefoot and only in trousers, scratching at his scarred and hairy belly with a scarred and hairy hand. He was given the appropriate style of Bearcat, as he shared so much with those beasts from the southern hill forests. Both were strong, squat of limb, and cantankerous as an overworked draft horse. And both had plenty of fur to protect them from the cold.

"I know," Brehems replied when Szathan explained the situation. His stubby fingers went from scratching his belly to probing the navel. "I was surprised when you gave the command."

Szathan stopped fastening his armor. His eyes bored markedly into his friend. Maybe it was the earliness of the hour, or maybe it was because Brehems had suffered one too many blows to the head, but it took the man quite a long time before he seemed to catch on. "Wait a moment, you didn't give the command?"

"*No.*" Szathan yanked the straps of his greave, forceful and angry and making sure everyone knew it. But with his other leg, he had to be gentler, as to not to agitate his long-injured knee. So here he was, fuming with ire, yet working his hands daintily. He felt a goddamn fool, but he didn't care. "He's acting without imperial sanction—and without my authority." An attendant stood on a wooden stool to help secure his spaulders—huge things they were, blackened steel segments that tapered to three falcate points, like the talons of the massive and majestic roc. He fitted his undercap and his open-faced helm, which was ornately embossed and forged with small black wings at the sides. He ran a hand through the center plume of bone-colored horsehair, then reached for his figured halberd, Nightwing, his eyes drawn to the blade-markings of wing and claw.

Szathan then turned to Brehems, gesturing to the man's bare chest. "You're riding like that? It's a bit cold, General, even for you." And before the puzzled man could ask, Szathan told him, "Yes, my friend, we are going after them."

The rising sun did little to alleviate the chill of the roadways. The swirling alpine fog did well to hide the light, but the distant mountains refused to go unnoticed, heaving up their white shoulders to align with the neighboring ranges. Spruce and fir ruled the land out here, the air thick with the smell of their needles. The occasional broadleaf stood hunched and cringing like an old man cowering before a stranger's wrath.

Szathan led his company on a buckskin charger, a huge beast bedecked in heavy barding, the most striking of which was a winged chamfron that matched the wings of Szathan's helm. The horse led him through the wooded paths while Szathan listened to the reports of the advance riders, which was more a gesture of protocol, since any old fool could follow the tracks of Fenerus's company in the snowpack.

It was just before midday when Szathan climbed a small rise and gazed upon the entire company: about five hundred young men in a column of black and gray, heavy horsemen with halberd and spear in the fore, lighter bowmen in the rear. Szathan scowled. *Goddamn those new bloods.* He whipped his charger into a run, galloping hard until he was past the rearguard and parallel to the main body. "HALT THE TRAIN," he shouted, his cold breath emerging before him. The men looked stunned by what they saw—their massive commander riding his massive charger, both armed and angry.

The column began to unthread itself, as some of the boys went to obey while others not so much, and a good number simply remained clueless to it all. Szathan kept on shouting until he reached the vanguard, where Fenerus Soffin broke from the line to face him. The general sat astride a fawn-colored charger, his face youthful and pale and resembling his uncle's only in its roundness. His hair was short and curly and already receding terribly, but his eyebrows were long and slim and black. And his eyes—those cruel and crescent eyes— they stared as if painfully bored by what they saw. "Ogre Mordall," he said, ignoring any sort of title. "How thoughtful of you to join us."

Szathan gritted his teeth at such blatant insolence. "By imperial decree, I stand as Commander of Thornberry, and as your commander, I did not give my consent for this. Disperse your company *at once.*"

Fenerus didn't offer a reply, didn't do much of anything except place the quirt that was in his hand into the leather loop of his saddle. Then he guided his horse closer, calmly, dangerously.

"It would be unwise to defy me," Szathan said.

Again, the general didn't respond, but his smug little gaze said enough. The man wanted to clash. Good, because Szathan was ready to strike down this young fool. It mattered not that he was outnumbered. Szathan refused to back down. By the gods, he'd sooner scrub an angry bugbear's rump than yield to this wretch.

The approach of riders broke the tenseness. Szathan's squadrons fell in line beside him. Brehems appeared to his left, his massive wolf-toothed mace in hand. Fenerus's crescent eyes narrowed. He didn't seem pleased. Neither did the soldiers behind him, despite their advantage in numbers. "You promised to keep the people of Thornberry safe," Fenerus said.

"And I have."

He balked at that. "If you believe that, then you truly are as small-minded as they say."

Szathan gritted his gapped teeth. "What do you think will happen if we go to war with the outlaws? Do you think Raas Dragath will remain idle in the south? His scouts are flying to his encampment at this very moment to report that Thornberry stands unprotected. Do you not realize that? You may think me small-minded, but only the gods might say what that makes you."

Fenerus frowned at that. Szathan took advantage of his silence to yank the reins of his charger and glare at the new bloods. Most averted their eyes from the grim faces of Szathan's veterans. "Now DISPERSE," Szathan roared. "ALL of you—back to the barracks. I give you but one warning." He pulled his figured halberd from its saddle ring.

The young soldiers looked to their leader for direction. Fenerus didn't oblige them—not at first, but only after a long, tense moment of silence. He raised an ungainly arm to signal the return to the city. Szathan listened as the soldiers went, but his eyes never left Fenerus's, not until the general's horse brushed past and he was out of sight. Szathan released his grip on the halberd and breathed in relief. Brehems, nearby, was raring to clash. "Take that churl's rank, I tell you. His insolence boils my blood."

"I want to," Szathan said firmly. And he did want to, and he wanted to even more the next day, when he awoke to learn that a soldier had been strung naked to a post of the watchtower and left to die overnight. When Szathan went to him, he saw the poor lad's face was black and distended from the blistering cold. Still, there was no doubt—it was the young messenger, the one who had earlier revealed Fenerus's unauthorized march.

When Brehems found out, he was ready to burst. "Goddamn monkey-faced mother-raping churl." He was bare-chested again, and scratching aggressively at his belly. "To hell with his rank, you need to take his head. Sabriel's nephew or not, take the prick's head."

Szathan nodded, his eyes holding the dead soldier. When he spoke his voice was solemn and distant. "Poor bastard didn't join the empire to be murdered like this." He ordered the young man buried with honors, then sat with his scribe and mulled over how he would address the soldier's surviving kin. It would be a long night, and Szathan wasn't very good with words.

CHAPTER TWENTY-SEVEN

H e spent the days crammed between tanned leather and burlap sacks of grain, tired and cold and sore of muscle. And every bump of the cart—no matter how small—caused his phantom limb to shriek with pain, and there always seemed to be a lot of bumps. His clothes were grimy and ragged and he felt a deepening chill down to the marrow of his bones. And so, after thirteen or fourteen days of this, it was no surprise that Alarin Athera was beginning to think being stuffed in a bullock cart wasn't the best way to get to Thornberry.

Still, it was a large cart, drawn by three yokes of oxen and overlaid with a roof of thatch, and today it wasn't so intolerable, as the icy grip of winter had relaxed just a bit, allowing the pain in his missing leg to recede. He was able to think about other things, the tranquility of his tower quarters, the comfort of his featherbed, and most of all, the wonderful fare of an imperial banquet. Useless thoughts, he knew, but they were the only ones that mattered now.

The cart ground to a halt, and Alarin lifted his head to peer through the uneven slats of wood. *Another imperial checkpoint*, he thought, slumping back down. They were all the same; a few minutes of forced chatter and greased palms and they'd be on their way. Sometimes the imperial soldiers came around to inspect the load, but it was always a lackadaisical effort.

They had to stop again later on, when the carter had to replace the axles and wheels of the vehicle. It was a laborious task, but necessary in order to remain in alignment with the deep ruts of the road. Alarin didn't mind. The respite allowed him a quick stretch and a quick piss in the snow. And when he was done he looked up to the cloudless gray sky and prayed for the day he'd be free of this damned cart entirely.

A few days later he got his wish. It was an especially cold afternoon; the carter had stopped for so long that Demien climbed out to see what was amiss. Before long, Alarin could hear the two men arguing with each other, and then Demien stomped back over and said they had to walk from here. "Here? Where is here?" Alarin questioned as he touched his good leg down onto the snow. "I don't see a city, I don't even see a hostelry."

"The carter's blubbering on about missing his wife and sons and all that," Demien told him.

"Wait, you're telling me the man has misgivings *now*? After checkpoint after checkpoint of greasing palms with *our* coin?"

"He said he usually stays north of the river, toward Indigo Cove—I don't know." Demien paused to shake his head. "He said it hasn't been easy, the last few checkpoints."

"I don't care. I don't care how goddamn difficult it is. There was an agreement. A promise of faith. Did you forget what that means, Lord Demien?"

"What would you have me do?" Demien snapped. He looked away, sighed, and seemed to think for a moment. "We'll keep along the outskirts of the Starwing Road. As the crow flies it'll lead us straight to Thornberry."

But traveling on foot was the absolute last thing Alarin wanted to do. And after but a single day of doing just that, he began to think it might be the very last thing he *would* do. Every step was a jolt of unrelenting ache, deep and burning despite the awful chill. After a few more days of this, he would've given his other leg just to be back on that musty old bullock cart again.

On the fourth day they were blessed again with balmy weather. Progress was rapid; by the late afternoon they had already forded an estuary and overcome a cluster of creeks and cliffs along the river's edge. And lamed though he was, Alarin did his best to keep up, and he often found motivation by cursing his companions, more Demien for being so fit and strong, but also the boy for being so young and agile. *They don't know what it's like to be old and broken.* Well, the boy was broken, sort of, but lacking a voice was not the same as lacking a leg. *At least not out here, not in these conditions.*

The companions occasionally heard riders on the main road. Greedy sots undoubtedly crammed the roadside inns by night, so Alarin and Demien had no choice but to rest elsewhere. It made for some difficult nights, but not without the rare respite. A few days ago they'd found a remote manor and paid the owner for shelter and food, and another night they squatted in an abandoned outbuilding. Last night they'd slept inside a temple that was built against a hillside. The high priest had been small and penurious, but he offered what little he had and never asked questions.

Over the next few days, they had to endure with snow caves and frame shelters in the woods. And as their foodstuffs thinned, the icy temperatures returned, and Alarin soon became weak, so so weak, and today he could barely drag himself along. Demien tried to help, but Alarin shoved him off and cursed and spat and said he'd rather slither on his belly like a goddamn snake before being carried by another man. It surprised him that even now his stupid pride ruled him, that even now he would choose his own suffering over another man's pity. *I was once the Thunder of the North,* he thought. *I was once in command of thousands of men.* He couldn't help being a cripple, but at least he could retain some measure of self-respect. It was all he had left.

The next morning Demien bought a horse that was paddocked in an old estate. It was a retired draft horse, old and half blind and weak from a lifetime of hard labor. But Silas adored it, so much so that Alarin mounted and rode only when the boy had taken his turn first. And although the saddle was stiff and hard and poorly stitched and made of poor-quality leather, he didn't complain. It was certainly better than limping along with cane and wooden leg.

When the companions stopped to rest, the boy constantly petted it and groomed its coat with a currycomb. Alarin couldn't help but smile at that. He wished he could be as a child, to be so carefree and so pure of heart even in the face of such tribulation. But Silas had the wonderful ignorance that comes with seeing less than a dozen winters; to him advanced age and death were surely no closer than the moon and stars. *Not so for me*, Alarin thought. *My days are behind me* now, *the good ones anyway*. Now every season of every year was as bleak and lifeless as this wretched winter.

Demien gave the horse a name, something like Sunspirit or Sun something or other, and a week later he killed it. He had to; the beast had gone from old and weak to feeble and bone-thin, so Demien killed it and leaned the carcass against a slope, belly up, and opened it from anus to breastbone. He removed its still-beating heart and took a bite, then offered it to his son. The boy looked absolutely grief-stricken, but he also looked hungry, and so he took his share. Alarin tripped on something and nearly landed inside the beast's open cavity, and when he looked up he found the boy was smiling at him, so Alarin continued to act the goof, and the boy's smile continued to remain.

Demien discarded the entrails and carved the best cuts into steaks and strips, and that night they ate like jackals. The boiled meat was barely chewed, the bones picked clean and sucked free of their tasty pink marrow. They smoked the rest into jerk and stuffed their packs for the days ahead. The beast's hide was fleshed and dressed and made to serve as an extra layer of warmth, and for the first time since abandoning the cart, Alarin allowed himself the slightest promise of actually reaching Thornberry in decent health.

Then they came to a tributary, its waters swift-moving and white-capped and offering no place to ford. Demien went to work stripping boughs and branches to build a crude raft. He used the horse's sinew as cordage, and the raft served them well for a while, until they hit a rock in the riffle and heard something *snap*, and all three travelers were thrown into the water. Demien hauled them both to land. Alarin didn't bother to argue; he was shivering and chattering and his body was already shutting down. Every moment spent soaked in this freezing air was a moment closer to death. Demien built a small platform and worked quickly to start a blaze, and before long the three companions were stripped of their wet clothes and sitting hunched and naked before the flames. A miserable sight, in truth.

"We need to get moving," Demien said after stamping out the blaze and dressing himself.

Later that night they broke their vow and took refuge at an inn, but the proprietor seemed a little *too* courteous and a little *too* eager to accommodate his guests. The moment Alarin and his companions were alone in their room they climbed out the window into the stableyard and fled.

There was only the vast, open land around them now. *I can't go on, not another moment*, Alarin thought, every single hour of every single day. Demien sometimes scouted ahead, but always returned without promising word. Alarin thought Demien was leading them in the wrong direction. He began to argue and became so insistent that Demien had to use a stick and shadow to prove otherwise. And even then, Alarin simply grumbled to himself and looked for something else to argue about.

Still, dispirited and pained as he was, Alarin couldn't help but feel a connection with the land. There was something honest about it, something admirable. It changed a man; Alarin felt it within himself, saw it in his companions as well. He began to understand how, in order to survive, a person would commit any act, even the vilest, if necessary. There was no room for morality—stealing a man's pig was no longer a terrible misdeed, invading a home for shelter and warmth was no longer considered an unthinkable act.

He understood this most of all when, after the longest, coldest, and most miserable week of traveling, they spotted a large estate with a surrounding wall of rammed earth. It was an oasis in the desert, a waterhole to a parched gaur—but when the owner refused entry, it was like a beautiful vista twisting into a nightmare. "I have nothing, no food. I starve," the owner insisted, speaking in a broken dialect of the Anir. He was of the Cothil, a lowland people dark-haired and pale like Anirians, but shorter and uglier and rather reclusive. Alarin hated this man, hated the way he spoke and hated the way he looked. Demien did too, even though the honorable fool would never admit to it. "Look at us, we're ragged," Demien remarked afterward. "I wouldn't welcome us either."

"I don't care if we just climbed out of an ordure pit. He's lying, that ugly cur is lying," Alarin said.

Demien said, "There's nothing we can do."

"Yes there is," Alarin said. "He didn't see the boy."

At dusk, Silas alone stood before the gate. He couldn't speak of course, but the boy certainly looked thin and glum and pitiable enough. But even then, the man didn't open the gate—well, not at first. For a while he just stood there, watching from the wall. Watching and waiting, waiting and watching. Alarin was about to break his composure, about to emerge from the brush and scream and curse at this wretched cur, but then the man vanished, and a few moments later the gate began to open. Demien stormed inside. As it turned out, the man wasn't lying, not entirely; his little clan *did* have quite a cache of grain, but there was no livestock. Demien remedied that by butchering the man's dog, and they ate well that night.

Once more they traveled on, and once more their bellies shrank and their bodies grew cold. They stuffed snow in their winegourds, dug for grubs and beetles, scrounged for wood garlic and grasses, and gathered crowberries wherever they could. They found mollusks clinging to the undersides of river rocks, and hunted whitefish and salmon at dawn and dusk, always wary of the occasional passing rider.

During the evening hours, the wolves serenaded them like mournful spirits. They seemed to always be in the shadows, always the same distance away. Then late one night a rustle roused Alarin from sleep; he could hear something creeping along the nearby snowdrift, could hear its guttural breaths. His gut told him it was a wolf, but Alarin was so tired and so weak that it sounded more like a bugbear or hobgoblin or whatever terrible creature supposedly lurked in these parts. He reached for the dagger in his belt, but when he saw Demien, eyes alert and clutching the hilt of his short sword, he knew he was safe.

A few days later, Alarin collapsed in the snow. "Let me rest a bit," he said. "I need to rest."

"We can't," Demien said, glancing around. "Not here, not yet."

"Just give me a goddamn moment, will you?" But it wasn't a moment he needed. Alarin spent the remainder of the day huddled against the bole of a naked tree, gazing at its snow-laden branches and the thin wisps of gray clouds overhead. He glimpsed a white fox padding daintily across the unbroken snowpack, its big ears fixed on some prey below. When it found what it wanted, it dived into the white, and sure enough, a marmot came bursting out, scampering for its life. Alarin lay there and watched until they were gone, and not long after he felt his eyes close and everything around him faded into darkness.

A voice roused him. "You say Alarin is inside, then take me to him." It was his brother Anseth's voice, and when Alarin looked up, he saw the man standing nearby, surrounded not by snow but by a land-scape of lush greenery. He looked different, older and thinner, but also harder. There was another man opposite him, a bit taller and black-eyed and frowning. He recognized the face. *Lord Lygrest of course. Lord Duren Lygrest of Amaranth Point.*

"Come then," Lygrest said to Anseth, "I'll take you to him."

Alarin called for his brother, but it went unheeded as Anseth moved ahead, following Lygrest. But then something strange happened. Anseth stopped suddenly; around him rose a circle of shadowy figures. Anseth drew his weapon, but it was too late—the shadows were too many, too encompassing. And when they rushed forward Anseth cried out—a brief and single cry, both terrible and piercing. Then he was gone.

Alarin tried to move but couldn't; he couldn't do anything but stare at where his brother had just stood. "Where are you?" Alarin shouted. "Brother. *BROTHER!*"

Nearby, someone rustled. "Be quiet," a voice said.

"Anseth, is that you?"

"No, was just a dream," Demien replied. "Now be silent."

No it wasn't, Alarin thought, but when he tried to speak he only coughed, and he realized he was sweating and hot, and yet everything around him was so cold and white. *It was the same as before, another dream, another omen. Anseth is in danger.* Alarin fished for his pack in the nearby snow, but he was so tired that he must've fallen asleep again, because next he knew it was dawn.

"Can you walk?" Demien asked, standing over him.

Alarin ignored that and reached for his pack, pulling out his inkstone and pot and brush. Despite cold and cracked fingers, he did his best to write. It was neither neat nor articulate, but it would suffice. He pulled out the kidskin pouch and slipped the letter inside. *By the gods let this find him in time*, Alarin thought.

From somewhere above, Demien sighed. "The letter pouch, again with this? I can't get your letter to Amaranth Point. Not now, not after we reach Thornberry."

"No," he said. "The letter must go to Aster Falls. It is meant for Lord Emeron Mathius only. Please, Demien." Lord Mathius was a childhood friend and sworn brother to Anseth—and likely the only man he could trust right now. Alarin recalled how green and warm the environment was in his dream. *The spring thaw*, he knew. "He's the only one who can help," Alarin blurted, "the only one who can warn him."

Demien shook his head. "You're not making sense, my friend."

Alarin coughed violently. "*Just take it*," he rasped.

Demien did. "Fine, but you can send the courier yourself when we arrive at Thornberry. I made a vow to get you there and I intend to see it through. Besides, my brother will be angry if I show my face there without you. Ever seen that giant man get truly angry? It's not very pleasant."

Alarin tried to smile, but he wasn't sure if he managed one. "No I haven't," he said, then coughed again, violently.

He lost much of his time to sleep. Light and dark came and went, and clouds passed in broken movement. Demien woke him with a bowl of some pottage, but Alarin wasn't hungry. Strange, he couldn't remember the last time he wasn't hungry. But he wasn't. Demien looked terribly despondent. "I tried," he said, over and over, while Silas looked on with the same sad eyes as when that old horse died. *Don't be sad, boy,* Alarin wanted to say, but couldn't. *I'm not cold, I'm not hungry, even my leg doesn't bother me.* It was a peaceful feeling. Death would be a welcome transition for a broken man like Alarin, a broken man whose life had little left for him save pain and more pain and the inevitable decline of old age. He drifted off again, sure to soon begin his journey to heaven.

But no, when next he awoke, he found himself being carried. "Goddamn it, Demien," Alarin said in a painful rasp. "Just let me *die* already." There was no reply. Alarin looked around as best he could. He was lying flat on his back, on a litter of some sort. Armed men clanged on each side. Demien wasn't among them. *They found us. Damn these imperial soldiers—how did they find us?* He demanded to know who these soldiers were, under whose authority they were operating, and most of all, where they were taking him. And the voice that replied was full and deep but most of all it was warm and familiar. "You are safe now, my lord, safe in Thornberry."

CHAPTER TWENTY-EIGHT

Demien Mordall followed his brother and his entourage into the outlying suburban villages. Soldiers carried the litter inside a compound of timber-framed and thatch-roofed houses, moving across the cobblestone courtyard to enter the principal room to the north. Szathan was so tall he had to duck under the lintel of the entranceway. Several attendants escorted them into a side room where food and wine and clean attire were provided. Afterward, Demien sat on a trestle bench and gazed out the large square window that faced the massive serpentine wall of Thornberry.

The cold clasp of winter had at last begun to recede, and signs of spring were quick to rise in its place. Sparrows and buntings fluttered on branches here and there, wary of larger magpies and crows. A weaver finch darted by, brilliant in its yellow breeding dress. The sights and sounds were surely enough to enrich the heart of any man, but Demien was still enmeshed in the bleakness of winter, still reliving the day Emperor Thavian was murdered. It was always his first thought upon waking, and always the last before sleep.

"Glad to see life at the palace hasn't made you any prettier, my friend."

Demien turned. Gilberon Brehems came trundling in from the center courtyard, a beaming smile on his wide face. When he greeted Demien it was with an embrace like a blacksmith's vise. Afterward, Brehems bent down to regard little Silas, who was crouching near his father. He reached out and mussed the boy's hair, then laughed a hearty laugh and said, "Now you look more like your father, see?" He rose and gestured at Demien's short chestnut tousle of hair.

Demien returned the gesture by pointing to that ugly thicket growing on Brehems's face. "What's this now?" He flicked at it with his fingers. "It looks like a marmot died on your face."

Brehems proudly stroked his beard. "Met this dark skin broad, you know, one of those Sijian types. Ever have one? What about you, boy? By the gods she was a lovely thing, dark as a coconut husk except for the littlest pink blossom between her legs. Anyway, she had me grow this in order to win her affections. I told her I'd already grown something else for her, but she didn't care." He twirled the hair with his fingers. "With this her legs spread easily enough. For a time anyway."

Demien nodded. "No more?"

"No more," he said. "Goddamn woman was mad, I tell you. Hips strong enough to push out a calf, but mad as a springtime hare, you understand? As it turns, the whore was abusing my servants and stealing from my households. So I had the magistrate strip her down and parade her through the public square. I tell you I'm done with all those mudhens, every last one. Keeping the beard, though."

A growing clatter drew Demien's eyes to the window. He stood and observed a mass of soldiers gathering at the foot of a distant hill, drilling hand-to-hand fighting and short weapons. There was a general with them, obvious by his battledress, though it was too far to distinguish the man's face.

"Fenerus Soffin," Brehems said, looking on. "That old prick Sabriel's nephew. Know the name?"

Demien nodded. "Heard he fought valiantly at the Horns."

Brehems's wide mouth curled into a frown. "Bastard's been boasting ever since. Claims no man can match him. And the others, those young bloods, they flock to him like swine to the trough. The Young Tempest, they style him. Some even compare his skills to yours, Demien. Do you believe that? What a mother-raping prick."

"A young peacock, eager to display. The ravages of soldiership will catch up to him. All the wars and injuries, you know. Soon he'll look like you, my friend."

Brehems lightened at the jest. He began to overdramatically nurse his left shoulder. "Still aches from that bolt at Black Sands, goddamn it. You took the heads of two generals that day. How long ago was that? Four springs? Five? Ah, by the gods, I can't remember shit anymore."

"It was six years ago," Demien said. "And I took the heads of three generals that day. Perhaps all that pillow-talk with the Sijian woman has clouded your mind, my friend."

"That or the wine," he replied, and both men shared a laugh when Brehems patted his paunch. Szathan entered the room. He wore no helm, but was strapped in heavy armor everywhere else. Blackened plates of steel on his chest, segmented spaulders on his shoulders, vambraces and greaves on his arms and legs. His general's cloak was fastened about him, gray-black and faded like old parchment.

Brehems acknowledged the tall commander, then turned back to Demien and placed a meaty hand on his shoulder. "Tonight, in our cups, we'll forget about all the gloom and doom of the dynasty. We'll reminisce about the good days, you understand? Until then, my friend."

Demien said his farewells, then continued to gaze outside as Szathan came to stand beside him. Both brothers were silent for a time, listening to the distant sounds of the drilling soldiers. At last Szathan said, "The day when the reinforcements arrived . . . it was strange to see Sabriel Soffin and not you."

Should've known it'd be his first concern, Demien thought. Szathan wasn't among the shrewdest of men, but his memory was something to admire, especially his grudges. "I mustered the Black Pine regiment and took the van," Demien explained. "But Lady Miriana commissioned me to stay. To stay and protect His Majesty. I thought it was some ploy to keep me subdued, but now I see the truth in it, and now it's too late. How is Lord Alarin?"

"Weak, but he's being tended. He'll recover, I reckon." He offered a winegourd to his brother. Demien declined with a slight, almost imperceptible shake of his head. Szathan leaned back and drank, then said, "The populace here, they'd weep at the dynasty's collapse had they any tears left. Truth is, Thornberry's been suffering since Raas Dragath's initial assault. Poverty and hunger and illness are rampant. Outlaws harass the merchants along the main highways to and from the city. Bastards are everywhere. Even if I could muster the entire garrison, it wouldn't be enough to force submission."

"I don't understand, you are the chief commander here, are you not?"

Szathan made a gesture toward the drilling soldiers. "That churl Fenerus Soffin has taken to his banner all the new bloods. He fills their heads with bold words and drowns me in ridicule. Did Brehems not tell you?"

Demien shook his head. "Not all of it, it seems."

"Fenerus defied me once by mustering a regiment to subdue the outlaws. I went after him. We nearly came to clash." He was silent for a length of time. "I don't know what to do anymore, Elder Brother. I've lost most of my veterans after the battle, and I've lost my chief strategist by defection." He shook his large square head and sighed. "It matters not now. I grow tired of this place, the defiance, the segregation, all of it. Let that churl Fenerus have it, you know? My life belongs to Lord Alarin now. Wherever he goes I follow."

Demien suddenly remembered the letter pouch; he pulled it from his belt and handed it to his brother. "This needs to reach the hands of Lord Emeron Mathius, in Aster Falls. At Lord Alarin's behest. Can you do that?"

Szathan nodded. "I'll send a rider at once."

"Good. His heart will be glad."

Szathan examined the kidskin pouch for a while, his finger tracing the details of the Sadralen head. He put it away somewhere, and only then did he seem to take notice of Damien's son, who was still clinging to his father's side, looking terrified by the giant man before him. "You were just a suckling when last we met," Szathan told him. "I'm your uncle, boy." The big general turned back to Demien. "A bit small, isn't he?"

"He is. What of your sons, are they well?"

He brightened at that. "Both are in the very bloom of health. Tall and strong but not cursed with the look of their father. I've been hopeful for a third, perhaps there's still time."

Demien gestured to the boy. "Your third's right here." It was meant almost as a light-hearted quip, but when Szathan looked at him with confusion on his face, Demien solemnly explained, "I need you to take my son with you."

"Why, where are you going?"

"The city. There's something I must do."

"Thornberry's no place for you, Elder Brother. There's still a mandate for your capture."

"Look at me," he said. "I look no more than a vagrant or beggar. Besides, I've never served in Thornberry. No one here knows my face."

"You bear a soldier's look, my friend. Enough to arouse suspicion. You should come with me."

Demien shook his head to that. "I can't, Brother. The dynasty is lost, and only I stand to blame."

There was a long silence between them. At last, Demien turned to his son, who was sitting on the nearby bench, fiddling with a small resin goat figurine one of the attendants had given him. "I have to go for a little while," he said. "Stay with your uncle for now. Goodbye, all right? Goodbye."

Demien didn't go to the city that day; instead, he visited a tavern along the outer roadway, to consume a sizable share of wine. And as the city gates groaned closed for the night, Demien observed from a grassy overlook, seated beneath the spreading boughs of an old oak.

It was such a climbable tree. The little boy in him smiled with glee at the twisted branches and gnarled boughs and intersecting limbs. *How I used to love to climb*, Demien thought. He remembered how Szathan would always try to outpace him, but his poor brother was just too large and too awkward, whereas Demien was far nimbler. He also remembered how his mother would praise him, and how cruelly she treated Szathan. He hated her for that.

Nightfall's descent rendered the surrounding wood a menagerie of clicks and chirps and unusual calls. A raptor's hoot, from some distance away, spared a moment's glance. The gentle glow of the first quarter moon bathed the city's massive walls, leaving the outer villages and stretches of threshing fields to recede into the shadows of the surrounding forestland.

Dreadfang slid from its sheath with a metallic *hiss*. Demien examined the weapon as though he'd never seen it before. The careful detail from the carbon steel tip to the rounded pommel, the beautiful, black-inlaid hilt, and the trembling hand that held it. *It's just the wine*, he told himself. *Too much wine is all.*

He went to his knees. The blade was turned inward, tip to chest, poised to thrust between the ribs and into the heart. It felt so heavy. He closed his eyes and took a deep breath. *Life and death are predestined. I've fulfilled my faith—there is nothing left for me to do. My death stands as but a welcome homecoming.* He steadied the blade . . . breathed in one last time . . . and that was when he heard it.

"*Father.*"

Demien spun. No one there, only darkness and shadows. *That voice —have I gone mad?* He looked closer. Wait, yes, someone *was* there, half hidden in the dark of the nearby wood. *Who is it?* He called out to it, once and then again, and finally the figure emerged into the moonlight. Little Silas.

"What are you doing here?" Demien demanded. "By the gods, boy, did you just speak to me? Did you? *Answer* me."

The boy said nothing. The area around him was left terribly quiet by Demien's shouting. "You shouldn't have followed me," he said. "You shouldn't have followed me." He moved toward him.

Silas took a few steps back.

"Where are you going? Get back here, bo—" Demien stumbled and fell, crashing hard onto the earth. He grunted and cursed and lay there moaning like a fool, like a drunken, idiotic fool, until at last the darkness came and took him away.

His eyes opened at dawn.

His head throbbed, his throat stung, and his body felt enormously heavy. He rolled over and saw Dreadfang lying in the grass, still and serene amid the chirping and singing of birds he was too groggy to name. He rose and staggered over to the fallen blade, slamming it back in its sheath. Then he glanced about the area. His boy was sleeping at the foot of the oak, resin goat in his small hand. He went over and roused him with a gentle shake. "Come," he said, turning back to the city.

Demien descended the knoll and watched as the land opened before him, a land imbued with the warmth and promise of the coming spring. The morning sky was clear and blue and filled with russet-bellied clouds. A beautiful day, but a day he intended not to see, a day he wished not to be alive for.

BOOK III: PRETENDERS

CHAPTER TWENTY-NINE

Seric reached blindly for the bedside nightstand, knocking down a taper or two before finding the small look mirror. In the predawn darkness, he saw only hints of its intricate design: the smooth, tortoiseshell inlay and meticulous accents of mother-of-pearl. He turned it over and wiped the film of dust from its reflective surface. Then he held it up.

There was only that awful scar.

It was like a ridge of pale earth, a jagged and hideous thing running across the apple of his neck. *How could I have let this happen?* Seric knew Raas Dragath had planned to retaliate, yet he was still caught unaware. Had he truly been blinded by his desire to win back Lady Miriana?

His lesser wounds had healed well enough; the black and purple welts on his face were gone, the vision in his left eye had returned, and not even the tiniest bump remained where a date-sized hematoma once distended his forehead. The complications of his injuries had also been few and fleeting. Headaches mostly, and occasional pain in his left shoulder. It'd been a welcome blessing for Seric to undergo treatment here, in the sickchamber of the palace, and under the direct care of Arden Lorian's son Orbrey. And yet, for all the physician's talents, he could do nothing for that hideous scar.

Seric sighed and tossed the mirror back onto the nightstand, but it missed and landed on the floor with a dull crash. From a nearby armchair, a silhouette stirred.

He thought it was Orbrey, but a closer look revealed his former wife, Nyvia. The plump woman blinked and yawned and looked around the room groggily. She appeared different right now—not in a bad way, but as if he hadn't seen her in a long time. She also seemed sad.

"What are you doing here?" he asked, not unkindly.

She yawned once more and then leaned forward to place something on the bed. It was a flat length of black silk, a scarf, no a neckerchief rather, and when he brought it closer, he could see the careful detail of the soft gray scrollwork and fringed edges. "I am not worth the time or fabric used in this," he said, but fastened it about his neck anyway.

She ignored that. "I saw my cousin yesterday. You know his trade has seen good fortune as of late. He's in need of an assistant to manage his accounts. You can use an abacus still, yes?"

"Nyvia—"

"*Please*," she blurted. Then, more calmly: "Listen, I don't know what kind of trouble you fell into. I don't even want to know. But I've already lost three brothers, and now . . . I nearly lost the father of my only child." She paused to sigh. "Just think on it, won't you? That's all I ask."

Seric told her he would. Account-keeping was quite a lowly profession next to his once lofty ambitions of imperial power, but when he reminded himself that the latter would never come to fruition, the former sounded a bit more reasonable. It would at least allow the repayment of his debts. But it was such a waste of his talent, not to mention how bored and restless the daily toils of mediocrity would leave him. He didn't know what to do. His fingers slid beneath the silk to touch his scar. "You speak as though your child even cares about his father."

"Veldries is young yet, he will come around. This incident has only made him realize how much he needs you."

A sharp rap at the chamber door gave him pause. The thick wood groaned as it opened, revealing an overweight man in loose ministerial robes. Thomen Zythara was the empire's Minister of Ceremony, but he was also serving as Minister Steward until a suitable replacement was to be found, whenever that might be.

Seric didn't mind; in fact, it was hard to dislike the minister. Thomen had a warm and avuncular manner about him, and big trusting eyes that seemed to see the good in even the darkest of hearts. His curly auburn hair was a few shades lighter than his smooth eyebrows, and when he bowed his head, hanks of it fell forward and he had to paw it aside to see. "My apologies for the sudden intrusion, my lord and lady." He raised a hand and spoke over the jingle of his garish bracelets. "Her Majesty Miriana Athera requests a private audience with Seric Dyre."

"Private audience?" Nyvia asked. "Why would she—"

"It's all right, Nyvia," Seric told her. He looked at Minister Thomen and nodded. "A moment, please, that I may dress."

Minister Thomen nodded gaily and turned about, his distressed gray robes trailing behind him as he left. Seric went to the bedrail and grabbed his clothes. Nyvia stood there, watching him, her eyes seemingly full of questions. She didn't get to ask any of them, as Seric gently ushered her to the exit. Moments later, Lady Miriana entered.

She was as beautiful as ever. Tall and graceful and draped in a frilled and sleeveless gown dyed the same mottled blues as her guardsmen's imperial cloaks. Her uncovered arms were alabaster pale against the black hair that cascaded down past her shoulders.

"The gods have favored you, Seric," she said as she crossed the room. The color of her dress made her eyes appear even bluer than usual, and when he caught a whiff of her perfume—that same wonderful perfume she'd worn months ago—he felt a pang of wistful longing. *Stop it, you spoony cur.* "What do you want, my lady," he said, as distant and cool as possible.

She seemed to be caught off guard by that. "Seric, I didn't know . . . the danger you were in. I didn't know Raas Dragath knew about your involvement in the Horns."

He considered her words. *She thinks Raas Dragath tried to kill me only because he learned that I was behind the victory.* He looked squarely at her. "The assassin, did he confess?"

She shook her head. "He tried to run but the night watchmen surrounded him. He slit his own throat."

He touched the scar beneath the silk and muttered, "Full marks for doing it right the second time."

She sighed at that. "Seric, I am not here to seek forgiveness, by the gods I dare not even ask it of you."

"Then what will you ask of me, my lady."

Her pale fingers toyed with the frills of her gown. "Emperor Thavian's death has shattered the realm. Pretenders are already planting the seeds of insurrection all across the empire. My own courtiers have turned against me. General Soffin has pacified them for now, but unless I take swift and purposeful action, public dissent is sure to rise once again. I fear I will lose my seat on the throne, or worse, my head."

For the second time in Seric's life, Lady Miriana was pleading for his aid. He couldn't believe it. *She has the gall to ask for my counsel now, after months of mistrust and repudiation?* And yet, a part of him couldn't help but admire her audacity. It was a reflection of just how strong she truly was. *I knew she'd come back to me,* he thought.

She was going on about the elaborate funeral of the emperor, about the days and days of mourning and the cancellation of the Winter Star Festival. Seric had no interest in any of this, so he urged her to make plain her point, and she did. "Merio Athera is mustering his forces to reclaim the capital. I can't allow that, but I am too ignorant to know how to stop him."

Seric pretended not to listen. "You sent me away to live like a wretch, do you not remember?" He could hear the insolence in his voice, but he didn't care; it felt good.

It felt even better when her eyes dropped to the floor, in a way he'd never seen before. "I remember, Seric."

"You only come to me now because you have no one else," Seric went on. "Never once have you cared for me."

She shook her head at that. "I *did* care, Seric, I do—"

"Spare your lies," he said at once.

She offered nothing in reply, and now they stood there, looking blankly at each other. "Forgive me, for intruding like this," she said at last, and turned to the door.

He sighed. "Wait."

She did.

Seric spoke to her back. "You may think Merio a wolf, but in truth he is no more than a whelp. If he desires to besiege the capital and claim the throne, your officers will have no trouble repelling him. Your sole concern should be whether Alarin is with him, because with Alarin as his military advisor he becomes the wolf that you fear."

Miriana turned to face him. "You think Alarin is with him?"

"I don't know, my lady. But if he is alive, no measure of clairvoyance is needed to foresee his taking refuge with Merio Athera. They are brothers, after all."

She had a strange frown on her face. "And if he does, what must I do?"

"Your best course is to reaffirm your position in the realm. Secure the cities of the heartland and those northward. Alarin will likely seek to bolster Stormhaven's forces, but with so few allies to turn to, he may look to unlikely sources for support. The southern Redlands included."

"He would seek an alliance with Raas Dragath? Never. Even he'd never resort to such a reprehensible act." But even as she finished speaking she seemed a little uncertain of herself.

"Nothing is reprehensible in war, my lady. Alarin is a man of wiles, he will undoubtedly consider the potential of obtaining the Redlands under his brother's banner. But now I've said too much, and I'll not say any more unless I am wearing the seal of the Imperial Advisor."

He thought she would deny him, perhaps even laugh at such a request. But no, he couldn't believe it—she was actually nodding. "It will be yours, Lord Seric."

"My lady, I pray this is not some cruel jape."

"You will be ennobled and enfeoffed and given earnings commensurate to a newly appointed minister of your experience and expertise. The truth of your victory at the Horns will serve as the preamble to your inauguration. You will chart the course of the realm and reveal it before the high council at the start of the next lunar month. Am I being forthright enough for you, Seric Dyre?"

He was silent for a moment. "My lady, appointing me will only further diminish your standing with the court."

"Yes, but when your course stands to reunite the empire, the hearts of the people will change. You know that."

He considered her words a little longer. "On second thought, I don't want it," he decided, shaking his head.

She seemed shocked at that, shocked and utterly insulted. "How could you reject such an offer?"

"Because if your husband recovers he will strip me of my rank quicker than you did his brother. He's already robbed me of everything once, I won't let it happen a second time."

"I'll not let him," she told him.

"You couldn't stop him and you know it."

"Seric, you're grasping at clouds. The man is soon to pass."

"Not good enough."

"Then what—what is it you want?"

"You still have the Mists of Midnight, do you not?"

She blinked, and her words came out slowly. "You want me to poison my own husband?"

He nodded. "I want him gone."

He thought for sure this time she would deny him, but after a long pause, she said, "And if I give my word, will you accept my offer?"

Oh, how truly desperate she is. "No," he said. "There's one more thing."

"What—what is it now?"

He moved to stand directly before her. "It is an empty title unless I share my rule beside you."

She softened at that. "You will, Seric, you will be beside me, of course."

His hand rose to caress her cheek. "Beside you, in all matters."

"In all matters," she agreed.

CHAPTER THIRTY

Alarin awoke in the dark. For a moment he thought he was back in that dreadful underground tunnel, but then he saw a sliver of moonlight sneaking in through the cracks of the shuttered window and he remembered Thornberry. He could hear someone breathing in the room, loud and through the mouth. A soldier's breathing, he knew, because only a soldier had a nose broken enough to render it useless.

Alarin looked up into the face of Szathan Mordall. "It's fourth watch, my lord," the general said in his sonorous voice. "The ranks are forming at the pass."

He offered no help when Alarin went to rise, and Alarin was glad for that. He grabbed his blackthorn cane and limped to the window and pulled open the stubborn old shutters. The night was crisp and clear and the moon was ivory like the foot of an abalone. A pleasing sight, though it would've been more pleasing had he witnessed it from the comfort of his observatory.

He turned away and gathered his belongings, then paused to glance up at the ceiling rafters, where a swallow had built a nest earlier last month. All through Alarin's recovery, the bird seemed to watch over him like some supernal guardian. It was only proper to say goodbye, and so he did, before he and his loyal general made their way out of the house and compound.

Outside, the great wall of Thornberry loomed over the outer suburban developments of the city, as longhouses and inns and shops all clung to its serpentine flanks. Farther along, Alarin saw scaffolding and wooden shutters and stacks of kiln-fired bricks, worksites where able-bodied men were pressed into labor from dawn to dusk to reinforce the wall. It was thankless drudgery, of long hours and little pay and constant pressure from the overseers, but necessary with the threat of the Redlands so near.

The two men were quiet as they climbed the low hills surrounded by oaks and maples whose rising canopies swayed and rustled in the night sky. Alarin had chosen to seek refuge with his youngest brother, Merio, who ruled the eastern province of Riverwind with many names and many titles. As much as Alarin loved him, he knew Merio as an inconsistent man at heart: bold in arms but indecisive in the field, faithful in duty but unmindful of deceit. Still, Alarin planned to remedy that by serving as the chief commander of all military operations, and together, the brothers would stand against Lady Miriana. But the thought of waging war against the capital was worrisome. For one, Zantherei was still alive. War would undoubtedly place him and his sister in danger.

He shook his head. *I won't engage just yet,* he thought, *but Miriana killed Kalen, and I'll not let that go forgotten.* There was so much to consider since the fall of the dynasty, and a small part of him still bore a wistful connection to his earlier, simpler concerns—when food and shelter and warmth were all that mattered. It wasn't so long ago that he was ill and weak and so close to death. And it wasn't so long ago that he'd made peace with the gods and prepared for that death.

The army waited at the foot of the pass. Not a large force, no more than a single regiment—or a thousand soldiers—but with the supply wagons and attendants and extra horses crowding the rear, it appeared as twice that number. Still, the bulk of the soldiers—the flying cavalry, the mounted archers, the infantrymen and pikemen and even the auxiliaries—all remained at Thornberry. *Fools and recreants, the lot of them,* Alarin thought. *Fools beneath the banner of an even greater fool, Fenerus Soffin.*

At the rearguard stood a pair of horses, saddled and bridled and waiting. Alarin struggled to mount his bay-colored charger, but once he took hold of the reins, he swore it hadn't been eight or so years since he'd last done so. Szathan mounted a buckskin charger as big and ferocious as he was, and together the two men moved through the ranks. There were no young bloods here; these men were veterans, scarred and grizzled and proud of their faded wool cloaks and battle-beaten armor. When they saw Alarin they bowed their heads with deference that Alarin had never thought he'd witness again.

General Gilberon Brehems waited at the van. The usually boisterous and uncouth man was all sternness and solemnity. He bowed his head and said, "At your command, my lord."

Alarin nodded and turned about. The rows of horsemen waited in silence. It was a surreal moment, a profound sense of empowerment that so few men ever experience. Alarin didn't want the moment to end, but he knew he had to take control, as any worthy commander would. And so he gave the word to march, then turned to lead the way.

The rising mountains hugged the pass at both sides, the channel before him barren and quiet and flooded by moon and starlight. He could feel the breeze flowing through what little hair he had left on his head. And when he heard the columns marching in formation behind, he couldn't help but smile. For at that moment, that glorious moment in time, Alarin Athera was no longer a cripple, but a general again, and behind him was a mass of loyal soldiers, eager all to obey his every command.

———

"From the annals of the earliest dynasties," Seric announced, "from the writings of oracle bones that were passed down by the kith and kin of our ancient predecessors, it was known then, as it is now, that as we stand upon the ashes of the Anir, we must endure steadfastly the governing law of time. And time decrees that a united realm will inevitably fall, just as a fallen realm will inevitably unite."

Lady Miriana observed him from the center seat of the table. Meetings of the high council always took place here, in the Hall of Sylvan Serenity. The room's tall pillars were carved as gray trees, though time and poor ventilation had left them cracked and weathered like the old, tired legs of giant treemen. Light from wall sconces shaped as tree hollows illuminated the nearby murals of uncharted forestland. The council table itself was a giant, flat stump, knotted and ringed and lacquered in gray.

Seric addressed the ministers while pacing the table's length. He was draped in carefully chosen raiment: silk trousers and tunic and sash, and an over-robe of dusky satin with flowing brocade sleeves. It was regal enough to warrant authority, yet not so much as to appear garish. He wore his seal of office around his neck, below the silk neckerchief. *He wears it quite well*, Miriana thought.

He also addressed the high council quite well, speaking to a score of the empire's most esteemed men as if he had done so countless times before. His rhetoric was strong, his manner open and cordial. And yet, it wasn't enough. The high council seemed only to respond with looks of discontent or downright disdain. They were misjudging him—the same way Miriana had in the past. *Not only have I misjudged him, I've accused him of conspiring with Alarin*. It was an accusation that proved unfounded when Vylas had showed her the secret underground tunnel. Evidence revealed that Alarin did in fact escape, but it was under the unlikely aid of Demien Mordall. *It seems our good commandant knew a thing or two about treachery after all*, she thought. And while it was clear Demien had no awareness of the emperor's assassination, he undoubtedly used the cover to get Alarin out of the city.

A hand touched upon hers. It belonged to her brother, Vylas, seated beside her. Miriana ignored the gesture and took another sip of wine.

He'd been a jealous little man as of late, and she still wasn't warm to his company, nor to his incessant bantering about his mistrust of Seric. "You are putting your faith in an undeserving cad," he'd told her, earlier in private. "That assassin wasn't sent just to silence the victor of the Horns. There was more involved."

Miriana had agreed with him, but didn't dare admit it, and so poor Vylas had only grown frustrated on top of being jealous. "Why do you trust in him so?" he'd asked.

"Because Seric Dyre is the *only* man who can chart the course of the realm."

Miriana Athera let go of the memory, focusing on the council. To the left of her brother were her ministers: the spare Korval, Minister of Judgment; the overweight Thomen, Minister of Ceremony; the diminutive Verenthal, Minister of Faith; and so on. The military officers to her right were men of far more impressive form, from the grizzled General Sabriel Soffin to the savage General Aldebron Pentagath. Pentagath was sitting with his arms crossed and head lowered, and though she hated to admit it, he rather frightened her. He looked half a beast, with that wild mane of dusty brown hair and wide, porcine nostrils that flared whenever he grew excited. The nose itself was flat and crooked, the same with the rest of his face—flat and crooked as though held down and battered by a smith's hammer. The single, lion-headed pauldron on his right shoulder rasped whenever he reached for a goblet of wine. The other shoulder was left bare, and when she'd once asked her husband why, he told her it allowed more fluid movement of his weapon, which she thought was strange until she saw the thing for herself. It was the largest battle-axe she'd ever seen, with a blade that could behead an ox with a single stroke. She wondered if she could even hold the thing.

"The realm seeks only to unify itself, to restore balance and harmony and wholeness," Seric was saying. "It is disinterested in the rising pretenders and designing usurpers that vie for power. Such concerns are ours alone. Foremost, of course, is Raas Dragath. The Red Terror is a traitor and a tyrant, but he is also a formidable opponent with a flourishing confederation. He holds the province of Barrowstone, and his southern lands enjoy the advantages of a warmer clime and frequent rainfall. His dominion extends east to the foot of Sijia, and northward to the city of Lakewood, where he himself currently stands poised. His field armies consist not only of Anirians, but of auxiliaries from the abundant southern tribes. His generals are loyal and fierce, his strategists adept and cunning." He paused and scratched himself beneath the neckerchief. "I seek to punish Raas Dragath with swift and exceptional fury, but understand that we must be patient in doing so."

In response, an unmistakably stentorian voice rang out: "Just like a mongrel to declare cowardice as strategy."

The high council went silent. It was as if every clink of metal or whisper of conversation had died at once. Miriana recognized the speaker as the Minister of Judgment, Korval Syr. Seric glared at the spare, old man for a long moment before replying. "You should give a care how you speak, Minister. I am the Imperial Advisor, after all."

"A title you do not deserve, churl."

"I may not share with you the distinction of being a pureblood Anirian, but—"

"You are a Zhoul. A mongrel," Korval said, then turned to the rest of the council. "Is the realm so far gone that men of noble birth and standing are forced to listen to the words of this baseborn mutt? Any man of reasonable intellect knows not to."

He was a bold one, Miriana gave him that. She needed to quickly staunch this flow of discord. She went to speak but Seric was quicker. "Minister, you are treading on dangerous ground," he said to Korval. "When you insult me you are also insulting my father, Nethan Dyre, a man who saw me fit enough to adopt into this life of nobility."

"Who speaks ill of Nethan Dyre," Aldebron Pentagath grumbled, stirring to life as if from some great slumber.

Korval only smirked at Seric. "And heaven made that old fool Nethan Dyre pay for his choice, did he not?"

A fist slammed onto the table. Pentagath rose to his full height, nostrils flaring. "How dare you speak ill of Nethan Dyre?" Sabriel Soffin rose to detain his general. Others followed. "No," Pentagath protested. "Get off me. By the gods I will bash this man's head through the table."

It was no secret as to why the general was upset. Aldebron Pentagath had personally served in Nethan Dyre's ranks for many years. His loyalty was the truest in form, and steadfast even after death. *Seric knew that*, Miriana mused. *He knew that and used it against Minister Korval. Clever man.*

The minister looked too terrified to speak, even as Pentagath settled back to his seat. General Sabriel Soffin said to Seric, "Enough of all this pointless talk. We wish to know your plans of action against the other pretenders. How will you stave off Merio Athera?"

"Our best course of action is to re-establish dominion over our three greatest advantages—the cities within the provinces of Skydeep and Cragspawn, both sides of the Grayling River, and the passes of the surrounding mountains. We must look to our northern neighbors first, starting with the city of Silverleaf."

"Silverleaf is under the governorship of Tavarin Valayne," Soffin replied. "It is well-known that Tavarin has fallen out of faith with Lord Zantherei."

"Yes, and I intend to restore that faith," Seric told him.

"He refuses to pay tribute. Such negligence is treasonous. Lord Zantherei has openly condemned him."

Seric nodded. "Yes, but Lord Zantherei is not presently with us, so I advise we sort through this misunderstanding and find a way to unite." No one said a word to that, and Seric gave a sudden sigh before going on. "Listen, all of you. I know it is the Zhoul people that harass Lord Tavarin by day. This is not some thinly veiled ploy to win a people with whom I share blood. I mean to crush them. And it will take the complete submission of the Zhoul people for us to secure this alliance. Three regiments will be mustered for this campaign. I personally intend to lead them."

Miriana wasn't sure if she heard that correctly. *You intend to lead them? You never told me this.*

"Three regiments?" Sabriel Soffin questioned. "You cannot subdue the Zhouls with three regiments."

Seric said, "General, I am sure you are aware of the most basic principle of military strategy is to know your enemy. Well, I know the enemy. By the gods my own father serves in their ranks." Before the council could fall into discussion about that, Seric said, "Now I have laid bare my heart and soul. And now I will remind you that Lady Miriana bestowed this honor upon me. She's given me not only the cord and seal, but her undying trust in my actions. My plan, though it may seem uncertain to some of you, is our best course of action. Put your faith in me as you would in heaven. Your Imperial Advisor has spoken, and that is all."

Later that evening, Miriana was pacing her chamber in wait. When Seric finally entered, she snapped him a glare that melted the triumphant little look off his face. "How dare you not inform me?" she demanded.

"Of what?"

"Your intent to lead the campaign. Why wasn't I told of this?" She didn't give him a chance to reply. "You think defeating your father in battle will bring your heart some sort of peace? It won't, Seric. Besides, wasn't it you who said strategies in one place often decide battles hundreds of miles away? You don't need to go. And Tavarin Valayne will never agree to such an alliance, even if you force the Zhouls to submit. The man's as stubborn as he is fat, you know. And you're a fool, Seric, for thinking you can change his heart."

"I know this, my lady," Seric said, calm and direct. "I know all this. The submission of the Zhouls is a mask, a means to win the populace, nothing more. True control of the province lies with the governor's wife, Perilia. And that is the real reason why I must go."

If his words were meant to comfort her, well, they failed miserably. "That's even worse. Lady Perilia despises me. She would sooner shove a dirk in her own breast than agree to an alliance with me."

He looked at her resignedly—as if he knew something he didn't wish to reveal. "She can be won."

"And how is that?"

He sighed. "The lady has made plain her desires for me before. Back when I was bound to Nyvia."

He intends to bed her. She was looking down, trying to hide her jealously, but it was a poor attempt, and she knew it. The thought of Seric sharing himself with that wretched woman made her stomach clench with ache.

"I meant to tell you," he went on, "but I didn't want you to stop me. I couldn't allow private matters to come before civic duty."

She didn't know what to say. "Tavarin's always with her. How will you get her alone?"

"I'll need your kind brother to aid me in that."

"Vylas?" She laughed at him. "He'll never ride with you."

"Then make him," Seric said. "It is well known that Tavarin loathes your brother, probably as much as your brother loathes me."

"What does that matter?"

"It matters because Tavarin has long suffered from declining health. I am told even the smallest measure of distress will render him bedridden for days. That said, a few gibes from your brother should send him off quite nicely."

She paused. It was a sensible plan, even though she detested it. "If I send my brother to accompany you, it will be as an honored guest, Seric. One word of mistreatment and I will—"

"Don't fret yourself," Seric told her. "He is the brother of Empress Miriana Athera. Please don't fret over that."

She wasn't fretting—not about that, anyhow. She had been sharing her pillow with Seric nearly every night as of late, and she couldn't help but feel wounded. *He's cruel to have kept this from me*, she thought. She was angry with him for that, angrier still at his cool indifference. It was as if he was punishing her for all those wrongful accusations. But no, the truth was probably nothing like that. He was not a vengeful man but an ambitious one, and as such he would do anything to fulfill his faith. Miriana knew this because she herself was of the same stamp, and she herself had done much worse in order to get what she wanted.

Still, knowing that gave her little relief. "Promise you won't enjoy it," she said.

Seric bent to a single knee and took her hand as gently as he would a child's. "Never." He placed a tender kiss upon her fingers. She had to fight back the urge to pull away. *For the future of my rule*, she told herself.

CHAPTER THIRTY-ONE

Dariok tore at a haunch of overcooked mutton. "You can attest to this man's honor?" he asked with a mouth full.

"Yes," Anseth said. *By the gods even his chewing irritates me.* "Are you ready to move? The envoy is waiting." He turned to the others of his escort guard, all stern men much larger than himself. "Once we're inside the city, be sure to keep covered. We are no different from Serkuts to these people."

Dariok's eyes narrowed at that, either at the insult or perhaps at Anseth's use of the word "we." Anseth didn't care to know which. In truth, he had little patience left for the chieftain's son—the man had been nothing but indignant ever since Lord Volduk had given Anseth command of two regiments. *This is my campaign, you cretin, so you can stuff that hostility up your arse.*

Dariok licked the grease from his fingers and said, "Piss on all those idiots, I am no Serkut filth."

"No, you're not," Anseth told him. "But you will do as I say, or you'll spend the rest of this campaign rubbing sheep's fat on saddles. Are you ready? We have to go." Dariok growled and hissed and muttered under his breath, but for once did as he was ordered.

Outside, the sky was bleak and gray, and despite the arrival of spring, the northern borderlands of the Anirian Empire were still cold. But the cold here was nothing compared to that of the Gray Plains. The wind was gusting, but not enough to drown out Dariok's incessant carping. There was something not right about that man, and Anseth couldn't help but feel contempt for him even though he should've only felt pity. *Just an oversized brute with the mind of a child, nothing more.*

The chieftain's son finally quieted at the sight of Amaranth Point's royal escort. Rich pennons and banners flapped boldly in the air, displaying the typical gray-black colors of the Anir. Not since Anseth's last campaign with the empire, nearly a decade ago, had he been greeted by such banners.

Provincial Governor Duren Lygrest stood in the center of the escort, a grim and grizzled man surrounded by a mounted escort of grim and grizzled soldiers. He looked older than Anseth expected, paunchier too, with a long, hooked nose and a stubbly gray beard. His pitted black eyes were as cold and unfeeling as ever, and with them he gazed down from the saddle of his mount, first at Anseth, then to the Vaskultans at his side. He frowned at what he saw, but that didn't mean much because Lygrest always frowned at what he saw. He had a face made for frowning, so much so that Anseth wondered if the man *could* smile even if he wanted to.

"It is good to see you, my friend," Lygrest said, polite but with as much enthusiasm as if he were addressing an old servant. "I trust my envoy was of good company?"

"He was, my lord," Anseth replied. And indeed, over the course of his journey to the south, he'd found Jarreth to be a kind and virtuous man, and moreover, he enjoyed conversing with a fellow Anirian in his native tongue after so many years of harsh Vaskulti. "My brother—is my brother with you?"

"Inside, my friend, he awaits inside the city." Lygrest scratched at what was left of his silvery hair. "Best you come alone. My people are

ignorant of northern cultures. They know only of the northmen who
raid their lands."

"I am aware," Anseth said. "But these are my men, and they will
stay at my side."

Lygrest's frown didn't move an inch. His pitted black eyes
continued to examine the Vaskultans.

"What's this piss-stain looking at?" Dariok said. Anseth told him to
be silent. He obeyed, but who knew for how long? Fortunately, the
Vaskultan insult went unnoticed by Lygrest.

Switching back to the Anirian tongue, Anseth said, "My lord,
please forgive my forwardness, but if Alarin is inside, then I'd like
nothing more than to go to him."

Lygrest nodded and gestured behind him with an outstretched hand,
drawing Anseth's eyes to the grand city of Amaranth Point. "Come
then, your brother awaits." He turned to lead the way. Anseth signaled
his men to follow.

The city itself was not so large as the Star of the Hollow, but it was
still rather amazing to behold, especially since Anseth hadn't seen a
city in so long. The walls stood over fifty feet high in places, made of
rammed loess coated with yellow clay. Armories and barracks and
watchtowers adorned the upper platform of the battlements, which
loomed over the wide moat and hardwood drawbridge. After passing
through the barbican, Anseth could see the drainage spouts and
machicolations and spiked cylinders ready to be rolled down upon
siege ladders. Between the gaping embrasures, armored sentries peered
down at the company, crossbows in hand.

The streets Lygrest chose were narrow and quiet. Jarreth said to
Anseth, "The eastern district avoids the main avenues and busy market
square." His froglike eyes gave a long blink. "Better to draw fewer
eyes, to be sure."

"To be sure," Anseth repeated.

The traffic here was indeed sparse, and the downcast eyes and
sagging shoulders of the populace spoke of lifelong hardship and
poverty. Shops and dwellings were crammed together like the teeth of
a comb, with many appearing foreclosed and abandoned. Peddlers of

pickled meats ambled by, while hawkers yelled from their market stalls, and traders bid combatively against one another. Urchins dashed to and fro. Dogs loped across the dusty roads, while cats took to higher perches, grooming themselves or lazing with half closed eyes.

The escort came to a sudden halt. Ahead, oxcarts blocked the roadway. Porters were arguing with one another. "Clear this at once," Lygrest ordered, even as his soldiers were already trying to do just that.

Anseth didn't mind the delay. In truth, he was a bit uneasy about seeing his elder brother again. *What would Alarin think of me? What will I think of him?* Eight years was a long time in a man's life. Alarin was forty-two now, and lame, but in Anseth's mind he only imagined that same tall and robust hero he'd admired as a child.

A hand grabbed Anseth's wrist. He went to twist free, but he was already free, and looking up he glimpsed a hooded figure in a homespun cloak darting away. Anseth went to point him out, but when he raised his hand he realized there was something in it, something small and light, a pouch of kidskin—*the* pouch, the Sadralen letter pouch he'd exchanged for years with his elder brother. He glanced around; his companions were focused on the commotion in the road. His eyes moved back down. Inside the pouch was a letter. He unfolded and read:

All of your correspondences with your elder brother have been compromised. Alarin is not in Amaranth Point but south, in Thornberry. He has reached out to me in the hopes of retrieving you from the danger you are in. Do not trust Duren Lygrest. He intends to murder you. Please, you must heed this warning. Your dear friend and sworn brother, Lord Emeron Mathius of Aster Falls.

Those five words stood out like an ugly sore: *He intends to murder you.* Anseth read them again and again, while his heart began to pound in his chest.

"Lord Revek."

Anseth looked up. The hooded Kirik motioned for him to follow.

Ahead, the path was clear. Lygrest's escort had moved farther along, and were now stopped and waiting. Anseth shoved the letter back into the pouch and stuffed it in his belt. He hesitated. Dariok groaned with impatience. What could he do? He moved on.

Roads passed and went forgotten, and soon, the escort came to the walled gatehouse of the governor's palace. Lygrest halted there and turned and began speaking to Jarreth, but had to stop when the great gate groaned to life. The noise was like a death knell to Anseth. He wiped his sweaty palms on his overcoat.

He intends to murder you.

The palace gate gave one last lurch before it stopped. Lord Lygrest went ahead, his escort in tow. Anseth's fellow Vaskultans moved to follow. "Don't," he said. The men turned, hooded and faceless and waiting. Anseth tried to speak but couldn't find the words.

Lord Lygrest called from inside the gate. "Come, my friend. Your brother awaits."

Anseth could feel his heart pushing up his throat. "I don't see him," he shouted back. "Alarin always greets an esteemed guest outside the palace." It was a lie, but it was all he could think to say.

After a moment Lygrest said, "Not with his infirmities. He waits for you inside. Please, come."

Anseth looked past the provincial governor, through the opened gateway, at a small shadowed courtyard. "What is going on?" he heard Dariok ask. Kirik was saying something, too. Anseth ignored both of them.

He intends to murder you.

"My lord, I've forgotten something—a gift, a gift meant for my brother. I'm afraid I can't see him without it. I must go, I must retrieve it."

Lygrest fiddled with the reins and looked toward the western avenues—a long look—before turning back. "It's not safe, the city," he said. "Your brother is waiting now."

Anseth shook his head. "I cannot greet him without this gift. I'll be back, half a watch, no more." He began to turn. The governor's voice called out, *"Retrieve it later."*

"What is wrong with you?" Dariok said.

Anseth said, "Follow me. Don't talk." He gave one last look at Lygrest, who sat mounted and frowning before the open palace gate. Anseth switched back to the Anirian tongue to address the governor. "My lord, do not fret, I will return in no time at all." After that he was off.

He could hear Dariok grumbling behind him. "What is going on? Severak, what did that fool say?" But Severak didn't reply to him—instead he said, "They're following us."

Anseth glimpsed back. Indeed, they had a tail of a score or so of Anirian horsemen. Anseth continued moving forward, calm and steady, until the company passed through the entrance of the closest ward. Once behind the dividing wall and out of sight, he whipped his horse into a run. The Vaskultans followed.

The world became a blur of motion, houses and buildings all sweeping by like faceless black hills. He remembered coming in from the north, so Anseth thought it best to make his exit to the west. But everything looked so unfamiliar to him now. He turned down the wrong corner. Yanking on the reins, he halted before the city's congested marketplace. People clogged the cobbled square like sardines in a jar. Anseth glanced back; the horsemen were closing in. Panic seized his heart. He tried to force his mount through but made little ground. The crowd grew tense now, a collective tenseness, as if formed from one giant source. There was nowhere to go. The pursuing horsemen shouted at them. The crowd parted. *There*—an alleyway. Anseth rushed for it.

He cut through the narrow path, turning left and then a quick right, before finding his way back to the main avenues. The western gate rose in the distance. Faster, he urged his company, faster, faster, *faster*. The next corner opened—to a waiting line of crossbowmen. Anseth cursed and yanked the reins. The crossbowmen shouted at the Vaskultans to hold. Dariok reached for his sword. His hood was down, his ugly face twisted with rage. "*No*," Anseth told him. "You'll die." He seemed like he wanted to disobey, and in a way, Anseth wanted him to, but then a bolt whipped past and struck the breast of a nearby Vaskultan horse.

The beast collapsed, throwing the poor rider from the saddle. Anseth wanted to go to him, but the trailing horsemen were closing in fast. He turned away and rode on.

The gate was close now. Faster they went, faster and faster, their horse hooves pounding down the avenue. Pedestrians dashed out of the way. Some yelled as they did. Anseth didn't stop. The portcullis was still open. *We can make it,* Anseth thought, *we can still make it.* The sentries waiting there regarded them with smug amusement, as if more annoyed than alarmed by this onrush of fools. But when the Vaskultans drew their steel and formed a wedge, the sentries fumbled and panicked like hares before the charge of wolves. Vaskultan steel cut them down. Blood splashed in Anseth's eyes, and when he wiped it away, he found himself beneath the great archway of the barbican, swallowed by a momentary darkness, then spat back out into the light of day. Bolts rained down from the upper guardhouse behind them. Anseth didn't stop. The crisp air buffeted his face. It felt good, so unbelievably good. But then he heard a terrible *thud* and when he glanced down, his mount was no longer beneath him.

The ground rushed up. *Smash.* Somewhere inside him he knew it was the sound of his body against the earth, even though it seemed so far away. He tumbled and tumbled and felt every tumble, then rolled to a stop with a fistful of mud in his mouth. *Get up,* he told himself. *Get up, get up, get up.* He staggered to his feet—wobbled and confused and expecting a second bolt to rip through his body. But it never came.

He didn't remember Kirik riding up beside him. He didn't remember climbing his bondsman's mount either, but next he knew he was slumped over the young man's saddle like a loosely girded baldric. He coughed and spat and listened to the thunder of horse hooves all the way back to the Vaskultan encampment.

CHAPTER THIRTY-TWO

"So the whore sends a Zhoul to further humiliate me."

Lord Tavarin sat on a high-backed throne, the skin of his plump arms hanging loosely over the carved armrests. He was an obese man, obese and cantankerous and likely made that way by years of chronic illness. It'd been an hour at most and already he'd complained of more aches than an ordinary man might in a year.

"I come to you not only as the newly appointed Imperial Advisor, but as a friend and fellow Anirian," Seric told him. "I seek nothing more than to restore the faith that has long been severed between us."

It had been a fifteen-day journey to Silverleaf, though another six or seven had passed before Tavarin finally agreed to this audience. Seric had spent the time in his guest chamber or in the lavish banquet hall, where his hosts entreated him with fine courses and delectable wines and charming entertainment. A grand show of hospitality, but he wasn't here to be fed and feted.

Tavarin's wife was speaking into his ear. Lady Perilia was half her husband's size, and comelier than Seric remembered, especially in that long pleated gown of ivory crosshatch. Her words caused her husband to frown and shake his head, like a selfish child who didn't get his way.

"My lord, I assure you, my intentions are most honorable," Seric went on. "All I ask is but a *private* moment of your time."

Tavarin looked at him. "You have only now. So speak."

Seric wasn't pleased. The seating here at the foot of the dais was roomy enough, but the tiled floor behind him was laden with trestle tables that were crowded with noisy, drunken diners. There was music too, zithers and panpipes and bronze bells, wafting loudly from somewhere along the far western wall, behind the screen of smoke. Servers poured bland wine into garish cups and brought dishes of bean soup, fresh greens and mushrooms, water chestnuts, and all cuts of duck. Duck wing, duck head, duck gizzard—and the tastiest of all, duck neck.

"I mean to do all that is needed to guide the House of Valayne back into prosperity," Seric said, after swallowing. "Subjugating the Zhouls is my primary objective."

That only seemed to make Tavarin more upset. He looked up from his trencher and said, "You must think me some great fool, Dyre. I know the truth. You're trapped. You're trapped and you're desperate. Lord Raas Dragath is choking you from the south, the same of the Graveland tribes in the north, and now Lord Merio Athera is mustering a campaign from the east. I have plenty of ears, you know, plenty of spies and sleepers and fast horses." A meaty hand clapped down upon the armrest. "You are here for your own interests, don't insult me by saying otherwise."

As much as Seric didn't care for the governor, his bluntness was almost welcome, considering all the weasels in the Hollow. "Forgive me, my lord. I meant not to offend you—"

"But you did anyway." He gnawed on some duck. "I sent petition after petition, pleading and pleading for aid, for more months than I care to remember. Your Lord Regent knew those Zhouls robbed us of our treasury, and yet he still expected tribute from me."

The growing thunder in the governor's voice was beginning to quiet the hall. "Lord Zantherei no longer holds the Imperial Throne," Seric told him. "I thought my presence here was an obvious testament to that."

Tavarin's chins jiggled when he shook his head. "It's too late now. I'll not give you want you want. You'll not have my city."

To Seric's left, Vylas spoke up. "This man you speak so discourteously to is not some lowly envoy, my lord. He is the Imperial Advisor of the Anirian Empire. You would do well to consider his offer, for the welfare of your people."

Tavarin's eyes narrowed at the one-eyed man, but when he spoke it was directed at Seric. "Keep your watchdog outside, Dyre. He's not welcome here." His wife whispered something, and he shook his head and said, "No, you know how I dislike that one-eyed wretch."

"And I dislike fat fools who open their fat mouths as if they have some standing of authority," Vylas replied.

Tavarin was about to take a bite when he heard that, and just like that he froze, eyes wide and mouth agape. At length, his plump fingers released the duck and closed into a meaty red fist. His face was red, too, and trembling with rage. "Only a fool dares insult a wolf in his own den."

"A wolf?" Vylas replied with a laugh. "Your wife must've hidden your look mirror. All I see is a fat and toothless old hound, wallowing in self-pity while his lady wife keeps the kennel in order."

Tavarin screamed for his guards. "*SEIZE THE WRETCH!* Blind him—blind his other goddamn eye!"

The guards advanced, drawing arms, but at Seric's signal the monster that was Aldebron Pentagath rose from his seat. The guards paled, hesitating. "My lord, I can't allow you to do that," Seric said.

It was a bold move, and yet Seric knew he was outnumbered, as the bulk of his army remained encamped four or five miles outside the city. Still, with him was a handpicked corps of elite soldiers, commanded by none other than General Aldebron Pentagath, who was like a good fifty veterans himself. "I offer you the submission of the Zhouls and the return of your treasury," Seric went on. "In return all I seek is your allegiance."

Tavarin's face twisted into a grimace—not at Seric's words, he realized, but of some sudden pain. His hand went to his belly, a telltale gesture that sent both aid and physician rushing to his side. They helped him off the dais, and guided him toward the nearest exit. The music stopped. The hall was eerily still. Seric could only shrug at what he'd just witnessed. Lady Perilia said, "Forgive my husband, he is weak with illness. May we reconvene at a later time, my lord?"

Strange, how stiff her words to me, Seric thought, agreeing with her request. Perilia rattled off orders to her stewards and hosts, then turned and followed her husband's groans to the exit. Seric watched her go. The music slowly resumed.

"Did I rile him enough for you?" Vylas asked. "I may need to dig my own grave now."

Seric opened his mouth to reply, but only laughter came out. "Did you see his face? 'Fat fools who open their fat mouths . . .' By the gods, Vylas, I can't believe you said that."

Vylas looked puzzled, and yet he was smiling as well. "I don't understand. You've been clamoring for his audience for six days—just to send him off again?"

Seric's laughter faded. He took a long sip of wine, even though the taste was a bit insipid for his palate. He set the cup down and his hand came back up to touch the scar beneath his silk neckerchief. "You were right, you know. About his wife. She runs this province."

Vylas seemed heavy in thought. "What does that have to do—"

"It matters not. You did well, counselor."

She came to him later that evening, her petite frame concealed by an oversized cloak of homespun gray. When Perilia removed it, Seric knelt and took her hand in his. "Thank you for granting my request," he said.

"Please stand, Seric, we're beyond such simple formalities. Besides, I should be the one to bend the knee."

He obeyed, now looking down at the small woman.

Perilia's face was quite comely once he looked past that small upturned nose and lack of a chin. Her eyes were large and expressive and easily her most attractive feature, that and the slight highness of her brows, which lent to her innocent, childlike visage. *A deceiving visage, in truth*, he thought.

She turned from him and began to wander about his guest chamber, gliding around in her long ivory gown like a lost specter. He guessed she was making sure he was given all the proper accommodations.

"How is your husband?"

Her wandering ceased, and she sat on the wooden couch. Shoulder-length tresses of dark hair quivered when she shook her head. "Your counselor has quite a tongue on him."

"It needed to be done." Seric took a seat beside her. He had history with this woman, so he knew he needed to tread carefully here. *She's a shrewd one, shrewder than her husband, and far more difficult to read.* "It is disheartening to know that your husband denies my hand."

She looked at him. "He has reason to, wouldn't you agree?"

"Such reason should be overlooked, Zantherei no longer holds the throne."

"Seric, the emperor is dead. The dynasty is lost. A *woman* sits on the throne. A goddamn woman—can you imagine? Not once in all the years of all the dynasties . . ."

"The Turyn dynasty," Seric told her. "When Emperor Regnus died his mother Aslena ascended the throne. And she held it for twenty-five years, until her death, and from what is written in the annals, the dynasty had never seen such peace again."

"Miriana is no Aslena. Miriana is a *whore*. I'll never crook the knee to her or any of her minions." She looked accusingly at him, a look that Seric didn't like at all. "Have I offended you?" she asked, her tone spiteful. "A thousand pardons for my grave offense." She went before him and bowed, a less than sincere gesture. Then she returned to her seat, and, with a snort of self-satisfaction, she said, "Tell me, Seric Dyre, is the leash tighter now that you're her imperial lapdog?"

She's goading you. "I wouldn't know," he said reservedly. "I came against Lady Miriana's wishes."

Her lips tightened at that. She raised a hand to caress gently his face. "A cheek so comely as this," she said, with that same hard edge to her voice. "It *must* belong to her."

"It burns you to think that," he said.

She hesitated before nodding. "Once, perhaps."

"No longer?"

"Seric, I'm not the same delicate blossom I used to be. I was young and weak, a fool to not realize you'd be gone once you were done with me."

"I had to leave. You were a wedded woman, and I was promised to Nyvia."

"You could've come back. After the annulment. I thought you would."

"I wanted to," he said. "But Zantherei ruined me. I had debts . . . I was miserable and I was ashamed. I didn't want you to see me, not like that."

She shook her head, as if disbelieving of such words. Her fingers began touching his silk neckerchief, the one covering that nasty scar, until he gently brushed them aside. Her hand went lower, to the seal of office around his neck. She cautiously traced its polished, circular edge. "You've become like all the others, with this."

"I am nothing like them. Believe me, my lady, I am here to prove there are still just men in the Hollow—"

"There are only wolves in the Hollow," she said. "Lurking in shadows, predators of ambition and power, never contented, never sated. They gulp and guzzle and grow fatter and fatter until they become bloated with coin and corruption. And even then, they continue to gorge themselves. They're all the same, all of—"

Seric wrapped his hand around her neck and brought his lips to hers.

She tasted sweet, of safflower and something richer, surely whatever balm was producing the cherry-red hue of her lips. And after he kissed her long and deep, he went to pull away, but she didn't let him, and so they kept kissing. Her hands took his, placing them on her body. Small as she was, Lady Perilia was blessed with firm hips and pleasing curves. He fondled those curves, and she purred and moaned and told him how aroused she was, and, like the sultry broad she was, she quickly peeled off her silks.

It was a task meant for purpose and not pleasure—but seeing her naked now, Seric knew only the latter. She had blossomed much since they'd last pillowed. Her breasts were larger than he remembered—certainly larger than Miriana's, although not quite as pale or smooth, and with nipples not quite as small and puckered. He only got a glimpse of them, as Perilia pushed him down to the bed, yanking down his trousers and spreading her legs atop him. She reached behind to guide his manhood into her. She was moist and she was tight, and the sensual way she moved up and down made Seric struggle to keep himself from an early climax. And just as she tightened her legs and threw her head back and moaned with release, Seric felt his own seed explode inside her.

Not long after, he was up and reaching for his trousers on the bedrail. She lay unmoving, watching him.

"You should get dressed," he told her.

She didn't reply, only curled a finger, bidding him to come closer.

"The hour grows late," he reminded her, glancing at the open window. "Dawn is not far off."

Her breasts jiggled when she lifted herself up by her elbows. "So? I'm not finished with you."

"Perilia, your husband—"

"That oaf will be gone for days. The tonic he's administered, it puts him out like an overworked ox."

"Still, the longer you remain, the more suspicious your courtiers will grow."

"I don't care." She was fidgeting with something between her legs, something small and faintly yellow—likely the rind of a halved lemon, a common contraceptive. "You are departing soon, yes? Until then, I require more, Seric, more before I affix my husband's seal to your edict. This is, after all, the true agreement of my husband's fealty, is it not?"

Seric stopped and looked up at her, like a child caught committing some misdeed. "I didn't—"

"Don't." She leaned forward. "I'm not the same delicate blossom I used to be, remember?"

He was about to reply, but was distracted by the hand around his manhood. She fondled it until he began to stiffen a second time. Then she smiled and lay back on the featherbed, opening her legs. Her voice was a libidinous whisper: "Now again, I say."

Seric obeyed.

CHAPTER THIRTY-THREE

When Demien's purse was empty, he was forced to sell Dreadfang. He'd spent days among the crowds of the city market, crammed like a fish in a hold, turning down offers that ranged from the subpar to the ridiculous, before finally settling on two hundred ounces less than the offer he had refused two days prior. All told, it was a quarter of the weapon's true value, and yet he had no choice—a man's hunger was both impatient and nonnegotiable.

Still, it was a small fortune to the folk of this city, and one that afforded Demien and his son many evenings of full bellies and warm featherbeds. And as he came to frequent the many hostelries and taverns and brothels of the city, Demien couldn't help but acknowledge that other, long-suppressed, desire.

The Golden Zinnia was not the most inviting of places—not with its worn façade, discolored windows of oiled paper, and cracked or missing roof tiles—but it was known to employ of some of the district's most appealing bawds. *It certainly seems to be a bustling place*, Demien thought as he brushed aside the old, piss-colored door curtain.

Inside, the common area was dim and smoky and obstructed by staircases and scrollwork panels and scarred wooden columns. Crowded among the tables were dozens of drunken idiots muttering dozens of drunken conversations. The floral sconces and hanging lanterns and assortments of wall paintings all seemed to hearken back to a more prosperous time. *A time long dead,* Demien mused.

The man who appeared to be the owner was a small gray fellow who barked orders from behind a serving counter. Years of slack posture left him stoop-shouldered, years of drink made him paunchy, and years of some untold hardship made him a miserable thing intent on making others as miserable as he. When Demien approached the counter, he saw at least forty summers on the man's face—forty long and unkind summers. "My friend, are you the proprietor here?"

The man scowled as if Demien had just smacked his firstborn son. "I am. But I'm no friend to you." His right hand was but a fleshy stump. Demien stared at it when he asked for wine, but the proprietor didn't reply, not right away at least. "I don't like your look," he said at length. "I've served enough filthy drunkards to know what kind of trouble you like to stir."

Demien could only frown at that, but with his unkempt hair and tattered hemp jacket and trousers, such treatment wasn't unexpected. And sure, he'd been in his cups earlier at another tavern, yesterday too, and every other day of recent memory. He reached inside his purse, snatching a handful of coins, but the proprietor had already turned away, to find someone else to bark at. So Demien had to wait. He felt little Silas clinging to him, and looking down, he saw the boy's eyes were fastened on the common area, where a handful of woman milled about or flirted with prospective clients. Most were pale of skin but a few were a shade or two darker, and one had that deep, chestnut tone that Bearcat Brehems seemed to fancy. Hairstyles ranged from straight and flowing to fastened in chignons, in shades of black and brown and gold and gray—one even had locks of bright red, like the throat of a frigatebird. Their physical features were just as varied: high cheek-bones, small lips, big noses, freckles, wide hips, big breasts, small breasts—whatever a man might possibly desire. Silas seemed mesmer-ized by them all, but Demien's eye was drawn only to one.

She was a tall thing, smooth of leg and strong of hip, her hair arranged in long black curls—just how he liked. He watched her for a time, sullen when she disappeared behind a screen or paneling, and gladdened when she re-emerged. He called again for the proprietor, but the little worm continued to ignore him, so Demien did the only thing he could do: he slammed a fistful of coins on the counter.

That sound—that unmistakable *clang* of metal—was perhaps the only sound that seemed to spark any life into the proprietor. He bounded over to Demien like an eager hound, watching closely while Demien pointed out his lady of choice. The proprietor called for her, and when she didn't respond fast enough, he shouted at her. That made her hustle. She stopped briefly to curse at a drunken lout for some indecency. *She's certainly a fiery one,* he thought. *And tall.* She was taller than most men, which meant she towered over the proprietor. Up close she appeared a bit older, and even the enhancements of cosmetics couldn't hide the dark pouches that tugged at her eyes. Still, minor flaws on an otherwise handsome creature. *Not everyone can look like Alana,* Demien thought.

"Twenty gets you the private screens in the back," the proprietor said. He gave her buttocks a perfunctory squeeze. "Between the silks, anything goes, both the lotus and the cave, if the latter's your thing."

"You're quite a large fellow," the woman cut in. Demien inhaled the cloying sweetness of her perfume. She touched him just beneath his chin, lifting it slightly to study his features. "Comely of cheek, too. You look like just the rare fellow to satisfy a lioness like me."

"As rare as any sot with enough coin," Demien told her.

The woman missed the gibe, or maybe she just chose to ignore it. Either way, she smiled and placed her hands on his broad shoulders. Demien went to speak but was distracted by the proprietor, who was talking to Silas. "What about you, boy," he was saying. "Plenty of young blossoms for you."

"The boy's dumb," Demien said.

The proprietor looked at Silas a moment longer, then back at Demien. He gestured to the woman. "Well, you want her or not?"

Demien got up and headed across the room to view the private areas. They weren't very private at all. Screens were shabby and dilapidated and torn, most offering no more privacy than what the smoky haze could provide. He could see intertwining lovers behind a few, man and woman or the less frequent man and effeminate boy. He shook his head at that and returned to the proprietor. "I want something better. A private room, the best you have." He pointed to the stairs leading up to the second story.

The proprietor gave him a price, which of course was exorbitant, and so the two men haggled for a while, before finally settling on an amount that didn't make Demien want to smash his head into pulp. Then the bawd led Demien and his son up a flight of rickety stairs and through a doorway that brought him to a tiny anteroom, which opened into a larger suite.

It was private, yes, but little else. It wasn't clean, wasn't fragrant; the rushes on the floor looked unchanged, the hanging black locust twigs had long lost their aroma, and the water in the washbasin was black and tepid. The adjoining privy chamber was so musty that Demien almost didn't use it. *That little worm cheated me*, he thought while relieving himself.

When he returned the bawd was sitting beside Silas on the rushes; the boy was showing off both the currycomb and the resin goat figurine he owned. Demien unslung his haversack and placed it on an uneven stand beside the featherbed. The woman came over, eyeing it coyly. She said, "You don't look like a man to have such a wealth of coin."

"And yet I do."

"What's your name?"

"Does it matter?"

"A simple question. You want to know mine?"

"It's Jasmina. I heard that worm of a pander call for you. And I don't care to tell you my name, no more than you truly care to know it."

"You talk funny," she said. "Are you one of those noblemen who dresses in rags to mingle with the commoners?"

The more she spoke the less he was beginning to like her. "Are you one of those whores who asks senseless questions? Take off your clothes." Demien grabbed the coverlet from the bed and handed it to Silas and told him to go to sleep. When he returned, the bawd had removed her red-ruffled outer jacket. Demien used the flint from his sack to light a pair of bedside tapers, then sat on the featherbed to watch her finish. She removed her chemise and came out of her slip, her naked skin glowing pale ochre under the candlelight.

She went to him, but he told her to stay there, naked as her day of birth. He wanted to take his time with her, to let his eyes absorb every curve of her body—from her silky dark curls to her soft womanly lips, and of course her breasts, those firm and youthful and uneven breasts. And despite the flattering candlelight, he couldn't ignore the faint scarring of her belly, an obvious indication of a previous birth. But her hips were strong and her legs were muscled and smooth to his touch, and warmer between her thighs.

She raised her left leg and planted it on the bedrail, showing off her delicate little flower beneath a soft patch of fuzz. It was pink and puckered and sweet of scent and even sweeter of taste, and as Demien licked her she moaned and moaned and for a moment he almost forgot that she was a bawd whose moans were done out of duty and not pleasure. Indeed, she was skilled—the way she grabbed his hair, the way her left foot stood on tiptoes, the way her hips thrust forward.

Demien stopped to remove his tunic. Her eyes glittered at his physique. "You are no ordinary man," she purred.

He didn't know what to say so he said nothing. She knelt down and removed his trousers and took him in her mouth, pleasuring him for a time, before Demien's passion overtook him and he placed her on the bed, one hand running through her hair, the other guiding his manhood inside her. Her legs flexed and tightened and she moaned after each thrust. His eyes closed and he thought of his late wife, and his climax came with a sudden, fierce shudder. And when he pulled away, he shuddered again, less so the second time.

She rose at once and padded off; Demien could barely see where, nor did he care to. He was depleted now, depleted and tired, and soon his eyes were fighting to remain open. He thought she'd left, but no, she soon came back to the bed. He took her hand and guided her fingers to his head, so she could stroke his hair the way his late wife used to. Before long, his eyes closed and the world faded into the darkness of sleep.

He was roused by a soft jingling, a faint sound, imperceptible to most —but not to a trained ear like Demien Mordall's. He raised his head. Jasmina was crouched on the floor, fully clothed and clutching something in her hand. It was his coin purse—the one he kept in his haversack. Demien sat up. Hearing him she shot to her feet and dashed for the exit. He sprung from the bed and grabbed her arm and yanked hard. The purse dropped with a *clang*, spilling strings of coin like metallic snakes. She tried to break free, but when she couldn't she cursed and spat and raked her pretty nails against the left side of his face. He shoved her—a little too hard—sending her sprawling across the floor. "*GET OUT!*" he roared. She staggered to her feet, disheveled and wobbly, and left.

CHAPTER THIRTY-FOUR

The ride across the imperial heartland had left Alarin Athera bone-tired and full of ache, yet the moment he saw his younger brother emerge from the gates of Stormhaven, all such grievances were gone from his heart.

The embrace between them was warm and long, and afterward Merio stood back as if to examine what the years had done to his elder brother. Kind soul that he was, he ignored Alarin's ever-thinning hair and aging face and pronounced limp, commenting only on how robust he still looked. Of course Alarin replied by calling Merio a liar, and both men shared a laugh. "The city of Stormhaven welcomes you, Elder Brother," Merio said afterward. He turned to the men of his entourage and raised a hand. "Bow your heads, you are standing in the presence of the Thunder of the North."

Merio was about eight or nine years Alarin's junior—the youngest of the four brothers, and the least like any of them. He was a handsome man blessed with sharp cheekbones and warm, nut-brown eyes that gave him a touch of effeminacy. Merio still had a full head of dark, wavy hair, and though it bore the look of a careless tousle, Alarin could only wonder how long it took his attendants to make it appear that way.

One needed only to glance at that hideous wardrobe to know that he was a man of grand extravagances. He wore a purple silk military robe embroidered with a slew of unnecessary fringes and furbelows, a pleated black sash, and fine boots embroidered in silver filigreed thread. The men of his honor guard—much like their lord—were slender and pale and beardless, and all were beribboned and draped in those garish Stormhaven colors of purple and red and white, colors that Merio probably referred to as mauve and maroon and ivory, the garrulous fool. *I'll take the ragged grays and blacks instead,* Alarin thought. *I am an Anirian after all.*

At Merio's side was a tall and lean fellow with humorless eyes and a stern jaw. He was dressed entirely in white—white armor, white cloak, white trimmings, white belts and straps. Even the plume of his helm was white—and glossy like feathers glazed in rime. He was none other than the renowned General Yuseth Valate, a man others referred to as the Lord of Winter, not only for the color of his dress, but also his icy disposition. Still, he seemed pleasant enough as he escorted Alarin and his host toward the mighty walls of Stormhaven.

The city sat on a promontory overlooking a meandering tributary of the Grayling River. A massive water gate directed the flow of pleasure boats and cargo-carrying junks, while land gates and turrets and a pair of defensive walls kept the populace secure. The outer wall looked no different from many of the Anir, its base a mixture of white ashes and soils and slurries, above which sat layers of gray, wind-beaten bricks. But once Alarin passed the gatehouse and found himself surrounded by the second, inner wall, his eyes were instantly drawn to the bands of marble-white, bas-relief sculptures running across it.

It was an elegant yet ostentatious display, a hodgepodge of ugly, malformed beasts mingling with young and beautiful women. And of course, most of the women were nude, and if you looked closely enough you could see the lewd acts they were engaging in. Alarin saw a long-haired maiden pleasuring a strange, centaur-like creature, its equine member both dark and engorged. Alarin stopped looking after that.

And yet, as intricate as the inner wall appeared, the city itself, at least the waterfront southern district, was anything but. Swill and sewage heaps and night soil left an ever-present stench to waft through the narrow, crowded roadways. A gaunt and bare-chested fellow lay on the outskirts of traffic, ignored by all except the overhead crows and a single quick sniff of an equally gaunt three-legged dog. Nearby, a merchant was chasing a fleeing urchin, leaving another ragged boy to abscond with the man's wares. Some of Merio's men laughed at that, but Alarin only shook his head.

The central district was no better. In fact, only when Alarin entered the northern palace district did he see a change, and what a dramatic change it was. Here, the wealthy lived in greater opulence than the impoverished masses could surely imagine. Everything was polished and gilded and gleaming. The furrows that ran alongside the boulevards were filled with a colorful assortment of blossoms, the stairs to the main palace white as snowdrops, the surrounding balustrade carved like leaves of icy pearl and marble. The huge five-paneled doors were painted a reddish purple—or plum, rather—and decorated with bold silver tacks.

Inside was no less luxurious. The wide corridors were bedecked with elongated statues and giant, enameled fish vases and richly detailed tapestries. Merio had General Yuseth escort Alarin's host to a guest wing, then led his elder brother on a personal tour of the palace. Alarin quickly grew tired of his brother's pontifications about the artistry and craftsmanship of each of his numerous statues, and he certainly didn't care to know the minute details of just how the clay was molded and coiled and pressed, or precisely how long each piece was fired in the kilns, or just how many apprentices each master artisan had under his wing. By the gods he just wanted to rest.

But Merio continued to ramble on, and hastened his pace while doing so. *Damn fool, he's like an eager child.* Even without this wretched limp Alarin surely couldn't keep up, and of course Merio didn't seem to notice. That was Merio for you—that was just the way he was. A different sort of man, mostly in the way he didn't understand certain, unspoken notions, no matter how simple they were. But Alarin had his own failings, too, so he tended not to hold a grudge. "Brother, I'd like to see all your attractions, trust me I would. But I'd be a far more pleasant guest after some rest and perhaps a change of garb."

He stood looking blankly at Alarin for a moment. "Oh yes, certainly. Forgive me, Elder Brother. I'll show you to your room first, of course."

It was a splendid semicircular chamber with far too much space and far too many servants. Alarin dismissed them all, then disrobed and washed his body and scrubbed his hands and foot in a washbasin of red jasper. He chose the drabbest clothing he could find—not an easy task by any means. Soon after, the palace chef entered, a snobbish man who offered to prepare dishes of sliced blowfish or octopus tentacles that wriggled while you ate them. When Alarin instead chose a much homelier offering of braised chicken, the chef left in a huff. Alarin lay back onto the softest, silkiest featherbed he'd ever felt, and he stared out the window at the fading afternoon sunlight, until his eyes grew heavy and closed.

Merio woke him not long after. His brother's arms were at his sides, while the dusky light at his back left his features dark and uncertain. "You're too much like Father," he muttered. "Why are you like that? You shouldn't be like that."

"What?" Alarin blinked.

"Your garb—so much gray. It's so drab, you know. So drab. I have much finer choices. Look at this"—he gestured to the scarf around his neck—"See this, the plum color here? It's made from the secretion of a very rare whelk. You wouldn't believe how many were needed just to make this. But it's the symbol of nobility, you know, of wealth and status and all that." Alarin gave a grunt, and Merio quickly said, "If you don't like the dye, we have others, you know. Woad as blue as the sea; weld as yellow as the sun. We have saffron and madder and kermes and—"

"Gray is fine, Brother. Gray suits me. I am an Anirian, *you know*."

Those last two words came out more derisively than intended.

Merio recoiled, like a priest hearing words of blasphemy. "So be it." He glanced over to a rounded table, where servers were placing Alarin's meal. "Oh, it took quite some time to soothe my master chef. Why do you insult him so? It is his duty to serve you his finest dishes. If you are fretting over the toxins in the blowfish, I assure you, not a single soul has lost his breath afterward. Well, there was one, but it wasn't the delicacy that killed him, the man was just plain *old*."

"What? I don't give a care," Alarin said. He got up and limped to the table.

"I'll let you eat. Then we can continue with the tour."

Alarin sighed at that, but obliged his request with a nod. And later, when the massive double-doors of the Rosebud Hall opened before him, Alarin was taken aback by what he saw. The hall was immense, with ornate pillars rising some fifty feet high, decorated in clouds that rose to the ceiling and scurried puffily across it. And suspended there, across the entire length of the hall, was the largest Sadralen Alarin had ever seen, as large as the annals described it to be. Each scale of its serpentine underbelly was like a man's breastplate, each ridged horn longer than a man was tall. Its massive, leonine head was fitted with a massive set of fangs.

There were other statues in the adjacent chambers and alcoves, statues of gods and deities and lesser deities, smaller but no less magnificent. There were creatures, too, ferocious beasts and wicked demons, many of which Alarin had never seen, a few he'd never even heard of. A giant wolf with two heads, a bizarre ungulate with six legs. He saw ogres twice as tall as Szathan Mordall, and bugbears twice as ugly. Such master craftsmanship was truly an honor to behold.

Afterward, Merio led him through a rear door into a small court-yard. It was a warm spring evening, alive with cricket song. Moonlight bathed the peach trees and the apricot trees and the beautiful rows of flowers. "I've been waiting to show you this from the moment you arrived," Merio said, then moved ahead to enter the door of the conservatory hall. "This is for your eyes only."

Inside, winding stone paths ran this way and that, each curving gently through a lush assortment of flowers, from rhododendrons of every color to other rare and tropical mountain specimens that Merio had no trouble rambling on about. It was truly a breathtaking sight, but Alarin was tiring of all this, and he simply plodded through the motions, hoping the tour would finally end. He followed Merio as he turned a corner to enter an alcove at the rear of the hall. A tiered stone wall rose before them, its planting beds home to the most splendid flowers Alarin had ever seen. By the gods, their petals were as white and fluffy as . . . cloudfalls? It couldn't be. No, cloudfalls had been extinct for hundreds of years. Or so Alarin thought.

Merio was smiling at him, at whatever expression was tugging on Alarin's face. "They are what you think," he said, moving to sit on a nearby trestle bench. Alarin followed. A servant appeared with a ewer of wine. He was a bashful youth, much like Kalen, his eyes never far from the ground, his reaction uncertain when Alarin thanked him.

Merio gestured to the cloudfalls and said, "It is said when Thalastor Siven stood before them, they radiated with the most remarkable light. Like starlight, but soft, not blinding. You know for years the man suffered cataracts in both eyes. The shining of the cloudfalls not only cured him, but awoke in him a greater wisdom, the wisdom of a man's slumbering mind. Of course he later went on to found the Anirian dynasty." He raised a goblet to his lips and drank.

"I know the tale," Alarin told him.

"Of course, Elder Brother," Merio said. He turned and shouted for the attendant. The sudden noise startled Alarin. When the lad came over, Merio chastised him for the blandness of the wine. Alarin sighed and let his eyes drift back to the wall of cloudfalls. They were so tranquil . . . so strangely comforting.

"You want to know where I got them," Merio said. "Well, I can't tell you. That is my secret alone, you know. But I will say this, it was easier finding them than it was transporting them here." He laughed at that, then seemed contemplative for a moment, as if taken by a sudden thought. When next he spoke, his voice was lower, more subdued. "They've never shone like that . . . like in the annals."

"That's because it's just a myth," Alarin said, waving a dismissive hand. It was the truth; the shining of the cloudfalls was just an old fairy story. And yet, as he stared at them, a part of him, a small, foolish part, couldn't help but wish the cloudfalls would open up and shine for him, just as they had for Emperor Thalastor. They would shine and heal his leg and Alarin would cease being a cripple and become the Thunder of the North once again. It was a nice thought . . . but the moment passed and he simply scoffed at the idiotic notion. Right now, he had matters of great import to discuss. He turned to face his brother directly. "Merio, if I am to serve as your director general, you must understand that you may not like some of my decisions."

He gave a shrug. "Your counsel has always been in the best interest of the realm."

"That is true, and that is why I must advise you to stay your campaign, at least for a time."

The attendant returned with their goblets once more, and this time Merio nodded his approval after sipping. Alarin did too, though it tasted no different from before. "So, will you do as I requested?"

"What? Oh, the campaign. Yes, of course, Elder Brother. A curious request, but yes."

Alarin nodded. "By now I'm sure you know that Seric Dyre has been inaugurated as the new Imperial Advisor. Don't scoff, Brother, he's not to be taken lightly. He's already doing what I advised Zantherei to do, he's marching north to reclaim the province of Skydeep under his banner."

"Does the wine not suit your palate?" Merio gestured to his brother's full goblet. "I have many other varieties, pomegranate, mulled ginger, quince, hawthorn berry perhaps?"

Alarin looked down at his goblet, then back at his brother. "Are you even listening to me?"

Merio nodded. "Of course. I just thought—never mind. Go on then."

"If Seric succeeds, the north will hold three provinces. That's eleven districts and six major cities."

"So let us muster the ranks, Elder Brother, between my garrisons and your—"

"No, Brother, we mustn't act so hastily. Besides, Seric's weakness is off the field. Imperial Advisor he may be, but he was born a half Zhoul, and I doubt such impure blood has earned him any love from the court or the populace. I have informants in the Redlands. I've recently come to learn some things about our little Imperial Advisor. I plan to spread this information throughout the city. Copies of these documents will be nailed to posts at every market and bridge and hostelry. The criers will spread its meaning swiftly enough."

Merio seemed unimpressed. "Lady Miriana will denounce it as a lie."

"Even so, it will only further tarnish his reputation. Perhaps enough to have him publicly removed."

Merio seemed heavy in thought for a moment. "So your plan is to smear him with calumny? I expected more, I must say."

"It's not calumny, Brother, and there is more," Alarin said. He stole a glance around the area before continuing. "My main objective is to take the Redlands without raising a single sword."

Merio didn't seem to like what he was hearing. "You must be jesting, my brother. Do you think Raas Dragath will simply hand over his land to us? You make it sound so easy."

Alarin paused. "It can be. Lord Dragath's wife has passed to heaven recently."

He nodded. "This is known."

"Well, a lord without a wife is like a bird without a nest."

Merio's eyes blinked once, then narrowed suspiciously.

"You have a daughter, my brother, a fine daughter in the flower of her youth. She remains unfettered, does she not? We extend her hand to Raas Dragath, with the promise of unification against a greater foe. Once agreed—"

Merio bolted to his feet. "Are you *mad?*" Anger flooded the soft features of his face. "You plan to give my daughter to the *Red Terror?*"

Alarin remained calm, which seemed to irritate Merio even more. "I didn't finish. It is a ruse. The wedding will be a coup. It's the only way to get close enough to strike Raas Dragath down."

"I don't care. My daughter will *not* be used as bait."

Alarin didn't understand why he was so upset. "My brother, it is a simple—"

"I once knew you to be a wise and capable man," Merio cut in, crossing his arms. "But I am beginning to think it was a mistake in bringing you here."

Alarin leaned on his cane and rose. "I said you might not like the counsel I have to give." His voice was stern.

Merio stood with his back to his brother. Alarin said, "You must understand, my brother, that our forces cannot stand against the imperial heartland alone. We must conquer the Redlands. But to do so, there must be risk on our end. It *has* to be a highborn woman. Raas Dragath will not even consider a proposal of insincere worth."

Merio was just standing there, back turned, facing the tiers of cloudfalls. It was quite some time before he turned around. "You'll bring disgrace upon our house."

"Don't be a child," Alarin said. "The House of Athera stands as the greatest of the realm, do you think that is by some coincidence? Capable men talk of honor and loyalty, but act in schemes and deception. This is known by all minds of great intellect. And do not doubt for a second that every great man has more secrets than there are stars in the night sky . . . even our beloved father."

Merio nodded, but it seemed not without reluctance. "I must seek counsel on this."

"No," Alarin said. "This city is bristling with Raas Dragath's spies. It's best not to reveal this to anyone right now—not your closest generals, not even your daughter."

Merio looked at him with loathing. "Not only must I put my sweet Cathia in harm's way, now you're telling me to keep the truth from her as well?"

"She will be in no danger, Brother."

Merio's hands were clenched at his sides. "Fine," he said at last, "extend your wretched offer. But if you fail me in this, Elder Brother, you will find that my forgiveness does not come easily." He glared coldly at Alarin. "The blood is on your hands, you know."

As it always is, Alarin wanted to say.

CHAPTER THIRTY-FIVE

D emien Mordall stood over the washbasin, scrubbing flakes of dry blood off his face. *Damn her,* he thought, *damn that thieving whore.* It was only the coin purse she'd wanted, but still, had she searched inside his haversack, she would've found an object of far greater value—the emperor's Imperial Seal. The very thought made his head pulse with ache. *Stop drinking yourself into a blur, or next time you might not be so fortunate.* It seemed a solemn enough promise, but not a few moments later did he reach for his wine-gourd. It was empty.

He just needed a dram—a single measure, no more. Just enough to make him forget who he was. *An accursed wretch who shouldn't be alive.* He looked over at Silas, who was tying the thongs of his ruck-sack. *He is so small and sickly and silent, but I just can't bring myself to leave him. He is my son, after all.*

They left the suite a few moments later. *Never will I return to this wretched place,* he thought. *And if ever see that whore again, she will get hers.* It wasn't until he reached the bottom of the stairs that he realized how quiet the common room was. Not a peaceable quiet, no this was a tense, ominous one—the sort of quiet that could fill a lesser man's heart with dread. Even at this hour, one would expect *some* degree of commotion. But no, it was quiet. Demien brushed aside the door curtain just enough to have a peek.

Tables were vacant, patrons gone. The little proprietor was standing timorously before three men clad in patched cloaks and brigandine vests. One lifted an arm and his cloak parted to reveal a sheathed saber at the hip. He was jabbing a long finger at the door curtain—right in Demien's direction.

Demien released the curtain and stood in the dark for a long moment. When he thought it safe he gave a second look, this time examining the entire room. Bawds sat clustered against the wall like sheep in a fold. A fourth intruder stood facing the opposite wall, his head lowered. *What is he doing? Oh, he's taking a piss.*

He was built like a muskox, that one, tall as Demien and burly as Brehems. A stature such as that would certainly befit a man of command, but no, when he sauntered back to the others, they didn't seem to regard him as one. *If the big one is not making the demands here, then who?* Demien studied the other three. *The older one is ignored, the reedy one with the horse face is treated as a greenhorn.* That left the bald one with the long beard the color of maple leaves in autumn. He was not a tall man, but he carried himself as if he were, and whenever he spoke, the others were quick to listen and to nod.

The red-bearded leader was speaking to the proprietor now, and Demien only needed a brief listen to learn that he was a ruffian and extortionist, a leech of a man who bled lesser folk to fill his own purse. And judging by his gestures and nods, the leader seemed interested in someone or something on the second floor, and that someone was likely the owner of a considerable purse of coin.

The younger, horse-faced thug grew bored and began teasing the whores, grabbing one and shoving a hand between her meaty thighs. When she tried to shove him off he squeezed tighter, and when she spat in his eye his fist smashed her teeth and dropped her to the floor. A subsequent stomp broke her pretty little nose. Another bawd went to pull him off, a brave but petite gal. Horseface threw her down and now seemed intent in having his way with her, one hand clenching her neck while the other worked the lacing of his trousers. Demien's anger rose. *Don't be a fool,* he told himself. *Turn around, get your boy, and get out through the back.* Silk tore and fell away. Trousers open, Horseface forced himself on her, slow at first, then hard and urgent.

Demien had seen enough. He yanked up the door curtain. All eyes turned on him—all except Horseface, who stopped only when a companion's hand rapped on his armored shoulder. He pulled up his trousers and rose. Behind him, the red-bearded leader nudged the proprietor. "That him?"

The proprietor nodded swiftly. "Stumbled in last night. Looks like a drunken cur, but I assure you, he has a heavy purse on him. My lady here doesn't lie. Tell him, woman."

Jasmina took a timid step forward. "Three thousand ounces of silver, maybe more," she said. "I assure you, I saw it."

Redbeard turned and sized Demien up. "This lady says you have something of mine, yes?"

Demien came forward. He feigned the slight wobble of a drunkard.

Horseface laughed, a cackle that matched his celery-rib frame. "The goddamn sot can't even walk."

Demien halted a few paces before Horseface. "I have no coin."

Redbeard turned to the proprietor. "If your little whore is playing me false by the gods I will carve out her teats and sew them to her eyes."

"It's in his room," Jasmina said, slinking over to the proprietor as if that scrawny weasel could afford her some measure of protection. "With his boy—he has a boy."

Demien's teeth clenched but he didn't look at her, didn't let his eyes wander from the ruffian before him. "I have no coin," he reiterated, then added, "for the hands of leeches."

They didn't seem to like that very much. Redbeard said, "I don't think you know who we are, my friend. You see, I own this place, I own all the brothels in this district. And today I am rather cross. I'm cross because I don't like having to smooth out the slubs of my operation. But the little proprietor here owes me quite a hefty sum, and when he promises me a purse that can fulfill it, well, I just had to come. You should feel fortunate, my friend, you are saving this man from losing his other hand. Now give me what I want."

Demien gave no reply. His hand remained at his side, fingers hovering over the dagger concealed beneath his tunic.

Redbeard twiddled his beard, a gesture of impatience, perhaps. "Look, I know you're a big fellow, but I assure you, my friend there is just as big, and twice as mean."

The big man brushed Horseface aside, squaring off before Demien. He had a spiked cudgel in his hand, and eyes that said he'd used it before. "You don't want this," he warned in a low voice.

Four against one, how unfortunate, Demien thought, *for them, that is.* He would've smiled at that except his heart was still, dead still, just as it was honed to be. It was that stillness that allowed him to see and hear what others would've let pass unnoticed—the sputtering of the oil lanterns, the creak of the floorboards when a man shifted his weight, the whir of the wind outside . . .

The *whoosh* of the cudgel rushing at his head.

Demien leaned forward and stepped in, just as he'd taught thousands of cadets in training. Lean and step, in and around. It required no more thought than fastening a greave or lacing a boot. His foot landed just outside the enemy's over-extended leg, in the optimum position to turn his hips and drive his dagger up into the man's neck, which he did, stabbing through skin and cartilage and bone. The force of the thrust staggered the man, but he was a muskox who somehow managed to stay upright. And yet, even though his eyes said he dearly wanted to retaliate, his body just wouldn't respond, and the floor yanked him down, *bang*, like a stone dropped in a lake. Blood gushed from his neck. By the time he seemed to even understand what was happening, he was already curling into the cold hands of death.

Three left, Demien thought.

Horseface watched in horror. He didn't even draw his weapon

when Demien stormed forward. Demien feinted low and sliced high, opening cleanly his throat. The man's eyes rolled back and he slumped to his knees, pouring blood and wheezing like a calf caught in white-water. Demien went over and grabbed the fallen cudgel, then calmly returned and smashed the man's head. Skull shattered, gore bubbled, and Horseface flopped facedown with his arms splayed over his head in a perverse simulacrum of a kowtow, his brains oozing in pale white globs that mixed with the red.

That leaves two.

The old man had his saber brandished, but his hand was trembling, and his heart seemed torn between avenging his cronies or fleeing for his life. Demien didn't have time for him to deliberate, so he rushed forward a single, taunting step that made the frightened man commit to a premature counterattack. The saber came forward, amateurish and limp; Demien parried it aside with his cudgel and stepped into the man, shouldering him to the ground. Instantly both arms were flailing, his lips blubbering pitifully for quarter. Demien silenced him with a blow of the cudgel, sending blood and teeth and spittle into the air. The man slumped to his side, still twitching for a moment or two before his body gave that final rattle of death.

And now, one.

Demien picked up the fallen saber and hurled it at Redbeard. The weapon soared just over his head, thudding deep into the thick wooden paneling.

Redbeard blanched. "Y-you goddamn cretin." He grabbed Jasmina by the wrist, yanked her close and placed the edge of his saber across her neck. "I'll kill her," he said.

Demien took a step forward. "Do it."

The poor woman's eyes were wide, staring at Demien the same way Dahlia had, right before she was forced out to face the cord.

"I will, I'll cut open her pretty little neck."

"The whore tried to steal from me. Do it."

He took a step back, his eyes incredulous. "Who the hell are you?"

Demien brandished the cudgel, its spiked head bespattered with gore. "Who am I?" He advanced a step. "I've clashed blades with the

greatest swordsmen of the realm—destroyers and killers and jugger-
nauts of men. And I've dispatched *every* last one." Another step.
Gobbets of flesh dripped from the cudgel. "I've unmanned ranks just
by the show of my face, routed entire wings with but a single shout.
I've gutted general after general and sent their armies fleeing like
sheep. You don't want to know who I am." He took another step
forward. "I am a *fucking* monster to you."

The man stumbled and the backsword fell from his hand. Jasmina
scrambled free. Demien moved to stand over him. Redbeard squeezed
shut his eyes and faced his death with a cowardly whimper. But
Demien didn't kill him. He only said, "If I see you again, I will peel
the flesh from your body and boil what's left to the bone. I don't sleep,
I don't eat. I come like the breeze and leave in a blaze. Five men or
five hundred, it matters not. Do you understand? Now leave my sight."

The man scrabbled to his feet and bolted for the exit. The door
curtain was left dangling back and forth. The rest of the room was still
as death. Blood painted the floor and the walls and in arcs across the
ceiling, looking like thirteen men had died in here, not three. Demien
had a way of doing that.

Neither the proprietor nor the women made a sound. It was as if
Demien was some rabid beast, expected to charge at anything that
moved. *They think me mad. Good. Maybe I am mad.* Jasmina was
cowering before the proprietor's counter. "I should open your neck,"
he told her. Then he turned his eyes on the proprietor. "Yours, as well."

Both seemed too frightened to reply. Demien remained there,
unmoving in the tense silence, until his hand opened and the cudgel hit
the floor with a sharp *clang*. The bawds blenched, startled. Demien
ignored them and took a seat at the counter. The proprietor seemed
unsure whether to stay frozen or go over and tend the customer as he'd
done countless times before. Eventually, duty won over, and he
approached, trembling, and by all the goddamn gods, the man had a
good mind to tremble. For who knew what this madman would
do next?

Demien asked for wine. This time, he got it.

CHAPTER THIRTY-SIX

The point of vantage was a tall escarpment that loomed over the quiet city in the valley below. It was a calm and desolate night; the stars were dim and distant, the moon hanging in the air like an overturned sickle, robed by ripples of black clouds. A soft shimmer swaddled the landscape below—the small fields of buckwheat and millet, the rude stockades and garrisons and primitive beacon towers, and the cluster of thatched-roofed houses of the Zhoul people.

Poor fools, Seric Dyre thought, *utterly unaware of the nightmare that's coming for you.*

What had begun as an uneventful march across lush and verdant flatlands, ended as a struggle across steep ridges and rocky slopes where mudflows had thrust deadfall and huge boulders across narrow paths. Seric had left the supply wagons to encamp along the anchoring foothills, where it was warmer and greener, before leading the army across the undulating hills and gorges, treacherous terrain even after mindful reconnoitering.

He fidgeted under the weight of his mail, then moved a hand to pat the sheathed weapon at his side. It was Zantherei's prized saber, the amber-hilted Sunburst. Lady Miriana had lifted it from the wall hooks and placed it into Seric's hands, imploring him to take it despite his protests. It proved a great comfort to him now, even though Seric had no intention of unsheathing it. In truth, he planned only to observe the ambush from afar.

Not the most morale-boosting move, sure, but Seric was exhausted. He'd already spent hour after hour in his tent, poring over maps and strategies and strategies and maps, detailing every movement to every officer, questioning them, replaying various scenarios again and again until every conceivable course of action was accounted for. Those days had passed in blurs—and the nights were sleepless. And now, just as his body was most depleted and his mind most drained, was it sensible to stand among the ranks and engage in battle? No, his part in this was done.

He could see his strategies now, like deer spoor to a hunter or notes plucked from his lute. Every move of his contingents: the vanguard of horsemen storming from the south, the detachment of spearmen from the east. He could see how the enemy would react to the pincer, could see them falling back to the northwest, to the Howler Pass. He could see the moment when General Pentagath and his crack lancers would appear to deter their escape. Under the assault the enemy ranks would buckle, and under the fusillades of the bowmen positioned along the defiladed ridge, they would break.

In his mind, Seric could hear it already—the paean of victory. It would fill the night sky, while the ground was strewn with kneeling Zhouls and their cast weapons. Seric's victory would not only satisfy his civic duty, it would elevate his standing and secure his title across the realm. And more, it would provide retribution against that cruel man from his past—that wretched Zhoulish father of his.

"You look troubled."

Vylas stood nearby, looking sidelong at him with his good eye.

"Not at all," Seric replied, but the lie was obvious, and Vylas was no fool.

"I can see it in your eyes," the privy counselor said, "Are you uncertain of victory?"

"Victory is all that I'm certain of," he said with a sigh. "What troubles me is the thought of facing the cruel man of my past, should he survive this night, that is."

"Your father," Vylas said.

Seric gave a nod. It was a long moment before he spoke again. "I am a man grown now, even one approaching his middling years . . . but there is a piece of that boy still inside me, and that boy is still afraid. I must sound craven to you."

Vylas shook his head. "You sound anything but craven, my friend. As a child you had the courage to abandon your homeland and make your way to the Hollow, where you somehow touched the heart of a great Anirian lord in Nethan Dyre. And now, by the gods look at you, you stand as the Imperial Advisor." He looked down. "It was not long ago that I loathed you, Seric Dyre. But even then I wasn't blind to all you had done to get where you were. Lady Miriana is strong just the same. Not so with me—my status was gained by tugging my sister's skirt-tails. What I mean to say is this: you are a radiant star in the prime of your being. What's to fear from some withered old brute who's never amounted to more than a low-ranking squad officer? I can see them—there."

Seric turned back to the valley. He could see them, too. A contingent of horsemen swarming the city like a great blob of spilled ink on a sheet of crinkled vellum. The sound grew from a tranquil quiet to a low hum of confusion and violence. From the crude Zhoulish beacon towers, basins of flame flashed to life. The night came alive. Seric watched it all, his fingers rubbing the scar beneath his black neckerchief.

Soon the reports began to arrive, each confirming what Seric's eyes witnessed below. The Zhoulish garrisons had been caught unaware, with many slain as they stumbled groggily outside, others before their armor could be strapped on. The survivors fled northwest. When Seric heard that he clenched his fist in triumph. *The paean of victory is soon to come,* he thought. But the quarter hours came and went, with no reports of victory to be had. The Zhouls did in fact retreat to the pass, but instead of folding under the onslaught, they were rallied by one of their generals. A general who not only led the charge to push the division of lancers down, but outmatched Aldebron Pentagath himself in battle.

Seric screamed when he heard that. "*Who* is this general?" The rider didn't know. In fact, no one did, and before long the men began calling him the Mad Wolf. One rider said when he fought, wolves howled and gathered around him, the next spoke of the wolves *battling* alongside him. By fifth watch the general himself was a nine-foot manwolf who wielded a tree with a blade lodged in it.

Damn all these fools, damn them all, Seric thought. "Drum the retire. All divisions. Get Pentagath out of there. *Now,* do you understand?"

The rider bowed and went off.

Seric fell to his knees and pounded the ground until his hands ached. *I was too close . . . too damn close to this.* There was a fine line given to preparation in battle—not enough and you were anxious and unready, too much and you become clouded by your own narrowing thought. *Wretched fool,* he screamed at himself. *One simple oversight and the battle is lost, maybe even the whole campaign. But what was it —what error have I made?*

The answer came to him much later, when he was back in his tent.

By then he'd forgotten just how much wine he downed, and in a drunken, half-blind rage he'd smashed anything within arm's reach— cooking gear, stools and chairs, sacks of grains, whatever. Then, when there was nothing left, he collapsed on the floor, cursing and muttering to himself. *I gave them no escape, no opportunity to flee . . . I made them desperate. A desperate man is worth the steel of ten others. I knew all this . . . by all the goddamn gods . . . I was too close.*

He went through the day unsure which caused his head to hurt most, the excess of wine, the sleeplessness, or all the goddamn talk about the Mad Wolf. Some spoke of the general's massive crescent-bladed halberd, whose broad, sweeping arcs beat back the foreranks and felled men two or three at a time. And when the Zhoul had taken an arrow in the shoulder and still pressed forward, his enemies faltered and gaped and backpedaled into a tangled mess of steel and flesh.

Pentagath looked rather discouraged when he finally entered the tent, bruised and disheveled and moving with a slight limp that he couldn't seem to hide. His single pauldron was cracked between its leonine eyes, his gray-black general's cloak torn and fringed by dark blood. And when he dropped to a knee and bowed his shaggy head, Seric saw blood dripping from a saturated bandage just above the knee.

"You're still bleeding," Seric said. He beckoned to his guardsmen. "Take the general back to the physician."

"*No.*" Pentagath's porcine nose flared as he shook his shaggy head. "I'm well enough to face death."

The poor fool faults himself. "General," he said. "The loss last night may weigh on your heart—but the blood is not on your hands. It was my oversight that caused the Zhouls this victory. My burden to bear."

"It's *shame* I bear," Pentagath argued. "The shame of misjudging my foe. I deserve death."

"I'll not give you what you deserve," Seric told him. "I need you, General, I need you to help set my vengeance in train. First, make sure your wounds are tended properly. Understood? We'll reconvene later. Await my call."

When Pentagath was gone, Seric summoned the two Anirian officers whose lines had personally faced the Mad Wolf. The first, General Nederion Perl, was a hard-eyed and imposing figure who fit the exact mold of what a high-ranking officer should look like. *Unfortunately a wolf in appearance doesn't always mean a wolf in heart,* Seric concluded, as he listened to the coward's ramblings of the Mad Wolf. He couldn't stomach what he was hearing, so he motioned for silence.

The other officer, Wyath Silth, was a former corps commander commissioned to lead the second division of the veteran Gray Talon regiment. His bowmen had been routed when the Mad Wolf led a detachment and struck the rear from an unchecked defile in the pass. "I saw no wolves, my lord," he explained, "only an enormous Zhoul whose ranks rose upon us with expert swiftness. We threw down our bows but our sabers were no match for their charging spears." He lowered his eyes.

"Your men were routed yes, but you rallied them back. You rallied them back and led them down the ridge to reinforce Pentagath's ranks in the pass."

He nodded. "I did, my lord."

"And it was such swift thought that may have saved the forward regiment. Raise your head, General, you've done well." Weeks ago, when Wyath had approached him in private, petitioning for command of such an experienced regiment as the Gray Talon, Seric saw only an eager man, still shy of thirty summers, with the narrow face and lanky build more fit for a scholar rather than a general. But it was his conviction that made Seric grant the man's desire. He was glad now, that he had.

General Wyath bowed and made his exit, leaving General Nederion frowning at what he'd just witnessed. "My lines held, his didn't. Yet I am silenced and he is praised?"

"Your lines held not for your actions, but for the experience of its veterans. You would do well to remember this: a worthy general knows how to carry his men, not only in the ease of victory but in the face of defeat. I learned of your actions from the reports, which your cowardly words only confirmed. You sicken me, General. Be grateful I don't strip you of your rank. Dismissed."

His face reddened. "*Cowardly* words? I spoke only the truth. Pentagath was outmatched by that Zhoul—we all were. None of us can stand against him. That is no falsehood."

"I said *dismissed*, General."

Nederion turned and stomped off. Seric shook his head at Vylas, who stood there biting his fingernails. The one-eyed man stopped to examine his work. Then he said, "I've told you once before, but I hope it's clear the cowardice in that one. He will do more harm than good, I reckon."

Seric nodded. "You're right about that, my friend. What more can you tell me, about the Zhouls, perhaps?"

He brushed aside the dark hair that had fallen over his halfmask. "Seric, I'm a counselor, not a strategist. I can't help you there."

"I don't need a strategist. I need fresh eyes. You may have but one, but it sees better than most with two."

He shook his head at that.

"Just tell me anything—whatever observations you've made, simplistic as they may seem."

Vylas was pacing now, across the scattered shards and splintered wood on the floor—remnants of Seric's earlier bout of rage. The counselor seemed to be speaking his thoughts as they came. "I don't know. Well, when I standing there, on that ridge, I remembering thinking how odd the stockades around their city looked. If fact, such a crude barrier seemed to speak of arrogance and overblown pride."

"That it does," Seric agreed.

He kept pacing. "There is weakness there, I have no doubt."

"Yes, there is, and if I could exploit such weakness, I may be able to draw them out of the pass. But I know not how."

"Yes, well I also think—" Vylas tripped on something, stumbling a step or two before clutching a wooden pole for support. Grimacing, he kicked at the shards on the floor. "You need to have all this swept, Seric. By the gods are you smiling? Only a small-minded man would find amusement in such things."

"Counselor, I'm smiling because you just gave me the answer I've been searching for. I need an urn. The finest in Silverleaf. Dispatch a rider at once."

Vylas's one eye grew wide. "An urn of wine?"

"An empty urn. No wine. Perilia was presented one years ago—at the Autumn Moon Festival. She'll know which. Have it brought to me at once. A cutter upriver would be fastest." For some reason Vylas's incredulous stare delighted him. "It's a tradition among Zhouls," Seric explained. "To offer a worthy opponent an urn of your most exquisite wine. There's no greater gesture of respect."

Vylas remained incredulous. "But you requested an *empty* urn. What purpose in presenting an empty urn?"

Seric smiled. "It won't be empty at all, my friend. It'll be filled with, well, piss."

CHAPTER THIRTY-SEVEN

"**L**YGREST!*" Anseth shouted. "You *will* answer for what you've done."

Before him loomed the barred gates of Amaranth Point; behind him, a sea of yak-tail banners and angry Vaskultan faces. Three thousand angry faces all told, with another thirty-five hundred divided between the other two gates.

A horse snorted and a man coughed, but from the ramparts came no response. Dariok, fuming with impatience, rushed his mount to the foot of the gate to hurl imprecations at the enemy. And vile and scathing though they were, they were nonetheless Vaskulti insults, many of which had no direct translation in the Anirian tongue. So even if Lygrest had a capable translator at his side, he'd have to possess a deep knowledge of Vaskultan culture in order to begin to translate effectively. Anseth himself had spent eight years among these men and he only grasped half of what was said. Still, even a simpleton could decipher the anger in Dariok's voice.

A handful of figures appeared on the ramparts, each clad in scales of gray and jet, wearing open-faced helms with decorated brow ridges in the typical Anirian fashion. The figure in the center displayed the gray-black officer's cloak and pheasant-tail headplume, and he looked very much like Lygrest, but Anseth's eyes were not so keen—certainly not so keen as the sharp-eyed Kirik, who could spot a hare moving in the brush twelve miles across the Gray Plains.

"That one there, leaning a hand on a merlon—is that him?" Anseth asked.

"What is merlon," Kirik asked.

"The stone . . . between the embrasures there."

A lip curled. "What is embrasures?"

Anseth groaned. "Never mind. Is that him or not?"

The bondsman nodded, his cold demeanor returning so fluidly it seemed to have never left. "That's the chieftain, lord."

"Provincial governor," Anseth corrected. Before Kirik could ask, Anseth added: "What's he doing?"

"Nothing. Frowning."

Dariok shouted at Anseth from afar. "Runt, look. The coward appears. How do I tell him I'm going to shove my spear so far up his shithole he can use it to pick the foodstuffs from his teeth? Never mind, you just tell him. Tell him I said it—runt, are you even listening to me?"

Anseth gave a brusque wave of dismissal, then shouted up at the wall, "I seek no harm upon the populace. You have my word on that. I want only you, Governor."

Lygrest's head made a sudden movement. When Anseth asked, his bondsman said, "He spat."

Dariok was laughing. "Did you tell him what I said? Did you tell that fucking prick?"

"By the gods Dariok, shut up," Anseth muttered. He looked back up and shouted at Lygrest. "I will know, Governor. I will know who turned you."

After that Lygrest withdrew from sight. Anseth remained there, staring up at the empty ramparts. His mare fidgeted and he adjusted his balance and pulled gently the reins to steady her. She was a bit unrulier than his previous mount—that frosty gray roan that Anseth had long favored. That horse could gallop for five miles without pause, and never once protested when he tightened her girth straps or overstuffed her saddlebags. But the poor creature had fallen under a hail of bolts, and Anseth was sent flying off, and by the gods, the way he landed should've left him dead or broken. But no, he'd remained unscathed, yet again. *By whose gods am I allowed to continually cheat death?* he wondered.

Something flew from the parapet, something dark and round—it spun through the air and landed with a dull thud. Dariok whipped his horse in retrieval. A second projectile soared over him, then a third, and that one landed close enough even for Anseth to discern what it was. A severed head.

Dariok came galloping back, clutching one by its dark tangle of hair. "He cut them *out*," he shouted, holding aloft the head to display the eyeless black pits where its eyes had once been. There was no mystery as to the owners of these heads—the three Vaskultans that had fallen during that frantic escape from the city.

"He cut them out," Dariok kept shouting. *"He cut them out!"* The act itself was despicable, of course, but to the Vaskultans, it was also an unforgivable offense. A spirit without eyes couldn't navigate his way up through the sky, and instead was left to wander eternally the Great Void. *I see you've done your homework, Lygrest, you scoundrel.*

Dariok reined up before Anseth. "You tell that pissant I'm going to gut him for that. Tell him I'm going to rip out his liver with my *goddamn teeth!*" He turned to address the serried ranks of light cavalry. Blood roused, they pounded their fists to their chests and struck the butts of their spears upon the earth.

Anseth glared at him. "Your father has granted me supreme command of this campaign. Did you forget? *Stand DOWN.*"

Dariok's puffy eyes were red with anger. "These men serve Vaskultan lords only."

"I have spent the last eight summers eating, fighting, and shitting with these men. I am of no different from any of them."

"You will *NEVER* be one of us."

"And what does it say of you," Severak cut in, astride a bay mare, "when the chieftain chooses an Anirian to lead his campaign over his very own son?"

Dariok gnashed his teeth. He couldn't seem to find a reply. Severak of course had that certain way of shutting him up, thank the gods, but even still, Dariok wasn't about to stem the fires in his men. Anseth watched him for a time, then went off shaking his head.

"He plans to cut the surrounding trees and build a battering ram," Severak told him, soon after.

Anseth scoffed at that. Dariok had neither knowledge nor experience in this matter, in fact no Vaskultan did. They were nomads, after all. And those walls were constructed to withstand the most powerful of siege weaponry, certainly beyond whatever subpar contraption Dariok might offer. "Lygrest may stand besieged," Anseth explained, "but the wretch is far from worried. And why should he be? He knows he's safe from the missiles of a mangonel or trebuchet, just as he knows no corps of sappers will seek to undermine him from below. And by all means, he is right."

Both men were silent upon hearing that. Anseth shaded his eyes to glance back at Dariok. The sun was fierce today, the spring air muggy and thick. The men had long shed their heavy overcoats and furs and felts, in favor of lighter garb to match the warm spring clime. Still, their leather armor wasn't providing much relief.

"I can't stop him," Anseth said. "But perhaps it's best that I don't." He studied the western tower. "I remember . . . it was some years ago, but I remember my father commissioning stoneworkers to repair the erosion of loess behind the sally port. The earth is likely weak there. If we deepen the channel that feeds the moat, we'll flood the city."

Severak's hard, hawkish face looked bewildered. "How can we do that?"

"We'll dig. We must be quiet and we must be patient—a little each night, just enough to remain unnoticed. Dariok's construction will serve as an ideal guise. I'll send riders to secure spades and mattocks from the outlying villages. Don't look so glum, Severak, it'll work. Trust me."

Time moved quickly through the subsequent weeks. By night Anseth was a drudge, by day he blocked out the light of his yurt in a vain attempt to rest. He always rose an hour before dusk and left the encampment to check on Dariok's progress, but today Dariok wasn't there. He returned to his yurt and found Severak waiting for him. The general looked in low spirits. "Dariok's taken ill this morning. The shaman said it's an imbalance of land over sky, likely borne of something ingested. Dariok is claiming poison. He accuses you, lord. He ordered me to send a rider north to apprise his father of your treachery."

Anseth said, "Make sure that doesn't happen. Did you question his bondsman?"

Severak nodded. "He filled Dariok's skin from a stream near the worksite. There were stoneflies about. The water was pure."

"Show me."

The stream was clear as quartz, but that of course meant nothing of its quality. Anseth treaded the widening banks through groves of aspen and white birch, upward across floodplains rich with flowers. A bull elk browsing the outskirts of a lake raised its massive head, a frond of pondweed clinging to its antlers. All around him woodcocks buzzed their nasally buzz, kingfishers flashed across the water, and woodpeckers drummed away on lifeless bark.

He came to a small village nestled against the riverbank. Flatboats and reed rafts stood moored and abandoned, tools lay discarded and grain baskets sat overturned. The village millstone was vacant, the powering waterwheel beneath it unmoving and silent. Around the wooden support beams bobbed something plump and white. Anseth leaned over a wooden rail to get a better look. It was a corpse. He saw others, farther down, scores of dead bodies, facedown in the waterways

—corpses large and small, defiled by scavenging invertebrates beneath the water's surface. Anseth waited for Severak to join him. Then he said, "There's your poison."

Severak made a tight-lipped frown. "This is Dariok's doing. He sent a picked force on secret raids to all the surrounding villages. He intended to pile all the bodies in the moat so his men could pass over it, but most villages were abandoned, so he gave up."

"Well, they surely got their revenge." Anseth shook his head and sighed. "That goddamn wretch. Come on."

Anseth returned to the encampment and headed straight for Dariok's yurt. A pair of guardsmen stood there, giants chatting with a young Vaskultan woman who was taking a break from her milking duties. One moved in protest but Anseth shoved his way through. Inside was dim and smelled of animal blood and the earthly smell of mugwort. The shaman rose; he was a small man, tiny for a Vaskultan, certainly one of the few that had to look up to meet Anseth's eyes. Beneath him, lying in a heap of ragged wools, wan and glistening with sweat, was Dariok. "I don't want you here." His voice was hoarse and weak. He berated his guards, then ordered them to seize the intruder, but they did nothing.

"You truly believe I poisoned you?" Anseth said. "You are a fool."

Dariok narrowed his puffy eyes. "You meant to stop me from continuing my work."

Anseth threw the skin at him. Water splashed, drunk by the wools. "You stupid oaf—the bodies of the villagers you butchered were in that stream. Are you a goddamn idiot? You *drank* from those waters. That's what made you sick, you wretch." Anseth shook his head and stormed out.

Kirik and Severak were waiting outside. "Goddamn him," Anseth muttered. Then to Severak he said, "Make sure the men continue on the ram. If not, Lygrest will grow suspicious." Severak bowed and went off.

Kirik raised a hand to scratch his half-torn ear. "If only his oath was honored . . . after the loss at White Throat Hills . . ."

"I'm aware, Kirik. I'm aware that I allowed him to live—you don't have to bring it up at every opportunity. I made a grave mistake, I see that, I should've allowed him to honor his oath by taking his own life. The gods know even his own goddamn father wanted him to."

CHAPTER THIRTY-EIGHT

Dawn was a beautiful canvas of pale gold and vermillion, sure to humble even the most supercilious of artists.

Seric Dyre watched the lone envoy gallop into it, wine urn fastened to the cantle of his horse. *The last dawn he'll ever see, and I've not the heart to tell him.* It was a wretched thing to do, but had he been forthcoming about the contents of that urn, he'd had no envoy to deliver it. *I'll seek your forgiveness in the next life,* Seric thought.

He rejoined the rank-and-file along the open plateau. What he saw here displeased him. Men bone-tired and weary, their faces heavy with grief or dread or both. Such was expected of conscripts and auxiliaries and greenhorns, but never of the veteran regiments and its officers. These men knew well the moil and ruck of battle—despair and doubt should be far from their faces.

He summoned his military council and led the officers through a path of bracken and other ferns, halting somewhere beneath the cool umbrage of larch and ash. Birds chirruped at their approach; a pair of young foxes ceased their gekkering and scampered off. A yellow and black striped butterfly fluttered by an officer. He looked ready to make a grab at it, but changed his mind at the last moment.

"By the faces I see before me," Seric began, "one might think *we* are trapped in that pass. You should be ashamed, all of you. You are supposed to inspire the lesser ranks, to show strength when strength is needed. But all you are doing is allowing a single man to turn my army into a flock of sheep. I cannot lead sheep to victory."

"You cannot lead us at all, it seems," said a voice—Nederion's, of course.

Seric turned to scold him, but the expressions of his other officers gave him pause. *They all think the same.* "I will prove my worth soon enough."

"How? You cannot stand against the Mad Wolf," Nederion said. "No one can."

Seric clenched a fist. He wanted to strike that craven general's face.

"The Mad Wolf is only a *man*," Pentagath boomed. "And a man can be killed like any other." He paused to hawk and spit a wad of phlegm. "If you make him into something more, he will become something more."

Seric nodded at that. "Pentagath speaks true." He looked down for a moment, collecting his thoughts. "Listen, I'm not here to gloss over defeats with glib speeches or meaningless rhetoric. But you must know that even the greatest minds of our age have made mistakes in their day. Emperor Thalastor's Imperial Advisor was immortalized as the greatest strategist of the Anir, but even he had his share of defeats. Now I do not dare compare my meager talent to a man of such remarkable merit, but I will say this: fight for me today, fight with your hearts bared, and this time, I guarantee victory. It's that easy. Will you fight?"

"We will fight, my lord," the officers replied. He made them repeat it, again until he was satisfied. Then he said, "Good, now no more talk of this Mad Wolf. The next soldier who whispers that name will lose his head. Now get out of my sight, all of you. Pentagath, a moment, if you will."

The officers departed, leaving the hulking general before him, his eyes dead and cold, his flat, porcine nose flaring.

Seric rubbed the scar beneath his neckerchief. "I need you at the van. I'm entrusting you *not* to let your heart give in to imprudence. You must fall back and draw the enemy after you. When the signal bomb bursts in the sky, the detachments will move upon their flanks. That is precisely the moment you turn and attack. Too soon and the Zhouls will see the deceit—too late, and we risk a true rout. Understood, General?"

The general nodded. "I'll not fail this time."

"Good. And make sure you take the Mad Wolf alive." He could tell Pentagath didn't like that much, but he didn't care. In truth, Seric had grown to admire this general they called the Mad Wolf. He would do well to have such a man under his own banner—or better yet, to have him as his personal guard, like Demien Mordall to the boy emperor. "Take the king's head if you wish, but leave the Mad Wolf for me. Understood? Now let us see how they liked our offering, shall we?"

The two men led a small host to the mouth of the pass. The Zhoulish king spotted their advance and signaled his foremost division to retire a bowshot. He was an old man, compact and muscular, with thick arms and squat legs and the olive-complected skin so common of the Zhoul people. Aside from some fisher trimmings, the king's battle-dress was no different from that of his guardsmen and generals: brown military tunics beneath lamellar cuirasses lacquered in dark olive, with spiked helmets and curved nasals and embossed cheekguards, all expertly forged by Zhoulish metalsmiths.

One figure in his retinue stood out. He was towering in height—a titan's frame—with a dour, unsmiling face that seemed carved of stone. He was carrying a crescent halberd that looked like it could sever a man at the waist. Seric pointed him out to Pentagath. "The tall one, to the king's left. Is that him, is that the Mad Wolf?"

Pentagath said yes.

Seric's eyes returned to the king, who had now brought forward both the tainted urn and the poor envoy who'd delivered it. The man was on his knees, hands bound at the wrists, eyes left to stare at Seric, at his lord who sent him off knowing this would be the result. It was an odd stare—neither cold nor angry—but one of genuine disbelief.

The king lifted the urn and smashed it over the envoy's head. Ceramic shattered and urine gushed out, matting the man's hair to his drenched face. Then someone handed the king a long, ornamented battleaxe. He tested its weight for a moment or two, before standing behind the envoy. The axehead came up—into the glare of the rising sun—and down. There was a terrible *crack;* the head split open, not clean but crushing.

The envoy flopped forward, legs quivering, arms flailing. One hand even managed to wander to his split skull, as if to somehow attempt to remove the axehead that was lodged there. The king raised a boot and shoved the envoy to the ground, then stepped on his back and wrenched free the blade. Blood and brain and bits of skull and all matter of gore poured out, staining the lovely spring grasses.

Seric had witnessed his share of beheadings, but never a head split vertically—and with such force as to make it burst like a winter melon. It was awful, and yet it was expected. These men were Zhouls, after all. "You do not care for our courtesies?" Seric asked in the Zhoulish tongue. "Perhaps the wine did not suit your palate?"

The king smiled a cruel smile. "I was eager to meet this Zhoul who mingles with Anirian vermin, but now that I have, I must say I am rather disappointed. I see no Zhoul but a mere mongrel, as ugly and impure as all the others of your stamp. You should be fortunate to have lived with Zhoulish blood in your heart."

"And you, for having Anirian piss in yours."

He scowled at that, his eyes narrowing venomously. "I will carve out your beating heart and force it down your throat, that I promise."

Pentagath twitched furiously to Seric's right. The general undoubtedly understood nothing of this exchange, but his fighting spirit was roused nonetheless. "Stay yourself," Seric murmured to him, before turning back to the king and speaking in Zhoulish. "First you drink my piss and now you long for my heart? By the gods, you think too much of me."

"You disrespectful little cockroach." He looked like he wanted to charge forward alone. "You are insulting King Balinor the Destroyer, Blood of the Mountain and last of the Fireborn."

"The Destroyer?" Seric questioned, "I prefer Balinor the Piss Guzzler. Yes, much better."

Rage twisted the king's features. Veins swelled on his forehead, eyes bulged, teeth gnashed. Heavy breaths escaped his lungs. The wolf general wisely put a hand on his king's shoulder to stay him, but only received a hard shove for his efforts. The king shot Seric one final glare, spun, and headed back to his line. Seric signaled his host to do the same.

Pentagath took the van and Seric made his way through parted pennants to join the midranks. For a time the two armies stood facing each other, waiting, waiting, waiting. The tenseness grew thicker and thicker until it became an icy claw that threatened to dull a man's mettle and leave him ultimately wondering: why am I here, and what purpose does all this serve?

The drums shattered all thought like glass.

BOOM, boom, bo-BOOM. BOOM, boom, bo-BOOM. It sounded like a gigantic beast stomping across the earth. *BOOM, boom, bo-BOOM. BOOM, boom, bo-BOOM.* Each drum was so large it required two men to handle: one to strap it to his back, the other to pound it. And under that relentless pounding, the ranks advanced. Banners waved and pennants fluttered. The ground trembled. Seric heard armor clanging and soldiers shouting, many just to assuage their nerves. Heavy feet churned up a gigantic wall of dust. The forward army moved as a single, hulking behemoth, ready to heave itself at the enemy with all its might.

And heave itself it did, for when the armies finally collided, the earth quaked and thundered as though fracturing at their feet. The drums were washed away by a great downdraft of violence, a sinkhole-spawning maelstrom that threatened to devour anything in its whirling path. Chaos and discordance ruled now: the crack of crashing bodies at breakneck speed, the ceaseless tang of steel against steel, the shouting and the wailing and the breaking of metal and bone.

The Anirian advance pushed forward, fifteen men abreast in the mouth of the pass, bottlenecked by ridge and rock. The Zhoulish infantrymen pushed forward as well, wielding sabers and clutching heavy iron shields, like a chain-linked armada easing out of a harbor. And just as the Anirian lines felt their sting and began to falter, Pentagath ordered the retreat. Soldiers spilled out of the mouth, rank after rank. The Zhouls raced after them. Men were knocked to the ground and trampled. The king stood at the fore, shouting soundless words — kill them all, most likely, kill them all and bring the mongrel to me. Seric bit his lip so hard he drew blood. He glanced to the eastern rise; the squadron stood ready. He gave the signal.

A guidon rose into the sky, red as blood, waving back and forth. The squad sprang into action, working their metal brands against the fuse of the signal rockets. But moments passed and nothing came of it. Something was wrong. "Light it!" Seric shouted. One soldier was shouting that he couldn't; the other kept shrugging. Back at the battle, the Zhouls were closing in—time was running out.

"Light it, you goddamn wretch!" Seric shouted. But the first fool only dropped his metal brand, and the other was shaking so much he could barely hold his. The first one tried to grab his partner's, but it too fell and went sliding down the rise. Both men raced for it, only to collide into each other. *NO, NO, NO, you worthless imbeciles.* The Zhoulish advance neared the edge of the flanks.

Seric broke from his line and rushed to the hill, shoving both fools aside and using his own tinder fungus to try for a spark. *Come on, come on.* He scraped and scraped and scraped—a hundred times, no a thousand, until finally he got one. He held it to the fuse. It caught. Seric dashed back to his line. About halfway he heard the rocket scream into the air, pause, then burst like a clap of thunder.

Anirian bowmen appeared along the outer flanks of the pass. Their arrows filled the sky like sharks in a frenzy, soaring down upon the exposed Zhouls, who immediately dug-in to defend. Then, under Pentagath's command, the forward army turned and charged. Seric drove the midrankers forward. He shouted at the men, shouted at them to tighten the formation and charge as one, but then a horde of Zhoulish cavalrymen appeared at his flank, and suddenly he was afraid for his life. The steel fangs of set lancers screamed past, some colliding with Anirian steel. Foemen toppled from their horses. One crashed into Seric, dropping him to the ground and leaving his left arm pinned under heavy lamellar plates. He gasped for air but inhaled only dust. His fingers clawed the earth but he couldn't pull himself free. Then a rankmate shoved the foeman off, lifting Seric to his feet. But before Seric could see his savior's face, a Zhoulish sword cut off half of it.

Rampant chaos now. Men were everywhere, stabbing everything. Sunburst tore open a Zhoul from lip to ear, leaving his cheek-skin to dangle like the tentacle of an octopus. Seric turned to find his next attacker. A Zhoul in heavy plates shouldered him to his knees. Seric couldn't breathe—he scrabbled for a way out. There was only dust, every which way.

He followed a crawling man, until a host of heavy cavalry trampled the poor bastard and left him broken and wailing. A wounded Zhoul lying nearby hurled a dagger at Seric, but when it missed he gave a shrug as though he were jesting, so Seric just left him there. A few more feet and more men tumbled in his path, kicking up dirt and debris that left Seric half blind and retching. When his vision began to clear he spotted a foeman searching for something on the ground. *What on earth is he looking for?* Whatever it was he never found it, as a spear smashed through his back, impaling him like a stuck mantid.

Seric found his way out by following the cracks of light in the dust cloud. *Where am I? Where the hell am I?* Before him, a contingent of friendly bowmen was breaking under a Zhoulish horse-charge. The Anirian general turned to flee—it was that coward himself, Nederion. Seric stormed after him—he didn't know why, but he did. Time slowed to a crawl. An hour had passed before he came upon the general, another two before their eyes locked. Seric watched as the coward's expression changed from unbridled fear to the glorious relief of seeing an ally. Then Sunburst came screaming for his throat.

Nederion jerked back. The blade cut through the clavicle and down into the sternum, biting through scale and flesh and tendon and bone. The general's mouth opened but no sound came out. Seric's next attack went right through his head. The general's body collapsed in a heap of gore, his officer's cloak draped over him like the shroud of ashes.

The bowmen didn't know how to react. Seric made it simple for them: he pointed his bloody weapon at their cowardly faces and told them to turn and wedge—and turn and wedge they did. Swords and sabers stormed at the Zhouls with renewed vigor. King Balinor himself appeared not ten paces away. When he saw Seric, he licked his blood-stained teeth and came forward. His great battleaxe thundered at Seric's head, narrowly missing. A cloud of dust blinded Seric. The steel axehead came barreling through, thrumming just past his ear, the haft crashing down upon his spaulder, hard, so hard it put the king off balance—and before he could adjust, Sunburst drove itself deep into his belly. The man groaned; the axe fell from his hands, but he refused to fall with it. Instead he grabbed Seric's fist, which still held Sunburst's hilt. Seric couldn't pull free; the king was too goddamn strong. With his free hand Seric reached down to snatch the haft of the fallen axe. It was useless to wield at such close range so he worked his hand to grip just below the curved head, and with one hand drove its steel point through the king's eye. The organ burst and he staggered and dropped, dead at Seric's feet.

When the Zhouls saw their fallen king they began to falter. Many regrouped with the Mad Wolf, who was engaged in a clash against General Pentagath, the latter looking tired and outmatched yet unwilling to give up. Each strike and consecutive counterstrike sent Pentagath farther off his footing. General Wyath appeared, but even the two men together couldn't overwhelm the Mad Wolf. Then Seric tossed the head of the slain king at his feet.

The sight of it sapped every ounce of fight in the Zhoul. A blow from the back of Pentagath's axe thundered against his cuirass; a second dropped him to his knees. A thwack of the heavy ash butt knocked helm and undercap from his head, exposing the Zhoul's shaved head. Pentagath lifted the axe, hands sliding down the haft, intent to bring it down upon the fallen enemy's neck.

Seric screamed at him to stop. The axe just grazed the Mad Wolf before plunging to the ground beside him. Pentagath stood there to breathe for a moment, then threw his head back and roared a thunderous roar—of anger and frustration and whatever else a man felt after killing other men with a giant axe. The Mad Wolf lay nearby, unmoving except for his eyes. Wyath held his blade at the Zhoul's throat. No one said a word.

A handful of Anirian guardsmen stood at Seric's side. He never heard them approach. "Send word to the Hollow," he told them. "To Tavarin, as well." They went off. Above, rays of sunlight were clawing through the dust, like the talons of some supernal creature. Seric had almost forgotten about the daylight. Seeing it now was like surfacing from an undertow, or pulling one's self from a mass grave. All around him, Zhouls were throwing down their weapons. It was so quick, like wildfire. Soon, the clangor of steel was replaced by the sweet, triumphant shouts of victory. And then, at last, Seric heard it—the paean of victory.

CHAPTER THIRTY-NINE

The change at the brothel was like the sudden wakening from a night terror. The ruffians and miscreants and cutpurses all melted away like hoarfrost in summertime, and evenings now were filled with upstanding patrons with courteous tongues and coin to spare. Fresh faces continued to arrive daily, each appearing wealthier than the last.

Demien Mordall observed it all from the window of his private, second-story suite. The late day sun was descending, yet the streetscape below remained teeming with all manner of merchants and fishmongers and drapers and diviners and porters. A surveyor offered a prospective investor broad promises of quick growth, while the master builder at his side gave details of just how it would be done. A neighboring silversmith waved a pair of tin snips to guide the unloading of his new equipment. It was amazing to witness such a bloom of commerce—and even more amazing to know that a simple farmhand from a simple village was the hero behind it all.

Demien was no hero, no more than he was a farmhand, but the locals had deemed him otherwise, and even now, weeks later, he would still receive the occasional gift, usually a brocade robe or bolt of satin or some fancy ornament made by some fancy artisan. Most were pleasing enough, but trinkets and baubles interested him none, so he kept them in a stockpile in the adjacent room, behind a screen where the boy slept. Silas was there now, playing a small pelletdrum, a gift by some elderly woman some days ago. He seemed to favor the annoying thing over his old currycomb and resin goat figurine.

The proprietor's name was Toben. He could still be a prick at times, but as business improved so did his temperament, and to Demien he was nothing less than magnanimous, providing a furnished suite and free fare and a generous wage to do whatever it was that Demien did around here. Demien did nothing, in truth, except deny wealthy men who offered huge sums of coin in exchange for some shady service, or turn down hopeful fathers who offered their daughters' hands. And every few days, a gaggle of young boys came begging for a lesson in arms, only to leave disappointed.

Not all visitors were denied, however. Demien had a weakness for the truly unfortunate, the insolvent and downtrodden and half-starved folks who'd come to him with slumped shoulders and lowered eyes. Demien would fill their purses and reclaim their properties and once he reunited a parent whose child had been sold into slavery. On rare occasions, he'd pay a visit to the corrupt moneylenders. Usually, his presence alone was enough to persuade the wretches to renounce their usurious ways, but for the stubborn types, well, Demien wasn't a cruel man, but sometimes cruelty was needed to straighten the crooked.

And yet, no matter how many unfortunate faces he brightened, Demien had remained somber. He was always in his cups, drinking and drinking until he'd forgotten why he began drinking in the first place. Then sobriety would inevitably return, and with it came the anguish of the emperor's death, and so Demien would drink again. A temporary peace was better than none at all.

A voice called from behind the door curtain—Toben's voice. "My friend, there's a lady here for you. She wishes a word."

Demien sighed before answering. "The hour grows late, tell her tomorrow."

Silence for a moment, then the reply came as a woman's voice, gentle and polite. "Might I see you now? I beg you."

Demien went over and raised the door curtain. The small proprietor stood beside a willowy young woman wearing a black satin blouse and ivory skirt, simple of cut yet a fine complement to her pale skin. Her face was angular and smooth, her eyes green as emerald raindrops. Her chestnut hair was tied in a perfect chignon, not a single strand out of place. Her hands were small and pale. "My heart is glad to look upon the hero's face," she said.

"You are kind," Demien replied, then gestured her inside, adding, "my lady."

She went in. Toben watched her go, flashing a lecherous smile. Demien replied to that by lowering the curtain in his face.

The woman made herself comfortable on a nearby armchair. "I have heard much about you," she said, smoothing her skirts. "The Hero of Seven Lakes."

"I'm no hero," he said.

"No man has ever done what you did to the Black Tusk." She spoke with civility and confidence, the voice of a woman who was used to getting what she wants. "I am told your given name is Ryden, is that correct?"

Demien nodded. Ryden was his father's name. The man was a criminal indicted by the magistrate and exiled when Demien was still a child. "And yours, my lady?"

"Lelana, of House Avelin. My father once served the capital as an imperial inspector, though in his advanced age he can no longer travel. He's retired here in Thornberry. Our name is known—"

Demien cut her off. "What is it that you require of me, my lady?"

She paused at his abruptness, then smiled at him, a smile that fit well with her petite nose and cheerful eyes. "I am an artisan," she told him. "A creator of ritual vessels and pottery. My wares fetch a high price in Indigo Cove, but traveling to the city has become dangerous with all the highwaymen. I need a worthy man to lead my escort. All provisions will be provided—weapons, tack, horses, anything you need. Payment stands as half up front, the rest after we return. Two hundred ounces of gold is a rather fair offer, is it not?"

Demien realized what it was about her that he was so drawn to: she reminded him of Alana, his late wife. It wasn't so much in any particular feature, but in her mannerisms as a whole—the graceful movement of her hands when she spoke, the way she pursed her lips, the enthusiasm in her eyes when she smiled. "There are plenty of buyers here," he told her.

She frowned at that. "I employ certain compositions . . . techniques passed down from various cultures. Angled brushes to paint the vessels' insides, which illuminates the porcelain under lamplight. Forgive me my bluntness, but the buyers here are ignorant of such talent. My clients reside in Indigo Cove."

Demien thought about it for a moment. "The southern road is heavily patrolled and dotted by imperial checkpoints. It's not quick, but it will provide safe passage around Wintersun."

"You don't understand," she said. "The springtime festival begins on the new moon. I've no time to delay—the swiftest route is what I must take."

Demien frowned. "It's too dangerous, my lady."

"That's why I need you. Any man who did what you did to the Black Tusk can certainly protect against outlaws."

"The outlaws of Wintersun are not some ragtag group of rogues. These men are hardened killers and military defectors, soulless brutes who will not hesitate to rape and ransom a pretty lady like you."

She seemed to blush, as if all she absorbed from that was the compliment he'd paid her. Then she said, "Three hundred—three hundred ounces, and not a single coin more."

"It's not about the money," he said. *You don't get it, woman. Once I was the Grand Commandant of the Anir, the head military commander of the whole empire. I had more coin than I could count, lorded over more fiefdoms than I'd ever care to visit.* But no, that was in the past now. What was he now? A simple farmhand. And no simple farmhand would ever reject the generosity of such a woman. Demien gave a long sigh. "Who else stands in your entourage?"

"My brother and a dozen hired swords."

"Are these hired swords of any worth?"

She nodded. "The best of this city, the best I could find, that is."

"The best of this city may not be enough," Demien said.

"With you it will be," she said.

Silas emerged from the side room, barefoot and rubbing the sleep from his eyes. When he spotted the lady he fled back into the room, his little eyes peeking out. "Is that your boy?" she asked. "The proprietor didn't mention . . . forgive me, my thoughtless words. I hadn't considered your loved ones."

Demien shook his head. "He's all I have. His mother died years ago. She was young . . . like you."

She heard that and smiled a small somber smile. "Not so young as I look. Twenty-seven springs and still I remain unwedded. My father has arranged many suitors, but I refused them all time and time again."

"Why?"

"I don't know," she replied. "I've always longed for a different sort, not a man of wealth, but one of strength, both in character and principle. I don't know why I'm telling you this." The armchair creaked when she leaned back. "What about you, do you want another son?"

"I did . . . once, but Ala—my wife—she was already weakened from her first. But the boy, he's a mute . . . and a puny little squib at that. I thought him unlovable. So I pushed for another. It was a selfish act, making her grow with another child just to satisfy my right to a proper heir." Demien shook his head. "He died the day he saw the world, and she a week after that. I don't know why I'm telling you this either."

That made her smile once more, this time with genuine compassion. "Forgive my candor, but a man such as you . . . were you to escort me safely perhaps I'd not reject your hand like I did the others."

He laughed at that. "I am but a crude rustic, you a woman of wealth

. . . what could you hope to gain from such a union? Besides, your father would never approve."

"It's not his choice," she said. "And you are not so crude as you say. There's intellect in you, I can hear it in your voice. You're a hero to these people, you know. The people sing of Ryden of Seven Lakes, the Queller of the Black Tusk. Please, serve as my escort to Indigo Cove."

"Toben needs me here."

"Toben already gave his consent."

Demien frowned at that. *How easily that man is bought,* he thought. *If he is so quick to be rid of me, maybe I should go.*

She rose. "Think on it," she said. "I'll return tomorrow at dusk. I'll have your answer then."

When she was gone, Demien went off in search of the proprietor. He found him in his counting room, abacus in hand, ledgers and books of account flung open, inkwell and brushpens scattered beneath the glow of an old oil lamp. At Demien's approach he pointed his stump to the sack of coin on the table. "Extra there," he said absently.

Demien loomed over him. "How much did she pay you?"

Toben stopped what he was doing and tilted his head up a bit. "Who?"

"Lady Lelana—how much coin did she use to grease your palm?"

He used his stump to rub his forehead. "I don't understand you—"

"How *MUCH.*"

Slowly, the proprietor placed his writing pen back onto its holder. "You single-handedly saved my establishment and turned this entire district into a pearl of commerce. You have coin in your purse, gifts in your room, the veneration of honest folk and a reputation that soars higher each day. You have more than any farmhand could ever dream to have, and yet you are that same miserable drunkard who first dragged himself in here. Why is that, my friend?"

Demien lowered his eyes; he didn't know how to answer.

At length Toben sighed and went back to his books. "There was no coin. I thought the lady might stir some fire in your lifeless heart."

Demien turned and left.

The next evening, when the lady returned, she and Demien shared a few rounds of wine together, and, instead of discussing her earlier proposition, they bedded each other. It was dark and she was drunk, but even still, Demien found her to be a passionate lover, gentle of touch and kind of spirit. And afterward, as she clung to him in the dim silence, he realized then that the decision had already been made. He cared too much to let her go to Indigo Cove without him.

CHAPTER FORTY

Miriana Athera stood in her husband's sickchamber, her eyes fixed on the motionless figure on the featherbed.

Master Lorian no longer tended Zantherei on a daily basis, and had since relegated the host of mundane and rather unpleasant duties to a trusted colleague. This colleague was a short, sluggish man who seemed more the reclusive, curmudgeonly type—until she asked him a question and his face brightened and his mouth never closed. By the time she managed to see him out, she'd learned the far-too-many details of what must be done in order to keep her husband's body from atrophying. Funny though, the moment the doors groaned closed and left her with the clatter of the rain and the howl of the outside wind, she *almost* longed for the little man's jabber.

Miriana moved bedside to look upon her husband's face. It was difficult seeing him this way—the once mighty Regent Zantherei Athera, Lord of the Hollow and Storm of the North. Gone were his hulking shoulders and tree-thick neck, the same of his fiercely set eyes and powerful hands. What was left was a shriveled thing, sallow of cheek and skeletal of frame—a corpse waiting to be interred.

He had lived in another time. A time before the emperor of the Anir was murdered, a time before Miriana became known as Empress Miriana. She used to tell herself that even without Zantherei's help, she would've forged her own path to nobility, but even she had not the arrogance to believe that. No, in her secret heart she would always know the truth: her rise out of the muck of mediocrity was caused by one man and one man alone, and that man was Zantherei Athera.

And this is how I repay him.

She looked down, her fingers fishing inside her gown, grasping the phial from inside a small pouch. *It's a mercy, not a murder.* She never did love him. She never thought of their marriage as anything more than a catalyst to further her own ambitions. And now, he was needed no more, and now her faith lay elsewhere. Seric Dyre had subjugated the Zhouls and restored the alliance with Silverleaf. He'd honored his word; now she must honor hers.

The wind howled outside; lightning flashed and thunder rolled. Her hand tightened around the phial. *You've done this before, Mir. You're strong and you've killed before. You were still a girl when you handed that wretched pander of yours a flagonful of poison. He deserved to die, just as the others deserved to die. The Minister of Finance died for knowing too much, the emperor's little consort died for what she might carry into the realm. You've done worse, Mir, you know that. You had Minister Sydrian beheaded—a man you once admired, and one of the very few to treat you as something more than a lowborn whore. But he was also a traitor, and so he was given a traitor's end. He and his entire clan . . . dozens of innocent faces, all dead by your command.*

She touched Zantherei's hand. *And now you must die as well.* Another flash of lightning, followed by a clap of thunder. It was strangely propitious, her husband's fall. At the time, their marriage had been hanging by a thread, him desiring a son that his wife couldn't bear. Still, she knew she would've done anything to remain in the palace. She'd known it then and she knew it now.

The wooden bung popped off, the liquid inside odorless. The wind pounded on the shutters—so loud it seemed as if a great monster was fighting to get inside. Her hands were trembling. *It's a mercy,* she reminded herself. *It's a mercy, a mercy, a mercy.* She parted his lips with her forefinger and thumb. Lightning flashed. *It's a mercy that will allow me to keep my status.* She brought the phial to his lips. *BOOM.* Thunder so loud she dropped the phial. *By the gods, where is it?* There, there on his chest. She reached for it. Another flash—so bright it illuminated her husband's face . . .

He was looking at her.

Miriana shrieked. A peal of thunder stole her voice. Her husband's hand began to twitch; the phial rolled off the featherbed. She lunged for it, banging her head on something hard, the bedpost, most likely. Pain seized her. The room spun. Her balance left her, there was a heavy *thump,* and everything went dark.

She was vaguely aware of the door opening. Footfalls swept inside, louder and louder until they were all around her, but it was only a single, wrinkled old face that greeted her. Master Lorian's face. He was framed in a glow of lamplight, small eyes squinting, face twitching like a whiskered mouse. Such an odd face—and one that looked even odder when viewed upside-down. *What is he saying?* He was asking her questions, idiotic ones, if she knew where she was, if she knew her own name. She went to get up and he bade her not to, but she was the empress so she did anyway. Lesser physicians stood huddled around the featherbed, a few spouting nonsense, stupid things, about the auspicious storm and the recent shift of the charts of the heavens. Between their robed outlines she glimpsed her husband's eyes—they were closed, she saw, and sighed with relief.

Miriana's eyes then searched the floor for the phial. When she found it she feigned dizziness and bent down to snatch it, and when she stood back up dizziness *did* take her this time. Lorian swooped down to her aid. "I need to get out of here," she told him, but when the old fool told her to remain still instead, she called for Vileron.

She could tell the captain's approach by the stiff shuffle of his gait.

"To my apartments at once," she commanded. Next she knew she was off the ground, feeling the breeze on her face, listening to Vileron's long, heavy strides, and the tiny steps of the trailing physician.

Inside her apartments, she was placed gently on her featherbed. Yana came in and gasped but Miriana told her not to fret. Then Master Lorian sent the poor girl off to heat some water, while he himself began working on a nearby nightstand, clinking bowl and stirrer and mortar and pestle, mixing this and that. When he was done, his offering was earth-brown and steaming. "Here, drink it quickly."

It tasted like something pulled from an ordure pit. "What is this? It's awful. And what did you rub on my head, it *smells*."

Master Lorian took the bowl from her. "A tonic to ease your pains. Angelica, ginseng, a touch of licorice root and a mix of—"

Miriana cut him off. "He looked at me. I *saw* his eyes."

Lorian gave no reply.

"He saw me—he saw me I tell you."

He looked at her as though she were a frightened child, and when he spoke, his voice was irritatingly calm. "His eyes may have opened, but I assure you they saw nothing. It will take some time before his vision returns, if ever. Even if by some miracle restoration has occurred, it's unlikely he'll remember much. It takes time . . . nothing like the famous tales of Quren the Awoken from the annals. A man cannot rise from so deep a sleep to even think clearly, not to mention immediately take up arms. And rarely does an awoken man ever retain the same vigor he once had. Excuse me a moment, Your Majesty. Yes, what is it?"

She looked up and saw Minister Thomen inside the chamber. She hadn't heard the door open. Lorian tried to send the minister away, but she stopped that and had Thomen approach.

The portly man's long ministerial robes trailed in gray ripples behind him. From a wide, embroidered sleeve, a pale hand emerged, plump fingers clutching a small stack of papers. "Your Majesty, these were confiscated from posts all over the city. They all bear the same words."

"Read it, Minister," she said.

He cleared his throat and began:

Like all the worthy people of the Anir, I mourn the terrible misfortune the realm has suffered this passing year. For the heinous crime of breaking the imperial line, the tyrant Raas Dragath is to blame, but I must implore you not to overlook that deceitful little rat who serves as your Imperial Advisor. Don't be fooled by his glib tongue, Seric Dyre is a traitor at heart. He will kill and usurp until he's taken the throne for himself. Let that scar across his neck serve not as a token of innocence, but as evidence to his treasonous ways. He is unworthy of our praise and our bows. Heed these words, gentle folk of the Anir, heed the words of a humble man who once bore the honors of administrative office. Alone, a single locust is of little merit, but together, a collective swarm can drive off even the largest intruder.

Miriana was silent for a moment. "This is nothing but slander and rot," she said at last. She reread the letter, as if unbelieving of its words, then she looked up at Thomen. "Cast a dragnet over the city, send riders to every checkpoint, request word from every watcher and informant. Since my privy counselor is on campaign I must lean on you to uncover this traitor, Minister." The man nodded, jowls jiggling, and hurried off. Next she had Yana fetch her inkwell and pen and paper, and sitting up she wrote as swiftly as the words came to her, and when she was done and the letter sealed she handed it to Vileron and said, "To Silverleaf at once. For our Imperial Advisor's eyes only."

CHAPTER FORTY-ONE

It was late in the evening when Seric found him.

He'd spent the entire day organizing the surrendered Zhouls and segregating those of appropriate age, then he scrutinized each face, one after another, hundreds of them, until the next looked no different from the last. And as dusk descended upon the encampment, Seric had grown too tired to continue. And yet, just as he was about to give the order to disperse, he found him.

His father wasn't nearly as large as remembered, which was expected, but what Seric didn't expect was how *old* the man looked. Wrinkles pulled and tugged at his face, leaving pockets of skin to hang like untreated leather. From the nostrils of his bulbous nose, thick curls of hair reached out, thicker than what was left on his balding head. And lower, both chest and shoulders were thin and feeble where once they were solid with muscle. At his waist both hands were bound, fingers callused and scarred and discolored by mottled skin. It was a sad sight, in truth. Nothing about this old man told of the heartless wretch he once was—nothing at all except those cold, cold eyes.

"I brought you here, Dederic," Seric began in the Zhoulish tongue. "To make it plain that you are the one responsible for the subjugation of the Zhouls."

The old man's eyes flickered at that, but he left the bait untouched. "Has old age taken your ears, old man?" Seric said. "Or would you like to know how that is?"

Still he didn't reply, nor did he look at Seric. He just stared ahead. *How unexpected,* Seric thought. He knelt and grabbed the old man's chin, forcing him to meet his glare. "You have no idea who I am, do you." He let go with a firm jerk. There was a long moment of quiet, where the only sound was the charcoal humming in the low braziers. Finally, the Zhoul said, "You're a mongrel." Though hoarse with age, his voice was just as powerful as it was in his younger days.

"Yes, but not just any mongrel. The one you had the privilege of naming."

His father's cold eyes studied Seric, but they didn't seem to show any kind of recognition. He made something of a snort. "I've named many mongrels over the years. Only my Zhoulish sons hold any measure of worth to me."

"And yet it was one of your mongrels that ended up conquering your kind." Seric leaned forward, glowering at his father. "The mongrel you beat until you grew tired, then beat again for making you tired. The mongrel whose flesh you bruised and whose bones you fractured with cudgel and mace. The mongrel you battered so hard he pissed blood for days." His voice was dripping venom. "You will suffer for him and for all the poor mongrels who felt your boot and cudgel."

His father was looking at him with a wry sort of amusement. "A man of my age is no longer moved by pain or death. So have your revenge, but know this, you will always be just another worthless mongrel, birthed by some Anirian cunt I had my way with. There were many, to be sure."

Seric gritted his teeth. Suddenly he was a boy again, powerless and alone. Nothing seemed to matter—neither the years that passed nor the tribulations that forged him into the man he was today. This whole endeavor was fruitless, his existence insignificant. *What did you hope to gain from this?* he asked himself. *You are a stupid, stupid man.*

The Zhoul seemed to enjoy the look on Seric's face. "You've been waiting for this," he concluded with a snort. "You've been waiting for this moment and now I've ruined it. I've ruined it, haven't I?" He laughed that guttural laugh of his.

Sunburst screamed from its sheath. The old Zhoul looked unimpressed by the motion. He spat a wad of phlegm, not in defiance but to prove he wasn't afraid. Then he lowered his head, offering the neck. "Be quick, mongrel. A single strike. Even you can do it with that fancy blade." Seric knew the man was goading him but didn't care. He raised the blade. The child in him yearned to see this old churl's head fall at his feet, to see his blood saturate the earth. *Do it!* the child screamed, over and over. *Do it! DO IT!*

But no, Seric wouldn't give in. He sheathed his weapon.

His father looked up at him and laughed. "You can't be mine. I've fathered no cowards."

"You're wrong. Do you know why? Because you're the biggest coward of all. And when I take the heads of each of your *worthy* Zhoulish sons, you will die knowing that you are the last of your line, and all that will remain of your legacy is the tainted blood of a mongrel bastard."

His face reddened at that. "You goddamn cockroach—I should've killed you long ago." Spittle flew from his lips.

"You tried. By the gods . . . you tried." He called for the guards. "But this mongrel had other plans. Take him."

At dawn, Seric had his father witness each of his trueborn sons face the axe. Thirteen in all, the eldest an imposing man of thirty-six, the youngest a lad of just eight. After it was done, the old Zhoul met his own end without a fuss, and just as his blood was spilled, the rising eastern sun blinded all onlookers with its radiant light. Seric returned to his commander's tent. He took three or four gulps of his winegourd, turned to his guardsmen, wiped his mouth, and said, "Now bring me this Mad Wolf."

The Zhoulish general had to bend to fit through the door. He dwarfed the guardsmen and made Vylas look like half a man. Not only was he tall but he was of fine proportion, legs like the boughs of oaks, hands powerful enough to snap a man's neck like a matchstick. The Zhoul was trussed up with enough cord to hold a bear, and yet, Seric still felt uneasy around him.

A guardsman's blow to the back of the leg brought the giant down to a single knee. Up close, Seric saw a rather homely face, beardless and bald, with protruding lips and sinister, arching eyebrows. He had a condition in his left eye that Seric couldn't ignore—an eyelid that never opened more than halfway. Odd as it was, it didn't detract from his fierceness.

"I admire the loyalty you held for your king," Seric said in the Zhoulish tongue. "Even though it went unrequited."

"He was my king." His soft-spoken voice seemed more fitting of a man of lesser stature—certainly not the voice of a giant whose howls had dulled the mettle of Seric's army.

"That he was. But tell me, does being a king allow one to regard his faithful subjects with such disdain?"

The general looked squarely at him, one eye opened wide, the other halfway. "He was my king."

Now Seric frowned. "A wise vassal chooses a wise king, just as the wise wolf selects the most suitable den."

The Mad Wolf offered no response. Nearby, Vylas was biting his nails, perhaps bored by the unfamiliar speech. Seric turned back to the Zhoul and asked his given name.

"I don't care to tell it, nor do I care to know yours," the general replied. "All that is remains for me is death. Now spare these carry-ings-on and get on with it."

"I think you misunderstand my intentions, General." Seric moved behind him, knelt and used a dagger to cut his bonds. Vylas protested, but Seric ignored that.

The Zhoul rubbed where the cord had chafed him. Then he rose to his full, towering height, casting his uneven glare upon Seric. "Is this some form of mockery, or are you just that much a fool? You *killed* my king." He took a step forward; the guardsmen behind him did as well, hands moving to the sheaths of their weapons.

Seric didn't back down. "I *killed* a small-minded tyrant who raided our peaceful lands. I *killed* a savage whose greed wasn't sated by the wealth of our treasury. I killed a witless and choleric man, and even though he promulgated your laws and dictated your policies, he was by no means a king." The Zhoul hesitated, and Seric went on, overbearing him. "And after I killed him I didn't destroy his lands, I didn't slaughter the old and the weak, I didn't defile the women and I didn't harm the children. And for the Zhoulish soldiers who waved the white, I want only to enlist their services as auxiliaries, to be paid well, fed, clothed, and issued arms. They'll even be afforded time to return to their families."

The Mad Wolf narrowed his arching eyebrows. "And what is it you want of me?"

"To serve as their commanding general—and also as captain of my personal guard. Know this, General, to have you at my side would be a privilege I'd not take for granted. Unlike your king, I do not demand loyalty from my men—I earn it through respect and camaraderie. No suffering in the field is without having been suffered first by me. No soldier grows thirsty while my winegourd remains full. No man grows faint with hunger while I do not. Consider my words, General. No Anirian save the empress herself will ever hold authority over you." Seric went to a knee, bowing his head, completely at the mercy of this huge Zhoul and his huge fists.

"What are you doing?" Vylas hissed. Seric said nothing. For a moment he thought he made a grave error, thought he was going to get pummeled, but then the general bent down to help Seric to his feet. "I am of the Revil clan. My given name is Zirian." He inclined his head slightly. "My king is to be interred in proper accordance to our customs, even if he may not deserve it."

To that Seric agreed.

A week later the army descended the tortuous mountain passes to emerge onto dry flatlands, a swift affair under the navigation of the Zhouls. From there it was a rather uneventful journey back to Silverleaf, and upon return, Governor Tavarin Valayne provided a week-long banquet to honor both the victory and the recovery of his treasury. Seric had never been showered with so many gifts or honored by such beautiful song and poetry, and never had he expected to be appointed such titles as the Tamer of the Zhouls and The Fist of the West. He'd responded to all that by bowing his head and offering simple words of gratitude.

On the fifth day Tavarin fell ill from overindulgence. That night, Perilia came to Seric in his guest quarters. She wasted no time pulling off her silks and offering herself on the featherbed, moaning and moaning while Seric thrust harder and harder inside her. And later, after Perilia's appetite was sated and she'd fallen asleep atop the padded silk coverlet, Seric sat on a nearby armchair, staring into the flames of a nearby brazier. He enjoyed the governess' touch no less than before, but the time away from Miriana was beginning to weigh on his heart. He longed to return to the Hollow. To return home, where he belonged.

An angry rap at the door startled him.

Seric stood at once. Perilia mumbled something in her sleep. A second rap came louder, and this time it brought along a man's irate voice. "*OPEN* the door, Lord Seric."

That roused her at once. "It's my husband," she said.

Seric pointed to the far wall. "Behind the arras, go." The petite woman padded naked across the room. Seric gathered her silks and stuffed them in a trunk at the foot of the bed. Zirian emerged from a side room, weapon in hand and wearing his skirted cuirass. The knock came again. "A moment, if you will," Seric called out. He glanced at the wall, making sure Perilia was out of sight, then he turned and told Zirian to let the governor in.

The overweight Tavarin Valayne lumbered inside, draped in bedclothes that looked humorously small since he was no longer in his slender years. He came to an abrupt stop before the huge Zhoul. "If you don't tell your tree to stand aside, I will have him hanged from a gibbet."

Seric motioned to let him pass. "Governor, the hour is late. What is it you need of me?"

Tavarin went to the bed, yanking aside the curtains and grunting at what he didn't see. He turned back and combed the room with suspicious eyes. "It seems I've misplaced my lovely wife. You don't happen to know where she might be, do you?"

Seric shook his head. "Of course not. Do you want me to organize a search?"

"No, I'll make the arrangements, if necessary." He came to stand before Seric, already drawing heavy breaths. A hand rose up—so quick Seric nearly blenched, but it was just to show a letter. "For the Imperial Advisor's eyes only." He shoved it into Seric's chest, then turned and waddled off. Zirian closed the great doors behind him.

Perilia emerged from the dark, naked and glowering. "It's from *her*, isn't it?"

"You need to go," Seric told her. "You're not safe here."

She ignored that. "She's trying to spoil our tryst." Her hands were planted on her hips, as she made no effort to cover herself from the eyes of the giant Zhoul in the room. And why should she? She was quite a stunning little thing. Seric meant to tell her to cover herself, but by then he'd already broken the seal and opened the letter, so instead he read:

My lord and Imperial Advisor, my heart is glad to learn of the alliance between the provinces and the submission of the Zhouls. But this message is not a simple note to extend my felicitations. There is unrest in the Hollow that demands your immediate presence. A written defamation has sullied your name and left your standing in question. I have already begun to formally address these allegations, but it is imperative that you return at once and quell this groundswell of dissent. Much more, when you return. - Miriana

Behind the lady's missive was the letter of defamation. Reading that, he tore it in two and fed it to the brazier. "I need to return to the capital."

"Loping back like a little lapdog already? How fitting, Seric. You must take me for some kind of fool."

"My reputation has been tarnished," he said. "I have to refute this calumny and restore my position. And you must return to your husband before he puts you to the cord."

"Oh please, the boor is all bluster and blubber. He'd never raise a hand on me and he knows it." She moved closer, her bare breasts bouncing softly with each step. Seric watched but all he could think about was the letter. It was as if someone had stuck a dagger in his chest, and each wasted moment drove it deeper and deeper. *I need to muster the men tomorrow—at dawn, no before dawn,* he thought. *I must not delay.*

"When will you return?"

We'll move double time by day, and continue marching by night. They'll understand. They'll have to understand.

"*WHEN WILL YOU RETURN!*"

Seric stopped. Perilia was frowning at him, her great big eyes filled with both anger and sorrow. "Soon," he assured her.

"When, Seric."

"I said soon." His hand rose to brush absently her hair, his attention drawn to the nearby brazier, where the letter crackled in the flames. *By the gods, how long have I feared this moment?* He always knew his past ties with the Redlands would arise to squash his life of prosperity. But why did it had to happen while he was away and unable to defend himself? *Ever and always my goddamn luck,* he mused.

Perilia was touching his neck, her fingers tracing the jagged flesh of his exposed scar. His neckerchief—he'd taken it off earlier. *Where is it?* There, beside the bed. He went to retrieve it, but she stopped him and reached down his trousers to grab his manhood. It took a moment, but it began to harden. "Do not forget," she told him, giving a firm squeeze. "*This* is the true seal of our alliance."

"I won't," he said.

CHAPTER FORTY-TWO

"South-southwest to the bridge," Eldrith said. "Another hour, maybe less."

Lelana's brother was graced with the same willowy build as her sister, but where her face was petite and comely, his was narrow and squinty like a stoat's. He reminded Demien of an old squad commander, a spear of a man whose tongue was quicker than his bowstring. *What was his name?* Demien wondered. *By the gods, I watched him die and now I can't even recall his name.*

The horse-drawn carriage groaned along the stony hillside rises. Inside it, Lelana sat half hidden behind curtains of sheer white silk. Silas was beside her, observing the small porcelain figurine of a smiling girl that Lelana had given him. He had quite a collection now: a currycomb, a resin goat figurine, that annoying pelletdrum, and the porcelain girl. Demien rode postilion, on a sand-colored horse with black points and a dark dorsal stripe running from withers to croup. A temperamental beast, but also one of the few large enough to carry him. He adjusted his balance and let his eyes drift eastward, to the remains of a razed village: fields and huts and cottages all burned and abandoned, granaries and millstones and plowshares all lifeless and broken.

It was a dreadful sight, but hardly an infrequent one. The company had seen plenty like it during its travel to Indigo Cove, and now, venturing back, no one seemed to spare the destruction a glance. Even Demien's own thoughts were more focused on that strange festival of last week. It was as bizarre a spectacle as Lelana had promised, with men and women of all sizes and colors in attendance. Demien had recognized some, like the Sijian and Cothil people, but others, like the Inrim—truly queer, those folks. Their skin reminded him of an unharvested pumpkin, gnarled and old and covered in a thick matting of dark hair from back to shoulder to knuckles and toes. The women were not quite so hirsute as the men, but in full garb no one could tell. Both sexes wore the same conical hats and the same oversized jerkins called tabards, as well as the same baggy pantaloons and even the same pointy shoes that had the most awkward heels. In truth, it took days of observation before Demien could distinguish the subtleties between the sexes—the slight roundness of a woman's face, the deeper slope of a man's forehead.

Lelana had sold everything to them, every vase and every vessel, even that tasteless sculpture of an elderly mermaid that Demien wagered no one would buy. To be fair, the detail in it was quite amazing, but it was still a hideous thing—all sagging arms and shriveled breasts and chipped scales. But the Inrim had an affinity for the grotesque, and so that moribund creature fetched quite a modest price at the bazaars.

The accommodations provided by the Inrim were no less peculiar. Lavish in presentation but lacking simple concerns for cleanliness, as in providing poplar twigs for cleaning one's teeth, a scoop for cleaning one's ears, or even a simple basin for washing one's feet. Their carpets were placed on floors rather than hung on walls, and they were odd, weft-over-warp rugs, knotted and dyed in lurid colors. Stranger still were the beds—rude wooden frames crisscrossed with taut ropes. Every night Demien and Lelana had shared one in mutual discomfort.

"To the east lies the Geistwood," Eldrith announced, plucking Demien from his reverie. "There are worse things than outlaws in that place, my friends. I was once told of a party of rowdy old drunkards who happened to make camp inside. One wandered off to take a piss, only to fall asleep in the brush. Come morning he returned to his party and found only corpses."

"What does that prove?" one of the listeners questioned. "'Worse things than outlaws' my ugly arse. The sot never saw the assailants. Why suspect anything but brigands?"

"Because of what they did to his company. Bodies raked with strange cuts, cuts that no human blade could make. A few had their limbs torn from their bodies. One was halved at the waist. Another's neck was twisted so far he was lying on his stomach and looking up at the sky. But that wasn't what unsettled this old sot the most, do you want to know what did? Nothing was taken. Coin, weapons, clothing . . . nothing at all was taken. What sort of brigand murders a man but leaves the loot?"

No one had an answer to that. Demien studied the wood. Deadfall and old growth skirted its periphery. The outermost trees leaned forward, like gaping black maws waiting to swallow any unfortunate intruder. It certainly looked uninviting, but Demien rarely trusted the tales of men, especially in matters of the supernatural.

"What a bunch of goddamn rot," someone blurted at last, sparking the men into a heated debate.

Demien shook his head and remained silent. There were fourteen hired hands in all; half were former military grunts, the rest outcasts or vagabonds. They were simple men, moved by simple things—power, coin, women. Lelana had made it clear early on that Demien (or Ryden, as he was called) was in command, but it was her brother Eldrith who seemed bent on undermining that. He was a brash, outspoken prick, the ideal type to draw the hearts of lesser men. Of course, Demien knew better. *It's often the weakest dog that barks the loudest,* he thought. And by the gods did that fool bark.

The broad-chested man with the cleft lip was the only one who seemed to share Demien's mindset. His name was Cal, and he was easily the most experienced of the lot, even though he talked a bit too much for a man who spent his entire military career behind the stockade of a grain depot. His close companion was the wiry-haired fellow who was competent with a blade but absolutely wicked in heart. His given name Demien didn't know, but everyone called him by the word carved into his forehead: Goatsticker. He wore the brand like a badge, not even bothering to conceal it with hair or headscarf. And the story of how he'd gotten it was long and tiresome and filled with extraneous details, but the point of the matter was this: he stole a goat and got caught, well, "sticking" it.

There were a few others in the company worthy of Demien's notice. The club-footed fellow who was adept with a bow went by the name Helgen, and that huge mace-wielding man with the gray eyes they called Bigmouth—an obvious moniker after taking one look at his face. In fact, his mouth was so large that men had whiled away hours betting on what he could fit in there.

The conversation moved to Helgen's awful mistake of paying for the services of an Inrim whore only to find out she was a man. "I didn't know—they're all so goddamn hairy," he argued in defense. The men only laughed harder at that, Goatsticker's cackle the loudest. Helgen turned to him and said, "You of all people should keep your mouth shut in this, friend."

The branded man waggled a finger from atop his horse. "And why is that? At least I can tell a hole from a pole."

Helgen went red, and the men roared some more.

The bantering stopped the moment they saw the bridge. It had appeared just as they wended their way through a wooded declivity—a rainbow of segmented stone enwreathed by the misty haze. It was an open-spandrel arch bridge, flying naked across the rocky riverbed below. Eldrith pontificated about its design, as if he engineered the masterwork himself. "Look at the convexity of the stone, how precisely the wedges fit. There are iron tension rods running in rows to reinforce the body of the bridge. Observe the cross-bondings, the joints, the iron clamps—notice those smaller arches within its frame-work . . . do you see? They serve to lighten the weight and release the water when the river grows wrathful."

The others nodded and murmured but seemed less than interested. Demien's only concern was how exposed they were. They had purposely avoided this route on their way to Indigo Cove, but when heavy rains had caused mudslides to spill down onto their intended roadways, they were left with no alternative.

The carriage groaned and horse hooves clopped along the bridge. Embedded wagon tracks in the stone spoke of decades of passing beasts of burden. Dividing the lanes were panels and balusters carved of mythical beasts, fierce of eye and sharp of tooth, undoubt-edly made to deter flooding. The river, thirty-feet down, was quiet today, its cool waters shimmering in the silvery light. Old trees and glacial boulders lined the banks and fled to touch the cloudless, azure sky. It was such a fine picture that it took a moment before Demien noticed the hooded figures gathering at the far end of the bridge.

They stood tightly packed, twelve at least, though it was hard to tell. The blinding sun was setting at their backs, casting long, gaunt shadows in front of them. Demien halted the caravan, dismounting and handing off the bridle of his mount. Eldrith stared dumbfounded and said, "Are those men? Why are they standing there?" Then after a moment he said, "We turn around. We turn around and leave the way we came."

Demien pointed out the bowmen in the rear. "They'll not allow that."

"Why not?" Eldrith asked anyway, his voice choked with fear.

"I see half a score," Cal cut in, shading his eyes. "Goddamn this sun."

Demien's hand drifted to the hilt of Dreadfang, sheathed at the hip. He was glad to have it at his side again. He'd paid that greedy prick three times the price he initially sold it for—but he was glad none-theless. He only wished now for the heavy battledress of the Grand Commandant—plates of blackened armor from ankle to shoulder. All he had was a brigandine vest with torn seams and poorly overlapping plates, along with simple leather bracers and dinted greaves.

"Maybe they'll let us pass," someone suggested.

"*Let* us pass?" Eldrith echoed. "Why *wouldn't* they let us pass?

"Be quiet," Demien scolded, but the stoat-faced fool didn't listen.

"Let's just give them what they want," Eldrith went on. "Coin, is it? Let's just give it to—"

Demien grabbed the man by the shoulder of his traveler's cloak. "Give them coin and they'll let you live, but your sister they'll pass around until they break and bloody her loins. Is that what you want?"

Eldrith, unbelievably, gave a nod. To be fair, the man was so terrified he probably didn't even know what he was nodding at. Still, he deserved a good shove for his cowardice. "Get out of my sight," Demien growled at him. "Go back to the carriage, maybe your sister will protect you."

Eldrith scurried off. Demien turned to rest of his company, barking commands until he had organized some semblance of a skirmish line. He took the lead and advanced. The sun dipped behind a hillcrest, allowing for better sight of the outlaws. Most were adorned in lamellar plates laced with doeskin, along with tattered, hooded cloaks. One wore a pair of vambraces while the next had none, and two in the fore held shields, both of black ox-hide with damascened steel bosses. Most carried medium-ranged weapons—saber or sword, axe or mace— except the large fellow at the fore; he was holding a three-pronged trident.

A breeze threw Demien's brown hair over his eyes; he pushed it aside. "We seek safe passage, nothing more."

"Your payment shall grant it," came the reply from the trident-bearer.

Demien made a quick glance of the surrounding area. "This bridge stands within the radius of Thornberry's jurisdiction. It belongs to the realm of the Anir, passage is free."

The outlaw was quiet a moment. "The bridge belongs to Wintersun."

"Show me the imperial decree that grants such authorization."

"Here's my decree," he said, jabbing forward the prongs of his trident. "Now your coin, your steel, and your boots." A long moment of silence followed. When it seemed clear his demands would go unmet, the outlaw gave a quick motion of his hooded head and his underlings advanced.

Dreadfang came free of its sheath. "Stay in form," Demien urged the men around him. "Don't break, and don't give chase." He thought they heard him well enough, but as soon as the enemy charged, they were gone from his sides. The first outlaw rushed at Demien both off-step and cocksure, and for that Demien stabbed him straight through the chest, with enough force to lift the man off his feet. Impaled, he slumped forward, dead. Demien yanked free his blade, then turned— just as the trident came screaming for his head.

Demien parried, but his sword became entangled in the prongs. The wielder reacted at once, adjusting his grip for a quick jerk that would disarm his opponent. It was a veteran's move, and one that Demien himself had trained thousands of other men thousands of times, so he knew not to fight against the trident's strength, but move with it, graceful as water. The sword slid free and Demien drove it into the man's side. Howling, the outlaw dropped the trident and turned to flee. He got four or five steps before Dreadfang thrust itself between his shoulders, dropping him face-first to the stone.

A row of enemy crossbowmen appeared in his place.

Demien dived for cover. Bolts burst through the air, screaming overhead like tiny steel-winged locusts. One man was struck in the face. Another's kneecap exploded. Three or four others fled. Goat-sticker, wounded, toppled over the ledge of the bridge, screaming as he plunged to the river below. A downed horse thrashed nearby, a bolt buried in its flank. Demien crawled behind it and waited as the cross-bowmen again raised their reloaded weapons. After a second round of bolts screamed through the air, Demien charged.

His legs pumped of their own accord, his mind examining each moment of their reload—from the notching of the bolt in the tillers, to the use of a foot stirrup and belt-hook to draw quickly the string. The crossbows came up. Dreadfang came down. An outlaw shrieked, his arm severed below the elbow; it fell along with his crossbow to the stone. The next bowman Demien took at the throat. The others fled.

Quick as that, it was over. Demien was left with clouds of dust and strewn bolts and wounded or dead men. Cal approached, breathing hard and wiping the blood from his cleft lip. "He's suffering," he said, pointing. Bigmouth was crumpled on the ground, hands spread across his belly, keeping his ropy innards from spilling out. The wound was lethal, his fate decided.

"Send him off," Demien said, then headed back to the carriage. He stopped to end a poor horse's suffering, then again to help a dying man unstrap his leather helmet. "That's fine, that's fine," the man said, then died shortly after. Demien peered over the ledge in search of Goat-sticker—the man was lying in a twisted heap upon a cluster of river stones, the waves lapping gently his dashed brains against the bank.

He found Lelana inside the carriage, unharmed but trembling with fear. Eldrith was beside her. Silas was sitting against the outer wheel, blank-faced and squeezing tight the porcelain figurine. Someone kept shouting, "*RYDEN! RYDEN!*" over and over, and Demien was about to yell for silence when he remembered he was Ryden to these people. He went over to find Helgen standing over a downed outlaw—the trident-wielder. The wretch was dragging himself forward with his hands, pulling his lifeless legs behind him. His hood had fallen, revealing a crescent of graying hair. The wound between his shoulder girdle left blood streaming down his back.

"Mercy," he said.

An expected request, but for some reason, it made Demien furious. A swift kick in the ribs sent the wretch sprawling. Droplets of red burst from his lips. "You dare ask for mercy," Demien said. He kicked him again. It felt good. "When you would have shown us none?"

A sudden glint betrayed the dagger in the outlaw's hand. Demien stomped on it, crunching fingers. The man shrieked and the weapon dropped to the stone. Demien delivered another hard kick to the ribs. "*Mercy*," came the reply, hoarse with anguish this time.

Demien went behind him and knelt. His hand reached over the man's head and lifted it by the hollows of his eyes, pressing Dreadfang flush against the lump of the neck. The outlaw began to moan and whimper in desperation—peculiar sounds, like the mewls of a dying goat. "Face your death, coward," Demien told him. Then Dreadfang opened his throat. The man's pitiful screams turned to shrieking wheezes as his windpipe struggled for breath. Bright blood spilled in soupy waves, painting red the cheerless bridge of old limestone.

CHAPTER FORTY-THREE

T he diverted channel roared upon the city like the waves of a coastal seaquake, smashing stone and leaching mortar and rendering everything it touched a whimpering shell of ruin.

Anseth had learned the details of the devastation from Jarreth, who sent notes fastened to arrows that were shot over the walls. Each had described in great detail the hunger and sickness and widespread panic that seized the populace of Amaranth Point. And yet, Lygrest had refused to terms.

Instead, he'd dispatched riders during the night to seek aid from the nearest cities. In response, Anseth had a contingent of heavy Vaskultan horsemen waiting outside the sally port, and as the Anirian riders emerged they were slaughtered to a man. That was three days ago. Another note arrived the morning of the fourth. Anseth perused it while breaking his fast. Then he summoned his generals.

When Dariok entered he was back to good health and back to his cruel ways. He plucked the note from Anseth's hand, only to frown at what he saw. The stupid oaf couldn't read—no Vaskultan could, not to mention these messages were written in the rather difficult language of the Anir.

"No terms," Anseth told his men. "The stubborn fool Lygrest plans to open the gates for one final sortie. He'll shove the civilians out to create a smokescreen, then armed soldiers will follow. They'll skirmish in small units to add to the confusion, while Lygrest sneaks out with a small host of riders." Anseth took a long gulp of his blackmilk. "Half a bowshot's retreat from the center ranks will allow the civilians to disperse, while detachments of mounted pikemen will break the Anirian columns before they can organize their units."

"I'll take the right," Dariok blurted. "Severak, you take the left. I assume you'll be taking the center, runt. Even though you seem less than eager to skewer the hearts of these pale-faced fools."

"We are not savages, Dariok," Anseth told him. "Only Lygrest is deserving of our wrath. That means the innocents are to be spared, and amnesty granted to any soldier who discards his arms. And most of all, I want Jarreth brought to me, *unharmed*. If so much as a bruise finds his skin I will take the head of the man responsible. And should he be killed during the sortie, the violator will suffer an eternity in the Great Void. A harsh punishment, I know, but that Anirian risked his neck to provide us with intelligence, and for that we owe him a great debt. Remember that, and make sure your men remember as well. That is all for now. We assemble in two days."

The air grew hotter as summer drew ever nearer, and on the day of the sortie it was sweltering. The Vaskultans formed their lines, baking in their leather armor under the pearl-white sun. The cold they could endure like no other, but this heat wasn't quite so familiar to them. They drank everything from blackmilk to lamb liquor to water even, and gnawed on slabs of meat that were wedged between their saddles. And as the setting sun stole away the last hint of daylight, so too did it take the Vaskultans' desire for battle. Morale was low, so very low. Even Anseth was ready to return to the yurts. He had already spent the entire day in battle, his enemies not men but heat rash and dehydration and fatigue.

But Anseth knew Lygrest was a calculating man. And a calculating man would wait until his enemies were at their weakest before he took action. So when that drawbridge finally jerked alive and those chains rattled and that windlass groaned, Anseth only shook his head. Tired or not, the sortie was upon them.

The thick wooden deck came to its resting place with a deafening *boom*. The overflowing moat washed across it like an angry breaker. Civilians piled against the latticed grille, jostling one another for a chance at freedom. A moment later, the portcullis whined its way upward. An onslaught of screaming faces and flailing arms emerged, like a herd of frightened antelope fleeing through the scrub. The quick and the able overbore the old and the weak, leaving them trampled and injured and cast into the moat to drown.

Anseth signaled his Vaskultan horsemen to turn and retreat. They reformed again to the south. The civilian horde unthreaded itself by then, men and women and children running every which way, east to higher ground, north to the river, south for the cover of the wood. A thick haze blanketed the area near the gatehouse threshold, blinding runners and causing a few to accidentally race headlong toward Anseth's line. Most managed to veer away as their sight returned, save one poor fool who met his end at the tip of some Vaskultan's lowered pike.

The Anirian soldiers emerged from the city soon after. Ignoring the anguished cries of the wounded civilians, they plowed their way through in tight columns of infantrymen. The moment the Anirian vanguard stepped across the drawbridge, Dariok's mounted Vaskultans swarmed from the left. Severak advanced from the right. The enemy broke like reeds in a gale. Many headed back inside the city. A great tangle of steel and iron and horseflesh clogged the gateway. The Vaskultans pushed forward. The portcullis began to close, only to open, then close again. Whine, jerk, whine, jerk—then the winchman must've died or abandoned his post because finally it stopped for good.

Anseth led the center forward, galloping across the flooded drawbridge and through the dark of the archway, to find himself in an open courtyard. Ahead, Dariok's detachment forced its way through the second gate, chasing the routed into the city streets. Severak wasn't far behind. The riders left behind scores of dead men, but a host of live ones stood on the battlements above. Crossbowmen, positioned along the crenels, rained bolts down, while others overturned giant pots of sizzling pitch. Arrows twanged from murder holes and other unseen places; one screamed past Anseth's ear. He ordered his men to form up and return with bowfire, then dispatched small teams to storm the flood-ravaged stairways and clear the upper walkways. Several died making their way up, but once above the backsword-wielding Vaskultans cut down the lightly armored Anirians and sent others plummeting off the battlements. All hit the courtyard with that same awful *thud*—except one, who broke his fall on the croup of a horse, shattering the beast's hindquarters and throwing the rider headfirst onto the flagstone with such force that his head could've been made of granite and it would've helped him none.

Cursing Dariok's reckless aggression, Anseth led the charge through the second lightless archway, emerging now in the southern district, where he was met by toppled buildings and blocked alleyways and streets filled with mud and black sewage. The dead lay everywhere, face up, face down, half sunken in muddied pools, on rooftops or dangling over sills of upper story windows. Vaskultans riders chased down anyone they saw, while footmen were hauling coffers and chests out of raided homes. Anseth screamed for them to return to form, but no one spared him a glance. And when his own lines began to disassemble, he spun to scream at them too, but his beast slipped in the mud and sent Anseth into the bog. He tasted sludge and swill and blood. *By the gods, it's no use,* he thought. Kirik came to him—good and loyal Kirik, never far from his side. Kirik and a few guardsmen and maybe a score of soldiers . . . the rest had scattered like the rabid dogs they were.

Nightfall moved in to darken the land, but fires fought to restore the light of day. Smoke twisted and curled skyward like thick black tendrils. A nearby workshop caught flame, blasting Anseth with a wave of heat that stole his breath and made his hair stick to his skin. Around him, Vaskultans killed without care or compunction. A fleeing boy of no more than ten was chased down and skewered by a Vaskultan's pike, while an arrow struck the fat and bare-chested man who went running after him. A nearby mother, surrounded, used a knife to pierce the hearts of her two daughters and then her own.

Anseth spat a wad of mud from his lips. The world was crumbling around him, and he had no idea why. Well, no, he did know why, he knew *exactly* why, in truth. *I let a madman live when fate arranged for his death*. But no, it wasn't just Dariok—it was all Vaskultans. *They're all acting like savages.*

Kirik was calling his name. "Just go," Anseth told him, "stop being my goddamn bondsman for once." But he didn't go. He just stood there, with his torn ear and reptilian face, and between his bowed legs given to years of riding, Anseth saw the governor's palace, small in the distance. He rose to his feet. "Come on," he said.

Carved and wounded men littered the avenues leading to the palace, and more lay sprawled before the walled gatehouse. In the inner courtyard, a wounded Vaskultan begged Anseth to carry him to a more suitable place to die. Anseth sighed; he didn't want to, he didn't want to help any of these savages right now. So he made Kirik do it, while he moved on, toward the main palace doors.

They were huge. And they were open.

Inside, winding pillars lined the length of the hall, stone-gray and decorated in vines that spiraled their way toward the ceiling. The corpses here were palace advisers and scholars and stewards, men of fine vestments and regalia, and men who never held a weapon in all their lives. Strewn among them were smashed benches and overturned trestles and shards of broken vessels that threatened to cut an incautious foot. And on the blue-tiled dais, the provincial governor's seat lay on its side, with Lygrest himself stretched out before a small postern door, weltering in a pool of his own blood.

Anseth didn't notice Dariok at first. The chieftain's son was sitting on the edge of the dais, clutching a backsword. Blood speckled his face and knotted his hair and spattered the leather helmet on the floor beside him. His cruel, puffy eyes stared at Anseth, seemingly without recognition. Then they went somewhere else, pointing at something. Anseth didn't see what. Dariok pointed again. He still didn't see it. Was this a game? He had no patience left. "What is it, Dariok, just say it godda —" Then he saw it. The diminutive Anirian counselor Jarreth Sorrel, lying dead on the cold stone floor.

Anger rose in him like a cyclone. "You killed him, you stupid mother-raping brute. You *KILLED* him. Do you not remember what I told—"

He barely saw the man move. Thick Vaskultan arms shoved Anseth to the floor. He went to rise but stopped at the sight of the backsword pointed at his face. *He's going to kill me,* Anseth thought. It was a sobering thought, and yet, Anseth wasn't afraid, only disappointed. Disappointed with himself, to not have seen this coming. By the gods, he'd wanted to return to his home one last time.

But no, Dariok didn't strike. Instead he lowered the weapon. "Do you remember what my father said? During the blizzard, the night Yugarak lost his head. Do you remember, runt? I do." His ugly, crooked face had always made him look a bit unsound—but now, drenched in blood, the man looked absolutely deranged. "Any man who betrays his lord will do the same to you." He flung the sword at Anseth's feet and left the hall.

CHAPTER FORTY-FOUR

Seric Dyre had long envisioned his return to the Hollow. Gray-black banners waving in the sky, drums rolling across the countryside, and an honor guard of the capital's finest approaching on horses that caracoled gaily to and fro. They would escort Seric into the city, through rows of civilians whose fanfare and applause would fill the avenues all the way to the palace district. And inside the Hall of Obsidian Light, a grand banquet would be waiting, with musicians plucking their instruments and stewards proffering gifts of silk and satin and silver-brocaded damask and framed mosaics of small tesserae. And later, when all the celebrations were ended, Seric would make his way to his private chambers, where the most desirable reward of all stood waiting: Lady Miriana.

The reality, however, proved a far different experience. No banners, no drums, and no honor guard—only a pair of dully attired riders who handed Seric a tattered cloak and led him quietly through the city. And inside the palace, there was no banquet and no music and no gifts, and most disheartening of all, no Miriana.

Instead it was his son Veldries who stood waiting for him. The boy looked older than his seventeen years, as he often did when clad in his full Anirian battledress of blackened scales and boots and cloak. Veldries was a handsome man, much like his father, and like his father he was blessed with smooth olive skin, innocent round eyes, and fine stature. Also, he shared his father's temper. "By the gods it better not be true," he said, scowling.

Seric brushed past him. "I expected more of you." He removed his filthy cloak, pausing to rub the scar beneath his neckerchief. The boy was glaring at him, probably the same way Seric had glared at his own father, not so long ago. It was strange now, to be in the opposite role. "Only small minds are turned by slander."

"Then we must live in a city of fools, because everyone here thinks you're a goddamn traitor."

"And I've returned to make it known that I'm not." There was a long pause. Did the boy believe him? He never wanted to lie to his son. But was it in fact a lie? His faith to the Redlands had never been fulfilled. He'd chosen to serve Lady Miriana instead. And Raas Dragath made it clear that all ties were severed the day he sent a man to cut Seric's throat.

"They may not believe you."

"I don't care. After I muster my army and lay waste upon Stormhaven, the whole realm will hear the truth from the cripple's mouth."

"Lord Alarin was behind this? How do you know?"

"The Hollow's spies work fast, my son."

Veldries didn't speak for a time. "I leave the Pit in a month," he said at last. "I want to join your campaign. To march beside you."

He looked squarely at his son. "You're not ready."

"You were my age when you rode into battle, were you not?"

"As a minor advisor. I saw nothing of battle until I was over twenty. Don't be so eager, my son. There's no glory to be had in the field."

"Deny me of this, Father, and I promise you I will find a lord who appreciates a man of my talent. When next you see me it will be from across the battlefront."

Seric paused. "You would stand against your own father?"

Veldries's smile was patronizing. "It's in my blood, is it not?"

"What the hell does that mean?"

"You *know* what it means. I'm aware of your personal interest in your most recent campaign. I know of your true father, the Zhoul. Mother told me all."

Damn her. "Your mother doesn't know when to shut her mouth."

"She said you would kill him. Did you, Father?"

Seric gritted his teeth. "Yes. I killed him and every one of his goddamn sons." Veldries's eyes widened at that, making Seric's tone soften a bit. "Listen, I know you don't understand, but that man was never—"

"I *do* understand, Father. I understand just what kind of man you truly are."

"Oh, spare me such rot. You are a fortunate boy, you know, fortunate to have been born into a life of privilege. Fortunate to have never suffered like I have suffered."

"Take me with you, Father."

Seric grunted in frustration, and yet, he couldn't help but acknowledge the boy's ambition. *Should it truly surprise me? He is my son, after all.* He was also the only good thing Seric had in his life. "It is difficult enough to lose an officer in the field . . . if I should ever lose you—"

"You won't, unless you deny me what I want."

There was a knock at the door. "My lord, Her Majesty requires your immediate audience."

"A moment, Vylas," Seric answered. He reached for his cloak from a nearby wall peg. It was among the finest in his possession—a soft cream-colored garment with a black fringe that matched flawlessly with his neckerchief. "You should go," he told his son. "We'll talk later."

Veldries didn't move. "Your answer, Father, or I'll not be here when you return."

Seric gave him a long look, but in the end he could only nod. "In private you are my son, but on the field you are my vassal. Don't you ever forget that."

"I won't." Veldries gave the slightest bow of his head, then turned and left the chamber.

Moments later, Lady Miriana appeared. She was wearing a flowing indigo gown that enhanced the color of her eyes, and a white enameled stone necklace that matched the paleness of her skin. Her long black hair flowed impeccably straight, held in place by several small clasps. She looked quite stunning, even if there was a certain sadness to her expression. Was it because of his time with Perilia? He couldn't say, but he knew he needed to reassure her. Perhaps a kiss might work.

It didn't. "My sweet Miriana," he said to her, "tell me what troubles you. Was it my sojourn in Silverleaf? You must know that I thought only of you—"

"No, Seric. No, that's not it."

The way her eyebrows narrowed annoyed him, as if such thoughts hadn't even occurred to her. "Then tell me already. I have enough to fret over, between the loathing of the populace and the distrust of my own son." He rubbed at the scar beneath his neckerchief. "By the gods, I had to convince him of my good faith. Do I need to convince you as well?" Without letting her reply, he went on. "I've subjugated the enemy, reformed our alliance with the west, and set my vengeance against a man deserving of his comeuppance. I've done everything I swore I would do, and by the gods, I even won the respect of your brother while doing it." He wanted to say more, but the words didn't come, so he fell silent.

"I know," she told him. "I know of all you've done. It's not the letter, Seric." She sighed. "I had but one task, and I failed."

It took him a moment to understand. "You mean Zantherei."

She nodded.

The news didn't bother him. It should've, but it didn't. He gently took her hand. The small sapphire stones of her silver bangles twinkled in the light. He led her to a seat on the couch. The light from the window illuminated the soft features of her face. She looked beautiful, and when he told her that, she smiled in reply, a courtesan's polite smile. "Has he awoken?"

She hesitated a moment before telling him no.

"Then right now he is of no concern. His elder brother, however . . ." He shook his head. "It was a grave mistake to think the winter would take him. Alarin is a resourceful man, and cunning at that. A cunning man will always seek victory without raising a single sword. You understand my meaning?"

She nodded. "Seric, you need to repudiate these allegations and allay the doubts of the court. Not only is your standing in question, but mine as well. It was I who recommended you for your position, after all."

"I will address the court." His tone was sharper than intended. "And the populace." He wanted to stroke her hair but feared it might be inappropriate. "And I won't be staying long."

She pulled free her hand. "Seric, you've only just returned."

"My vengeance burns, Mir. I cannot delay. Summer is come, it won't be long before the sun begins to weaken. I'll not risk marching in winter."

She frowned at that. "Your anger is making you rash. Alarin has Szathan Mordall at his side, likely Demien Mordall as well. And Merio Athera has Yuseth Valate. These are powerful generals, Seric. And not only that—"

"I know what they are," he cut in. "I'm not a fool to rush blindly into Stormhaven. We still have allies this side of the Grayling River— Duren Lygrest of Amaranth Point and Lord Emeron Mathius of Aster Falls. I intend to personally visit each of these men to reinforce our bonds and place their armies under my banner. Then I'll move south to descend upon Stormhaven. And this time, when I return to the Hollow, I expect to receive all the adoration and praise that I very well deserve."

"Seric, you didn't let me finish. Spies report of talks between Lord Dragath and Merio Athera, talks of alliance through marriage. These are not falsehoods, so I suggest you drop that smirk. If an alliance between Riverwind and the Redlands is established, our enemy stands to hold two provinces, fourteen districts, and an army nearly as large as our own."

"It matters not," he told her. "Either way, it matters not."

"Why?"

He was no longer looking into her eyes, but past her now, at the soft spears of light shining through the scrollwork windows. "Because I will *kill them all.*"

BOOK IV: DECEPTION

CHAPTER FORTY-FIVE

"**G**et *inside*," Demien ordered. There was a sternness to his voice, one that Lelana was wise to heed, as she quickly urged Silas and headed inside the household gate. Demien turned back to face the armored company of Anirian soldiers approaching from the city avenues.

He had long expected this. Word of his smashing of the outlaws had spread like wildfire throughout Thornberry, and before he knew it citizens had presented him with a slew of new gifts and conferred on him new titles he'd already forgotten. The Golden Zinnia had become busier than ever—not for the gambling and the whores, but for a chance to meet the great hero of Seven Lakes.

Naturally, it was only a matter of time before the military caught wind. A summons had arrived first, sealed by none other than General Sabriel Soffin. Demien knew he should've left the city then. But he couldn't—not without Lelana. So instead he'd taken refuge in her household. A few weeks had passed before word of his name began to fade. A few more and he'd thought himself forgotten. But he was wrong.

The commander removed his helm and dismounted from a fawn-colored charger. He was a man of poor posture; head hunched between slumped shoulders, arms long and gangly like those of a baboon. He was General Fenerus Soffin, Demien knew, even without ever setting his eyes upon the young man. *So this is the great Hero of the Horns,* Demien thought, unimpressed.

Curious onlookers peered down from upper story windows. Passersby stopped in front of buildings or huddled beneath shaded eaves to whisper to one another. The general seemed to take no notice. His bored, unmoving eyes seemed more fitting of an old veteran's rather than a man who had yet to see thirty. "The tales of your stature do no lie," the general said. He had an edge of haughtiness in his voice that Demien didn't like. "Too bad only a cur would think himself above an imperial summons."

"Forgive me, I am but a country rustic, neither cultured nor worthy of a great commander's time."

Fenerus ran a hand through his short crop of curly hair. "You sound like no rustic. Where are you from?"

"Seven Lakes." Demien said. "I am but a simple farmhand, I assure—"

"No man is simple," the general cut in. He plodded a few steps closer, drawing his saber. Demien didn't move. "You don't fear me," Fenerus said. He pointed the tip at the ground. "Get on your knees and submit to your imperial commander."

Demien's pride kept him standing tall, that and his intense dislike for this snub-nosed little fool. Fenerus observed him for a moment or two, then shook his head. "An affront to me is an affront to all that is sacred to the Anir." The signal he gave was lightning quick, but unmistakable to Demien, who had spent a lifetime issuing that very same command. A line of bowmen advanced, their arrows aimed at Demien's heart.

This was not a group of unskilled roughnecks, Demien knew. They were trained soldiers, men whose adept posture and steady hands were given to endless hours of practice and repetition. Demien had nowhere to go, had nothing but a thin layer of hemp to protect him. He could feel the cold fingers of death reaching for his heart. Strange, how comforting they felt. After all, this was what Demien had wanted. Wasn't it? He wanted it since the moment he found young Thavian's body. He wanted it beneath the oak tree, when he tried to plunge Dreadfang into his heart. And he wanted it now, at the hands of these trained bowmen. A homecoming long overdue.

"A shame," Fenerus muttered. "I came to greet a hero, but found only a scoundrel." He motioned to loose.

"*STAY! STAY YOUR FIRE!*" It was a woman's cry—Lelana's, undoubtedly. Fenerus motioned to hold. His eyes narrowed as Lelana rushed over to stand between Demien and the bowmen. "If you strike this man down you are committing a grave injustice."

Fenerus looked at her as if she were no bigger than a mouse. "Injustice? Contumacy is punishable by death. This man ignored an imperial summons and refused to kneel before his imperial lord."

"That's because it is you who should be kneeling, not him."

Surely Fenerus wouldn't even consider such a ludicrous statement, but no, by the gods, the stupid wretch took the bait. "And why is that?"

"Because this man is the Grand Commandant of the Anir," she declared. "Surely the name Demien Mordall is known to you?" Her words were like daggers in Demien's heart. He called out to her, but she ignored that. To Fenerus she said, "Now lower your weapons and bow your heads and be gone."

Fenerus's crescent eyes had gone wide. He glanced at his subalterns for answers, but received none. When next he spoke, he seemed more careful with his words. "Demien Mordall is a fugitive of the empire. I am bound by the mandate of Empress Miriana Athera to take him back to the capital. There is no honor left in him."

Dreadfang screamed from its sheath. "You arrogant wretch," Demien growled. "If you try to take me to that corrupt woman, I swear I'll cut out the hearts of half your company before these hands are bound."

Fenerus opened his mouth but nothing came out. A long spell of silence broke between them. In the end, he motioned for the bridle of his charger and mounted. He looked down at Demien. "My uncle will know of this." Then he went off, his soldiers clanging behind him.

Demien grabbed Lelana's arm, spinning her about. "You *knew*," he said. "How long?"

"Let go. You're hurting me." Her eyes were strangely defiant, as if she'd done no wrong.

He released her. "You deceived me." His thoughts came rushing at him, like the pulse of a sudden tide. "When you came to me, in the brothel, you knew already, didn't you? You knew who I was. You didn't want an escort, you wanted the claim on my house. You lying little wench."

"Yes . . . no! I didn't lie. Not about that. Please, I lied only about my father. My father is no imperial inspector, he's an informant of the Hollow. He knew all the details of the Grand Commandant's treason. He was there, in the brothel, the day you made those men look like boys. I didn't mean to . . ." Her hand went to his cheek.

Demien pushed it away. He glimpsed Silas standing just outside the household gate. "Come, boy. We're leaving." He turned and started on his way.

Lelana stood before him. "Don't go."

"Get out of my way." When she refused, he shoved her aside. That made her angry. "What sin have I committed? Such a small wrong, to be treated like this. You act like I killed your wife to get to you."

He stopped. "Don't talk about her." *She knew about Alana, too. She knew just how kind of a woman Alana was.* "I said we're leaving, boy. *Now*." Silas was tentative as he followed, his eyes glancing nervously at Lelana.

"I wronged you," Lelana went on. "I admit, but . . . what I told you, that night at Indigo Cove . . . either baseborn or noble, it is a man's character alone that matters to me." Her small hands clutched his forearm. "I meant what I said. I don't care about the man you *were*, what matters to me is the man you are now."

Demien tried not to listen. There were eyes everywhere, people staring at him, at the hero farmhand who was no hero farmhand. "I put my life at risk so you would have yours," Lelana was saying. "Is that so wrong?"

Maybe she was right. Was what she had done so terrible? She'd deceived him, no doubt, but did it matter now? He looked down at her. Such a comely face. For a moment he thought he could forgive her . . .

No, he didn't ask for this. He didn't ask to be saved. Death was all he deserved, and death was what she denied him of. He couldn't stand the sight of her. He needed to get away, to go somewhere, anywhere. She was no different from every other dishonest wretch in this city. He was tired of everyone, tired of everything. Demien shouldered his way through the busy avenues, shoving aside porters and peddlers and pouring men who snapped curses at his discourtesy. One moment Silas was struggling to keep up, the next he was gone. Demien didn't care. If the boy had any sense about him, he'd know the only place where this drunken coward knew to go.

CHAPTER FORTY-SIX

The target was a crude butt fashioned from worn leather and twisted straw and wooden legs that jutted out from a mound of peat. An audience of hundreds observed from the grassy sward to the north, wine-drunk and wealthy old nobles, obvious by their lurid robes and tacky jewelry.

Alarin Athera looked upon the spectacle from high atop the tower terrace. His white-lacquered seat was fashioned to look like the petals of a cloudfall, but it was an uncomfortable thing, especially the armrests whose long peduncles dug into his arm even through the sleeves of his robe. To his left, Lord Merio's thronelike chair had an upper crest that was outlined in mother-of-pearl, or nacre, as he liked to call it, just as he liked to ramble on about its true iridescent shine, especially when compared to the inner shells of lesser mollusks.

It was only an archery competition, yet Merio was dressed for an emperor's coronation. His long outer robe was bright purple and decorated with silhouettes of trees inside gilded roundels, while his dark red inner robe was secured by a fringed sash and belt. His headdress was tasseled and studded and fitted with the curved horns of a Sadralen, but it was an oversized piece in need of constant adjustment, and each time Merio raised his hand to do so, the obnoxiously wide sleeve of his robe would block Alarin's view.

His brother looked like a fool, and yet, the highborn toadies at his side all fawned over his garb. Even his fat, foppish wretch of a steward told Merio that he looked 'scrumptious.' Alarin wanted to shove his cane down the man's gullet and ask him how scrumptious that tasted, but of course he had more self-control than that. *Anirians are simple men of simple garb,* Alarin wanted to say. *We don't speak in flowery drivel and we don't smell of cloying perfumes and we don't dress like some grandiloquent performer at a Sijian opera.*

A burst of applause drew his eyes below. From the west, a pearl-white horse curveted forward, a man in white astride it. Yuseth Valate looked like a great snowy owl, dark-eyed and mysterious and adorned in overlapping plates of polished scale. He galloped up the line, then back down, a second time and then once more. Notching an arrow, he drew and loosed. The target thrummed and cheers erupted. The arrow had struck the bull's-eye.

Merio didn't hesitate to brag about his general. "To loose at that speed, from a hundred paces, at exactly the moment the steed's four hooves touch the ground . . . well, I don't need to explain such precision to you, Elder Brother."

Alarin wasn't really listening. Truth was, he had more important matters on his mind. The southland advisor Ravathyr Aeryn had arrived two days early, and had since been enduring his share of half-hearted entertainment in the Rosebud Hall. An insolent gesture, but Merio didn't seem to care. He was only interested in the contest, or the quality of the wine, or the serving lad who refilled his wine. The boy couldn't have been no older than fifteen, and with his smooth white skin and small-shouldered frame he looked almost as much female as he did male. Merio thanked the lad and sent him off with a playful squeeze of the rump. Alarin pretended to ignore that.

General Szathan emerged onto the field astride his great buckskin stallion. Unlike Yuseth's pristine battledress, Szathan's serrated hem cloak and dinted black armor spoke only of the drudgery of battle. The general cantered forward, then fell into a full gallop, and with a *twang* he loosed. The target quivered, straw fluttered to the ground—but there was no second arrow, only the one Yuseth had fired. Someone gave a derisive shout, and a great hubbub arose.

Merio turned to his brother, a triumphant smile on his face. "No shame in not matching the skill of my general, you know."

Below, the tallyman was waving his arms and pointing at the lone arrow that Yuseth had loosed. Whatever he was saying was making the crowd begin to cheer. Alarin already knew what it was. "Szathan's arrow struck exactly where Yuseth's had struck, splitting it from the fletching," he explained.

A pause, then Merio began to laugh. "By the gods, you knew all along, didn't you? That is one splendid general you have at your side, Elder Brother."

Alarin nodded. A handful of lesser officers took turns next. Just as they finished, Alarin said to his brother, "I must insist, the envoy shouldn't be kept waiting."

Merio's smile dissolved at once, as if Alarin had just confessed to burning his brother's favorite outfit. "I didn't ask him to arrive early," he complained.

"Still, it is unwise to insult a man whose favor we seek."

Merio's frown deepened. "You seek it, not me, you know." He sounded like a selfish boy who didn't get his way. "I'll offer him a seat here, would that satisfy you?"

"He's not here for the festivities," Alarin reminded him.

Merio gave a halfhearted shrug and turned back to the competition. Servicemen were wrapping lance tips in felt and dabbing them in lime, in preparation of the next event. Merio clapped his hands in anticipation.

Alarin stood. "I'll not make him wait any longer."

Merio waved a dismissive hand. "Go on then."

He limped his way to the arched doorway. Gilberon Brehems stood there, chewing on something and toying with the curls of his beard. "Gil, you don't want to watch this, do you?"

The husky man thought about it for a moment, then spat a mouthful and followed.

The tower stairs were narrow and difficult for an old cripple like Alarin. By the time he reached the bottom, his leg was burning with ache. The long palace corridors stretched out before him, festooned with floral sconces and wall carvings and all the typical showiness that Merio seemed to enjoy. Brehems seemed uncharacteristically dour, and when Alarin pointed that out, the man said, "I always stood by you, my lord. Even when you lost your leg and traded your steel for silk, and when you disappeared in that tower of yours and did whatever it was you did. Point is when people disrespected you I shut them up. But this . . . no, I won't stand among the clay dogs of a murderer."

Alarin stopped. "What are you saying?"

"I'm saying I'd sooner gut myself than fight alongside Raas Dragath."

"Gil, my friend, you have nothing to worry about."

"You are meeting with a Redlander emissary to discuss a possible alliance. Now that sounds like something to be pretty goddamn *worried* about."

"You must trust in me, that's all I ask of you. All will be told soon enough."

"Szathan said the same goddamn thing. Are you planning something? Help old Gilberon understand, because right now you're twisting steel in my gut."

Alarin tossed him his best reassuring smile. "I can't. Not with that wild tongue of yours—too many know how to get it to wag." He pointed to the winegourd at the man's hip.

They entered the hall through doors ornamented in golden clouds and glimmering raptor feathers. Brehems, having never set foot in the Rosebud Hall, gave one look at the massive Sadralen suspended from the ceiling and muttered, "By all the goddamn gods." Servants moved about the area, some cleaning the straw mats on the floor, others tending the incense burners.

The Redlander advisor sat at an oblong table, surrounded by bustling attendants and blathering stewards. At Alarin's approach, he rose and introduced himself. He was a man of many contraries: tall in height but dressed in too-short robes, nimble in movement but wizened in appearance, solemn in aspect yet cheerful in voice. Alarin liked him at once.

"The Thunder of the North," the man said with a sweeping bow. "I am truly humbled by your illustrious presence, my lord."

"Please," Alarin said, motioning for him to take his seat. "Don't tease an old goat, my friend."

The skinny man went to speak but paused to allow his attendants to fill a pair of goblets. "Lord Dragath gratefully accepts your gifts and condolences to his late wife," he said after.

"Meager tokens, though not without my utmost sincerity. What of my proposal?"

He smiled at that. "A plain-spoken man, how commendable. Lord Dragath is truly honored by your offer, my lord. But he fears, in his advancing age, that a beautiful woman in the very flower of her youth would not desire him."

"Nonsense. Lady Cathia is eager to stand behind the Lord of the Redlands," Alarin said.

Ravathyr paused to take a sip. "And your good brother, is he eager as well? Because it appears he finds the twanging of bowstrings more compelling than the dealings of the realm."

"Forgive him," Alarin said. "Merio is a good man."

Ravathyr smiled an infectious smile. "Yes, well, he is also a man who likes to speak but not listen, a man who likes to lead but cannot decide." He gestured to the furnishings around him. "And by what I see, he is a man whose lust for superficialities has left him devoid of ambition."

Alarin also glanced about. "You see that? I just thought he had poor taste."

Ravathyr gave a hearty laugh. "I like you," he said after. "And if I may speak candidly . . . if this were your brother's proposal, I'd not even be here. Few men have the respect of Raas Dragath, friend or foe. You are one of them."

"My heart is glad to hear that," Alarin told him.

"And I can tell you keep loyal men at your side." He looked at Brehems. "You must really not like your lord's proposal, because you are peeling back my skin with your very eyes."

"Your goddamn lord has committed terrible atrocities," Brehems growled in reply.

Ravathyr held the goblet to his lips, but didn't drink. "Haven't we all, General?" he said with a chuckle.

Brehems's face darkened. "Does talk of regicide amuse you?"

"General," Alarin warned.

Brehems ignored that. He took a heavy step forward. "Maybe I should rip out your goddamn liver, now that'll be quite amusing, don't you think?"

"N-no, of course not," Ravathyr stammered, clearly afraid now. "I didn't intend—"

"Then *what* did you intend?"

"*Brehems*," Alarin cut in. "That's enough." He looked at Ravathyr. "Forgive him."

The Redlander advisor took a few moments before responding. "Nothing to forgive. Would that all men were so honest of heart." His voice sounded even enough, but when he reached for his goblet, Alarin saw his hand was trembling.

Alarin attempted to soften the mood by speaking of small things for a while: the travel, the competition, the warm and fertile lands of the south. Ravathyr soon became his calm self again. Perhaps it was the wine, but Alarin found him to be an easy man to talk to. Almost too easy. And Ravathyr seemed to enjoy his company just the same. Was it all a mummer's act? Perhaps not, since Ravathyr eventually said, "It pleases me to find such high-minded company as yourself, my lord."

"High-minded," Alarin repeated with a chuckle. "You don't need to flatter me, my friend."

Ravathyr waggled his finger at that. "It's true, my lord. You're not at all how Lord Seric painted you to be. Not that he spoke so poorly of you."

Alarin blinked at him. *Did he just make a mistake? Or was it intentional?* Alarin thought for a moment. "You know Seric then."

"Is that a question? Because you already know the answer to that, I reckon."

Alarin wasn't sure how to respond. "How do you mean?"

"That letter you had posted at all points of the Hollow, about Seric and his traitorous ties with Raas Dragath. It's all true. Everything your spies reported."

Alarin thought for a moment. *This is no mistake.* At length he said, "It was you. You wanted me to find out. How come?"

He gave a noncommittal shrug. "I never liked him much. Seric, I mean. But I wasn't foolish enough to underestimate him. By the gods if someone of his talents had joined Raas Dragath's side . . ." He paused. "Well, obviously he never did. He severed his faith. I still know not why."

"Seric's personal ambitions far outweigh his provincial loyalties. Miriana must've offered him something more."

Ravathyr said, "Well, he does serve as the Imperial Advisor now, so . . ." He left the statement go unfinished, and a spell of silence passed between them. They shared another round of wine. Ravathyr's eyes began wandering around the room. Alarin said, "Fret not, my friend, I will make sure the grounds of this union will appear in a manner fit for a true lord of the Anir."

"And where exactly will this union be held?"

"The banquet will take place here in the Rosebud Hall, then the bridal procession will proceed to the temple grounds just north of the city. After all the official services and sacrifices and formalities, a private chamber will be prepared for consummation."

"I'm sure she will prepare a fine trousseau. I hear Merio's daughter is a lovely young woman, is she not?"

"Lovely, yes, if not an overindulging sybarite, much like her father."

"Well, perhaps Lord Raas Dragath can remind her of the beauty in simplicity," he said with a small nod.

Later, Alarin found Merio in his private chamber. The glowing braziers made the room far warmer than it needed to be on this cool summer night. Merio was sitting on a divan, primping in front of an attendant's look mirror. Orange light flickered against the profile of his handsome face. "The alliance is off. I don't want Cathia involved in this."

"It's too late," Alarin said. "She'll not be in any danger, I promise you."

His foot stamped down on the floor with a loud *whump* that made his attendant give a start. "I decide what is or isn't done."

"You were too busy with your games," Alarin reminded him. He could tell that his baby brother was not used to such outright refusal.

"The proposal is off," Merio repeated.

Alarin sighed. "Raas Dragath has already agreed—" He stopped, his frustration running over. "Were you even listening before? Sometimes it amazes me to know we share the same blood."

Merio was examining himself in a small look mirror. "You've changed, Elder Brother. You never used to speak to me in such a way. You've changed, you know, and I don't like it."

Alarin threw an arm out, to mock all the extravagant décor around him. "I've changed? Look around you, Brother. This isn't how Father raised you."

Merio didn't like that comment one bit. "Don't. I am not the same boy you could once so easily scold."

"Yes you are. You are but a boy writ large. Are you a pederast too?"

"How *dare* you." Merio rose, approaching his brother with gritted teeth. "I am Merio of House Athera, Lord of Stormhaven and Keeper of the East. No man speaks to me in such a way. *NO MAN*, do you hear me? The proposal is *OFF*."

Alarin punched him. A hooking right that clipped Merio's jaw, sending him staggering back. A pair of purple-cloaked guardsmen took a step forward, but Alarin's glare sent them back another two. Merio lowered his hand, revealing a small welt on the lower left of his face. "I am a greater man, so I will forgive you for that."

"Oh yes, you are so great, Brother. So, so great. Did you know, Raas Dragath would not have even considered this alliance had I not been involved? What does that say about you? About the great 'Lord of Stormhaven'? I want to know, Brother."

Merio's lower lip quivered but he gave no reply.

"You should be ashamed of yourself . . . living in such excess while your people suffer so."

His eyes narrowed at that. "I treat my people well."

"Do you? I'm inclined to think otherwise. Ravathyr agrees. He passed through your city. He saw the squalor."

"Poor harvest this year. Lack of trade, unsafe roads. The vicissitudes of life, you know. We've all suffered hardships."

He was enraged by that remark. "Look at you—at your garb. What hardships have you suffered? You look like a goddamn hedonist from Zirce. And you smell like a whore." Alarin limped closer. Merio stepped back, as though afraid to get hit again. But Alarin only said, "Never have I seen a more polarizing figure than you. You surround yourself with your voluptuaries, while the true heart of this city suffers in poverty. You may hold the province under your banner, but the common folk surely do not love you." Merio opened his mouth but Alarin spoke over him. "Greed makes a man blind. Fancy trinkets and colorful silks only serve to dull his ambition. Do you not remember Father's words?" He gestured to his own garments. "It is always the most timeworn clothes that fit the best."

Silence for a moment, then something unexpected happened. His little brother wept. He fell to his knees and wept. Tears were streaming down his face.

Alarin motioned all the guardsmen and attendants to leave the room. Soon the clamor faded, and he was left only with his little brother's snuffling. He didn't know what to say. Fortunately, Merio spoke first. "You're right, you're right, my brother. Even without your leg you're still strong, strong and smart like father was, like Zantherei and little Anseth, too. By the gods even Nyvia is more capable than I am. I am such a goddamn *fool*."

"That's not true," Alarin told him. He didn't know what else to say.

"Don't lie to me. I have enough toadies who do that, you know. Father sent me here because he deemed me too stupid to deal with the capital's principal affairs. He sent me here to run a purposeless city."

Alarin reached down to help Merio up. Pain flashed in his limb, but he grunted it away. "Stand up, my brother," he said.

Merio straightened himself, sucking in snot and wiping the tears from his reddened eyes. Sweat matted his wavy hair. "I cannot lead a kingdom. Look at me." He gave a small embarrassed laugh. "I don't know how to win the people. I try to offer kindness like father, they laugh at me. I try to be strong and firm like Zanth, they despise me. Tell me what I need to do, Elder Brother. Please, tell me, tell me, tell me."

"You are an Anirian still, are you not? Then rule your people as a true Anirian would. Shred all the colorful patterns, discard all the pomp . . . become accessible to your subjects. Show that you are not above them. The people will rejoice—they will see the truth in your heart."

"I will, Elder Brother," Merio said, sniffling. "I will, I will."

"Good. And most of all, place your trust in me. Trust in me and I will extend your kingdom and reunite the realm under its true and rightful house."

"I will, I will," he said once more.

CHAPTER FORTY-SEVEN

"**L**ord Demien."

Demien lifted himself from his featherbed, his eyes darting to the closed door curtain. He recognized the voice, yet it wasn't the hoarse speech of the proprietor, nor had Toben ever referred to him as 'Lord' or 'Demien'.

"Lord Demien," the voice repeated.

He threw on the nearest tunic crumpled on the floor. Then he raised the door curtain.

General Sabriel Soffin regarded him with his close-set eyes and round, cherubic face. He was fully adorned in the gray-black Anirian battledress, helmet tucked under an arm, its headplume folded back. "My lord, a thousand deaths could not attest for my nephew's lapse in judgment. He still has much to learn."

"He acted as any loyal servant of the Anir should," Demien replied. He stole a quick glance past the general, searching for others in the shadows. "It was his official duty to have me bound and brought back to the capital, just as it is yours now."

Soffin balked at that. "You're talking rot, my friend. You know men of steel and blood never abide by the robes of the court. May I?"

Demien stood aside to let the aging general enter. He found a seat on a nearby armchair, declining an offering of wine. His eyes wandered about the room, to the old trunks and hempen rags and empty bowls that all lay haphazardly about. "Much has happened since your disappearance from the Hollow, my friend. War threatens the realm and men are scrambling for footholds to power. Alarin Athera is forging an alliance with the southern Redlands, offering Merio's daughter as his dowry."

Demien frowned at that last statement. "Your reports are false."

"I'd thought the same, until defectors from the east began arriving at my gates. It's true, Demien, it's true and yet your brother remains beside Alarin."

He shook his head. "Szathan would never ally himself with the Red Terror. Not after all he's suffered at Thornberry."

"Still, I do not wish to face that man in battle. With you at the head of my vanguard, I'll rest easy knowing I won't have to."

"Lady Miriana will know of this treason."

"Her Majesty will absolve you of any crimes. She owes me a debt, you can say." His close-set eyes made another quick scan of the room. "You don't belong here, my lord. You are an officer of the Anir, not some base vagabond. I'll send for your battledress, your halberd, too. Word of your return will reinvigorate the spirits of my soldiers."

Demien shook his head. "I can't, old friend."

His cherubic face formed a frown. "We need you, Demien. The realm is in dire need of the great Savior of the Anir."

"Sorry, I'm not that man any longer."

Sabriel seemed to mull over that awhile. Finally, he gave a sigh, rising to his feet. "You're wrong, Demien. You will always be that man. He's in your blood. You can't change that any more than you can change the ebb of the tide or the turn of the moon. Anyway, you know where my quarters are. Come to me when your heart is ready."

Demien spent the remainder of the day in his room and in his cups. He left only to fetch a supper of millet stew with radishes and mallow. Silas just sat there toying with the porcelain figurine Lelana had given him. The poor boy seemed to miss the woman as much as Demien did. Indeed she was an exceptional woman—who wouldn't mourn the loss of her company? Demien missed most the nights they'd spent entwined as lovers in Indigo Cove. *Just go to her already, you stupid stubborn fool. Why prolong your misery?*

Silas placed the figurine in his hand. Demien looked at it, truly scrutinized it, from the details of the girl's flowing robe to the end-blown flute in her left hand. Her little smile made her seem so happy. Demien handed the figurine back to his son. "I miss her, too," he told him. He sat there for a bit longer. Then he got up and grabbed his boots.

Outside, the setting sun bathed the streetscape in shades of muted red. The market was all but empty save a handful of hawkers who were recounting their wares or tidying up their stalls. Demien found himself quickening his pace. He knew she was waiting for him. Waiting for him to come to his senses, to tell her that he forgave her. Her household was just ahead. Strange, the gate was open, but the keeper was nowhere to be seen. Inside, he found the main chamber vacant, the same of the adjoining wing-rooms. He headed across the courtyard, making his way past the cherry blossoms and rockeries, sure to find her in the rear chamber . . .

He did, eventually, find her there, although he dearly wished he hadn't.

She was lying in a twisted heap, naked and bloody and facedown, the stink of her emptied bowels spreading through the humid summer air. Demien knelt and brushed aside the blood-slick hair from her face; a terrible grimace was plastered there, a horrifying delineation of the last moments of her life. He found cuts on her arms and back, and more on her belly when he turned her over, but the one that had likely killed her was a laceration across the thigh, a deep gash that drained her life away. Her legs were folded over and stiff with rigor, her sex sticky from the spent seed of her rapers.

Something *crashed* behind him. Demien turned; Silas was standing there, the porcelain figurine broken at his feet. Demien meant to send him away, but hesitated as something began to stir behind the boy, something in the shadows there. He went for a closer look. It was a man still alive—his nose was smashed and his eyes were swollen shut and the top of his head was stained in dark blood, but he was alive. Demien recognized that weaselly face at once. Eldrith.

The impact and pattern of the wounds told Demien the attacker had used a mace with a long-handle and melon-shaped head. Such weapons originated in the far south, and were far less common than they were a decade ago, which meant they were most likely in the hands of brigands and criminals. But Demien needed to be sure. "Eldrith, look at me. Was it the outlaws—was it the outlaws of Wintersun?"

Eldrith spat a glob of bloody phlegm. "I-I can't see." He tried to raise a hand but couldn't seem to find the strength. "My eyes—please."

Demien wiped away the blood from the man's face. Swollen eyes looked upon Demien. "It hurts."

"Tell me who did this to you, Eldrith. *Tell me*."

"Please, I don't want to die."

Demien grabbed him by the collar of his cloak. "Neither did your sister. Now answer me or I'll kill you myself."

The man's only response was a low moan, so Demien let him go. He returned to Lelana. She had to have left something for him. *Anything*. Her left hand—yes, there was something beneath her left hand. It was hard to see from here but when he went closer . . . yes, she had written something in her own blood. He cupped her hand and lifted aside fingers whose nails were broken and encrusted with black gore. It was a word, a single word, smeared and nearly illegible. Wintersun.

He left the rear hall and found a spade somewhere. In the courtyard he dug and dug and dug, and when he was done his back ached and his hands were raw and blistered. The thought of Lelana's death moved him none. How could that be? He even tried to reach inside himself, as if to pull out some dormant mass of anguish and anger, but there was nothing.

Eldrith was dead by the time he returned. He wrapped Lelana in the silk coverlet of her featherbed, the one they'd shared many nights beneath, and carried her out to the courtyard. It was so dark he nearly tumbled into the open grave. He dumped her in instead. Silas helped pile the loose earth atop it. Then Demien went back inside the main chamber, and drank enough wine to topple a draft horse.

He barely remembered walking through the city, but suddenly he found himself standing before the interrogative torchlight of a pair of armored sentries. They were blocking the stairway that led to the commander's quarters. The one to his left—the ugly one with an underbite—was demanding answers from him, answers Demien didn't know, so he simply tried to push past, only to come to an abrupt halt before the gleaming tip of the man's saber.

"I will gut you, cur. Step back."

"Do as he says," the one holding the torch put in. He had a smaller frame and younger face, but could've easily been over thirty.

Demien demanded an audience with Sabriel Soffin, or slurred something to that effect.

The youthful one's brow furrowed. "What's on him—what is that, blood?"

"The torch, hold it here. It *is* blood." The ugly man's voice grew hostile. "Is this your blood, cur?"

Demien said something but couldn't remember what.

"Goddamn drunker," the ugly one said. "I should throw you in a cage cart." The two sentries spoke to each other for a moment or two, then the one with the underbite was gone, leaving Demien with the torchbearer. He was the more amiable of the two, at least until Demien threw up all over his boots. Then he was all grumbles and scowls and curses. For some reason Demien wanted to laugh, but then he heard movement from somewhere above. Heavy footfalls plodded down the upper stairway. "Bring him up," a voice said.

More night sentries waited along the upper wallwalks and turrets and outside the commander's quarters. Inside, Sabriel Soffin was bare-chested and barking orders. Scars covered his arms and belly, most of them small, except a particularly nasty cut that had sheared off half his left pectoral muscle. It was almost a decade ago but Demien still remembered it as though it were no more than a fortnight. Back then Sabriel still had the frame of a general, not the body of an aging man he was now.

Sabriel brought him to a stool. His eyes looked heavy from being roused. "Lord Demien, are you all right? Lord Demien." He looked elsewhere. "Fetch the physician, have him prepare a tonic." Someone went off. Others remained, talking in low voices.

"You were right," Demien said.

Sabriel motioned his men to be silent. "Right about what, Demien."

He paused to belch. "They killed her, you know. They *killed* her."

"Who, Demien?"

He shook his head. The room was awhirl with motion, but his thoughts came clear enough. "I have but one condition."

"Name it."

"The hills of Wintersun. I want them drenched in outlaw blood."

CHAPTER FORTY-EIGHT

Cathia Athera wore only a silk slip, but the constant swarm of attendants around her was like a dressing screen all the same. Somehow, in all the chaos, they were managing to comb her lustrous brown hair and apply a powder base to her cheeks and dab oils onto her skin.

Alarin turned his attention to the attendant kneeling before him. The stout young man had undone the straps of his wooden leg, and was slowly easing it off. The pain was dreadful today, but Alarin expected as much, given the overnight storm that had broken the heat. The warming oils soothed his stump well enough, but the physician's rough and inexperienced hands only made him miss Kalen all the more.

Merio was standing near his daughter's dressing table, observing the young woman and offering instructions to her many attendants. In simple gray robes he looked unusually plain today, though he matched well with the newfound homeliness of the surrounding inner chamber. Gone were the carved statues and long-necked vases and gold leaf mirrors, replaced by Anirian banners and unassuming wall curtains that could've easily been found in any chamber of the Hollow. It'd been over a week since the entire palace had been denuded of its finery, and still Merio would occasionally maunder on about how everything looked so 'gray' and 'bleak'. Alarin had to remind him that this was how an Anirian palace was meant to look.

The steady discordance of drunken voices continued to echo from the nearby Rosebud Hall. It'd been three days since the crimson-cloaked Redlander soldiers had first clogged it, sitting shoulder-to-shoulder and stuffing their mouths with food and drink and more food and drink. Each day Alarin had regaled Lord Dragath with fine courses and entertained him with praise, even as Alarin's own soldiers continued to defect. Merio had provided little comfort in the matter—in fact, he'd done little but argue over the most insignificant details. Typical Merio.

Today, however, was different. Today was the wedding day. The last day of celebration, the last banquet, the last day to endure the cacophony from the hall—and above all, the last day of Lord Dragath's reign.

"You look sweeter than a snowberry, my dear," Merio was saying to his daughter.

"It's a bit bland, my gown. Don't you think, Father? I look no more colorful than a raincloud."

"Too much cinnabar," he told the attendant tending Cathia's cheeks. "Too much, too much. She's the daughter of an esteemed lord, not some baseborn bawd. A faint hint of rouge is all that is needed. See? Like the underside of a rose petal." His voice softened when he spoke again to his daughter. "The colors of the Anir may be a bit bland, my dear, but you give them radiance."

Alarin could only agree—indeed, Cathia looked radiant. She was dressed in a high-collared gown of flowered silk, gray with black brocaded edges and a matching silver and onyx tiara. "The Red Terror will salivate over you like a hound over a trencher," her father said with a smile.

"I don't see what's so terrible about him," Cathia said offhandedly. "He seems rather harmless to me."

Merio's mirth vanished at once. "Don't be a fool, girl," he warned. "They *do* call him the Red Terror for a reason, you know."

"Your father speaks true," Alarin cut in. "Raas Dragath is vile man, a usurper who kills without compunction or restraint. He'd skin a man alive with no more thought than an old farmhand gives threshing wheat. And for the truly disfavored, he has them removed of limb and stuffed in the lower dungeons, to live out their miserable days in darkness. Trust me, my lady, when Dragath first carved out his southern kingdom, his city endured constant raids from neighboring barbarians. Instead of engaging in a long and costly battle, he paid the barbarians off with gold and valuables taken from a peaceful city to the south, and then cut off the heads of its citizens and returned claiming they were the heads of the barbarians. Make no mistake, the crimes and cruelties of this man tower to heaven itself."

The attendants had all stopped moving. No one spoke. The discordance from the nearby hall seemed to echo even louder. Cathia looked nervously at her father. "Perhaps I'm not yet ready for this."

Merio threw a scowl at Alarin. "You've frightened the girl. Was that necessary?"

"Her fear will make her cautious."

Merio didn't seem to agree, but he let it go. "How long must she be alone with Dragath?"

"For the consummation? No more than minutes. At her signal Szathan and Yuseth will move in."

"You are aware that Dragath's soldiers will search the bridal chamber as a precaution, yes?"

Alarin nodded. "It matters not. The storeroom is well-hidden behind the center wall curtain."

"Good, because if anything should happen to my daughter . . ." Merio let the warning drop. His eyes glanced up and behind Alarin, where Szathan Mordall stood. "You rush that dastard the moment her wine goblet hits the floor, you hear me, General?"

"I know the signal," the huge man replied. "I assure you I'm not so witless as I look."

"Yes, well, you haven't *looked* the same since your deputy general defected, have you now, General?"

Alarin hissed at that. "*Brother—*"

"I am displeased," Szathan shot back. "But even I'm smart enough to see that Gilberon Brehems is not a man who could be sworn to secrecy."

Alarin added, "I sent out a company of riders at dawn. I cannot risk anything more. My heart tells me that he'll return upon learning the truth."

"We will find out then," Merio said. His daughter came to stand before him, pleasing in her bridal gown. "Come along now," he said, taking Cathia's arm in his. "One more day with these Redlander louts. By this time tomorrow their heads will all be piked."

CHAPTER FORTY-NINE

They left the city of Amaranth Point a heaping mass of smolder and ruin.

Southward they went, southward across swollen floodplains and engorged riverbanks that meandered here and there like the watery veins of a blue heart. Anseth led the Vaskultans around intertwining confluences, where rivers met and diverged in opposite directions, west to join with the Grayling, south toward the Azure River.

Their constant companion was the Sparroc Mountains to the east, white-crowned and forested and hazy. Shimmering lakes lined the deep slopes of the valleys, and along the western mountainside, armies of larch and cedar and straight-trunked pine stood at attention. A patchwork of wildflowers dotted the meadows above the timberline, and at the greatest heights snowfields clung to every cranny and ledge to be seen.

Anseth found comfort in these lands, to be surrounded by lush, earthy aromas and a windswept sky. Above, broad-winged hawks swirled along the air currents, while badgers and large-eared deer crept below, and once he spotted a black bear with a paw full of chokecherries. He traded with drovers and moved through villages whose inhabitants were too tired to care about the strange passersby. They used hardwood instead of dung for fires, and on warm nights they slept beneath the lovely, star-besprinkled sky.

Before long they'd come before the curved walls of Aster Falls. The city drew much of its commerce from the surrounding waterways, which were teeming with shallow skiffs and flat-bottomed boats that often housed entire families. Fisherfolk settled along the banks themselves, on single-room homes raised on wooden stilts. And farther out, in the widening headwaters that led to the main stem, Anseth could see the ribbed sails of the distant river-going junks.

He had arranged for Governor Emeron Mathius to meet him in a guest yurt outside the encampment. It was the peak of summer, so Anseth had the bottoms of the single-layer felt walls rolled up for better ventilation. He stood before the entrance now, watching the Anirian banners bobbing up and over the hillcrest. He noted the extensive company of mounted guardsmen accompanying the governor's sedan chair. Dariok made it obvious that he didn't like what he saw. "Make him retire his guards," he said, scowling.

"No, it's enough that he's agreed to meet me in the yurts," Anseth told him.

"I don't give a stoat's prick," Dariok countered. "Make him retire his guards."

Anseth swatted at a pesky wasp. "I said no. Emeron Mathius is a man of honest virtue and unwavering faith."

He snorted at that. "You said the same of that other pissant to the north. That was before he cut the eyes out of three Vaskultans."

"It would've been more had Emeron's letter not found my hand."

"Lord Revek knows what he's doing," Kirik cut in.

Severak, also nearby, said, "Get out of his way, Dariok."

Dariok grunted but moved aside, allowing Anseth to approach his childhood friend. It was such an odd feeling, reuniting after so many years. Anseth was not the same man he once was. Would Emeron know that? Would he think him a savage?

His greeting to Anseth came as a most heartfelt embrace. "It's you, my friend," he said. "It's you, truly."

Governor Emeron Mathius was not a tall man, no taller than Anseth himself, but where Anseth's face was narrow and pale, Emeron's was round and ruddy and fixed with an upturned nose and carrot-tip chin. He was dressed in a long ash-colored gown, trimmed in ermine and tied at the waist by a plaited black sash. Age had given him a few extra pounds while making off with most of the hair on his head, but he was still the same calm and thoughtful man, with the same indefinable charm that seemed to shine from the inside out.

His personal guards were outfitted in feathered cloaks and the gray-black colors of the empire. To the Vaskultans they must've looked no different from Lygrest's soldiers—and they stared grimly at one another, the tension quickly growing palpable. Emeron tried to diffuse it by bowing deeply to the Vaskultan officers, but his warmth went unreturned. Dariok simply glared down at him as though he meant to run him through at any moment. Anseth put an arm on the governor's shoulder and turned him about. "We'll make this quick," he said, indicating the yurt's entrance. Emeron nodded and went inside.

They shared a seat around a low table. Emeron's eyes ventured off to study the peculiar furnishings of these northern tribespeople: the various blankets and knitwear, the leathers and saddle stands, the unusual patterns painted on the stools and storage chests. Seemingly satisfied, he returned his gaze to Anseth. "My friend, you look as fierce as the men you command."

"That I do," Anseth agreed. "And yet nothing comforts me more than to see you as jovial as ever. Forgive me for bringing you here, but my men bear no love for any Anirian, not since Lord Lygrest tried to run us down. But you saved my life, my friend, and for that I owe you a great debt."

"It was your brother's doing. I served only as his messenger."

"What news of Alarin? Tell me."

"He remains in Stormhaven with your brother Merio. They are

preparing for war against the Hollow. Seric Dyre marches eastward as we speak, with as many as fifteen thousand under his banners. He serves as Imperial Advisor now. I've no doubt he is expecting my allegiance."

"Will he have it?"

"You were both once dear friends to me, but I've always pledged my faith to you above all others, my friend. Do you not remember?"

"I remember a child's promise."

He looked insulted by that. "Does that make it any less true?"

A pair of young bondsmen interrupted to place some finger foods on the table. Emeron stared at the colorless squares of jellied sheep's head, opting for one of the biscuits instead. Anseth enjoyed one as well, washing it down with a horn of blackmilk. They spoke of the empire for a while, with Emeron imparting all the information that Anseth had missed since losing correspondence with his elder brother. He listened in silence, his face unmoving, impervious to emotion, just as all Vaskultans were taught to do. But inside, he was despairing. To hear that the emperor was murdered, that Zantherei lay poisoned and the realm had fallen into disunity—truly, it burdened his heart. War was brimming everywhere. Old friends like Seric Dyre were now among his enemies. In fact, the three of them, Anseth, Emeron, and Seric—how many days had they spent running through the avenues of the capital, making mischief wherever they went? They'd been inseparable young men once. By the gods, that time was over.

"I'll stand with you against Seric's army," Anseth said. "I have but four thousand Vaskultans, but I will stand with you."

Emeron's ruddy face jiggled when he shook his head. "You saw what happened earlier. Your men would be of no use to me."

"Still, you have what, thirty-five, thirty-six hundred here?" Anseth reminded him. "Seric has *four* times that number."

"The Burning Wolves—are you familiar with this maneuver, my friend?"

Anseth nodded. "Divert with fire and attack on all sides, yes. Seric will see it. He is far too clever for that."

"Unless he has no reason to look," he replied. "Listen, I have Seric's trust at the moment. I plan to use that against him."

"Let me aid you. I'll not sit idly by."

Emeron Mathius shook his head. "That you won't. You will continue to your elder brother as planned. I'll apprise him in a letter and have it sent at once. He'll be expecting you."

Anseth gave a nod. He pulled out the kidskin pouch from his belt, handing it to his friend. "Send it in this."

Emeron studied it. "For months I feared having to send word of your death to Alarin. How deeply relieved I am to be free of that burden."

That made Anseth smile. "If I were meant to die, I would be dead already. By the gods I *should* be dead already." A commotion was rising from outside the yurt—it sounded like Dariok, belligerent as usual. Anseth stood. It was time to end this little rendezvous. "It gladdens my heart to see you again, my friend."

Emeron went to his feet. "Mine as well." He set his plump hand on the protective leather of Anseth's shoulder. "Perhaps you are alive because you're meant for greater things, Anseth. Perhaps you've arrived at the most auspicious time."

———

The sounds of the bridal company grew and grew until at last the double doors of the chamber burst open and a whirl of drunken, cheerful voices flooded inside.

Hidden in the nearby storeroom, Szathan tensed himself, listening through the tiled wall. He glanced over to Yuseth Valate, who appeared as no more than a faint silhouette in the musty dark. *I pray you're ready,* Szathan thought. *The time is come.*

After the closing rituals of the marriage ceremony, Szathan and Yuseth had made their swift escape through the temple's rear chamber, moving unseen down a concealed path and into a small grove, where grooms waited with their mounts. Under the cover of darkness they'd raced back to the palace, entering the bridal chamber unseen, careful not to disturb the nuptial candles or ribbons or swirls of flower petals that skirted the connubial bed. The storeroom was located behind the center wall curtain; a tight space, fit for a man of average stature, but uncomfortable to the point of painful for a giant like Szathan Mordall. He'd spent the last hour feeling like a bear stuffed in a hollow log, his nose clogged with dust and his hands itchy from cobwebs.

Someone cast a lewd remark at the bride and groom, and laughter ensued. *Goddamn Redlander fools making this nothing like the stately affair it should be,* Szathan mused. At last the double doors came to a close, drowning out the wall of noise. All became quiet.

He could hear them speaking to each other, the deep rasps of Raas Dragath overpowering the soft murmurs of Lady Cathia Athera. Armchairs creaked and wine goblets clinked against lacquered tables. A short while later someone climbed into the bridal bed—it was Dragath, who beckoned his bride to join him. Szathan heard the girl's tiny footfalls of compliance. The low speech resumed for a time. Then, silence.

Szathan waited and waited, but the drop of the wine goblet never came. *What is she waiting for?* He glanced at Yuseth for an answer, but the general made no move. By the gods, Lord Merio would take both their heads if they allowed this brute to get on top of his precious daughter. Still, Szathan was hesitant. *Did she somehow forget?* A moment later he heard a moan—a woman's moan, long and soft and filled with pleasure.

Damn her. Szathan pulled free the hinged panel of wood and tile-work, then crawled out beneath the wall curtain and into the light of the chamber.

Twin charcoal braziers cast their dim light upon the canopied bed. Shadows moved behind the drawn, silver-spangled bedcurtains, back and forth as lovers move. Yuseth crept silently across the room, to stand in place beside the bed. He was wearing a simple hooded cloak, not his usual white but earthen brown in color.

Szathan could hear Dragath's grunts mixing with the woman's pleasured moans. *Why hadn't she thrown the goddamn goblet?* he thought, moving in front of the bed. A dagger slid into his hand. He nodded at Yuseth, who gave a quick pull to draw the curtains open.

Szathan lunged forward, seized Raas Dragath by a meaty arm, and yanked the naked wretch from the bed. The silk coverlet whirled in the air, coiling itself around the old warlord's body. Cathia shrieked. Dragath, slick with sweat and grunting like a boar, kicked and clawed at Szathan. The dagger fell. Dragath broke free of Szathan's hold, and was now fleeing across the chamber, his broad, naked body jiggling with each step. Szathan scooped up the dagger and chased him down, launching himself forward and stabbing the man's buttocks. Dragath tumbled headlong onto the floor tiles. A flurry of flower petals puffed into the air.

Dragath began to rise. Szathan wrapped a massive arm around his neck, then, drawing his saber, he leaned back and drove it straight through the bare flesh of the man's back, through skin and tissue and bone, to exit out the front. Dragath made a strange *buurk* sound, then dropped to his knees, slumping over on the blade. Szathan slid it out. The Redlander tyrant teetered there for a moment or two, then came crashing down on the floor. His toes twitched, but that was all. *He's dead,* Szathan thought. *At last the wretch is dead.*

Cathia was screaming. It was all Szathan heard now—the loud, piercing screams of a terrified woman. *What are you doing, girl, have you gone mad?* Yuseth was trying to calm her down, but it seemed the more he tried, the louder she screamed, which only made him grow more forceful. He was shouting at her now, shouting and squeezing her arms. "Don't harm her," Szathan roared. Yuseth threw her down to the floor. She gave a cry of pain.

Szathan was so mad he nearly struck the Stormhaven general. *What is wrong with you? She's Merio's daughter, goddamn it.* Yuseth was trying to tell him something, but Szathan ignored it and went to her. She was still naked, her breasts small and pale and pointed, her sex hidden beneath a soft black bush. Szathan looked up at Cathia's face. *Wait a moment.* No, not Cathia—not Cathia's face at all.

It was as if until now Yuseth had been speaking in an unfamiliar tongue. "It's not her. It's not *her!*" the general kept shouting, even as

Szathan left the young woman and went over to the lifeless form of Raas Dragath. He knelt for a closer look. This man had the telltale silvery hair and grizzled beard of the old warlord, but the face . . . the face was not the face of the Red Terror.

What in all hell? At first he thought that perhaps he'd been hiding in the wrong room, as foolish as that sounded, but then his wits returned and he realized the deceit. He looked back at the young woman. Yuseth had a dagger at her throat, shouting, "Where is he? *Speak!*" She sputtered an incoherent reply, her tears ruining her ash and antimony eyeshadow.

The double doors burst open. A handful of Anirian guards stormed inside. Lord Alarin Athera followed in a limp. He spotted the dead man on the floor and his face glowed in triumph. But it was a triumph that slowly melted away when he went over and bent down to see the truth of the man's identity. Szathan had no words inside him. It felt like someone punched him in the gut.

Alarin rose and shouted at his men to bring back Cathia at once. He offered promises of coin and fiefs for any man who returned with Dragath's head. Then he went over to the naked girl. He raised her chin to meet her eyes. "A little thin, but comely enough," he said to himself. "Why did you do it? Was it land he offered you? Status? Strings of coin?"

She nodded frantically at all of them.

"Which was it, my dear?"

She seemed too distraught for sensible thought. "H-he said no harm would come to me. H-he said—"

"That's enough now," Alarin said. He turned away from her, rubbing his balding pate with long fingers. More soldiers hustled through the open chamber door, this time with Lord Merio at the fore. Szathan heard Alarin curse. The youngest Athera brother crossed the chamber hesitantly, as if wading through a den of vipers. General Yuseth went to his side, speaking in his ear. Merio's hands closed into fists. He barked orders and the general went off at once. Then he approached his older brother.

"We'll get her back," Alarin told him. Merio said nothing to that.

He simply stood there, his brown eyes fixed on the young woman who was not his daughter. For a moment it looked like Merio would strike her, but he only turned and uttered a command to his guardsmen. The clean-shaven pair hurried out to the antechamber, where Szathan could see Redlander men kneeling in surrender. The guards chose a robed and unarmored fellow and brought him inside. It was the southland advisor Ravathyr Aeryn, hands bound and head slumped between gaunt shoulders. Merio turned to his elder brother. "You are not the only Athera who's full of tricks," he said.

CHAPTER FIFTY

The sharpened stakes of the outlaw's mountain stronghold glowed like amber fangs in the waning afternoon light. Even at its weakest points, the palisade rose over ten feet, with a tight, gapless construction more formidable than expected. Still, Demien Mordall wasn't concerned. The amber hue soon faded as the sun sank behind a thick pall of clouds, rendering the surrounding hills both dreary and gray. Moments later the drizzle returned, a cold drizzle, one that hinted at the coming of autumn.

Ahorse, Demien continued to ride up and down the wall, taunting the enemy, cursing every drop of blood in their craven bodies. His surcoat and oversized cloak were made of thick undyed wool, which did well to conceal his Grand Commandant's armor beneath. His massive halberd, sixty pounds of ash and snowflake steel, lay socketed in his saddle. Dreadfang clung sheathed to his hip. "I am but a single man," he shouted up. "Are you so filled with cowardice that you will take a woman's life and hide from a single man?" He feigned a swig of his winegourd. "Show yourselves and prove your damn mettle."

On the wooden wall-walks above, cloaked outlaws observed in silence. The clappers of the watchmen had long grown silent, but the beacon that warned of Demien's presence still burned bright. Demien could feel the crossbowmen aiming at him from the rude wooden hoardings. And even though his voice was terribly hoarse, he continued his tirade of taunts and jeers, his fury repeatedly renewed by the image of Lelana, dead and naked on her chamber floor.

The stronghold had no moat, only a single gate of iron-studded wood, which began to open now with a slow and terrible whine. From the haze emerged some three score footmen, in a double crescent formation that Demien knew as the Feral Goose, though this version was not so disciplined. The outlaws were a ragbag of ill-fitted armor and mismatched leathers and variegated cloaks, with those in the front-line brandishing spears and lances while those in the rear held cross-bows. Demien sighed at their numbers. *They mean to kill me and be done with it.* But then a center pathway opened, revealing a lone figure, a burly figure, mounted and draped in heavy coat of lamellar and scale beneath a leopard skin cape. On his head was a feather-crested conical helm, with a nasal that came to a point just above his mane-thick mustache, which he carelessly stroked as he spoke. "You must have eaten a tiger's gall to dare come alone."

Demien tossed his winegourd to the ground. "Are you the one who took my lady's life?"

"In Thornberry." He nodded. "That I am." The rain grew stronger, clattering against the outlaw's cape from a sidelong angle. "Her life for the brother of mine you took at the bridge." The burly man nudged his steed forward; in his hands was a great axe. "And after I split your skull, I'll use it to sip my wine later tonight."

Demien pulled his halberd from its socket. The outlaw's mustache rose as his lips curled into a grin, as if he couldn't wait to make the weapon his own. *Such confidence in this fool,* Demien thought, whipping his horse into a run.

The outlaw came in screaming, his axe cutting through the air.

Demien's halberd parried it in a steel-sparked clash. The man turned the weapon—skillfully, to strike from an off-angle. Again, Demien parried. Their interlocked weapons grated against each other. Demien looked into the outlaw's eyes—and smiled. The outlaw's mustache twitched in reply. Then he turned and galloped off, his axehead trailing along the sodden earth. Demien raced after him. The outlaw turned in his saddle—not with axe but bow in hand now. The tip of the drawn arrow glistened in the rain, and, with a sharp *twang,* it flew.

It was a maneuver that might've fooled even a veteran cavalryman, but Demien Mordall was of course something more. Already he had Dreadfang out, and with a shrill *clang* the arrow was deflected off the flat of the blade. The outlaw, still galloping, fired again. Another clang. The man's eyes went wide. He tried to nock a third arrow, but Demien circled from the flank and cut off his movement. The outlaw had nowhere to go. For a split second he looked as if he finally knew what kind of opponent he was facing . . . and then Dreadfang was upon him.

The sword cleaved through the leather gorget of the man's neck, opening the pale flesh beneath. A second cut and the outlaw's face ripped wide open, helmet shards and mustache hairs and blood all spitting into the air. Something of a garbled hiss spilled from his torn lips, and he toppled from his saddle, landing with a dull *plop* on the mud-soaked earth.

Demien wheeled around to face the others. There was no noise, not a clink of armor, not a single voice, nothing. The outlaws simply stood there, leaderless and directionless, fear and consternation plastered on their faces. They seemed ready to break; Demien didn't want them to break. *Think quickly, you fool.* He yanked the reins, turning to flee. To flee is to goad a man into chase. And chase they did.

He could hear them charging across the saturated earth. *That's it,* Demien thought. *That's it, run me down.* He led on toward a nest of hills, which were jagged and uneven and perfect for concealing men. Down a slope and a bog rose up, engulfing his steed to hock and knee, slowing it to a desperate stagger. The outlaws were gaining ground. Bolts whizzed past. One struck the crupper of his horse, but the beast pushed on. A second tore through Demien's cloak, a third glanced off the iron plates of his right cuisse. He urged the beast on and on until it roared free of the bog, then he raced forward until the hills around him rose and came alive.

Two thousand mounted Anirian soldiers stormed from the hillcrest in two massed battalions. The pursuing outlaws scrambled desperately for safety, but no matter where they turned, the unyielding, inexorable force of the cavalrymen was there to steamroll through them. Demien turned about and joined the rear ranks, beside the fire squads whose wheeled platforms groaned forward and launched bitumen-tipped arrows that streaked across the sky and set the palisade ablaze.

Sabriel Soffin led the van, wearing his black halfhelm and serrated hem general's cloak. His nephew Fenerus rode beside him, shouting orders as his soldiers rammed through the crude wooden gate and flooded into the stronghold. Demien followed across a hilly sward interspersed with thatch-roofed longhouses and timber-framed wattle and daub cottages. On meandering cobblestone paths outlaws darted here and there, most either trampled or cut down or driven back to the safety of the distant keep.

It was a crude structure, the keep, its bailey yard enclosed by a second palisade, smaller and less formed than the first, though ringed in a defensive moat. Before that moat gathered six rows of outlaw foot-men. Demien joined the vanguard of the Anirian ranks to engage the enemy. From the rear, the fire squads launched salvoes of blazing arrows at the raised timber drawbridge and surrounding stakewall. "Burn it *down,*" General Sabriel was shouting, as he thrust skyward the tip of his long-handled saber.

From watchtowers above, bolts and stones and buckets of scalding oil rained down upon the battleground, showering friend and foe alike. Anirian archers fired back, sending outlaws toppling off the upper platforms, to scream a horrendous scream as they plunged sixty feet to the earth. It was so abrupt, the silence that followed when their bodies hit. Demien never looked, just kept killing and killing, even as a burning man landed mere feet from where he stood. He had dropped his halberd earlier but he couldn't recall when, and in his hands now was Dreadfang. He used the sword to gut foe after foe, while blood splashed higher and higher up his killing arm.

Without warning, the watchtower wobbled in the air, spurting bright orange flames and billows of black smoke. Wood snapped and splintered and suddenly gave way, and with an enormous crack like a quake ripping the sky, the tower came crashing down. *BOOM.* Demien didn't remember being thrown to the ground, but there he was, eating mouthfuls of mud. Ash and debris covered the area around him. There was a strange silence, a sudden lull in the chaos, before the sounds of battle swiftly resumed.

The fallen watchtower had taken down a section of the palisade wall, and now the Anirian soldiers were piling the wreckage into the moat, building a rudimentary bridge. Around them corpses bobbed in the murky water, among split logs of fire-chewed wood and patches of black oil. Demien pushed his way through, eyes burning and face drenched in sweat. Ahead, he could see a throng of outlaws charging down the motte; behind them, the wooden keep was a blaze of ruin. Demien moved forward, rankmates at his sides, to meet this last desperate sortie.

The first foeman that came for him was no more than a boy. Demien swept his leg and tossed him to the ground and pierced his heart. The next man he slashed across the upper torso, shredding leather like linen. He took down one more and now the outlaws were no longer fighting back. Were they frozen with fear? Demien didn't care. He struck down another. Then another. The next he took at the throat. Another. Another. Then another, and . . .

A hand clamped down on Demien's shoulder; he whirled about. Sabriel Soffin stood wide-eyed and blood-matted from boot to hip. "Demien," he rasped, harsh as though he had said it a thousand times. "It's over, Demien." His breathing was so heavy. "Can you hear me? It's *over.*"

Only then did Demien begin to realize . . . only then did he begin to see the cast weapons and white rags being waved by the surrendered outlaws. He also saw charred men, decapitated men, men with all manner of wounds, littering the area, among the remains of the palisade wall or in piles at the foot of the motte. An acrid gust of smoke tightened his throat. Severed hands and arms and feet peered from their deathbeds in the mud, some mere spans from where Demien stood.

He took a step forward—and stumbled. Weakness overwhelmed him; he dropped to a knee. An arrow shaft, he saw, protruded from his chest, a deep wound, halfway to the fletching, with blood drooling from the broken scales of his armor. He went to speak but gobs of blood came out instead. Then the muddy earth rose up to take him.

Next he knew he was looking up at the sky, watching tendrils of smoke coalesce into the gray. Rain sprayed his face, sharp and winter-cold. Sabriel was shouting but Demien couldn't hear over the heave of his own lungs. Every breath became tighter and tighter. He clutched at Sabriel's cloak, squeezing so hard he wrung it of rainwater and blood. With each movement he could feel the arrowhead tearing at his insides. The pain was a white-hot agony that drilled deep inside the core of his being. He needed to stop it—he'd do anything to stop it. His hand came down to grasp the arrow shaft. He clenched his teeth, ready to pull.

A hand stopped him. "No," he heard Sabriel say. "You'll die."

"I know," Demien replied. He tried to push the man's hand away but the old fool wouldn't budge. He tried and tried until what little strength he had left also abandoned him, and soon, the world began to fade. The smells, the voices, the pain in his chest and the pattering of the rain—all of it gone. In its place was light, radiant and measureless white light. In it stood a woman. Was it Lelana? No, it was his wife. Sweet, beautiful Alana. She was standing beside another . . . beside Emperor Thavian Siven, tall and stately and smiling his most heart-warming smile. Demien felt himself smiling, too. He closed his eyes and drifted toward them . . . toward the vast and coruscating light.

BOOK V: INFERNO

CHAPTER FIFTY-ONE

It was late when Miriana Athera moved along the outskirts of the palace district, the hood of her tattered cloak pulled tight against the clattering rain. Her heelless boots sloshed ankle-deep across the avenues, leaving her garb muddy and her toes cold. To her left, Vylas hurried to keep up, while opposite him, Captain Cyrille Vileron walked with long strides. Both wore hooded cloaks, homespun and undyed, the same as her own.

Waiting in the guesthouse was her unexpected visitor, a general by the name of Gilberon Brehems. River patrol had found him along an eastern arm of the Grayling. She assumed deception was at play, knowing well his lifelong devotion to General Szathan Mordall. Still, she'd made sure to offer this man a most welcome stay, having arranged for him an abundance of wine and warmth and the women of his choice.

A shout from behind made her stop. Turning, she saw a wet pair of night watch guards approach with lanterns upraised. Cyrille went ahead to address them. A moment later she saw the guards fall to their knees in the mud-soaked ground. "Get up," she went over and told them. "I'll not punish a man for doing his duty. It is more than can be said of all the other halfwits that let me pass. Now keep your lips tight about this and I'll have my steward reach you with a generous reward."

The men gushed with gratitude and Miriana moved on. She entered the guesthouse through an arched gate, tracking rainwater and mud across the antechamber's mosaic tile floor. The waiting guards ceased their idle chatter and bowed their heads deeply. One particularly reedy fellow raised the door curtain to the inner chamber, allowing Miriana and her two companions inside.

The room was a mess of strewn mats and overturned wine cups and heaps of shabby clothing slung across armchairs and bedrails. Dim light flickered behind a sateen screen. Even with her cold and stuffy nose Miriana could smell the sultry mix of perfume and passion. It made her think of Seric. She stepped behind the screen and found a great, hulking, hairy man, sipping from a wine goblet while three dark-skinned courtesans lay clinging to him in a swirl of silken sheets. One was fondling his chest, the second kissing and purring against his neck. The third was hunched between his legs, head bobbing up and down . . . and given only the view of the woman's backside, Miriana could still tell its owner at once. *"Yana!"* she gasped.

The handmaiden spun, her bare breasts jiggling in the dim ochre light. She scrambled sheepishly away from the naked man, wiping the slaver from her lips. Miriana's eyes were drawn to the general's manhood, fat and slick and rising from a bramble of black hair. "You're not a Sijian broad," the man muttered. "But you're tall as a hollyhock. Perhaps I'll make an exception. Come here, lady, into the light so I can better see you."

Miriana growled at her brother. "Why is Yana with him?"

Vylas gave a shrug. "You said give him any courtesan he wanted. He wanted Sijians. He wanted her."

Miriana stared at the husky general. He was breathing heavily, his fuzzy shoulders glistening with whatever oils the courtesans had rubbed on him. Wine dripped from the tangles of his beard. By the gods he sickened her. The thought of her sweet little Yana being pounded by this ugly beast of a man . . .

The general used the silk sheet to cover his manhood. Then he stood. As blubbery as his belly was, his chest was quite the opposite: thick and muscled and covered in scars that looked like pink, hairless worms across his body. "Who are you?" he asked.

Miriana stepped into the light. "I'm the woman who arranged your accommodations. Are you enjoying them, General?"

His eyes went wide. "Forgive me, my lady." He began searching for his clothes. "I wasn't expecting you so soon. Forgive me, forgive old Brehems. I'm a drunkard and a fool." He threw on his smallclothes and trousers, then searched aimlessly for his tunic.

She took a seat on an uncomfortable armchair. "General Brehems, I am told you have honorably served the Anir through all its good fortunes and bad. They say your loyalty is as firm as a rock."

"Six years under General Szathan Mordall," he said. "Four under your husband and five under Lord Lasarin." He went back to searching for his tunic.

"Forget your garb, General. Please, sit. Tell me why you've come."

He went over to a stool and joined her. Perhaps it was the wine, but he seemed to have a hard time sitting still. "To speak plainly, my lady —Your Majesty—I don't care for you any more than I do Lord Merio. But Raas Dragath's alliance with Stormhaven . . . it's an injustice to heaven and a goddamn stain upon all that is sacred to the Anir." He seemed to think for a moment on what he just said, then smiled as if amazed that he was able to get all the words correct.

"An injustice indeed," she said. "But is such an alliance truly worth abandoning your lord after all your years of service?"

"Slow down there, my friend, or you'll have nothing left to chew later on." Brehems was looking at Vylas, who was gnawing on his fingernails. The privy counselor froze, the unmasked side of his face turning red. Slowly, he removed his fingers from his mouth, and Brehems gave a hoarse snicker.

"Go on, General," Miriana said.

He quaffed a draught of wine before continuing. "That's not much more to say, Your Majesty. I served honorably your husband for many years—to follow you now would satisfy my heart's blood. I'll never serve that wretched Redlander tyrant, no I won't."

His words annoyed her. *Does he think me so gullible?* She clutched the arms of her chair, her knuckles going white. *No*, she decided, *he couldn't be this stupid.* She looked him up and down. *A waste of time, this one.* "You disappoint me, General. I was expecting to hear something a bit more . . . persuasive." She turned to her guards, "See this man to a cell. Tomorrow his head will find the East Gate."

Metal clanged as her guards went into motion. General Brehems didn't move at all. He had this wild, disbelieving stare, the look of a man who'd just lost his home to a terrible storm. But when the guards put their hands on him, he threw his head back and burst into laughter. It was a chilling sound, mirthless and loud.

She raised a hand to stay the guards. "Do my words amuse you, General?"

His red-rimmed eyes peered up at her, and when he spoke his voice was somber. "You poor foolish woman. Turning away honest and loyal men while keeping snakes at your side . . ." He gave a rueful laugh. "I guess old Brehems expected too much from a lowborn bawd."

"How *dare* you speak to your empress that way," Vylas snarled.

"What snakes do I keep, General?" Miriana asked.

Vylas said, "Sister, it's a dilatory tactic. The man obviously has nothing—"

"Be *quiet*, Brother," she said, then urged Brehems to continue.

The general's voice retained its somber tone. "I've chosen the wrong lord, and for that, I blame myself. It's pointless to despair. You've condemned me to die. What I know will die with me."

She studied him for a long moment. "Leave us, all of you."

"My lady," both Vylas and Cyrille protested.

"Be gone, Captain. You too, Brother. I command it."

Both men sighed and went off, the guards following behind. She was alone with this man now, this hairy, drunken oaf of a general. Miriana had long dealt with men of his stamp, and yet, she found herself feeling more vulnerable than she cared to admit. *Am I making a mistake?* She did her best to hide her unease. "General, you know I've spent many months dealing with alleged defectors like you. Men who come to me, offering to bend their knee, but only to reveal a dagger concealed in their boot. I know all too well the eyes of deceit."

"Then let my goddamn life be forfeit," he said. "I do not fear death."

Miriana got up and approached him, her boots tapping against the tiled floor. Without heels, she still stood a hair taller than the general, and yet, she felt so tiny next to him. The man had the frame of a woodland bear, his hands twice the size of hers. One was busy scratching at his crotch, but she knew he didn't need both to strangle her little neck. "General, forgive me if I've misjudged you. I am more than willing to offer you a full pardon . . ."

He nodded at that. "Spare your little dance, my lady, I'll tell you what you want to know." He studied the floor for so long that she assumed he was stalling, as if he had nothing to reveal all along. But then he said, "Your snake is Seric Dyre."

Anger rose inside her. "Rot. Seric serves the Anir, heart and soul. Were it not for Seric we'd not be having this very discussion. It was his victory at the Horns of Vermilion—"

"I fought at the Horns," he cut in. "He wasn't there."

"It was Lord Seric's stratagem that gave you your victory, General."

Brehems regarded her coldly. "That may be, but it was also Seric Dyre who planned to defect to Raas Dragath's side. He fed the Redlander bastard intelligence for months. The letter Lord Alarin posted all over the Hollow, everything he wrote was true, all of it I tell you. That wormy little Redlander emissary, he revealed it all."

"I need more than just your words, General," she countered, still angry.

Brehems walked off to rummage through his belongings. Miriana watched him absently. Indeed, Seric's reaction to Alarin's proclamation had always struck her as odd, especially the hostile and emphatic way Seric denied it. Still, this could all be part of the general's ruse; she mustn't forget that.

"Is this enough?" He returned and placed a tattered letter in her hand. "I stole it the night before I deserted. A man of my size, you wouldn't think I could move as quietly as I do."

She unfolded it. It was a letter to the Redlands, in Seric's handwriting, incriminating words, words that corroborated a clandestine agreement between Seric and Raas Dragath. She only read three or four lines before her stomach weakened. *Could this hulking fool be telling the truth?* she wondered. If this letter was a forgery, it was a masterly one. *What have I done? I've placed a traitorous man at the fore of the realm. Oh, how foolish you are, woman!* She tried her best to remain calm. "My scribes will verify the authenticity of this letter. If it proves true, you'll be given a formal apology and a place in the ranks."

General Brehems said something in reply, but Miriana was no longer listening. She left the chamber soon after, her thoughts racing. Vylas appeared but she barged past him. "Sister, are you all right?" he called after her. Outside, cold rain streamed down her face. She didn't bother to raise her hood. Vylas was still calling for her. She halted only when he grabbed her arm and turned her about. "Sister—"

"You were right," she told him. "You were right about Seric. He betrayed the capital. He betrayed us *all.*"

CHAPTER FIFTY-TWO

T he letter arrived inside a familiar kidskin pouch.

Alone at his writing desk, Alarin Athera studied the lines and curves of filigree and the horned Sadralen head burned in the leather. The letter inside bore Emeron Mathius's provincial seal, the soaring ivory crow. He broke the seal but didn't open it. Instead he rose to visit the privy and also to refill his wine goblet. Then, contented at last, he settled back in his seat to read.

My lord and dear friend, nothing warms my heart more than to inform you that your brother Anseth has arrived in my city alive and in good spirits. He plans to make his arrival at Stormhaven before the season's turn. While I regret being unable to attend your reunion, I am certain it will be a most glorious one.

In other matters, Seric Dyre is soon to reach Aster Falls. He will find my gates open and my knee bent, but I intend to have his head soon enough. With Seric gone the Hollow stands to be devoured by the east. Heaven above bears witness to my vow. You have my aid in all exigencies of the realm. - Emeron Mathius, Provincial Governor of Whitecrow and Lord of Aster Falls.

Alarin couldn't help but smile at the thought of reuniting with Anseth. He needed his young brother, now more than ever, since Merio had spurned him after Cathia's abduction. Alarin had spent summer's end here in his chamber, or occasionally in the palace conservatory, where the tiers of cloudfalls breathed life into his old soul. They were so gentle, so tranquil—their nebulous petals like downy puffs of heaven upon the earth. In his secret heart he'd hoped they would release their brilliant, ensconcing light, both healing his infirmity and revealing his purpose in reuniting the realm, just as they'd done for Emperor Thalastor in the Annals of the Anir.

But they never did. Of course they never did. It was just a stupid fireside story, and only a stupid man would consider otherwise. *You are, and always will be, a cripple,* he told himself.

With a sigh Alarin rose, limping to the window. He unlatched and opened the shutters to observe the crisp autumn landscape below. Sea-worn junks bobbed along the meandering tributaries, their lugsails glowing in the pale midmorning sun. On land, tree boughs and branches rustled and swayed in the wind. Closer, shaggy bark hickories and maples dropped their golden and crimson leaves onto the outer courtyards below, where the thud and thwack of practice swords meant young men in training.

Alarin looked away. The solitude here was far more lacerating than that of the Hollow. He had none of his tomes to read, and no armillary sphere to keep him busy looking to the heavens for hours. And back in the Hollow, Kalen and his sister had often visited him, just to make sure he was in good health. Here, no one came. Not Merio, not any of his stewards, not even his attendants.

Of Szathan Mordall, well, he'd sent the big general west. The look Szathan had given him before he departed was chilling. Still, Alarin couldn't blame him—not only had Alarin driven away a loyal officer in Gilberon Brehems, he'd done the very thing he promised he would never do: ally with the Redlands. Still, Alarin had no choice. Cathia was Raas Dragath's prisoner now. The Redlands warmonger had used her to force Alarin's hand, demanding he send Szathan and a regiment of soldiers to join under his banners. What could Alarin do? Having Ravathyr in custody wasn't enough of a bartering tool, much to Merio's dismay.

Alarin placed his hands over his face, his fingers rubbing at his balding pate. He needed to question Ravathyr, to find out why the advisor wasn't worth his ransom. He'd tried once already, but the prison guards had brusquely sent him away. This time, however, would be different. Alarin fetched a small sack of coin and tied it to his belt, then reached for his cloak from a peg above the bedpost. He clasped it over his shoulders and exited the chamber.

The expansive corridors were once again furnished with all the fancy décor Merio had once promised to get rid of. It was a spiteful gesture, a gesture of rebellious immaturity, which of course was expected of Merio. Alarin exited through an arched doorway at the far end of the wing, crossing the courtyard and heading into an entry hall. The downward steps leading to the lower prison chamber were uneven and difficult, causing a deep, penetrating ache to course through his leg. At the bottom, he found himself in a dim and musty corridor, with a wrought iron door at the far end. Inside, a pair of unshaven turnkeys sat at a table, playing a gambling game on a square board.

A row of hanging torches lit the cells at their backs. When they saw Alarin they sighed and put their game pieces down. One rose. He had a distrustful look and disk-shaped eyes that made hard, pronounced blinks. "Lord Alarin, no one enters without Lord Merio's consent. Not even you, my lord."

"I am still the chief military commander of Stormhaven. Now let me through, I need to speak to the Redlander."

The turnkey crossed his arms. "You know I cannot do that, my lord."

Alarin untied the sack of coin and placed into the turnkey's hand.

The man judged its weight, then gave a satisfied nod. Alarin went to move past, but the second turnkey rose to stop him. He was the same height as the first, but broader of shoulder and bearing an odd, flattened face. "Forgot about me."

Alarin gestured to the sack in his friend's hand. "That's more than enough for both of you. More than your yearly wages, I'm sure."

The broad one didn't budge. "But my friend here is a greedy man."

Alarin glared at him. *Miserable wretch.* He had nothing else to grease this fool's palm with—he had to think fast. He gestured to his wooden leg. "As you can see I am a lamed man. And for a lamed man, the walk to this prison chamber is terribly long and terribly painful, especially those godawful stairs."

The turnkey looked unconcerned.

"Now, I didn't intend to endure this ache just to be sent away again, so this time I made sure not to come alone. At the end of the corridor are men, soldiers. If I am forced to return to them unhappy, then my soldiers will in turn be unhappy."

The turnkey said nothing, but his eyes darted behind Alarin, searching the darkness there.

"Now if my soldiers are unhappy, then I guarantee they will make *you* quite unhappy. Do you understand what I'm telling you?"

The turnkey just stood there looking at him. Alarin knew if he had expressed just the right amount of confidence, the lie would be believed. And it was. In the end, the turnkey produced a bronze key from his belt, then went to the prisoner's cell and opened it with a dull click. The other man handed Alarin an oil lamp. "Be quick," he muttered, as Alarin moved into the waiting darkness.

Ravathyr was sitting on his chamberpot, his trousers down around his ankles. He shielded his eyes from the sudden light, the palms of his hands black with encrusted dirt. He brought them down to hike up his trousers. His hair was filthy and knotted, his cheeks cavernous, his eyes pale and rheumy. "Lord Alarin?" he asked. "How long have I been . . .?"

Alarin set the lamp down. He handed the advisor his winegourd, watching Ravathyr drink with utter abandon. "Just over a lunar month," Alarin told him. "I need to know if you had anything to do with Raas Dragath's escape."

Ravathyr was mumbling to himself, not listening.

"The wedding, Dragath's escape," Alarin repeated firmly. "I need to know if you had any part of it."

The sternness in Alarin's voice grabbed the gaunt man's attention. "You think so little of me," he said. "Of my admiration for you." He pushed the hair from his eyes. "His military advisor, the young general who betrayed you at Thornberry. He's the schemer you seek."

"Hiriam Thraves," Alarin said at once. It was no surprise—Hiriam was certainly among the craftiest of men. "I believe you, my friend." Alarin went to the ground, the hinge of his knee squealing as it bent. "As I hope you believe that I had no part in your capture," he confessed. "I offered you as an exchange for Merio's daughter, but Dragath wanted no part of it."

Ravathyr gave a dejected sigh. "Of course not. Does the alliance remain in good faith?"

Alarin nodded. "Raas Dragath plans to march upon Thornberry. He has demanded two thousand of my men, with Szathan Mordall to lead the vanguard."

"Was the demand met?"

Another nod. "He threatened to pike Cathia's head if I didn't."

"He means it. Sever your faith and the girl will die."

"But what of you? Even he is not so savage as to let his chief advisor die for nothing."

"My life is worth spit to him," he said. "And yet it shames me that I don't wish for death. My dear wife and children, they'll have nothing without me. Save this poor coward's life, and I will honor you the rest of my days."

The turnkeys called for him from outside the cell. Alarin rose, his phantom leg flaring with ache. "I'll talk to Merio. He will listen. I promise you, my friend, I promise to get you out of here."

That night he lay in bed, listening to the howling wind bang against the latched shutters. He could feel himself falling in and out of sleep, his mind a wasteland of wandering thoughts. It seemed he'd made the right move in sending Szathan to the Redlands, and yet, he couldn't help but resent Merio for it. After all, the worth of a general like Szathan Mordall was far greater than the worth of a man's daughter. But this was Merio's daughter, the daughter he'd doted on every day of her young life. If Cathia were murdered, Alarin would be outcast. Merio would never forgive him.

His thoughts turned to Anseth. He visualized the moment of their reunion—what his brother would look like, what his brother would say. Anseth had lived among the northern nomads for years. *Nine years.* So much had befallen the realm since: a regent poisoned, an emperor murdered, an empire torn and plagued with pretenders and their uneasy alliances. Good men had become traitors. Friends had become enemies. Seric Dyre came to mind. The newly appointed Imperial Advisor was marching from the north, unknowingly to his own death. Would the people grieve for Seric? Would Nyvia? Their marriage had ended years ago, but she did bear him a son. A son that would likely desire vengeance. Alarin sighed beneath the coverlets. *And ever the cycle turns,* he thought, allowing his eyes to close.

A noise, from outside the window. Not the typical howling or banging of the wind, but more of a scratching sound, like a wildcat kneading a snag. Alarin raised his head. There it was again—that same scratching, faint but noticeable. He rose and limped over to the window, listening closely. *Skrrt, skrrt, skrrt.* It sounded like something —or someone—was trying to get inside. *That's not possible,* he thought. *I'm forty feet above the ground, and there's no balcony.* But there it came again. *Skrrt, skrrt, skrrt.* Alarin limped back to his feath-erbed, grabbing the dagger he kept concealed by the nightstand. He returned to the shutters. *Skrrt, skrrt, skrrt.* He unlatched them, opening
. . .

It was Ravathyr—or Ravathyr's head, his severed head, floating in the darkness, pale and soaked with rain. Blood poured from his open neck, streaming like bright red ribbons. Cold, lifeless eyes locked onto Alarin's, then the advisor's mouth opened, emitting a horrific shriek, a tortured and guttural sound that frightened Alarin to the very marrow of his bones. He thrust the dagger into the open mouth, driving the blade as deep as he could. The head fell away, its shriek fading in the gale.

Alarin just stood there, shaking, numb, speechless. He reached up to close the shutters. A pair of hands appeared, belonging to Ravathyr's headless body. It was clawing up the window, clawing its way inside. Alarin grabbed the thing by its shoulders and shoved it down, hard as he could, shoving and shoving as blood from its open neck spurted like a blowhole in his face. He pried its cold fingers from the sill, and gave one final, heaving, *shove*. The headless body shrank into the swallowing darkness. Alarin slammed the shutters closed.

Then he woke up.

CHAPTER FIFTY-THREE

"Lord Emeron Mathius is most eager to see you, my lord," the steward said. He was a tall, cheery-eyed man with a perfect band of white hair wrapped around an otherwise spotless pink dome.

Seric Dyre nodded. The escort ferry dipped and bobbed as it made its way through the canaled streets of the city, the motion causing gentle sprays of water to splash upon the oarsmen and deck. To Seric's left, the waterfront residential buildings rose tall and narrow, with household members working busily on the private wharfs, either washing vegetables or dumping waste or haggling with boat merchants. Around them small children tottered and played, tied at the waist with fat, floatable gourds in case they fell into the water. Above, the midday sunlight beamed down warm and bright, shimmering against the latticework of waterways and bathing the surrounding rooftops and walls.

It pleased Seric to see the port city of Aster Falls so alive and bustling, especially after hearing the grim reports of Amaranth Point's fall at the hands of the northern barbarians. Not only that, but it'd been a terribly arduous journey across the realm, and after months of uninhabited terrain and stale pottage and discomfiting bedrolls, Seric was eager to indulge himself in whatever amenities this beautiful city had to offer. And a simple glance to the generals at his side—towering Zirian, fierce Pentagath, even-tempered Wyath, and youthful Veldries —proved he was not alone in his sentiments.

They passed through a great double gateway equipped with spiked barriers and an algae-coated water sluice. Boatmen standing on the quay moored the craft to wooden bollards, bringing Seric and his generals on land. Sun-bleached wood creaked underfoot and the smells of pickled fish and spoiled fruit and roasted waterfowl filled the air. Crowds of self-important men and quick-footed women moved busily along the surrounding harbor district.

Lord Emeron Mathius waited on a promenade near the entrance to the palatial grounds. He was a stout little man draped in white robes— mourning robes—and a waistcoat embroidered with both the sigil of the Anir and his province of Whitecrow. His armored guardsmen wore white mourning cloaks that were feathered about the shoulders. They stepped aside and the governor embraced deeply his old friend, and when he smiled his infectious smile, Seric couldn't help but return it with one of his own. Afterward, the governor motioned the balding steward to lead the entourage onward. They followed him up a steep stair and toward a three-ringed building that rose out of the urban landscape like the shelf of hard coral.

Semicircular walls of rammed earth stood on a cobblestone foundation, each ring rising higher than the last. A narrow path meandered to the waiting doors of a private hall, and once inside, Seric and his generals were met with rows of tables and benches in preparation of the feast, along with daybeds to relax on and washstands to clean themselves. Waiters and attendants in feathered garb moved busily about, while on wooden couches women in fitted silk gowns eyed the guests coyly.

In the adjacent alcoves, songbirds chirruped and sang and cocked their curious little heads while hopping from perch to perch inside their rattan and reed cages. Their colors were resplendent: red canaries with smooth, frosted wings, yellow-breasted finches, green-faced and orange-crested parrotlets. Seric had forgotten just how fond of songbirds his old friend was. As a young man Emeron would spend all day observing them, often scrawling lengthy notes on their habits and activities. Seric had always teased him for what he considered a petty man's avocation. They were just birds, small and loud and irritating birds.

Strangely enough, his son Veldries seemed to take the most interest in them. The young man was nodding while the balding steward rattled off just how many birds his lord had in the palace. "Of course these are but a paltry sample of my lord's entire collection," he was saying. "The real gems are in the palatial aviary. There you'll find birds from the tropical jungles of the south. Blues brighter than the brightest sapphire, reds deeper than the richest ruby. Would you like to see them? It will be a moment or two before the feast is ready. Come then, all of you brave men. Come see some of the most exquisite creatures you'll ever lay your eyes upon." Veldries and the other officers went to join the steward—all except Seric, who stayed at Emeron's behest, and General Pentagath, whose eyes remained plastered on the seated courtesans.

"My eyes are content enough here with all these exquisite creatures," the battle-scarred general remarked. His fellow officers shared a laugh at that.

Emeron observed the departing men with his plump hands behind his back. Afterward he turned to Seric and said, "This will take but a moment of your time." He exited through a small central door that led to a shaded veranda. It followed a small courtyard that was outlined in peach and almond trees. Seric hadn't realized that Zirian was still with him, not until Emeron looked up and said, "What an impressive figure you are. Surely you must be the great Zhoulish warrior I've heard so much about. Do you speak our tongue, my friend?"

"Little," Zirian answered.

"He's a remarkable man," Emeron commented to Seric. "All of

your generals are, in fact. And your son . . . last I'd seen him he was but a boy, but now, he's truly a man grown."

Servants handed them slender ivory goblets, both rim and base studded with garnets. The wine was the best Seric had tasted since leaving the Hollow. He mentioned that, then, after a second gulp, asked, "Is it safe to say I have your faith, old friend?"

"My city is yours, Lord Seric. Whatever you need—supplies, arms, horses. That said, I cannot guarantee the discipline of my soldiers."

When Seric asked why, the man's ruddy face dipped into a frown. He rested his hands on the veranda's wooden railing. "After those wretched barbarians sacked Amaranth Point, well, their bloodlust was not sated. They moved against us, but our lance wall repelled their cavalry and a last moment detachment flanked their mounted archers from a secluded rise. We drove them off, but we were not without our own losses. General Xavien Vorn was struck down during the final advance, mere minutes before the horns of victory sounded. My best physicians were at his side, but none could offer any relief. The funeral took place just days before you arrived. I'm sure you can tell by all the white robes around you."

"Grievous news," Seric told him, nodding. "And rather poor timing. Had I arrived a week earlier, your general might've been saved. I have the Grand Physician's son with me, Orbrey Lorian, surely his name is known to you?"

"Of course, my friend. My heart weeps to hear you say that. General Xavien Vorn was the greatest military commander this city has ever known. The man was pivotal in driving back the northern hordes. Without him, my soldiers are bereft of morale and stand in utter disarray."

Seric rubbed the scar beneath his neckerchief. He had met General Vorn before, had even shared the field with him years ago. His death was indeed a serious blow. After all, Seric had come to Aster Falls to acquire a powerful military force, not a floundering mess of grieving regiments. They were useless to him—no, worse than useless. *What else could go wrong?*

Emeron's eyes were studying something in the courtyard. It was

awhile before he spoke. "I've never been a man of strong military presence. I'm no pillar of authority or model of sternness. But you are, old
friend . . . yes, certainly you can make a difference." He reached up to
place a hand on Seric's shoulder. "I implore you to take my soldiers
under your wing."

Seric considered that a moment. "Their low spirits will plague the
hearts of my own regiments," he said at last. "I didn't come here to
mend broken soldiers."

"I know," he said. "They're not broken, just mismanaged. An inefficient leader leads inefficient men. The presence of the Imperial
Advisor and his stalwart generals will change all that. I implore you,
dear friend—"

"Don't fret yourself," Seric said, sighing. "I'll take them in."

Emeron let out a deep breath. "That is good. I can have them
assemble and move into your camp in two days' time."

"Today, before dusk," Seric told him. "I'll be waiting at the eastern
gate of my encampment. I have a lot of work to do, and I don't intend
to stay long." He turned back to face the entrance to the hall. The
wafting smell of roasted meat made his stomach rumble. "I believe the
feast is ready, shall we?"

Emeron nodded, and the two old friends made their way back to the
hall. For the remainder of the day, they spoke no more of war and
death, and instead spent it laughing and reminiscing about times
long past.

CHAPTER FIFTY-FOUR

S zathan Mordall felt more like a prisoner than an ally to these Redlander brutes.

He sat on a stool inside the commander's pavilion, the great warlord Raas Dragath standing over him, grilling him with questions, one after another. Behind him a large map lay on a crude table, a military map depicting the Redlander troop positions, distances and orientations, marching stages, and various locations of terrain. An abundance of small paper flags were used to represent both the Redlander forces and those of Thornberry, making things appear more complicated than they needed to be. Not that Szathan Mordall thought himself among the cleverest of men, but after overseeing the city of Thornberry for nearly a decade, he knew the details of things no surveyor could ever provide.

The southern warlord looked fierce in his long crimson cloak and burnished plates of scale armor. His unkempt hair and bushy beard were both the color of old snow, after time turns it into gray slush. His eyebrows were bristly like two black caterpillars. A pink scar curved down below his right eye. Another ran across the bridge of his nose. He huffed a lot and moved in short, angry bursts, as an unpredictable and violent man often does. Earlier, when one of his lesser officers arrived late to the military council, Dragath's gauntleted fist had smashed the man's face with such force that pieces of his teeth had to be collected from the ground.

Szathan should've felt rather uneasy around the volatile brute, but he didn't. In fact, his only concern was the young officer beside him. Hiriam Thraves, the defector of Thornberry. Seeing him now made Szathan's gorge rise. He had trusted this man with his life once, and for all that he'd received only betrayal in return.

A gauntleted fist slammed on the table. "Withholding intelligence is a crime against heaven," Raas Dragath warned. There was a deep scowl on his face, one that made him look even more barbaric, if possible. "If you don't keep talking, giant man, I *will* take your head."

But Szathan was tired of talking. He'd already explained where the city wall was the least defensible, where time and weather had eroded away the loess and rammed earth, which turrets were weakest, which officers were least respected, which slept late, were feckless, cruel, indecisive, cowardly, or simply spent too much time in their cups. All that and yet, it wasn't enough. Dragath also demanded to know the exact battlefield movements of Thornberry's formations. Things Szathan couldn't possibly predict. Still, he did his best. "Infantry units will likely gather here, flanking cavalry here and here. Sabriel Soffin will lead the advance; his nephew Fenerus will likely take the left. Focus on the nephew to win the battle."

"Fenerus Soffin is the stronger warrior," one of the officers remarked. "Are you trying to thwart our campaign?"

A quarrel began to arise; Szathan silenced it with his sonorous voice. "Fenerus is strong but reckless. He can be easily goaded into moving forward, which makes him susceptible to flanking." He placed a finger on the map. "Plant a detachment in the copse here. No, this is wrong. The copse is a quarter mile west of this area—whoever made your calculations was either negligent or a novice."

Raas Dragath crossed his burly arms, studying the map. "You are certain of this?"

Szathan nodded. "I am." No one spoke for a long moment, so Szathan gave a sigh and rose to leave. "I've had enough for one day. Take my head if you will, I don't care."

Dragath didn't stop him. Not until he reached the tent flap. "General, one more thing," he called. "I want you to lead this detachment."

Szathan gave a curt nod and exited the pavilion.

Outside, thin clouds streaked across the vivid blue sky like wispy white snakes. Redlander tents stretched across the flatlands as far as the eye could see, all dyed the same crimson as their cloaks. Banners and ensigns were decorated with the two-headed serpent known to Anirians as the Zythrai. Bringers of blood, they were called. Ancient texts spoke of the Zythrai as mounts used by the gods during the first battles of the realm, before the earliest of men populated the land.

Szathan's gray-clad guardsmen drifted to his side. He turned to say something to Brehems, only to frown when he remembered his old friend was long gone. In his place Szathan had promoted some wiry old fool he had little faith in. He looked at the man now, but decided to close his mouth and move on. He thought back to the Red Terror's last words. Even though he despised Raas Dragath and all these Redlander fools, he had to admit there was something beneficial about this arrangement: to see that young upstart Fenerus Soffin slain. It shouldn't be difficult; from what the reports had told, the soldiers were still recovering from the battle against Wintersun. Sacking the outlaw stronghold had taken quite a toll on their ranks.

Still, it troubled him to have to muster his soldiers and move against a city that had spent years under his protectorship. Against men he'd commanded for years. Where did his loyalties lie? Everything had become too complicated. Szathan was a simple man. He didn't wish to face General Sabriel Soffin in battle. And yet, he couldn't break his faith with Alarin. The life of that young girl Cathia was in his hands. *To hell with you, Alarin, for placing that burden on me.* He shook his head. And what of Demien? Last he knew his brother was still in Thornberry. He could still be there—maybe Szathan should go to him.

Maybe he should defect. By the gods he would were it not for his wife
and his children.

"General," a voice called from behind.

Szathan turned. Hiriam Thraves was taller than his youthfulness
made him initially appear, his face sharp and white and never far from
a snooty smile, as if he knew something about you that you didn't want
him to know. The edges of his crimson cloak trailed along the grass
behind him—seeing him in those Redlander colors still didn't sit well
with Szathan. "I've nothing to say to you," he growled.

The young general spoke calmly. "We are allies now, together we
fight a common enemy. Best to put aside your personal concerns in
favor of public duty."

"I will never look upon you as anything but a traitor of the highest
degree."

Hiriam opened his mouth to reply but Szathan cut him off.
"Because of you I lost half my garrison at Thornberry. Because of you
good men died alone and racked with infection and illness. I should
carve out your liver right now, in front of all your men. It's more than
you deserve, you gutless wretch."

Hiriam's youthful face darkened. "Fate commands life and death,
General. My choices were made out of my obligation to the empire.
We both know power has been in the wrong hands for far too long.
Zantherei Athera was a tyrant who rode roughshod over his administra-
tion. He mistreated the wise and twisted to realm to fit his own needs.
Now the tyrant lies on the brink of death, and his goddamn wife holds
the throne." He spat, then shook his head at the notion.

"And you think Raas Dragath is a man of greater worth?"

"His Lordship's measures may be harsh, but he is a determined and
decisive man. A far greater hero than that cripple you crook the knee
to. Alarin Athera is but a shell of himself, a man ruined by self-sabo-
tage and conflicted thought. In your heart you know the truth. General
Brehems did, that's why he defected. Tell me, is he no more treasonous
than I in your eyes?"

"Gilberon Brehems had more loyalty in his goddamn prick than
you'll ever hope to have."

"And yet he is not at your side. Why is that, General?"

Szathan glared at him long and hard, then turned and went off.

He got about ten or so paces before Hiriam's voice called out behind him: "I pity you, Szathan Mordall. Still the same giant man with the same small mind of a child."

CHAPTER FIFTY-FIVE

"Lord Seric."

Seric opened his eyes. He was wrapped tight in his bedroll, knees drawn to his chest. A hand rose to his neck, fingers rubbing beneath the neckerchief.

"Lord Seric," the voice came again. *Zirian's voice,* he realized. The soft-spoken man sounded deeply unsettled.

Seric rubbed the sleep from his eyes. He studied the ridgepole of the tent, and the attached linen canvas whose underside glowed against the dim light of the low brazier. "What is it?" he asked in the Zhoulish tongue.

"Reports of fires, my lord. Fires near the eastern gate."

Seric sighed, raising himself up. "Likely some drunken fool's mishap. Have the night watch commander see to it, and don't disturb me aga—" A war horn blasted to life, its howl tearing across the land. Seric sprang to his feet. This was no mishap—this was a call to arms.

The big Zhoul rushed to the front of the tent, one hand clutching the haft of his crescent halberd, the other pulling back the entrance flap. Moonlight flooded inside. Seric girded on his armor. He slammed Sunburst into its sheath at his hip, then exited behind Zirian. Outside, an officer collided into the Zhoulish giant. The smaller man fell on his rump, exhaling strenuous breaths and rambling in a panic-stricken voice. "My lords . . . all four gates are surrounded . . . it's an ambush—"

Something exploded nearby, sending Seric lurching forward. Next he knew he was on his hands and knees, the world above him spinning. Waves of suffocating heat rolled over his body. Everything was quiet—no, not quiet . . . he had a terrible ringing in his ears, and an odd sensation that bugs were crawling through his head. Then sound returned, hitting him like a blast of headwinds, so tremendous that he had to slam his hands over his ears. "Firestorm bombs!" he shouted. "They're launching firestorm bombs at us!"

It took him three tries before he could get to his feet, and just as he did, another blast threw him like a rag doll. Light blinded him, the heat so intense he thought it might crush his lungs. He managed once more to stagger back to his feet. The panicked officer opposite him never did. Soldiers were running this way and that, churning the pathways into clouds of obscurity. Shouts broke the air, drums rolled, horns blasted, wooden clappers clacked . . . it was all a slow blur, and yet, everything moved so fast.

Someone grabbed Seric's arm—he reached for Sunburst's hilt, then slackened when he saw it was Zirian. The light of the guttering fires bathed the Zhoul's face, highlighting the blood speckled on his shaved head. His good eye looked unnaturally wide compared to his half-lidded one. "We must go. My lord. *Now.*"

Seric went. He couldn't tell where he was going or whom he was running from, but whenever a shadowed figure came too close, the Mad Wolf's weapon whirled through the dust-choked air, and a wreath of blood spurted in reply. Seric kept glancing to his right, and soon he could see the rows of giant artillery engines standing in rows along a small rise, some eighty or so paces away. Thick moonlight glazed their semi-pyramidal bases and dangling ropes and pivoted throwing arms. Squads of soldiers manned each engine, all working in tandem to launch those hulking slugs of gunpowder into the air. Like small spheres of light they first appeared, growing larger and larger until they screamed upon the encampment like meteors from the sky. Tents collapsed, bursting into flame; soon, the encampment lit up like the streets of the Mid-Autumn festival at the Hollow. Volleys of enemy arrow-fire hissed down at timely intervals, cracking like timber when they hit their mark.

A soldier stumbled past Seric, his hands clutching the hilt of a dagger lodged in his belly. He spotted Seric and scowled and raised a hand to strike, but collapsed from exhaustion before he could do so. Seric saw he was wearing the feathered cloak of Whitecrow. *White-crow? No . . . no, it can't be.* But it was. *Emeron Mathius, you have the gall to betray me?* He noticed Zirian nearby; the big man was hunched over. Was he wounded? No, he was trying to pull the head of his halberd free from a dead foeman's skull. It took three or four tries before it finally loosened, and when it tore free a blob of gore splattered itself onto the Zhoul's skirted cuirass. He took no notice. "My lord, this way."

Deeper they went, deeper into the chaos. The acrid smell of smoke and ash and struck metal burned his nostrils and made his eyes tear. Zirian cleaved through another foeman's skull with a single arc. Seric leaped over the corpse but stumbled on another. Wait, this one wasn't dead; he was reaching up at him—for what, Seric couldn't say. He slashed down with Sunburst and ran on, wondering if he'd just struck friend or foe.

Zirian led him away from the firestorm bombs and toward the western gate of the encampment. A line of mounted shadows appeared at their flanks, scores upon scores of halberd-wielding figures, their banners obscured by the dark. *We're doomed*, Seric thought, or said, he couldn't remember which. But then a massive figure emerged into the light—General Aldebron Pentagath. The shaggy-haired man waved his great axe and roared something Seric couldn't hear. *Good Pentagath,* he thought, *good, good Pentagath.*

A soldier appeared, holding out the bridle of a black charger in full defensive bard. Seric mounted. He whipped the beast into a run, galloping alongside Pentagath's rallied battalion, which was now driving toward the gate of the encampment. A large enemy host of spear-wielding men-at-arms was positioned there. Their ranks tightened like a hedgehog's spines. Pentagath raised his axe and gave a roar so loud it dwarfed the surrounding din. Other rankmates joined in. Seric shouted as well, shouted something, anything, "For the ANIR!" perhaps, whatever words came to his lips. Sunburst rose into the air, steel gleaming in the moonlight.

BOOM. The collision of lines was like a great rock detaching itself from a cavern wall. Men and horses and banners and pennons crashed and tangled and stabbed and kicked at one another. The enemy's spear-wielding forerankers impaled the Anirian advance like shrews on a stick, but there weren't enough to hold the cavalry down, and by sheer will Pentagath cannoned his forces through, pouring through the enemy like winnowed grain. The enemy lines bulged inward; a gap opened in the center of the ranks. Seric galloped inside it. He felt drunk and on strings, striking at anything he saw, anything in this thick whorl of dust and violence and senseless chaos. Enemy faces came and went, Whitecrow faces, men that were his allies mere hours ago. Then he saw him.

General Xavien Vorn.

Their eyes met only briefly, no more than a blink. Then he was gone. It almost seemed as if it hadn't happened, but no, that was indeed Vorn—Seric knew well his narrow, vulpine face and curled mustache and wavy chin hair. He meant to turn and find him, but suddenly the gap was closing. Like a giant black hand it tightened and tightened until it seemed to suck the very breath out of Seric's lungs. His world began to darken . . . growing darker and darker and . . .

He breathed out. He was free. Free of the darkness, free and fleeing into the night. Whitecrow riders pounded after him, in disorderly files from opposing flanks. Zirian appeared to dispatch the enemy, swinging his halberd as though it were a hollow staff of pine. He decapitated one

and left the headless rider careening off, feet still perched in the stir-
rups of his mount. The others slowed after seeing that. *Yes, fear the
Mad Wolf,* Seric thought.

Seric led the Anirian soldiers onward, the enemy in hot pursuit.
Around him, thick unspoiled wilderness belted the rising hillside paths.
Horse hooves trampled across raw earth and leaf litter and old, dead
wildflowers. Boles and boughs whirred by in darkened blurs. Soon,
rugged and uneven ridges claimed their view. They passed honey-
combed rock and old boulders eroded into strange formations, a man's
face one, a beast's head another. Seric galloped across natural bridges
and alongside scenic overlooks, onward and onward until the distant
ground suddenly fell away, and a great gaping maw of darkness
yawned up at him.

He yanked the reins and shouted.

Horse hooves skidded across gravel and dirt, tottering to a halt on
the very brink of the cliff. Behind him, Seric could hear his fellow
riders fighting to do the same. A few didn't make it. They hurtled off
the precipice, screaming down into the darkness below. Seric
dismounted to stop the oncoming rush. General Wyath was there, on
foot and doing the same. It took some time before order began to
prevail.

Afterward, Seric left his men and climbed a nearby shelf of rock, to
gaze down below. The enemy hadn't pursued. They were circling the
base of the hill, their torches illuminating the area like streaking red
serpents. Seric sighed. *We're trapped,* he thought. *We're trapped like
goddamn dogs.* Nearby, officers were barking orders to the men, re-
organizing the soldiers into divisions and smaller squads. Orbrey
Lorian and the other surviving physicians were organizing lines for the
wounded to be served. Men were frantic, in despair.

Veldries came to Seric's side. The boy was bruised and cut and the
scales of his armor were chipped and dulled by grime, but thank the
gods he was alive. Seric fought off the urge to embrace his son. The
young man was obviously wearing a mask of bravery; Seric could tell
the ambush had truly dulled his mettle. *Damn it, boy, this is what you
wanted.*

"Half a regiment," Pentagath shouted. He stood nearby, huddled with a group of officers. "I need half a regiment to take that traitor's head."

Wyath replied, "General, if you march down that ridge, their forces will swallow you whole."

"We must strike now or die like rats in a cauldron," Pentagath told him. "The hearts of my men are still ablaze—we must strike before their fires dim." His porcine nose gave a twitch as he turned to survey the cliffside.

"You'll send good men to their deaths, General," Wyath told him.

"Better to die a brave man than rot as a coward up here," he said. Before long an argument broke out. Officers were cursing at one another. Seric stopped listening. He didn't care.

"My lord," he heard Zirian say urgently.

Veldries said, "Do something. *Father.*"

Seric glanced at his son. The boy meant the world to him. He couldn't lose him, not here, not like this. He stomped over to the officers. Three men were holding Pentagath back, his massive hands aiming to wrap themselves around a minor officer's throat. Seric moved into the middle of the fray. *"ENOUUUUGH!"* His voice cut a hole through the night. The officers stopped at once, their eyes downcast. Seric stared long and hard at their faces before speaking. "He's right. General Wyath's right. It is folly to fight our way out. Our position is checked. Even getting a rider out is of little gain. The Hollow is half a realm away, and we have only days of water to sustain ourselves, weeks if we bleed our horses. Those Whitecrow bastards will be patient."

"So, what is your plan?" Pentagath asked gruffly.

It was a rare moment for Seric to find himself without speech. He simply didn't know what to say.

"My lord," Wyath called. He was sitting on his haunches near the precipice, gazing about the area. "Look around. Creepers and vines growing in the furrows of the stone, some are thick, easily thick enough for a man to grasp. We can lash them into ropes and descend here, down to the tall shelves of fir and spruce below."

Pentagath balked at the notion. "You want thousands of soldiers, each weighed down by how many pounds of steel and goddamn iron, to just shinny down the goddamn cliffside? Are we a bunch of monkeys?"

"No armor," Wyath said. "We won't need it. If we descend before dawn, at the last interval of fifth watch, we can quietly surround the enemy. They'll wake up with sword tips in their faces."

Pentagath groaned at that, but Seric wasn't so quick to dismiss it. Looking around, he couldn't help but notice the thick web-work of vines spread across the mountaintop. Wyath was right. *This can be done,* he thought. *This definitely can be done.* His eyes wandered off the cliff's edge, ignoring the sensation of vertigo that sought to over-whelm him. "You sure this can be done?"

Wyath gave a firm nod.

There was silence then, long and reflective. The young general's plan seemed a reckless one, and yet, Wyath had delivered it with such confidence, such certitude. What other choice did they have? The thought of Emeron Mathius's false courtesies and duplicitous words drove Seric to anger. "You have the lead on this, General," he said to Wyath. "Our lives are in your hands."

CHAPTER FIFTY-SIX

"We'll discuss it tomorrow," she told Minister Thomen, again, for what seemed like the sixteenth or seventeenth time. The overweight man was standing before the braziers, his long ministerial robes flowing around him. When at last he turned to withdraw, Miriana gave a sigh of relief. *He's grown rather persistent, that one*, she thought. *Sydrian was never so stifling.*

It was some time after nightfall, and Miriana was at last free to relax in her private apartments. The day had passed terribly long and terribly tiresome, another day filled with meetings to attend, councilmen to appease, and courtiers to oblige. Her ministers were acting more and more like a nest of baby birds screaming for their mother, while Miriana in turn had to pretend she had all the answers. She was tired of pretending. Tired of being strong. Tired of telling herself she was strong.

Yana peeled off Miriana's silks and freed her hair from the tight clasp that had made her head ache. The Sijian woman then guided her to a wood-framed daybed, where Miriana lay on her stomach, naked and at the gentle mercy of her handmaiden's massaging hands. The deep rubbing felt good on Miriana's stiff muscles, and the fragrant scent of her warming oils—mandarin and sandlewood and cinnamon bark—put her mind at ease. She turned her head to the side and closed her eyes. She was so tired.

Yana's hands moved from Miriana's thighs up to her buttocks, which often led to other things—but tonight she halted the young handmaiden's advances, in no mood for sensual pleasure.

"No?" Yana asked in her heavy Sijian accent.

"Not tonight," Miriana replied.

The woman went back to her regular duties.

Miriana's thoughts turned to Seric. With the reports of Amaranth Point's destruction recently coming to her, she knew she should warn Seric, and yet, no rider emerged from her gates. More, the alliance between Riverwind and the Redlands had been cemented, and now Raas Dragath's recruited and conscripted troops were planning to move against Thornberry. But with Seric gone, Miriana had no strategists of worth to rely on. All she had was her military generals, and while she doubted not their valor, it was their lack of cunning that ultimately dispirited her. A part of her wished to forgive what Seric had done. But she couldn't do that. *He is a traitor,* she thought. *How can I allow a traitor to remain at my side?*

A knock on the door broke her reverie. Cyrille Vileron's raspy voice called for her, and Miriana gave a groan. "Not Minister Thomen again? I told him I'd discuss it in the morning."

"It's your brother, Your Majesty," Cyrille said.

"Oh . . . well, send him in."

Vylas appeared a moment or two later, with goblets of wine and a tray of steamed sponge cakes. "You had a long day. Thought you might like something to—" He halted at the sight of her nakedness. "Another time, perhaps?"

"Now is fine," she said, urging him forward. She accepted a goblet and took a generous gulp. "I'm a bit too tired for modesty, Brother."

Vylas sat down on a nearby armchair, goblet in hand. He wore a straight-cut black robe, tied at the waist by a sash of pale gray scroll-work. The warm glow of the adjacent brazier cast a dim yellow light on the profile of his masked face. "Still not sleeping well?" he asked at last.

"Not well at all," she answered. "Higher, please." Yana's massaging hands moved accordingly.

"What's troubling you, Mir?" he asked.

She sighed at the question. "I don't know what I'm doing, with the court. I just tell them what they want to hear."

He nodded at that. "Sometimes that's all that is needed. The court needs to know that this so-called alliance will not last long. They need to know that even with the enemy's combined forces we will still drive them back."

"But such words are meaningless," she said.

"I don't believe that," he assured her. "Thornberry will hold. General Sabriel Soffin will not falter, trust me on this."

"You're right," she said with a wan smile. "You're always right, my brother." Then, after a pause: "I wish you weren't always right . . ."

He seemed to think on that. "You mean about Seric," he said at last. "Do you regret your decision to take his head upon his return?"

"No." She wasn't sure if her brother believed her. The wine was making it hard to tell, not to mention hard to keep her eyes open.

"Good, because it is the right decision," he went on. "We still have thousands of worthy men and capable generals. The loss of Seric will be recouped tenfold."

She nodded sleepily at that, then yawned and allowed her eyes to close. Vylas continued speaking for a time, though Miriana's mind began to drift elsewhere. She couldn't help her heart from aching . . . even though she knew she could never forgive Seric. If the court knew of his transgressions, Miriana would be exiled without question. She'd not risk losing everything for a man whose ambitions outweighed his devotion to the empire. No, she had to kill him for what he'd done, for being the treasonous wretch he truly was. Never would she allow herself to grieve for this man . . . no matter how much her heart yearned to.

The room had grown quiet, save the pattering of the soft autumn rain against the scrollwork window. Darkness came and went for a time, until next she knew Yana was no longer massaging but combing through Miriana's hair with her fingers. Soft and soothing caresses, combined with an occasional kiss on an arm or shoulder. Miriana gave a low moan. Soon, the hand trailed down to the small of Miriana's back, caressing her tenderly, shyly, as if for the first time. Then it went lower, to her buttocks, between her legs.

"Not tonight," Miriana purred, groggy from sleep. But the caressing didn't cease. In fact it became more lustful, more urgent. Fingers rubbed and pushed inside her moistening sex. "I said *not* tonight," Miriana ordered. Still, the stupid woman didn't stop.

She reached back and seized Yana's hand. No, it wasn't the dark-skinned hand of her servant, but a pale, thin one, fingers nail-bitten and skeletal. *Vylas?* She spun her head, staring up at her brother's face. "*Stop that!*" she cried.

He tried to kiss her then, but she shoved him back. "I said *stop*."

He cocked his head to better look at her with his one good eye. "Why?" he asked.

Her eyes were scanning the room. "Where's Yana?"

"I sent her out." He moved closer.

Again, she pushed him back. "Vylas, are you mad?"

He was staring at her naked breasts like a drunken lecher. "I deserve you, Mir. I belong to you."

"I'm your *sister*."

"*Half* sister," he corrected. "And even that may be untrue."

She made a disappointed grunt. "I am still Lord Zantherei's wife."

"That didn't stop you from bedding Seric."

Her mouth was open, but she found no speech. He took hold of her hand, his fingers wet from her sex. She pulled away, which made him frown. "I assure you my faith is undying, unlike the mongrel's," he said.

"You're not yourself. You're drunk."

"That I am," he agreed. "But in wine there is truth, is there not? The truth of what I've wanted to do for years."

She pushed herself off the daybed, in search of something to cover herself with. She found a black silk robe, but before she could put it on, he came over and yanked it from her hands. "Stop it, Mir."

She slapped him.

Vylas staggered back, his hand moving over his cheek. The blow had knocked his halfmask askew. He lifted it all the way off, revealing that hideously scarred eye. He pointed to it. "It's because of this, isn't it?"

"No, Vylas."

"Then what?" he demanded to know. She didn't answer, mostly because no answer was needed. He was her brother, her one-eyed, scrawny little brother. When he closed in again she warned, "Touch me again and I will call the guards."

"Call the guards then," he growled, narrowing his good eye. He looked rabid right now, a drunk and rabid little man. "Call your faithful little pet, Cyrille. How is it you have him so trained? You must be spreading your legs for him, too."

She gaped at him. "I think you should go."

He ignored that. "You know your husband would certainly be interested in what his good lady has been doing while he lies in a comatose state."

"How dare you . . ." She slapped him again, harder, right across the jaw. A cold sting ran through Miriana's hand. She picked up the fallen silk robe and threw it on. "Vylas, you are my brother and I love you as such, but I promise you, if you dare threaten me again, you will deeply regret it."

"You would dispose of me as easily as the others?"

"If I must," she said. "Yes."

He sucked at the blood from his split lip. The look on his face had turned from lustful to morose. When he spoke, his voice was no longer firm but pleading. "I've done everything for you, Mir. I stood by you, endured all your suffering and all your grief. I've defended you from all the men who abused and betrayed you. Everything . . . everything I've done was for you."

"And everything I've done was for you, Brother."

He looked doubtfully at her. "Everything *you've* done was for you and you alone."

That made her angry. "Look at where you are now, your residence, your status. I've given you more wealth than a man such as you should ever possess. What more do you want from me?"

The words hung the air for a long moment. Then, without reply, Vylas turned and left.

Miriana was left prickling with irritation. *Curse you for trying to make me feel guilty. I've always taken care of you. I don't owe you anything.* She let out an agitated grunt and sat on her bed. She felt violated by his touch, a feeling not unlike those of her early years as a lowborn bawd. She never wanted to experience that again.

She lay back and pulled the silk coverlet over herself. Somehow, from somewhere, tears began to form in her eyes. Vylas was the last man she truly trusted . . . and now, even that might be taken from her. *He's just drunk*, she told herself. *He'll sleep it off and everything will be back to normal. Come tomorrow he'll not remember this, and we'll go on as if nothing happened.*

CHAPTER FIFTY-SEVEN

The night grew ever colder, and the winds threatened rain.

Seric cursed under his breath. Rain would turn a difficult descent into a treacherous one. They very thought of trying to grasp at slippery vines made his chest ache. But he couldn't override his decision now—for one, Wyath and his crew had already spent hours anchoring the vines to the cliffs and securing knots with lashers, and secondly, Seric removed the head of a Whitecrow emissary who had earlier come to offer terms.

He tried to walk along the precipice for a time, as if that would somehow drive back his fears. It only made things worse. When he kicked a small stone off the edge, seeing it plummet made Seric dizzy. He had already pissed three times in the last watch. He would've emptied his bowels, too, had he eaten something in the past fifteen or so hours.

Of all things to occupy his mind, he found himself thinking about Miriana. He longed to touch her, to hear her honeyed voice and observe her sweet smile. By the gods if he were to survive this night, he would never leave her side again. *No matter what.* He gazed up to the night sky. The stars glittered like a thousand pearlescent eyes. *I pray you are thinking of me, my dear sweet Miriana. I need your strength, now more than ever.*

He didn't hear General Wyath's approach. "We're ready, my lord," the narrow-faced man said. He looked incredibly spare without the bulk of his battle armor. "You can remain here, if you choose, until victory is ours."

"And if it doesn't come?" Seric said at once. He usually praised the young general's self-assurance, but right now it only annoyed him. "It is my duty to stand beside my men. I'm ready. Let's get on with it."

The soldiers were waiting by the cliff face, clothed in worn tunics and cloaks and the occasional undercap or sash. Sabers and short swords were sheathed at their sides or scabbarded on their backs. General Aldebron Pentagath looked just as fierce even without his full battledress, his shoulders large and square, his hair a wild mane. Veldries, however, looked very much like the boy he was. A lean and rugged boy, sure, but a boy nonetheless.

Wyath went ahead, pacing the ledge, bending down to test the pull of the vines at every point of descent. More than once did he double back to a specific spot, making sure it was secure. When he seemed satisfied he turned to face the others, delivering his instructions one last time.

Seric had long committed the words to memory. He knew what to do if a hand slipped or if his body swayed into the rock face. He knew how to position his feet, how to distribute his weight, how to rest on the knots if needed, and how to use cracks and finger pockets in case the vine gave way. Seric knew all of this, and yet, he quivered at the thought of actually doing it. Fear clawed at him and yet he could do nothing about it. He was the Imperial Advisor of the empire, and the chief commander of the greatest army of the realm. How could he show any measure of apprehension?

The first row of soldiers lined up before the precipice, maybe fifteen or sixteen across. They looked so goddamn calm. At Wyath's command they grabbed the vines, dropped down over the ledge, and disappeared. The only sound for a time was the faint huffs and grunts of the climbers. Wyath signaled the next row to line up. Again, not a single face showed any hint of fear or reluctance. *By the gods I must be the only coward here,* Seric thought.

File after file descended in a steady pace, soldier after soldier vanishing into the darkness. When Veldries moved to his turn, Seric went to his side. The young man turned to his father, his face obscured by the dark. "My hands are shaking," he said. "Am I the only one?"

The boy's admission bolstered Seric's own courage. "Every man around you is afraid, your father included. But like most of these men, I'd rather face death than endure the shame of losing this battle."

Veldries nodded at that. Somewhere below, a terrible *crack* rent the air, the sound of timber snapping. A shout followed, muffled and abrupt. Men shot to the edge, peering down. Wyath pushed his way through. He studied the scene for a moment, then turned around. "Stand back. No one's harmed. A broken bough, that's all. Now stand back." The soldiers exhaled in relief, all except Veldries whose eyes had gone wider than before. Seric gave him his best reassuring nod, and the boy cautiously dropped down over the ledge.

Seric was next. At Wyath's signal, he bent down and moved himself off the precipice, taking the thick vine in his hands while clamping his feet on a knot. Dirt from the rock face crumbled, smelling of roots and earth. One hand reached down, then a step, then securing his footholds he committed his weight. Again. One hand reached down, then a step, then securing his footholds he committed his weight. Steady and slow. Wyath was somewhere above him, reminding the men to be patient, to be sure of their positions before moving down. Seric nodded and nodded but all he could think about was the vine snapping, and the terrifying plunge to a gruesome end.

Stop it, you coward, he told himself. One hand reached down, then a step, then securing his foothold he committed his weight. Along the vines to his right, soldiers moved like nimble tree shrews down an oak. Seric in turn was a sloth, slow and ungainly and terribly awkward. One hand reached down, then a step, then securing his foothold he committed his weight. The cold mountainous winds blasted him against the rock face. He jammed his feet into pockets of stone and waited for it to pass. *I'm almost there*, he thought. *I must be almost there.*

He felt something tap on his head. Something wet. Rain. Tiny droplets of rain. *By the gods, not now.* One hand reached down, then a step, then securing his foothold he committed his weight. More tapping, a soft drizzle now. *Am I almost there? I have to be almost there.* One hand reached down, then a step, then securing his foothold he committed his weight. The wind plastered his cloak to his back, while the rain pattered against it, louder and louder, until it was all he could hear. Panic seized him. *Don't look down, don't you dare look down.*

He looked down.

The great vast darkness reared up at him like the jaws of some ungodly behemoth. Cascading rain vanished into it. He was not even at the halfway mark. *Not even halfway?* His heart pounded so hard he thought the vibrations might knock him off. *Keep steady, keep steady now.* One hand reached down, then a step—then a sudden gust of wind knocked his grip from the vine. He slid down, fast, his hands grasping at rain-slick knots, clawing for purchase. Dirt loosed and stones broke and fell. A nest of rock-clung creepers snagged his arm, and he jerked to a stop, his body smacking the rock face. He tried to twist free, but the creepers only tightened. He hung there, helplessly entangled, the wind screaming in his ears and the rain pelting him in sheets. Seric's heart was ready to burst out of his chest. He couldn't breathe. His bladder released.

A voice called from above, so small and distant. "The vine, my lord. Use your legs to grab the vine. Then your dagger to free yourself."

Seric was too afraid to move. *I can't, I can't do it. I'm going to die here, I'm going to fall and I'm going to die.*

"Your hips, turn them to reach the vine. Use the rock, just as I showed you."

Seric tried but couldn't do it. The rain hammered harder. *Fuck you!*

he wanted to scream at it. He resigned to remain where he was, like a frightened tomcat dangling from a tree limb, until the horrific image of his plummeting to the ground spurred him into action. Reaching out with his foot, he pulled the vine close enough to seize it with his free hand. Somehow, he managed to unsheathe his dagger, and bringing the blade up he sliced through the creepers, freeing himself. Cheers rang from above. For some reason, that irritated him. Seric hugged the vine for a few moments longer, then one hand reached down, then a step, then securing his foothold he committed his weight. Again and again. Steady and slow.

The bristling conifer needles against his legs made Seric exhale with profound relief. A single foot ventured off in search of a steady limb. When he found it, he pushed off the rock and grabbed hold of the tree, inhaling the scent of rich, wet bark. Crouching, he dipped each foot and found the next step. It came easy at first, until he nearly slipped on a bough. After that, he moved slower. Soon, the great vast darkness gave way to solid ground, and Seric ignored all caution, descending quicker and quicker, pushing through sharp needles and scratching branches, his hands caked in pitch. The ground rose up, and at last, he pressed his feet into the waiting earth.

He was standing on a small sloping hill, surrounded by screens of pine and clusters of wind-twisted oaks. The rain had stopped on this side of the mountain, but the scree beneath Seric's boots was uneven and jagged, and halfway down he lost his footing, and now he was racing down the slope, his boots gliding across the scree as though it were water. Jagged rocks whipped by his head, some dangerously close, but somehow, *somehow*, none hit him, and soon he regained his balance enough to zigzag out of the way.

He stumbled to the bottom, seeing the tumbling stones, some as large as a man's head, roll to a dusty halt at the base of the hill. Seric wiped away the dirt that masked his face. His eyes stung. He tried to take a step but his ankle buckled, and pain lanced through his left foot, sending him down on his rump. Wyath came down the slope a moment later, quick like a sidewinder across a dune. He immediately went to his fallen lord.

"Lead the assault," Seric told him. "Strike the enemy now, go on."

The narrow-faced general turned and sped off. From behind the curtain of pines to Seric's right, Zirian approached with a handful of Zhoulish guardsmen. "You too, General," Seric said. "Go on. Protect my son."

The Zhoul obeyed, but ordered the guards to remain at his lord's side. Seric sat there for a time, removing his boot and rubbing at his ankle. It was terribly swollen, but fortunately he felt no dislocation. When the pain subsided a bit, he struggled to his feet and started back to the others. He got maybe halfway before runners flew to him with reports of victory. Those Whitecrow fools never knew what hit them; they'd surrendered at once.

Dawn broke by the time Seric reached the battleground. Defeated Whitecrow soldiers were kneeling in rows, their relinquished arms being stockpiled by their Anirian victors. His officers were there, Zirian and Veldries and Wyath, all overseeing the matter. It was all very orderly. General Aldebron Pentagath was barking commands nearby. When he spotted the Imperial Advisor, the shaggy man rushed over at once. "General Vorn escaped. South, with four or five scores of riders. On your word I'll gladly fetch his head."

"Let him go," Seric said. "I want only Emeron Mathius. Tell me you have him."

Pentagath nodded. "Bastard tried to run himself through, but I wrested the dagger away before he could finish." His porcine nose flared aggressively.

"Bring him to me," Seric ordered.

Pentagath lumbered off. Seric turned back to address the surren-dered soldiers. Poor souls looked miserable—quite the opposite of the fiery spirits he'd faced several hours ago. "Pledge your lives to the empire and you will be spared. It is Lord Mathius himself alone who deserves my vengeance." The soldiers bowed and nodded, some even falling from their knees to the ground in gratitude. Seric looked past them, at the city of Aster Falls, its walls and towers glowing under the golden light of dawn. To General Wyath he said, "Enter the city and calm the populace, reassure them that no harm will come to any citizen. I will personally address them later."

"Yes, my lord."

"Oh, and General," he added. "The city is yours. Good work."

"Thank you, my lord." Wyath went off to appoint his escort. Seric's gaze returned to the city, holding it there until Pentagath returned. The shaggy general shoved forward the much shorter Emeron Mathius, whose plump hands were bound at the wrist. Dark blood stained the feathered robes of his chest. His face was no longer ruddy but pale.

"He had this," the general said, handing Seric a letter. It was an unsealed, unfinished proclamation of victory, written to a nameless recipient. Seric tore it to pieces, letting them flutter to the ground. He looked at Emeron and smiled. "A little soon for celebration, don't you think, old friend?"

Mathius looked up at him, matching the smile with a tired one of his own. "So it would seem."

"What astounds me is not that you betrayed the empire," he said. "But that you betrayed a dear old friend. Tell me, who are you bending the knee to?"

The smile faded. "You know I won't answer that."

Seric sighed, giving a slow nod. "I know."

A mournful silence passed briefly between them. Emeron broke it when he said, "My wife and daughters—"

"Your family will be spared, only out of respect for all the years of friendship you've given me. I'm a sentimental sort, you know."

Emeron nodded. He seemed to want to say more, and did so only after a long moment of thought. "My lord is to the south," he said quietly. "Please, bury me facing the south."

Seric shifted his weight off his sprained ankle, studying Emeron from a sidelong angle. Despite all the false words and all the treachery, Emeron Mathius was still a good man. A man who had always spoken kindly to all men—even the poor and unfortunate and those who could do nothing for him. Seric thought back to their younger days, when he and Emeron and Anseth would spend so much time together, either practicing archery or swordplay or just running amok through the streets. He helped his old friend to his feet. "The south it is, my friend. You will be interred with honors."

Emeron's face softened then, and his eyes became clear, as if finally contented to die. "My heart is glad," he said, then lowered his eyes as the axeman came to take him away.

CHAPTER FIFTY-EIGHT

T he clash of their polearms was like the shattering of delicate crystal.

Szathan Mordall backed a step, both hands clutching the haft of his figured halberd Nightwing. Before him, Fenerus Soffin wielded a long-handled saber, hooked and tasseled and notched with silver rings. The young general's cruel and crescent eyes glared up at the much taller foe. Even with Fenerus's long arms, Szathan still had a reach advantage over him, and his quick jabs and thrusts did well to keep the shorter man at bay. Fenerus was clearly frustrated. Scratches and dents marred his blackened scale armor. He thumbed the sweat from his brow, then quietly circled his foe, ignoring the furious battle that thundered all around him.

Szathan's mounted detachment had smashed Fenerus's overextended left, leaving the ranks of enemy soldiers formless and buckling on the open fields before Thornberry. Szathan himself had fought like a man possessed, fought endlessly and tirelessly as torrential rains drenched him to the bone. His horse had been cut down, his rankmates dropped from his side. But Szathan fought on. He fought on and on until at last he'd come face to face with the Young Tempest himself, Fenerus Soffin.

The long-handled saber jabbed for his head; Szathan parried it aside, once and then again. The young general was already slowing, tiring. But he was a tough bastard, not a man to easily lose heart. Szathan drove forward now, shifting his feet right-left and left-right as he thrust and cut and withdrew. He forestalled him, pressured him, moved in quickly but slashed with calm precision. He blocked Fenerus's attack and stepped back, only to dash forward just as the general began to relax. He was forcing Fenerus to think, to hesitate. To make a mistake. And that was exactly what the young general did.

He overcommitted a thrust. A split-second misstep, but enough that Szathan drove the butt-spike of his weapon into the man's armored abdomen. Fenerus fell to one knee and grimaced, but quickly pushed to his feet again. Szathan countered his next thrust. Another ear-splitting clash, and then another. Szathan's third strike connected, a sweeping cut that sent Fenerus sprawling to the ground. The rain hammered him, as if trying to keep him there. He staggered to his feet, though not so quickly this time. A gauntleted hand wiped the mud from his face. "Fuck you, Ogre."

Fenerus dashed forward, long-handled saber thrusting. Szathan knocked it aside, grabbed the shaft mid-turn, then shoved its wielder to the mud. Fenerus rolled, jumped to his feet, short sword now in hand. Szathan circled on the outside, striking in quick jabs, waiting for an opening to show itself. Once it did, he brought Nightwing down in a heavy arc, so powerful it might've taken a horse's head clean off, but it goddamn missed. It missed and Szathan somehow slipped in the mud. There was a terrible metallic shriek as Fenerus's sword bit into his forearm, probably would've severed it had he not strapped on his vambraces earlier. A follow-up strike missed, but the hilt of the blade smashed the armored knuckles of Szathan's gauntlet. Nightwing fell from his hands, swallowed up by the mud. Szathan unsheathed the saber at his hip, and once more the two men circled.

Soldiers tumbled in his path, wounded and fighting and dying, but like always, Szathan didn't spare them a glance. His only concern was this general before him. Not to say he wasn't aware of his surroundings —he certainly was, but like always, his senses were unnaturally heightened during these times of intense combat. He had this inexplicable ability to *feel* what was happening around him, his thoughts both focused and precise. To explain this to a civilian would be an impossible feat.

Fenerus lunged, sword slashing. Szathan blocked the attack but Fenerus pivoted and drove the blade up across Szathan's shoulder. Metal screeched, scales broke, leather straps snapped. Pain surged up his arm. Fenerus moved to deliver another blow, but Szathan threw himself forward, smothered him like hot lacquer, and now they were pushing against each other, both men struggling for an advantage. A deadlock. Then, cat-quick, Fenerus broke free, pushing himself back to proper range. Szathan's saber came up; Fenerus's sword did the same. It happened fast. Szathan couldn't defend. By the gods he couldn't. His eyes snapped shut as glittering steel came screaming for his head.

Something wet touched his face. Blood—but it couldn't have been *his* blood. No, Fenerus's blade never touched him. Somehow it missed his big square jaw. His own blade didn't miss, however, and looking up he saw Fenerus staggering backward, blood spewing from a grisly wound that started at his neck and tore through the plates of his chest. He looked at Szathan, and then he fell. Just like that. He fell and this time he didn't rise.

Szathan used a single boot to push the man onto his back. Metal creaked dully in the rain. Fenerus's wound pulsed wetly, leaking streams of bright blood. His eyes were still aware. He was trying to speak, but the din of battle deafened his words. Szathan knelt at his side. He still couldn't hear. *What is it? What do you want to tell me?* He moved closer, lowering his head, his ear to Fenerus's mouth. The general spoke in a pained whisper. "I turned . . . I turned my hips, my step was precise, my cut swift . . . how did I miss?" He wheezed a long, ghastly wheeze. "Goddamn it . . . it's damn cold."

Szathan raised his head. He watched the rain fall upon the dying general, dancing on his halfhelm and glazing his face. Fenerus's eyes blinked once, twice, and then he was gone.

———

"Piss on this rain," Severak complained. "Our progress is being undone." It was unusually cold today, and yet the Vaskultan general wore only a single layer of mud-drenched felt. Head to toe he looked exhausted.

"We'll toil through the night," Anseth told him. "*All* night if we have to. Seric's army is six days to the river. We have little time left."

Severak's hawkish face frowned at that, but he said nothing.

"I'll help," Anseth said. He fastened his heavy wool Vaskultan overcoat.

Nearby, Kirik said, "An ominous sign, the rain. Surely an offer of sacrificial blood will appease the Skybringer."

"No," Anseth said at once.

Kirik shrugged. "Perhaps a little jig would better suit you?" He began to dance an exaggerated little dance.

Anseth didn't laugh. "You ready?" he said, shoving a mattock into the bondsman's hands. Kirik only stared at it, his reptilian face confused and frowning. Anseth turned and exited the pavilion before the man had a chance to protest.

The news of Emeron Mathius's death had forced Anseth to abandon his march to Stormhaven. He knew his outnumbered Vaskultans were no match against Seric's regiments, but the Vaskultans still had their spades and mattocks from the earlier siege against Amaranth Point, and Anseth designed to make good use of them.

The Amber River was a large branch among the network of tributaries and distributaries of the Grayling, its rich, alluvial waters running just north of Stormhaven. A timber arch bridge called the Starling provided crossing for traffickers. He knew Seric was too clever to fall to an ambush there; Anseth had to be more inventive than that. So he'd sent soldiers to collapse the bridge, while the rest of his men toiled to dam the upstream riverbed. Still, as narrow as the waters were, halting its flow was proving a mammoth undertaking, and worse, the heavy rains were making the waters swell and overflow, a dangerous situation to be sure.

He could see the men laboring along the riverbank now. Carriers plodded past, hauling heavy sandbags to the teams of setters who methodically placed them into the water. These men were tied at the waist with hempen ropes, in case the river decided to snatch them up. The diggers toiled along the sandbanks of a nearby estuary. They had the most backbreaking work, though in truth every task was dirty and dangerous and damn exhausting, which was why Anseth beamed with pride in seeing such diligence from his men. They must've regretted their savage ways at Amaranth Point, because they all seemed to possess a newfound respect for Anseth—well, all except Dariok, of course. *Where is that brute anyway?* He'd wandered off sometime ago, where Anseth couldn't say. Nor did he care.

He joined the workers along the sandbanks and put his mattock to work. The others paused to watch him for a bit, passing odd looks to one another while wiping the mud and rainwater from their filthy brows. It baffled them to see their commander toiling away as a common drudge. Before long the notion went forgotten, as Anseth became the same as they, soaked and filthy and sore in places he hadn't used in some time. It was strenuous work, but Anseth pushed on, as hard as the others, which said a lot considering most of these men outweighed him by a good forty or fifty pounds. But as Anseth pushed on, his Vaskultans pushed on, and soon the hours slipped away, hours he spent grunting with his men, complaining with them, joining in on their quips and jeers—whatever made the time pass.

His hands eventually became so raw that it was difficult to hold the goddamn mattock. Even still, he grimaced and pushed on. Each sandbag he filled seemed heavier and heavier. *Just one more*, he said after every one. He didn't remember when, but his body went numb. He knew he should've stopped, but the work came easier this way. Tonight, he knew his body would punish him for his stupidity, but right now, he simply pushed on.

"What are you doing?"

He turned. Dariok stood watching him, his eyes half hidden behind locks of wet and disheveled hair. Anseth tried to act irritated by the interruption, but in truth, he was glad for it. By the gods he was tired. "Digging," he said.

"I know that."

"Would you rather I stand here with my prick in my hand like you?"

Dariok's face darkened. He didn't offer a retort, thank the gods, and only gestured behind himself, at the approach of a man, one of Volduk's principal riders, a grim Vaskultan with deep-set eyes and a long knotted beard splotched with gray. His name was Urryk. Something about his demeanor told Anseth this was important, so he handed his mattock off to a neighboring worker and approached the two men.

"Lord Revek," Urryk said. He went to bow his head and speak the traditional Vaskultan greeting, but Dariok was too impatient for that. "The runt's waiting. Speak your message. Now. Out with it."

The Vaskultan's eyes didn't waver from Anseth's. "Lord Volduk is dead."

Anseth's chest heaved. Questions spilled from his mouth. How. When. Why. Whatever came to him.

Urryk was very calm. "His last moments were spent in his own yurt, surrounded by his wife and his children, with General Kaigon at his side, and thousands of warriors kneeling outside."

The Vaskultan in him should've felt relief upon hearing that, but Anseth was too distraught to care. "What of the Nidrak tribe? Last reports stated they were fleeing north, up the Iron River."

The man shook his head. "The enemy escaped along the causeway. The chieftain's death left the Vaskultans in disarray. General Kaigon needs you, lord. He asks that you return to the north to reunite the tribe as one."

Dariok had been strangely quiet until now. "We go north then."

"No," Anseth blurted. "Not yet, we can't leave yet."

Dariok's eyes settled cruelly on him. "The chieftain's dead, runt. The father's reign passes to the son." A smug smile crossed his face. "I stand as chieftain now."

Anseth groaned inwardly at that. *Does he even care about his father's death?* A silly question, no doubt.

Urryk was reaching inside his overcoat, fishing for something. After his hand came out he went over and placed whatever it was into Anseth's hand. The Earthstone—it was the Earthstone, the official mark of Vaskultan overlordship. Was this a mistake? Anseth didn't know what to say.

"Lord Volduk's last will," Urryk said. He took a step back, dropped to his knees, and exclaimed, "ALL HAIL LORD REVEK! ALL HAIL THE LORD CHIEFTAIN!"

Anseth, startled, stood back. The man said it over and over, his voice like an undying peal of thunder. Others came forward, looking on, joining in when they understood. Anseth didn't know how to react. A part of him didn't want it, a part of him even hated Volduk for willing it—but then, in his heart, he knew Volduk had only done what was best for his people. Anseth was the only man capable of leading the tribe. His fingers closed around the stone, and his hand rose skyward.

More Vaskultans came over, each man falling to his knees. *"ALL HAIL LORD REVEK!!! ALL HAIL THE LORD CHIEFTAIN!!!"*

Dariok, still on his feet, was foaming at the mouth.

CHAPTER FIFTY-NINE

The fighting ceased at nightfall.

Drums pounded the return to the encampments. Soldiers broke into squadrons and worked quickly to light cook fires, tend weapons, set broken bones. There was a strange quiet that came over a man during these times. Physically he worked through his duties as normal, but something in his heart was undoubtedly missing. Nothing moved him. A man ate, a man slept. Or at least, he tried to.

Szathan had no luck. Every time he closed his eyes Fenerus would appear, thrusting forward his long-handled saber as if the fight had never ended. After a few hours of this he got up and wandered out into the night. The rain had ceased but the air was cold, winter cold, cold even with his layers of heavy wool and blackened scale armor. He thought about Fenerus but he also thought about the other young men he had killed, the new bloods. He didn't like having to end their young lives. But what could he do? It was his duty as a soldier. Diplomacy was as distant to him as a mangonel was to a wainwright.

Along the outskirts of the encampment, Szathan climbed a knoll covered in bluestem grass that appeared more red now in autumn. To the north stood Thornberry. He had never seen the city like this, from an outsider's eye. Like a giant steel serpent, its thick ramparts meandered and curved in the moonlight before softly fading into the dark. To the common man it must've appeared impregnable, but Szathan knew this city like a mother knew her babe. He knew every stone of every turret, every alcove and every crevice. To him this great stone serpent was nothing more than an old, sun-dried worm.

Turning, he almost didn't notice the figure standing at the foot of the knoll. In a flash Szathan's saber found his hand.

"My lord," the man squeaked, holding up empty palms. Clad only in homespun, he trembled as he gazed up. Szathan didn't recognize his face. He looked too young and too craven to be a Redlander. "Who are you and why are you following me."

The man's pitiful hands rose higher after each interrogating question. By the gods the poor bastard looked ready to piss himself. "I bear a m-message, a message is all."

"What message? *SPEAK.*"

"Your brother . . . y-your brother waits for you in the nearby wood." His eyes focused on the tip of Szathan's blade. "P-please."

"Demien?"

The man nodded fiercely. "Yes, my lord. I'll take you to him, my lord, if th-that would please you, my lord."

Szathan stared at him a moment or two longer. Then he said, "Go on then."

The man lit a torch and hastened through the wooded paths, farther away from the city and toward the neighboring Drakewood Forest. Szathan didn't like this at all, but he followed anyway, probably because he was a fool. The surrounding thicket was dark and ominous and filled with all the typical buzzing and clicking you'd expect to hear at so late an hour. And each time the wind made the trees sigh, Szathan stopped to look around, never once finding anything unusual.

The path narrowed to squeeze through a dense cluster of evergreens. Inside, Szathan found himself in a grassy circle illuminated by glowing shafts of moonlight, some so bright they almost seemed unnatural. In the center stood a large figure. Could be Demien, but it was hard to tell. Szathan moved closer until the figure's face became clear. General Sabriel Soffin. Szathan's first reaction was to turn and chastise his escort, but the sneaky little man was nowhere to be seen.

"Sheathe your weapon," Sabriel said, his voice firm but not unkind. Battle fatigue pulled on the heavy features of his cherubic face, rimming his close-set eyes in red. He wore no helmet, but his heavy general's cloak did little to hide the bulk of his armor beneath.

Szathan didn't sheathe the weapon but lowered it, and only by a little. His eyes peered at the surrounding trees, expecting the shades and shadows to form into armed men.

"There's no one there," Sabriel said. "I only want to talk."

Szathan didn't believe him. "Talk about what? I killed him. I killed your nephew."

"I know."

Szathan could feel his thick eyebrow ridges pushing together. "What do you want from me? Vengeance? The man was a despicable wretch. I'd slay him a thousand times if the heavens allowed it. Now where's Demien?"

Sabriel looked at him long and hard for a moment, then his round, gray head shook gravely. "Demien succumbed to his wounds at Wintersun."

Szathan's chest tightened. A burning rose in his throat. "His body —if Miriana gets hold of—"

"She won't. I arranged a secret procession to his homeland of Seven Rivers. The men who interred him gave their lives to preserve the location of his final resting place." Sabriel gestured over to a small area of grasses. A boy sat there, gazing up at them. Little Silas. He was absently toying with a small broken figurine in his hands. Sabriel watched him a moment longer before he spoke. "I want you to take the boy."

Szathan wasn't sure what to say. He knew this wasn't the only reason Sabriel had arranged this little meeting, but he couldn't guess what else the man wanted. He wished he were smarter. "Men rarely risk their necks for nothing in return," he said. "You must want something more of me."

Sabriel gave a nod at that, like a schoolmaster surprised by a pupil's insightful answer. "I want to give you something." He took a step forward. "I'm unarmed. Sheathe your weapon. We are comrades in arms, are we not?"

"Once we were," Szathan said, but sheathed his saber all the same. Sabriel moved closer. He had something in his hand, the haversack that once belonged to Demien. "Take it, I want you to have it."

Szathan did. Its weight told him it wasn't empty, but he didn't open it. "What else?"

"I'd like my nephew returned to me, that I can properly bury him. His family grieves, you know. His boy is not yet five, but he weeps like an old widower."

After Szathan had killed him, he cut off Fenerus's head and held it up to put fear into his enemies' hearts. Later he stuck it on a pike at the gate of his encampment. The body he'd left undefiled, out of respect to the man's name. He was glad to have done that. It allowed him to satisfy Sabriel's request with a nod.

"I know what my nephew was," Sabriel went on. "I'm not blind. But he was still my blood." He paused to give a quick sigh. "Listen, I don't want your head. I don't want vengeance. All I want is the goddamn robes of the empire to stop making honorable men kill each other. Lady Miriana is not fit to hold the throne, but the Hollow will crumble without her. Alarin was capable once, but now he's broken. Merio's just too goddamn weak. But Raas Dragath is worse than all of them. I can't stomach the thought of the Red Terror ascending the Imperial Throne."

Szathan nodded without realizing it. Everything General Sabriel said made sense. He was a good speaker.

"I'm growing old now," the general went on, "too old to change the course of the realm. But you are young yet. You have the power to influence men."

An image of Lady Cathia popped in his head, held captive against her will. He opened his mouth to reply but it took a few moments before anything came out. "I can't."

Sabriel's cherubic face turned hard. "Countless men will suffer and die if Dragath takes this city. Are their lives worth nothing to you?" He didn't wait for an answer, thankfully didn't seem to expect one. "Your brother was the very pillar of loyalty and righteous faith, a man gifted with the highest standards of rectitude. He lived and died unmoved by wealth and power and everything else that drives a lesser man. He was the purest form of honor. I do hope but a touch of his greatness has also been passed to his younger brother." He gave a brief pause to rub his temples with a free hand. He looked stressed. "You hold the key to the empire," he said at length. "It is your burden now. Yours to give to whomever you see fit." He gestured to the haversack in Szathan's hand.

Szathan looked down, suddenly remembering what he was holding. He untied the thong and pulled out whatever was inside. A single object, a patterned box of flawless ornate design. Inside it, five inter-twining Sadralen set in a meticulous inlay of silver and black jade. *By all the goddamn gods . . .* It took Szathan a good moment to realize he was holding the Imperial Seal of the Anirian Empire.

CHAPTER SIXTY

T he military train groaned to a slow and tired halt.

Mounted on a brown and barded charger, Seric waited impatiently for the reports, his eyes wandering to the officers and guardsmen around him, fingers moving absently beneath the cloth of his neckerchief. The rain had stopped but a deep chill still clung to the air, as if the thick colorless clouds strove to hinder the rebirth of warm sunlight.

It'd been weeks since the army departed from Aster Falls, having moved southward across the Grayling River and into the province of Riverwind. The supply wagons, weighed down by the booty of their defeated foe, had dragged the march down to a sluggard's pace. Worse, the province had proved a labyrinth of intertwining waterways, all given life by the massive glaciers of the eastern Sparroc Mountains. The army had forded shallow headwaters and negotiated high lakes and traversed broad valleys, all while the cold grew deeper and the late autumn wind pressed harder. Still, no one complained. These men had seen much, much worse.

General Pentagath rode up frowning a deeper frown than usual. Not a good sign. Chips and scratches marred his chest plate and lion-faced pauldron. "The bridge is out," he said gruffly. "Destroyed."

The news was grim. Crossing the Amber River would've left a mere six or seven days until they were to descend on Stormhaven. Now, who could say how long it would take? Still, Seric only smiled at what he'd heard. "Find a fordable point," he said to Pentagath. "The army will encamp here for the night, under the lee of the hills." He glanced briefly at the sky. "The passing rains have been strong, but don't lose heart, the gods may yet favor us."

The next morning, Seric awoke to find Veldries in his tent. The boy was seated on a stool, breaking his fast with Zirian. His scale armor and gray-black Anirian battledress gave him a formidable look, yet his eyes hadn't been the same since their near-defeat at the cliffs. Seric rose and joined them, helping himself to a bowl of bean porridge and a square of hardtack. Only after Veldries finished his serving did he speak. "Why did you smile?"

"What?"

"When you found out the bridge was destroyed . . . I saw you smile. Why?"

Seric gave him a measured look. "Tell me why you think, my son."

Veldries took a moment to consider, but in the end only shook his head. "Destroying the bridge stalls the march."

"That is true."

"The passing rains will likely leave us with no place to cross. We may be forced to build a pontoon bridge."

"Also true," Seric admitted.

His brow remain furrowed, his green eyes curious. "But that will take time and manpower. We can't afford such a delay, not with winter so near."

"Yes, all true, but your thoughts are too narrow. Consider Alarin Athera. What does the act say of our saboteur?"

"It says Alarin is aware of our position. He expects us, knows of our coming."

"That it does," Seric agreed. His attention turned to Zirian, who had placed his empty bowl on the ground and now sat with his arms crossed and head lowered. He always seemed to fall into a sort of quiet contemplation during discussions in the Anirian tongue, as if his mind saw fit to venture off elsewhere. Still, Seric had a sense that the big man was simply translating the words in his head, working to master the nuances and intricacies of the language. The Zhoul already knew quite a bit of the Anirian tongue, more than he'd have you believe.

"Just tell me, Father," Veldries said, obviously frustrated by his father's reticence.

Seric looked at him. "I smiled because at that moment I knew we would crush them."

Veldries threw him a confused look. His mouth opened, closed, then opened again, before finally he spoke. "How do you know that?"

"By destroying the bridge, it only shows how truly frightened Lord Alarin is."

The boy's confused look turned into a slow nod, as if some esoteric principle had just been revealed to him. He seemed to study his father in quiet admiration. "I still have much to learn," he admitted at last.

"Don't fret yourself," Seric told him. "You will be a great man someday. I can see it in you now, the way your men talk to you. They respect you, you know. Not an easy feat at your age."

"They respect me because of my father's name," he said.

Seric smiled at that. "They respect you. Don't fret about why. You are young yet. You've been blessed with all my strengths, and none of my faults."

"I see no faults," Veldries said, but then added, "no wait, you're too trusting of old friends." He smiled a dimpled little smile.

That made Seric chuckle, but when he spoke his voice was more somber than he'd meant it to be. "Emeron's betrayal still grieves my heart."

Veldries's smile vanished. "Forgive me, Father, for rattling old bones. But you never did tell me why he betrayed you."

Seric wished he could do more than shrug. "I still don't know myself."

A guardsman called from outside the commander's tent. Both Veldries and Zirian rose to see to the disturbance. Seric was left with his thoughts. It pained him to have so misjudged Emeron's motives. The old cripple Alarin couldn't have turned him. No, Seric would never believe that. Still, it'd been many years since the three of them—Seric, Emeron, and Anseth—had all sworn lifelong friendship to one another. So many years and yet it seemed like yesterday. Seric and Anseth were young then, no more than sixteen. Emeron was eighteen. It was just after the Steel Gauntlet, the empire's annual contest of arms. Alarin Athera had defeated both Duren Lygrest and Tavarin Valayne to take home the prized silk robe. And little Anseth, by the gods . . . he was so puffed up with pride about his elder brother's achievement that one disrespectful remark from Seric boiled his blood. He tried to push Seric into an ordure pit, but Seric fought him off, and in the melee poor Emeron got thrown in instead. That was hilarious. Yes, it was that day the three had pledged lifelong friendship. Sworn brothers, as it were.

"Father. *Father*. Are you listening to me?"

Seric looked up. Veldries was standing by the exit, arms crossed. "It's the scout leaders," the boy said.

Seric nodded and slowly rose, his foot still aching from when he'd sprained it on the hill. He was fortunate to be alive—he probably wouldn't be were it not for General Wyath. Seric was still unhappy about leaving the general behind, but Aster Falls was Wyath's home now, as he governed the city and commanded the surrendered White-crow soldiers.

Two men entered, one lean, the other leaner. Both knelt and bowed their heads. Seric urged them to rise and speak.

"We found dry crossing four miles south, one west," the leaner one said. "The local fisherfolk said the rains haven't touched that whole stretch of the river for weeks, maybe more."

Seric nodded at the report. "Good work." He turned and saw Veldries staring at him with that same look of admiration as earlier.

"You were right, Father," the boy said. "It seems the gods have favored us, after all."

———

The battle had roared since daybreak.

Szathan Mordall and his Redlander allies had driven the Anirian soldiers back, forcing them off the open field and into the tight and tortuous dirt paths that bordered the Drakewood Forest. General Sabriel Soffin's men eventually dug in along a narrow defile, crammed between a steep drop-off and a tall tangle of thicket. Ranks were compressed to eight against eight, the Redlands' numerical advantage made null. Worse, Soffin had sent small detachments in and out of the surrounding woods to harass the Redlander flanks. What had started as a clear-cut victory turned into a bitter stalemate.

Raas Dragath reconvened with his military officers just after high sun. His gray hair was bedraggled and bloody and his battle armor was filthy and worn, but he looked more angry than fatigued. "My men are getting *cut down*," he bellowed. "Goddamn it, Hiriam, you *need* to do something."

The strategist's pristine battledress made him look odd in the face of the battle-drenched warlord. And though he seemed intent on calming the fiery man, whatever he said only made Dragath angrier. "I don't care," Dragath replied in his usual shout. "*I don't care.*" He shoved the young strategist, leaving Hiriam scowling at the offense.

"You *should* care," the young strategist countered. "I advised you *not* to follow—"

"*DO SOMETHING*," Dragath roared. "DO SOMETHING before my men all feed the GODDAMN worms in the dirt."

"I DON'T KNOW WHAT TO DO," Hiriam shouted back. It was rare to see the strategist so muddled. He took a long moment, as if to collect himself. "I told you not to pursue. You didn't listen. Now he lured you in and he's picking you apart with surprise skirmishes. It's a simple rule of any military text: feign weakness where you are strong.

Only a goddamn *fool* would—" The young strategist halted. Clearly, he'd forgotten whom he was talking to.

Raas Dragath's face was ice. The frantic anger he'd shown just moments ago melted away into a murderous stillness. Halberd in hand, he approached the young strategist. Szathan needed to do something. As much as he disliked Hiriam, he despised Dragath more, and he didn't wish to see any man lose his head so dishonorably. "I know the outer roads," he blurted.

Hiriam quickly gestured to Szathan. "General Szathan! General Szathan knows the roads, my lord. I'd wager he knows them better than Sabriel himself. Right, General? Can you get around that bastard? You must know a way."

Raas turned his head slowly to Szathan. *Do you?* his dark eyes asked.

Szathan gave a firm nod. "I do know a way."

That was enough for Dragath. "Then do it." He began stamping his foot impatiently as an attendant hurried over with the bridle of a fresh charger. Shoving the young man to the ground, Dragath mounted. "Don't you fail me in this, General," he warned Szathan. "I will cleave that highborn bitch from cunt to crown. Do you understand? I *want* this goddamn city." He made a few motions to his men, then whipped his horse into a run, off to rejoin the battle.

Hiriam sank to his knees, leaning over as if someone had stolen all the muscles in his body. Szathan shook his head at the young strategist. He wanted to say something, to tell Hiriam that he wasn't as shrewd as he thought himself to be, that he was a fool for choosing to stand beside the Red Terror in the first place. But the moment passed and Szathan couldn't find the right words, so he just said nothing. He did manage a big, gap-toothed, told-you-so smile, even though he knew it made him look like a fool.

Szathan went off to mount his charger and return to his detachment of veteran cavalrymen. They stood in formation, half a regiment or about six hundred men, their faces worn and grim and telling. They despised Raas Dragath, and no longer could they stomach fighting at his side. Szathan felt the same. He dearly wanted to tell them that, but he couldn't. *Your faith has been sworn,* he reminded himself, *you must hold true, even if that means seeing Thornberry fall to that goddamn tyrant.*

The midday light dimmed like a worn-out flame the moment they entered the wood. Here, dirt roads narrowed and twisted and fled in a thousand different directions. But Szathan knew them so well he could navigate his way through the dark of a new moon. And for all his ineptitude with words, he was damn good at sensing direction and noting landmarks in his mind. He made a left at the sight of an old, cankered oak, and another after passing an aspen covered in swollen knots. A patch of oyster mushrooms prompted a quick right, and wending his way around a narrow bend he made a final left at a split stump. He could hear the sounds of battle in the distance now. Once more, conflict rose in him. Yes, he'd given his oath to Alarin. But what about what Sabriel had told him? *Countless men will suffer and die if Dragath takes this city.*

A diverging fork opened before him, both paths twisting off in opposing directions. The right ran in a long curve that ended at the rear of Sabriel's host. An ambush there would leave the Anirians with little chance to defend. Raas Dragath would certainly win the battle, and Sabriel Soffin would certainly lose his life. Szathan looked to the left. The path curved only slightly before moving on, dipping here and there on uneven ground. This would take him to the flank of the Redlander soldiers, a perfect position to ambush. Szathan didn't know what to do. A hand moved to touch the Imperial Seal, concealed in a pouch beneath his armor. He closed his eyes and asked himself what Demien would've done . . . and after a long and quiet moment, the answer came to him.

"My lord?" his deputy officer cut in. "We should hurry. Lord Dragath's command . . ."

Szathan turned in his saddle. "He is *not* my lord, is he yours?" The officer looked as though he wanted to say no, but didn't for some reason. Szathan said, "Raas Dragath is a tyrant and a murderer." His voice had grown loud, loud enough that all his men could hear. They stared at him now, listening closely, expecting him to further explain.

Szathan swallowed hard. "I know that I . . . I despise him, I despise him as you all despise him . . . and yet you continue to fight, continue to remain loyal to your lord." He paused. *You're not making any sense.* Goddamn it, this was too difficult. "What I mean to say is . . . you are all virtuous men. Far more than the general you serve. You are virtuous because you've remained at my side . . ." He stopped. Another pause. "You see I made an oath, to follow my lord as you follow yours. But I'm not like you. I'm not virtuous and I'm not loyal . . . because I cannot allow Raas Dragath to take the good city of Thornberry. Our city."

The soldiers were beginning to understand. Fire flashed in their eyes, boldness to their breasts. Encouraged by this, Szathan pointed Nightwing toward the far-off Redlander banners. "That is our true enemy," he said, his voice steadier now. "The tyrant who took Thornberry from us once before. He *murdered* our brothers, our comrades in arms. No oath is worth serving a traitor to the empire. You've stood by me all this time, now I stand by you . . ." Szathan ran out of words.

The soldiers seemed unsure if the speech was finished, but when nothing more came forth, they began to roar and clash their weapons and stamp their boots in the dirt. Szathan straightened himself in his saddle, grabbing the reins of his charger and turning about. The divergent paths stared at him. Szathan's chest suddenly ached, heavy with the realization of what he'd just done. He regretted his words. He wanted to turn back and call off the whole goddamn thing. But no, that would be stupid. The decision was already made. Done. Over. Nothing he could do.

He chose the left path. *Forgive me, Lord Alarin,* he thought.

CHAPTER SIXTY-ONE

They reached the ford just after midday.

Seric stood along the outer banks, observing the vanguard division of the Anirian army make its way across the riverbed. It had seemed a narrower crossing from a distance, but now, standing before it, the river stretched fretfully wide. To the east the upper course snaked its way downstream, twisting through gorges and thick limestone outcrops. Westward the channel meandered and widened to leave lakes and natural levees behind. The sky above yawned cloudless and blue, and despite how gleefully the sun shone, the air was still a bit cold, not intolerable but just enough for snow.

Bridles in hand, the soldiers of the next division led their horses through the shin-deep and muddy waters. In files they went, cautious and orderly, reminding Seric of the organized descent down the cliffs of the Blue Wolf Hills. The thought of that harrowing night still put knots in his stomach, and no matter how hard he tried, he couldn't push it out of his mind. Always it would rear up at him, like a croc lunging from a waterhole.

Seric's eyes flicked eastward. He thought he heard . . . no, it was nothing. Wait, there, he heard it again. A rustling. Faint, like a gentle susurrus of leaves in a passing autumn breeze. Maybe Seric was just hearing things. But no—louder, the rustling grew. A few others began to hear it now, too. They were looking off to the east. "What is it?" Veldries asked from behind. Seric motioned him to be quiet. Louder, the rustling grew. Chargers began to fidget, their riders struggling with their bridles. An unexplainable wave of dread washed over Seric. Something was wrong.

Louder, the rustling grew. Standing puddles of river water began to ripple from some unseen tremor. Louder, the rustling grew. The wind began to stir, like the opening dance of a winter gale. Louder. The once gentle susurrus now turned into a harsh sound, like the hissing of a thousand hognose vipers. *Louder*. But it wasn't a thousand goddamn vipers. Of course not. *LOUDER*. Seric knew what it was. *LOUDER*. He knew exactly what it was . . .

It was the river.

Embankments exploded as angry white breakers surged downstream. The waves blasted against limestone and knocked aside boulders like a child kicking over an anthill. Seric watched it all happen and yet his mind refused to believe it. The mass of his troops was still in mid-crossing—hundreds of them, perhaps a thousand. There was a host of shouts, an attempt to escape, but then the rushing whitecaps roared upon them like the charge of some gigantic leviathan.

Seric turned and shoved Veldries back. "Get out of here. *RUN!*" The boy only looked at him, mouth agape. He went to give another shove but something struck him so hard he thought all his ribs had shattered at once, like a look mirror dropped on stone. The world flipped and spun. River water rushed down his throat, faster than he could spit it back up. The moment he found a breath he used it to scream for Veldries, but the boy could've been an arm's length away and it would've made no difference. Seric was powerless.

The river flung him somewhere against the muddy banks, where he scrabbled at anything to keep from being pulled back into the current. Hard, watery fists smacked him, force-fed him clumps of sediment. His nails raked against broken slabs of stone. He found a rocky ridge and pulled himself out, clawing his way until he was safe from the pull of the river. Between coughing up mouthfuls of water, he listened to the waves roaring behind him, ferocious and unstoppable waves, like those of a sidewise waterfall, if that could somehow be possible. The bloated banks hungrily snatched up anything that drifted too close.

Seric tried to rise but pain blazed through his foot, sending him back down. Soldiers scrambled past, fleeing this way and that, formless and in sheer panic. A nearby officer was struck from behind and fell face-first to the rocks. Seric saw an arrow shaft protruding from his shoulder. *An arrow?* Seric didn't see any foemen. When the poor guardsman lifted his head the bridge of his nose was so purple it looked almost black. But still the tough bastard refused to stay beaten —at least until a spear crashed down into his spine, skewering him like an overturned lobster. His mouth twisted open, but Seric couldn't hear his scream. Well, not entirely. He heard it in his mind, and it was awful.

A hand seized the haft of the impaled weapon, jerking it free with a gruesome spurt of red. Seric could barely make out the foeman's face. *Who in the hell are you . . .?* There were several of them, tall men in heavy overcoats and leather helmets. They spoke thick and guttural words, in a language Seric didn't know. These were *not* Stormhaven soldiers. By the gods they weren't even of the Anir. They were barbarians—northmen. Their long spears thrust and stabbed at fleeing soldiers. Blood flew through the air like crimson spindrift. Soon, the Anirians had nowhere to go except back toward the river, and in the ensuing chaos they pushed their own comrades into the raging waters, to drown miserably in their heavy armor.

Seric needed to move. *Now, you fool. NOW!* He crawled somewhere, anywhere, wherever he could go to hide. He slid into a muddy depression, settling beside the body of a dead soldier. He dragged the corpse over him and became a corpse himself. The barbarians trampled the earth around him, their spears piercing the Anirian soldiers as easily as hunting fish in a dried-up pond.

He couldn't say how long he lay there, but it was long enough that the initial swarm of violence began to abate. The river had settled somewhat in its course, its crimson banks now filled with the groans and wails of wounded and dying men. Haunting sounds, and yet the sun continued to shine down bright and blissfully ignorant of the carnage below. The weight of the dead man pushed Seric deeper into the mud, so much so that he feared he might suffocate. But he didn't have the strength to get this waterlogged bastard off him. He tried and tried and tried, but his arms were limp as noodles, his legs numb and useless. He was just a head, barely getting enough air to breathe. *I'm going to die,* he thought. *I'm going to die here like a fool, like a goddamn miserable fucking coward. No, please, I can't die like this. Please, someone help me.* He begged every god he could think to name: Azrial the Protector, Mersis the Warrior, Elysa the Wise. He begged them all.

A shadow appeared overhead. The weight of the dead man lifted. Seric raised his head, coughing and taking in gulps of precious air. A pair of strong hands dragged him out of the depression, its owner tall and grim and wearing boiled leather armor beneath an unfastened over-coat. Seric couldn't reach Sunburst, so he pulled out his dagger instead. A boot stamped on his wrist; another kicked the weapon from his fingers. Several barbarians loomed over him now.

A blade cut the straps of Seric's gorget, then a hand yanked it off, taking the silk neckerchief with it. Seric felt something cold press against his neck. He thought it was water, but no, it was the steel of the barbarian's blade. Seric's eyes followed the weapon to the man's face. By the gods he was an ugly thing, his features withered and flat like a bat's. Cruel, puffy eyes glared down at Seric. The barbarian's arm tensed, his wrist turning to cut.

"LRAK REGARAK, DARIOK!"

The shout came from somewhere nearby. Seric had no idea what it meant, but it must've been a command of some sort, since it made the barbarian stay his hand. They were arguing now, the two of them, the ugly one and the other, much shorter commander. *"Do it,"* Seric cut in. "Kill me. *Kill ME!"* Seric shouted it again and again, hoping to goad him. He didn't even know why to be honest. But after seeing all the dead men in the mud and muck around him, he suddenly realized he needed to join them. He wasn't afraid. He couldn't live with yet *another* defeat, no, not again. How could the great Seric Dyre have been outwitted like this? *Kill me*, he shouted. *Kill me.* When the barbarian made no move he called him a coward. A filthy fucking coward. But the bastard probably couldn't understand a word he said, so Seric spat at his face. That seemed to get his point across.

The blade pressed harder against his throat, drawing a thin line of blood. Again, the short one shouted. More commands, more words Seric couldn't understand. Or did he? Yes, he did understand—the man was speaking in the Anirian tongue now. Telling Seric to be quiet. That voice . . . there was something familiar about that voice. *Have I lost my mind?* Seric looked closer at the speaker. The little barbarian's face was hidden beneath the length of his black hair, but when he brushed it aside, Seric saw not the dark and leathery skin of a northman, but a pale face with sharp features. Anirian features. *Who are you?* Seric pawed away the glops of mud and grime in his eyes, and then at last he saw . . .

He was staring at the face of Ansetheral Athera.

———

"LET HIM GO, DARIOK," Anseth shouted, for what seemed like the thousandth time. And for the thousandth time, the brute refused to obey.

"The coward deserves to die," Dariok argued, the blade of his backsword flush against the apple of Seric's scarred neck. Behind them, the waves rolled along the overtopped banks, splashing river water just yards from where they stood. Occasionally, a rush of spray would lunge at the two men, but neither seemed to notice. Seric was simply staring up at Anseth, his eyes helplessly wide. *He recognizes me,* Anseth thought, studying his old friend in return. The half Zhoul was mud-covered and filthy and exhausted, but he was still the same Seric, still the same handsome face with the same green eyes and dimpled chin. The jagged scar across his neck was new, but that was all.

A rustle to the west drew Anseth's eye. Emerging from the wood was a massive man, larger even than Dariok, or most Vaskultans for that matter. In his hands was a crescent-bladed halberd. He wore a dark olive cuirass, long and skirted, with a crested halfhelm and the ragged, gray-black cloak of an Anirian general. But he was no Anirian, this one. His skin tone was only a shade lighter than his cuirass, and his features were more rounded. This man was a Zhoul.

When Dariok noticed he spun on the man, keeping the blade at Seric's throat. The big Zhoul only gazed at him, calm and unperturbed.

"Let him go, Dariok," Anseth said in Vaskulti. "Let him go or I swear I will clap you in a cangue."

Dariok, at last, lowered the blade. Was it because of Anseth's warning or because of this new threat? Anseth couldn't say. But whatever it was, Dariok released Seric and squared off against the big Zhoul. It was rare to find a man to make Dariok look small, but clearly the Zhoul did, and he could tell Dariok didn't like that one bit.

"Step back, Dariok," Anseth commanded.

"Shut up," Dariok told him. "I'm going to gut this big pissant."

Anseth scowled; he had enough of this. He turned to his guardsmen. Severak was among them, his black wolf fur torn at the shoulder where an enemy's blade had cut through it. On Anseth's signal the men sprang forward and grabbed Dariok, hauling him back. The brute cursed and struggled but in the end was no match for the three Vaskultans. He gave in.

Anseth spoke to the Zhoul in the Anirian tongue. "Take him. Take your lord." The huge man didn't move. *Does he even understand?* Anseth repeated the command, but the Zhoul's attention was still on Dariok. His left eye looked half closed, as if someone had stitched it there mid-blink. "Take your lord. Take him somewhere safe."

The big Zhoul's stare detached itself from Dariok. He moved slowly and cautiously, like a starving fox approaching a nest of abandoned eggs. He bent to a crouch, placed down his halberd, looked this way and that, and scooped Seric up as though he were no heavier than a babe. Then he threw the man over his shoulder, grabbed his halberd, and disappeared back inside the concealing wood.

Anseth was left staring at where Seric had just been. He wondered if he'd made a terrible mistake. Would Seric have done the same for him? They had sworn their friendship once, but that was many years ago. Anseth sighed and turned—and found Dariok scowling in his face. "You are a coward to let that chieftain escape."

Anseth tried to ignore him, but Dariok wasn't about to make it so easy. His backsword flashed in his hand—or maybe Anseth hadn't seen it until now. The brute came forward, but thank the gods Severak was still there to step in the way. Dariok tried to push through, and when he couldn't, he spat in Anseth's direction. "You don't deserve the stone around your neck." Anger made his eyes look extra puffy. River water matted his hair to his withered face. "It's *mine*. I am the rightful chieftain. I am challenging you. The cage of bones. Either kill me or die by my hand."

Severak gave him a fierce shove. "Have you gone mad?"

Dariok staggered back but made no further move. All traces of fury seemed to dissolve from his face, but what remained was a deep, smoldering mask of hatred. A hatred that was directed at Anseth. "Accept the blood challenge," he growled. "Or deny me and be cast out of the tribe. Make your choice, *runt. MAKE YOUR CHOICE.*"

It wasn't much of a choice to make. Anseth had long known this would happen—he knew it the moment he put the Earthstone around his neck. No, before that, when Lord Volduk first told him he wanted Anseth to rule as his successor. He also knew he'd never defeat this brute in the cage of bones. And yet, despite that, he looked calmly at Dariok. His heart was still tense from the battle and his mind was still reeling from the sight of Seric's defeated body, but somehow, he managed to look calmly at the brute. "I accept," was all he said.

BOOK VI: ASHES

CHAPTER SIXTY-TWO

Y<i>ou wound me so.</i>
Those four words were tattooed on Alarin Athera's mind. Four words that greeted him when he woke, four words that lay down with him at night. Four words that held the whole of his fears.

You wound me so.

Alarin was looking down now, at those four simple words. Scrawled in the center of an otherwise blank sheet of white silk, its seal belonging to the Redlander warlord. Alarin had stared at that seal for at least a week before finally mustering the courage to break it. To this day he wished he never had. And to this day, he put forth no response. What would it matter? Nothing could assuage the Red Terror's wrath. Merio's daughter would die because of Szathan Mordall's betrayal.

The general had turned his coat at Thornberry, leading an ambush that broke the Redlander ranks and saved the city. It was a bold move, courageous even, but—and this was an important but—Raas Dragath had escaped with his life. The Red Terror escaped, and now, Alarin could do nothing but wait for the tyrant's undoubtedly malevolent response.

While Szathan's betrayal certainly stung, strangely enough Alarin wasn't angered by it. In a way it shamed him to have ordered Szathan to ally with Dragath in the first place. *I had no choice,* he thought. *I'd failed in my attempt to rid the realm of the traitor.* Still, he should never have forced the general to dishonor himself so that Alarin might correct an oversight. Alarin had thought he could keep all the pieces together, but no, either there were too many pieces, or Alarin simply wasn't the competent man he used to be.

He had written a letter to Szathan. Why did you do what you did? How could you go against my orders? Question after question. He burned it when he realized he already knew the answers. There was only one question left, and it was for Raas Dragath himself. What will you do to that sweet, innocent girl?

You wound me so.

Alarin placed the four words into the brazier. He watched the letter curl and blacken at the edges, then shrivel completely under the devouring flames. When all that was left was ash, when those four words were utterly eradicated, it made no difference. The words were long immortalized in his heart.

It was winter now. The days grew shorter and Alarin slept longer. Merio still never came to see him. The palace of Stormhaven had become a foreign, lonely place. Alarin was useless, a commander without a battalion, a man without a leg. He spent long hours in his chamber staring out the window, observing the landscape like a wistful vagabond trapped in a hanging cage. He mapped each jagged peak of the distant mountain ranges, and counted the many arms that split from the Amber. He tracked the courses of the merchant junks traveling to and from the city, an undemanding task since their numbers were far fewer than those of the Hollow.

He often found himself returning to the conservatory to sit on the benches before the tiers of cloudfalls, either relaxing quietly or engaging in mindless chitchat with the gardeners and maintenance workers. Sometimes he'd visit the private staging areas where performers and sword dancers perfected their acts. If he felt especially vibrant, he'd visit the potter's workshop to watch the young apprentices toil away with their clay bins and glazes and mixing vessels. He did anything and everything he could do to stay busy, and yet, he only felt more and more lifeless. Truth was, Alarin had become but a lonesome prisoner, a prisoner waiting for the hour of his execution . . . and finally, late one evening, it came.

"*NOOOOOOOOOOOOOO* . . ."

The sound startled him awake. He hadn't been in a deep sleep, but enough where you don't realize you're actually falling asleep. The moan had brought him out of it at once, and in the ominous silence that followed, Alarin rose and dressed himself in his gray robes. When that was done, he simply sat on an armchair. And waited.

He long heard the commotion growing outside his chamber, and yet, when the door burst open, it was with such force that Alarin still gave a start. The flame of the nearest braziers dimmed under the sudden gust of wind, and in the doorway Alarin glimpsed a silhouette. Merio's silhouette. Behind him stood Stormhaven soldiers, a score at least. They flooded inside the room. Merio entered last. He was dressed in heavy furs and fine silks of mismatched colors, as if he'd just picked anything and went with it. Cradled in his hands was a plain leather sack.

Alarin rose and did his best to remain calm, but the look on Merio's face unnerved him, like an injured woodsman hearing the growl of a bear. He'd never seen his young brother look so goddamn angry. In fact, he looked *more* than angry—he looked absolutely mad, mad and murderous and disheveled and a dozen other things Alarin didn't have time to point out. And when Merio came to stand directly before him, Alarin could think of nothing to say save one single word. "Brother . . ."

Merio shoved the sack into Alarin's arms. It was wet and encrusted in old snow. "A gift," Merio said, his voice close to breaking.

Alarin tried to look unruffled.

"Open it," Merio urged. He began untying an imaginary sack by its imaginary thongs. "Open it."

Alarin looked down. His fingers worked quickly, pausing only once to dry them on his robe. The room remained quiet. The only sound was the occasional crackle of the braziers, that and the pounding of Alarin's heart. He slid one hand inside the open sack, slowly, like a man reaching into a barrel of crabs. His fingers touched something stringy and knotted—the unmistakable texture of human hair. He grabbed a fistful. Slowly, ever so slowly, he brought it out . . . out of the darkness and into the light of the chamber.

Cathia's head.

Her face was so frozen and so twisted that Alarin barely recognized it at first. Both ears had been removed, her nose too, leaving gutted black craters in their place. Her mouth was split and the few teeth that remained were jagged and broken. All traces of her former beauty were gone, replaced only by the hideous, distorted mask he saw now. Alarin didn't want to look at it any longer, but neither did he wish to look up at poor Merio. In fact, few things in his life had been so difficult as lifting his head to meet his brother's eyes.

And what did Merio do? He simply grabbed his daughter's head and pressed it to his breast, swaddling it like a mother does a babe. After that, the man wept. He wept and he moaned, and they were the most heart-wrenching sounds Alarin had ever heard. Even the guards around him looked ready to weep, so great was their lord's grief. It was the grief of a loving father who'd just been given his daughter's decapitated head in a sack. Alarin averted his eyes and said nothing.

Eventually Merio planted his face in the crook of his arm, sniveling softly into his robe. It was a muffled, almost soothing sound, like a child snoring against his mother's breast. When he was done, he raised his head and wiped his eyes, then from a sleeve he produced a letter. He held it out to his elder brother. His hand was trembling. "Take it," he said. His voice was trembling, too.

Alarin took it and ran a finger across the broken seal of Raas Dragath. He swallowed a lump in his throat, and hesitated.

"Read it," Merio said, urgently.

Alarin unfolded the letter and looked down.

She was a beautiful thing, a woman whose heavenly grace could turn the moon or cast light upon the darkest sky. And yet, to her kith and kin, she meant nothing. Alarin stopped. He'd read enough. He wanted no more of this. But Merio gave him a furious look, and he had no choice but to continue. *She wept when I cut off her hair, she screamed for her life when I cut off her ears and nose. When I cut off her fingers she began to squeal like a swine, so a swine is what I made her. I cut off her arms and her legs, and I placed what was left of her in the dark of the lower dungeons, where she died alone and in agony. I am told if you listen closely enough you can still hear her little voice, crying out for her father, asking why, why, why. I share that same question, Lord Merio. Why? Why did you betray me? I do hope your answer is worth more than the suffering of that sweet little girl.*

The silence that filled the room was thicker and more dreadful than anything Alarin had ever known. His brother's eyes were redder than red, his glare so malicious it made the normally stolid Alarin want to melt into the floor. "If you were any other man you'd suffer a most horrendous death," Merio said. "But you are my brother . . . so another will have to die in your stead." He turned to address his men. "Bring him in."

The guards returned with Ravathyr Aeryn. The advisor's tall, lanky body was slumped over like an old, dehydrated carrot stick, his face bloody and bruised and battered as if an angry drunk had taken a truncheon to it. "*NO!*" Alarin shouted. He lunged forward and latched onto his brother's arm, nails digging into flesh, as if hurting the man would somehow save the advisor's life. Merio threw Alarin to the ground. His wooden leg twisted and drove itself hard into his stump, sending pain up his body. He tried to get up but couldn't. Grimacing, he said, "Ravathyr is not involved in this, by the gods he's *innocent.*"

Merio's eyes glittered with rage. "There was only one innocent in all this, and she is *DEAD*." He whipped around to face his captive. A dagger appeared in his hand. "Hold him," he ordered. The guards obeyed. Ravathyr's terrified eyes remained fastened on Alarin even as the blade tore open his throat. Streams of crimson poured out, and the body toppled forward, landing facedown on the floor. Blood spread through the cracks of the surrounding tilework.

Alarin crawled to his dying friend. He tore a strip of his robe and tried to staunch the flow, but the wound was too deep, the artery gruesomely severed. Merio stood over him, the tip of his dagger dripping blood onto the floor. "I'm mobilizing the ranks and I'm taking the van. I'll not rest until I tear Raas Dragath's heart out with my own goddamn teeth." He paused for a moment, as if considering something. "When I leave on campaign, I want you gone, Elder Brother. I want you gone from my city." With that he turned and left, his guardsmen trailing behind him in a great metallic roar. Soon, the doors slammed shut and Alarin was alone, alone with the poor dead advisor. He rose and limped over to the nearest armchair and sat, lowering his head into his bloodstained hands.

CHAPTER SIXTY-THREE

When sleep did come, it was filled with blood and breakers and barbarian steel, and every dream began with Seric Dyre battered on the riverbank, cowering before the might of the northmen. The faces he saw would all become Anseth's face, every one of them, all twisted and malformed but undeniably Anseth in their own way. The faces would then chase him, and Seric would run and run and run and run, but always they would catch him, and just as cold steel flashed across his neck, Seric would awake.

He opened his eyes now to find a mousy face leering over him. Orbrey Lorian's face, the son of the illustrious Grand Physician Arden Lorian. The small man had extended his services to Seric before, most notably after the Redlander assassin had sliced his throat. But as skillful and diligent as Orbrey was, Seric only found him more and more tiresome through each passing day. "Drink, my lord," Orbrey said, offering up an earthenware bowl of some dark tonic. It smelled foul and tasted fouler, and Seric told him that. He said it tasted like old dirt and rotted fruit and he even compared it to the stink of a man with a terrible digestive disorder.

But Orbrey was persistent, so Seric had no choice but to sip and sip, his nose runny from the steam of the liquid. When his free hand wandered to his silk neckerchief, he found only a piece of linen, wrapped around him like a dirty old rag. He let go of the fabric and balled a fist, perhaps in frustration, perhaps in anger, likely a mix of both. His thoughts returned to the ambush at the Amber River, to the sight of Ansetheral Athera. It all made sense now. The reason for Emeron's betrayal. Only Anseth could've turned the man against Seric. But how did Anseth survive all those years in the Gravelands? Not only did he survive, he'd risen to become a *commander* to those men. Anseth was always tough and resourceful little lord, but this . . . this was something more. It was some kind of divine providence, as if Azrial the Protector had been guiding him.

But in the end, Anseth had made one grievous mistake. He let his old friend Seric Dyre live.

Orbrey removed the bowl and urged him to rest. *I am fucking resting*, Seric wanted to say. *That's all I'm doing. That and staring at your goddamn ugly face.* Truly Orbrey was an eyesore of a man, with his mousy features and horrendous overbite. His ears were big and droopy, his nose red and bulbous. All that remained of his hair was a scattering of thin brown locks like shreds of seaweed on a sandbar. Worst of all, his breath stank. Seric could smell it right now, as the physician's upside-down face stared down at him from above. Still, Seric did his best to temper his irritation. He knew the physician was only doing his duty, but at the same time, that was what irritated him. Seric didn't have *time* to rest. He needed to get moving. He needed to get his *soldiers* moving. But the pain in his foot—the same foot he'd injured at the cliffs—left him at the mercy of Orbrey's foul concoctions and persistent urgings.

Sleep came and when next he knew, Seric was back along the river-bank, fleeing from the horde of barbarians. When they caught him, steel flashed, and Seric awoke with a start. He might've been scream-ing, but he wasn't sure. Footfalls came scampering over, and Seric groaned when Orbrey's face appeared. "You're safe," he said, "you're safe, my lord. Just rest now. You're safe."

"What the hell are you administering to me?" he complained. "It's giving me terrible dreams."

"It's just a little mugwort," Orbrey replied. "And a bit of dried peppermint. You swallowed a lot of salt water. It made you sick and dehydrated . . . near feverish."

Seric tried to rise, but the sharp pain in his foot forced him back down. "My foot," he moaned.

The physician drew the heavy wool blanket back over him, then gave Seric a disapproving look. "It's a minor open fracture, no infection. It should keep. But you *need* to stay off it. You need to rest."

"I can't rest any longer," Seric said. *"Please."*

Orbrey shook his head. "I've debrided and drained the wound of bad spirits. The bone is set so don't touch the dressings. It's only a minor break of the large toe, my lord, but still you must be patient. The process cannot be rushed."

Just the toe? It felt like Seric's whole foot was on fire. He turned to his side and gave a long sigh. They were stranded somewhere along the foothills of the Sparroc Mountains. Nearly a third of his conscripted infantry and about a quarter of his veteran regiments were either lost or dead or dying from their wounds. The Zhoulish auxiliaries were the only soldiers to remain fairly strong, having lost only a fifth of its numbers. Still, Seric couldn't afford to be injured, not in this goddamn winter. He needed to address the men, to re-establish logistics and supply routes, to survey the land for the march back to the Hollow, to find his son, to—

Orbrey pushed another steaming bowl in his face. Seric grabbed it and threw the goddamn thing across the tent. It landed with a crash somewhere, prompting a gasp from the physician. *"Get this shit AWAY from me!"* Seric's throat felt raw enough already, worse now after shouting. He took a moment to calm his thoughts. "Listen to me, I need to get these men moving. There's not a village around that can supply us, and we're all slowly weakening. Don't you get it? With these heavy snows it'll be an ordeal even if the men were strong. I need to send a missive. Where's my bag? My bag, Orbrey."

He watched Orbrey's silhouette flit across the room. The physician fumbled around until he found Seric's military satchel, then he rushed back to hand it over. Inside Seric found his brushpen and ink. He also found a letter. "What is this?" he asked. Then he remembered. A rider had delivered it the very day they were to ford the Amber River. Seric had no time to look at it then so he simply stuffed it into his satchel, where it went forgotten.

He examined it now. A plain silk letter, unsealed and without any identifying marks. Unfolding, he read:

This is but a secret warning, written by a secret friend. Lady Miriana knows of your clandestine meetings with the Redlander advisor. She knows about the intelligence you shared with Dragath, and about the position of director general you were promised. She knows about it all and she plans to execute you for your crimes. Do not think you can reason with Her Majesty. If you dare return to the Hollow you will find yourself bound and arrested at the gate. This is but a secret warning. I suggest you heed it.

Seric stared at the letter, disbelieving of what he'd just read. One hand rose to his head, squeezing a clump of hair so hard that when he brought his hand down, stray hairs clung to his sweaty fingers. He was shaking. His throat grew tight. He gnashed his teeth so hard he thought they might break.

Then Orbrey was there, telling him to drink this and drink that, to do this and do that. Seric obeyed, too weak and too tired to do much else. Before long, the great hand of darkness overtook him. He was running along the riverbank again, running and running while the barbarians chased after him. Hands seized Seric's chest, the ground rose up, and a blade flashed at his throat. Once more, Seric woke up.

His thoughts returned to the letter, though for a moment he wasn't sure if the letter was just part of the dream. Then he saw it lying nearby and the truth rushed at him like a hot poker. He grabbed it and crumpled it and threw it into the low center brazier, but it only bounced off the outer rim and landed somewhere among the nearby furs. He sighed.

Everything was ruined. Everything was ruined and only Seric was to blame. And just when he needed Miriana the most, he'd lost her. He lost her and he lost every inch of power he'd so arduously attained at the Hollow. He wasn't the Imperial Advisor any longer. He was nothing. Tears rose in Seric's eyes. He wept softly and he wept silently, and when he was done he didn't bother to dry his eyes. Instead he closed them, wishing for sleep. To sleep and never wake up. But when he did sleep he dreamed a horrific dream, and when he awoke Orbrey came over and quietly urged him to rest.

CHAPTER SIXTY-FOUR

Miriana Athera exited the hall and made her way to her private bedchamber. Another prolonged council, another headache, another evening ending in exhaustion. All she could think about was that one empty seat at the table. Vylas's seat. It was the first time she'd held council without him, and it left her heart heavy with ache. She hadn't spoken to her brother since the night he . . . well, since that dreadfully awkward night. She'd tried to but her summonses went unrequited, her personal visits all met with pleas of illness. As of now she had no idea where he was, if he was still in the palace district at all.

The corridors were eerily quiet at this hour. She walked alone in the dimness, stopping to observe the cast-iron statues poised in the recesses of the walls. True masterworks they were, each depicting a powerful god or deity or some great figure of a faraway dynasty. She must've passed these statues at least a thousand times and never once had she truly observed the detail in them. Funny, how the eyes only see what they want to.

It wasn't long before she heard footfalls behind her. Miriana turned to see Cyrille Vileron and a handful of his imperial guardsmen approaching. "Your Majesty," Cyrille called out, his sickle-shaped eyes wider than she thought they could go. "You shouldn't wander off alone."

"I'm fine," she said.

Master Arden Lorian was among them. The little old man slipped through the larger bodies, almost tripping on his long gray robes as he came to stand before her. Worry tugged at his old face, deepening his already deep wrinkles. "Your Majesty," he began. "Have you heard anything new . . . any new reports?"

"No," she told him. And not for the first time. Like some of her other ministers, Master Lorian's persistence was beginning to irritate her.

"Oh," he said, despondently. "Forgive me, but my son . . . my son was at Amber River . . ."

"I know," she told him. "Like I said before, the moment I hear word of Orbrey's whereabouts, I'll have you informed."

He nodded at that, but it didn't seem enough to satisfy him. "Can we go over everything once more, Your Majesty? Please . . . if you may be so kind."

The guards opened the door to her bedchamber, and Miriana went inside. Lorian followed. He was like an old housecat clinging to her side, unceasingly annoying whenever his mealtime came late. "Forgive me, Your Majesty, but Seric assured me Orbrey would be unharmed in this campaign. He *promised* me."

"Not the first time Seric's broken a promise," she muttered.

That made the old physician's face blanch. "Do you think my son . . ?"

Miriana gave a sigh.

"Please . . ."

"Your son's likely fine, he is a physician not a soldier. But until I know for sure, I need you to remain patient." She went behind a screen to her wardrobe, removing her silk outer jacket and stripping off her long skirt. She went to hand them to Yana but realized Yana wasn't there. Miriana cursed. "Goddamn it, Yana. Where the hell—"

"I sent her out."

Miriana looked out from behind the screen. At the far end of the chamber, half hidden in the darkness, stood Zantherei Athera. "Hello, my wife."

Her mouth fell open and she nearly shrieked. Zantherei came closer, taking small, slow, uneven steps. "I can't see so well," he said. It was strange, his voice, familiar yet so unfamiliar. She watched him, speechless for a long moment. Then she threw on a silk bedrobe and emerged from behind the screen. Her eyes went right to Master Lorian. "It's m-my husband, I . . . why didn't you tell me?"

The Grand Physician looked more surprised than she. "I didn't know either, Your Majesty."

Zantherei stopped before the center brazier, the flames throwing red-orange light onto his face. The man was a skeleton. He stared at her with hollow eyes, eyes that were more misaligned than she'd remembered. His hair was thinner too, and messy, while his face was freshly shaven but incredibly pale. A pink rash trailed down to where his powerful jaw once sat. "I'd thought you'd be delighted to see me," he said, frowning a frown that made him look a decade older.

"I-I . . ." she stammered. *Act delighted*, she told herself. *Act delighted that he's awake!* "You're . . . I'm just . . ." Her bedrobe had fallen open, revealing the racy little slip she wore beneath. Without thinking she jammed it closed. His eyes narrowed and she feared she might've offended him. "I just . . . I don't believe it." She lifted one foot from its place, then the other, slowly moving closer to him. Barefoot, she always had to tilt her head up slightly to meet her husband's eyes, but right now, he seemed small. Small and hunched and shriveled, like an old mutt after a lifetime of receiving its master's boot. She forced a warm smile. *Does he know? Does he know all I've done?*

"'Your Majesty'," Zantherei said, mimicking the way Lorian had said it. A bony hand rose to touch her cheek, his fingers cold and alien.

She had to stop herself from pulling away. Looking into his wife's eyes he said, "Why are you still here, Master Lorian?"

The Grand Physician straightened and spun and scurried off, spry for a man in his sixties. He didn't even glance at the empress for permission of leave. It was at that moment Miriana knew all her imperial power was gone. She was no longer an empress, but a courtesan again, a courtesan and a servant to her husband. And like a good little servant, she remained meek and silent.

The chamber door closed, leaving her alone with Zantherei. He was looking deep into her eyes, examining her, drinking her, as if he intended to later paint her from memory. She didn't like it. Tired as she was, she probably looked no better than he did. Relief flooded her when at last he turned away. He stood with his back to her, his frame noticeably gaunt even with his loose-fitting robes. "Nyvia told me everything," he said. "The coup, the conspiracy, the emperor's death . . . *everything.*"

His words made her heart pound even faster. *Does he truly know everything? Does he know about Seric? No, if he did, I wouldn't be here, talking to him like this. I would've been given the cord before I knew what was happening.* She watched him now, her mind filled with questions, endless, endless questions. But she couldn't gather the courage to ask any of them, so all she said was, "I am sorry . . . for all that's happened."

He made a half turn. "Don't be. You've done everything in your power to keep the realm united." Something about the way he said that didn't sit well with her. Zantherei finished the turn to fully face her. "And to me, you have remained faithful."

"I have," she lied.

He seemed to want to say something more, but instead his expression folded into a tight grimace, as if struck by sudden pain. It was a familiar grimace, what with all his old aches and pains. Still, it made him look feeble and broken, the same way Alarin looked after losing his leg. Zantherei leaned against the nearby pillar. His eyes wandered the room as he spoke. "I have . . . difficulties, still some things I cannot —" He stopped abruptly, his voice turning hard. "Where is Sunburst?"

Miriana followed his eyes to the empty wall hooks. She tried to speak but faltered. She didn't know what to say.

"Sunburst. My *saber*. Where is my saber."

"S-Seric . . . Seric took it, for protection on campaign."

His eyes evinced no hint of emotion, though his left hand began to twitch. At length he said, "I want you to arrange a high council for tomorrow. I will enter and take my seat on the Imperial Throne. As emperor. Emperor Zantherei Athera. I'd adorn myself with the Imperial Seal but I'm told someone stole that from the palace as well." He shook his head disappointingly, then glanced once more at the wall before placing his eyes back on her. His voice carried a familiar edge of harshness. "Your choices of late have left the capital buried by loss, defection, and defeat. But you are only a woman, and I cannot condemn a woman for a man's faults. Don't fret, you still have worthy generals and experienced soldiers at your side. And most of all . . ." He pushed himself off the pillar. "You have me."

"Please, my husband, you shouldn't place yourself in a war against Alarin—"

His fury was so sudden it made her flinch. "Do *NOT* speak his name." She lowered her eyes. He said, "I will send an edict to Stormhaven, demanding nothing short of his full submission. If he agrees, I'll personally welcome him back to the Hollow. If not, then he stands as my enemy. The same goes for that little brat Merio. The fate of our familial bonds will be theirs to decide."

She nodded but kept her eyes lowered. Silence passed between them, long and uncomfortable. Zantherei raised a shaky hand to re-open her silk bedrobe. The low-cut slip beneath revealed more of her breasts than she would've liked to display. He began fondling them, gently, one and then the other. She closed her eyes and felt a whore again, a whore under the power of the man who bought her. And like any practiced whore, she would give him her body and escape with her mind. This should be over quickly . . .

But no, he stopped. He simply stopped touching her. Miriana opened her eyes. Her husband was staring at her, not lustfully or sensu-ally but rather oddly, the same stare a client might give after being informed of her high price. At length he spoke. "Now that I am reclaiming the throne, I have but one request for my wife. A request I've made before."

"What is it?"

"Give me a son."

Miriana promised she would. Then her eyes fell once more to the floor. Inside, she wept.

CHAPTER SIXTY-FIVE

S leep came and went, and despite the terrible dreams it brought, Seric still longed for it when he woke. Asleep, he didn't have the anguish, the shame, the crippling sadness. Asleep, his heart wasn't tormented by Lady Miriana and her beautiful, beautiful face. Asleep, he didn't see himself bound and kneeling before the axeman.

Awake his head hurt and his foot throbbed and he was hungry and cold and surrounded by an army of soldiers who were also hungry and cold. They were desperate men, men who wanted things from him. Things Seric couldn't give. Why not? Because he had no logistical plans, no provisions en route, and no reinforcements to speak of. He had nothing.

Days passed like this, long and miserable days. The pain in Seric's toe had eased enough for him to walk again. Too bad he had nowhere to go, other than to piss or shit or rifle through his belongings in search of something edible. His body had grown gaunt and weak. Malaise and dizziness assaulted him. And even though Orbrey Lorian remained at his side, the physician bore no more interest in Seric. His only concern now was his own failing health. Seric pitied him none. *Stupid wretch, I told you this would happen.*

Zirian came to him sometime later. The broad and powerful wolf general had become a mangy old mutt, sallow of face and listless of bearing. His left eye, the one with the cast, no longer made him look dangerous, but half dead. And while still enormous in size, he didn't seem quite so imposing. He usually approached with the same old plea for Seric to take control of the men and lead the march, but today he said nothing. Seric thought him a fool. A fool for not abandoning his miserable commander weeks ago. Seric told him that, and then he told him to leave, to go away. But the giant Zhoul seemed to have no desire to make things easy today.

Zirian's massive hands yanked back Seric's blankets. He tried to hold on but the Zhoul was too strong, and Seric felt the burn of the wools as they zipped through his palms. Zirian gathered them up and tossed them outside the tent. Seric cursed at him. "What the hell is wrong with you?! It's goddamn cold."

He came back over and spoke in a voice so grave it was almost unnerving. "We cannot stay here any longer."

"We?" Seric countered at once. "There is no 'we'. I told you to leave."

The Zhoul gave him a grim look. He seemed to want to say something more but didn't. It mattered not—Seric already knew the gist of it. The soldiers were suffering and morale was dangerously low. Many had already deserted to brave the winter wilds on their own. Those that remained, well . . . they were ready to storm the commander's tent and cut off Seric's negligent head. And they probably would've done so already, had Zirian left him like he was ordered to do. "I don't want your protection, you purblind oaf," Seric told him. "I want you to leave. Now *LEAVE*, goddamn it."

The Zhoul rubbed his stubbly face and sighed. "I can't."

"If you don't you will die. Your soldiers will die."

"Such is my lord's will."

"No," Seric told him. "It is *your* will. I freed you of your oath, remember? You are no longer my vassal. Take your Zhouls and return to the mountains."

"Your soldiers will mutiny," he said.

Seric placed a hand on the snow-encrusted fur draped across Zirian's shoulders. He spoke calmly, softly. "Listen, my friend, you've done more than enough for me. Now you must go. Save yourself and your own." He couldn't help but admire the Zhoul's steadfast loyalty, and yet he pitied him for it as well. *I never should've recruited you,* he wanted to say. *I should've known better than to think anything good would ever come of my life.*

The Zhoul's voice broke the silence like a hatchet splitting wood. "I won't break my oath."

Rage welled up inside Seric. "*FUCK* your oath. Don't you get it? *I WANT* to die."

So loud was his outburst that even Orbrey stopped doing whatever he was doing. The physician didn't know a single word of the Zhoulish tongue, but the anger of a man was of course universal. Seric lowered his voice and continued on. "Listen, my officers are dead. My status in the Hollow revoked. The woman I admire wants my head on a pike, and I'm too damn weak and hungry to think straight. My life ends here." He gave a slight pause. "It ends here."

Zirian laughed, a hard and humorless laugh. "Your father was right. You *are* a miserable wretch. Certainly not the great strategist you claim to be."

Seric didn't know what infuriated him more, the mention of his father, or the smug way the general said 'great strategist'. "I am a great goddamn strategist," he shot back. "The greatest in all the realm."

"So a great strategist would choose to die here, alone and at the hands of his own soldiers?" His pale lips curled back in anger, like a wolf baring its teeth. "I see no strategist but a goddamn fool. A fool who focuses on what he doesn't have, rather than what he does."

"Spare your pitiful attempts at rhetoric," Seric said, scoffing. "You couldn't persuade a drunk to down a nightcap. My life is at its end, I tell you. I have nothing left."

"You have me, and you have some five thousand Zhouls. You have General Wyath to the north, that other city to the west . . . the fat man's city. What name do you call it?"

"Silverleaf."

"Seel-ver-leff," Zirian pronounced in the Anirian tongue. He switched back to Zhoulish. "You received a letter, warning you not to return to the capital. Whoever wrote that letter is your ally. You need to find out who that is."

Seric hadn't thought of that.

"And your son. He may yet be alive—"

"My son is *dead,*" Seric said. The very mention of Veldries put a heap of stones on his chest. "I've worked my scouts to the bone. Every inch of these foothills . . . there's no sign of him."

The harshness fled from Zirian's voice. "No sign means he may be alive."

"He's dead. He was standing right behind me when the river hit. Trust me, the gods wouldn't have it any other way. They enjoy making me suffer."

"Still, you don't have to die here," Zirian replied. "None of us do."

Seric gave him a long, weary look. "Maybe not, but how do you propose to get me out of here alive?"

Zirian gave a halfhearted shrug. "I'm not the great strategist here."

Seric said nothing to that, and in the ensuing silence he retreated into his thoughts. Surely he could arrange a way to slip out in the middle of the night . . . but is that what he truly wanted? To slink away like a mutt with its tail between its legs? No, he didn't. And as much as his soldiers were ready to take his head, he still disliked the thought of abandoning them. A great strategist would devise a way to regain their faith and comradeship. But how? *Come on, great strategist, think.*

A sneeze broke him from his thoughts. Seric's eyes turned to its source. Orbrey sat huddled in thick blankets, wiping his nose. Seric silently cursed the physician for the disturbance, but then . . . his mind began to turn, like the waterwheel of a clock tower. An idea came to him. Yes, it might work . . . it just might work. He looked at Zirian.

"Tonight, during fourth watch, meet me at the eastern exit." He made a quick motion to the physician. "Bring him with you. Understand?"

Zirian furrowed his thick brow. "My lord, what does he have—"

"You want to get me out alive? Then do as I say, General. No questions."

The Zhoul agreed.

It was deep into fourth watch when the three men exited the encampment. Seric was dressed in layers of fox fur and winter wool and fitted with doeskin gloves and long cowhide boots, the warmest he could find. The blizzard that had assaulted them throughout the day finally began to ebb, but the wind kept howling on, stubborn and insistent on punishing anyone foolish enough to intrude on its domain.

Their boots crunched faintly in the snowpack. *Crunch crunch, crunch. Crunch crunch, crunch.* Seric's own steps were mid-paced and determined, Zirian's long and steady, Orbrey's quick and erratic. To their right, black foothills rose like misshapen lumps of volcanic clay. They traveled high enough to where Seric could observe his army's military tents littering the lowlands below. The sides of their ridged canvas roofs bowed inward, laden with ice and crusting snow. Seric could picture the poor men crammed inside, hungry and weak and huddled together for warmth. There were no horses. The soldiers had already butchered them and eaten them and drank their blood. Soon, they'd do the same to their dead comrades. A barbaric thing to do, sure, but hunger drove a man to do barbaric things. Things only a man who's ever been truly hungry could possibly understand.

The three men continued along the outer reaches of the hills, careful not to slip on the strewn patches of ice. Maintaining balance was especially difficult for Seric, since he had to put most of his weight on the heel of his foot, as not to aggravate his wounded toe. When a terrible gust blew a spray of white in his face, he slipped and probably would've gone tumbling down the hill had he not grabbed on to a nearby cedar for support. Shoving down the apprehension at his throat, he tightened his cloak, lowered his head, and moved on.

The path narrowed into a thick enclosure of spruce and fir and limber pine. Darkness swallowed the men, then spat them back out into an open clearing, where twisted stretches of frost shimmered like rime in the moonlight. Seric stopped here. The physician looked around, groggy and shivering and obviously irritated. "My lord, you know I am loyal to your every command, but this . . . what hour is it?"

"Late," Seric said. He offered the small man a gourd of warm wine. Orbrey took it at once, taking a long gulp. Seric had to shout to be heard over the wind. "You have been a great help to me, even when I made things difficult for you."

"Any other physician would have done the same," Orbrey replied. He seemed more concerned with the cold than about what he probably perceived as idle chatter. He kept looking back toward the encampment.

"I'm afraid I have to ask for help just one more time," Seric went on.

"Of course, my lord," was the noncommittal reply. "However I can." Shivering, he took another gulp of wine. "I can fulfill this request back in the tent, I'm sure. Might we head back?"

Seric didn't answer that. He looked up and down the path, a long look, making sure they were alone. Then he said, "You have something I need in order to quell the threat of mutiny."

"What did you say?" The wind had picked up.

"I said you have something I need in order to quell the threat of mutiny."

The physician sucked up a wad of snot through his bulbous nose. "Of course, of course," he replied, his breath visible in the air. He was so eager to get out of this wretched cold he probably would've agreed to anything. "What is it from me you need?"

"I need your head."

The man didn't respond, not at first. He was still looking around as before, cold and antsy to leave. But then the words slowly sank in. He stopped shivering. His eyes narrowed and fell upon Seric, as if truly questioning what he'd just heard. Seric said nothing. The two men were left looking at each other, silent while the wind screamed past. Then Zirian moved, his heavy footfalls crunching soundlessly in the snow. He seized the small physician from behind. The sudden force made Orbrey gasp. The winegourd fell from his grip.

Zirian bound the physician's hands while Seric stoppered his mouth with a rag of linen. When the man lost the ability to speak, suddenly speaking was all he wanted to do. And when he couldn't, he shook and swung his tied hands and kicked wildly at the snow. Zirian put an end to that, with a hard shove that sent Orbrey face-first to the white ground. The Zhoul then stripped off the physician's furs and unfastened his cloak. Orbrey moaned and whimpered but didn't fight back. Seric saw he had pissed himself, the steam rising in the air.

What have I done? the physician's terror-stricken eyes seemed to ask. *What have I done to deserve this?*

Seric tried to ignore it, but Orbrey wouldn't stop looking at him like that. It grew irritating. "What do you want me to say? I'm a wicked man, I know." He pushed the physician's head forward, exposing his pale neck. Orbrey gave only the slightest of twitches, like a fish long out of water, after it stopped struggling and just waited to die. Zirian's gloved hands gripped the haft of his crescent-bladed halberd. Seric motioned for it. "Let me do it."

The Zhoul handed over the weapon. It was heavy, probably a good sixty pounds, though it felt twice that in Seric's malnourished arms. Nevertheless he raised the weapon, slowly, then eased it back down, to calculate his aim. He tried to bring it back up but the goddamn thing was so heavy he ended up resting the flat of the edge on Orbrey's neck for a moment. Removing it, he took a chunk of the man's skin, leaving a blotchy patch of red on the back of his neck. The physician's muffled moans turned frantic. He wouldn't stop, by the gods he just wouldn't shut up. *Hurry, just get it over with,* Seric told himself. He gritted his teeth and took a deep breath and raised the weapon over his head. The wind gave a gentle nudge, and the blade came screaming down.

Brrrrraaaakkkkkkk. Cold steel tore through tissue and bone. The head popped off, leaving the body to squirm like a wounded snake. Blood sprayed from the open wound like a gushing red fountain in a beautiful winter garden. *Thump*. The body hit the ground, thrashed for another moment or two, then lay still. Steam rose from the open neck. Seric dropped the halberd into the snow. Even with his gloves on he saw his hands were shaking, and it wasn't from the cold.

Zirian went over to retrieve the physician's head. The goddamn thing had traveled a few good yards before finding a home in the snow. The Zhoul grasped it by a hank of thinning hair, lifting it out of its bloodstained grave. Seric's eyes wandered to Orbrey's face. He expected to see an ugly grimace, the tortured, twisted, petrified face of a man in his last agonizing moments of life . . .

But no, it was just a face, a normal and unexpressive face. Seric stared at it, taking a few moments to gather his thoughts. "I want his head on a pike in the center of camp," he said to Zirian. "Make sure it stands firm against the wind. I want every soldier to see it come dawn."

"What is the charge?" Zirian asked.

Seric took a deep breath before answering. "Physician Orbrey Lorian was punished under military law for purposefully prolonging the Imperial Advisor's injuries and preventing the march of his army. His crimes of subversion and neglect were fulfilled by death. That is the announc—" The wind howled in his face, forcing him to wait. "That is the announcement I will present to the soldiers in the morning. Understand?"

Zirian gave him a dutiful nod. "Yes, my lord."

"Good," Seric said. "I'll send word to General Wyath. Tomorrow we march to Aster Falls."

CHAPTER SIXTY-SIX

"Your hands are trembling, lord," Kirik said as he handed over the wooden cudgel. It was no longer than a backsword, with a large misshapen head covered in blunt points like a knobbed mace. A primitive weapon, fit for a primitive people.

"I'm afraid," Anseth admitted. The Vaskulti word for fear was not the same in the Anirian tongue. In truth, there was no word for a Vaskultan to express such a cowardly admission. The word Anseth had used implied a feeling of tenseness, and even that was frowned upon by Vaskultan warriors. Anseth knew this but was too afraid to care.

Kirik moved behind him to re-adjust the fit of his lord's boiled leather armor. "Don't say that. There's no place in a chieftain's heart for that."

Anseth shook his head. "How many times have you fought in the cage?'"

The man hesitated. It was a rhetorical question, since no bondsman could ever make a legitimate challenge for the Earthstone. "Well, none, but—"

"Then I'm pretty sure you shouldn't be speaking right now."

Silence broke between them for a spell. Anseth used the time to collect his thoughts, and when he finally spoke he managed to sound much calmer. "I play it over and over in my mind, and every time I find myself unable to beat him." He gave a heavy, dejected sigh. "I'm going to die today."

Kirik shook his head. "The Skybringer has kept you alive all these years. He won't let you die here."

Anseth scoffed. "Dumb luck has kept me alive. Luck that I won't have when I face that brute alone. Unless the Landforger himself reaches up and yanks that bastard to the ground, he's going to kill me."

Kirik worked silently for a moment. "Perhaps you shouldn't do this, perhaps there's some other way."

Anseth shook his head. "You know what'll happen if I don't accept the blood challenge. I'll be cast out, exiled."

"You were already planning to leave, were you not?"

Anseth turned to face his bondsman. At first he thought the young man was jesting as usual, but Kirik's reptilian face betrayed no hint of humor. "I am no coward," Anseth said. He threw on his overcoat and left before Kirik finished his adjustments. The bondsman called after him, but Anseth ignored it.

It was another cold and dreary day. The winter sky was a deep, despondent gray, like the ashes of a funeral pyre. Anseth could've smiled at that, since he was likely heading toward his own funeral. But of course, Vaskultans didn't have pyres or processions or any kind of funeral ceremony. His body would be given to the Landforger, while his soul would ascend to the Skybringer. Basically, he'd be left in the dirt to rot. Anseth shook his head and spat. A child could've developed a more complicated system of theological principles. *Stupid Vaskultans and their stupid traditions,* he thought bitterly.

His heart began to race when he observed the size of the Vaskultan crowd, thronging together about a hundred feet away. Men, women, children, all waiting to watch their beloved chieftain get his face bashed in. Upon Anseth's advance the bodies spread like river water around a stone. He could feel their eyes on him, could hear their hails and encouraging cheers. Anseth ignored it all and focused only on the cage ahead. It was not a square but a misshapen structure, its latticed walls constructed with ill-assorted bones all lashed together by heavy knots of gut and rope. Sheep bones, goat bones, human bones—all arranged in no discernable fashion, other than to perhaps look as macabre as possible. The entrance was a simple gate, nearly twice Anseth's height. It opened soundlessly under the clamor of the crowd. Anseth stepped inside.

A single Vaskultan stood waiting for him. Dariok, cudgel in hand, stretched his neck side to side and grinned like a master torturer who never missed a day of work. It was hard for Anseth to focus with all the Vaskultan spectators everywhere. They weren't just around him, they were *above* him, clinging to the bones of the overhead cage like the rungs of a ladder. Dariok seemed to relish the attention. He turned and waved his muscular arms like some heartthrob competitor in a midsummer's tourney.

Cocksure bastard, Anseth thought. He pulled out the Earthstone talisman and threw it in the dirt between them. That caught Dariok's attention. The big Vaskultan observed it for a long moment, his eyes glinting like a thief with a stolen coin purse. When he was done, he placed his gaze back on Anseth. There was nothing methodical about Dariok, nothing strategic about his mind. Anseth knew there would be no feeling-out process, no cautious circling or gauging of skill. He knew the brute would just rush forward and strike—and that was exactly what he did. But by the gods, the brute rushed *fast* and struck *hard.* As prepared as Anseth was, he scarcely had time to raise his weapon and block, and even as he did, the force of the blow knocked the cudgel right out of his hand. *That's it,* he thought. *I'm dead already.* Dariok spun like a spider on his feet and gave a great upward swing. Missed. He goddamn missed, and now the brute was off-balance. *Not done yet,* Anseth thought, as his cudgel came up—but then something exploded in his gut, and he crumpled to the dirt.

He never saw the attack. He had no idea where it came from, no idea how Dariok managed to even hit him from that angle. But none of that mattered now. He was in trouble. He couldn't get to his feet, couldn't do anything but cringe as waves of terrible pain blazed through his upper abdomen. Even with his armor on he couldn't bear it. And by the gods Anseth was no weakling—hell, no man could endure being struck in the liver like that. It completely shut a man down, rendered his body powerless. Ask any veteran soldier and he will tell you the same.

Still, his mind was clear enough, and it screamed at him to take action. *Get up, get up, get up!* Anseth rose just as the big brute's cudgel came down; the weapon *whooshed* past his head, no more than inches away. A second blow struck Anseth's shoulder, sending pain pouring down his arm. Anseth scrambled for safety, remaining on his feet despite the agony that sought to yank him to the ground. He found his weapon and snatched it up. He turned but Dariok was already upon him, cudgel smashing into Anseth's ribs.

His lungs heaved and his body quivered, but he grimaced away the pain. He retaliated with his own strike, but the larger man ate the blow like a shark, then replied with a backhanded thwack that knocked Anseth's leather helmet off his head. The world spun, shifting from sky to dirt to bones to sky to dirt. Another blow hit him and maybe one more, then Anseth dived forward into Dariok's arms, closing the distance to stop the barrage. The big man tossed him aside like a child. The bones of the cage rattled when Anseth crashed into them. He tried to dart away but Dariok cut off his angles. Anseth was trapped. He lunged at the brute again, only to be flung aside once more.

How Anseth was still standing he couldn't say. He'd been hit so many times he couldn't even tell what was hurting anymore. Dariok's ugly face split into a smug grin of triumph. Anseth tried to knock that goddamn grin off his face, but Dariok countered the blow and struck Anseth again in the ribs. But this time his cudgel became stuck in the arm of Anseth's overcoat, and when the brute couldn't pull it free, he let go of the weapon and drove a fist into Anseth's face. Another punch, and another. Anseth threw up his hands but the brute pounded his way through. The world flashed and darkened, like the flame of a sconce flickering on and off, on and off. Anseth's legs were gone but somehow he was still standing. How? Dariok was holding him against the cage, using his free hand to pound Anseth's face. On and off, on and off . . .

Then something happened. That last punch made Dariok grimace. It was the tiniest, tiniest grimace, so small that Anseth had almost missed it. But no, he didn't miss it. Dariok stepped back. He shook his wrist, like a man shaking dirt from his sleeve. Anseth got his answer. Dariok hurt his hand.

Anseth sprang forward and clobbered the brute across the face. The big Vaskultan staggered back. For the first time since the beginning of the fight, Anseth was spared a moment to breathe. Of course he had to do his breathing through the mouth, as his nose was utterly destroyed. He swallowed a lump of blood and wiped another sheet of it from his face, then turned back to defend himself from Dariok's next attack. But no, the brute hadn't come forward.

He was just standing there, taking in huge gulps of air. A thick gash empurpled the flesh above his eye, leaking red strings down his cheek. He stared at Anseth for a long moment, before deciding to press forward. He moved slower now, less determined. His focus was off. He was tired. He was probably thinking about his hand. Still, a broken hand didn't mean he was no longer dangerous, but Anseth was much quicker and not as exhausted, despite the awful thrashing he took. He hopped back to avoid the brute's tired swing, then darted in and whacked Dariok on the shoulder. Now it was Anseth moving forward, his cudgel twirling and swinging, while Dariok, for the first time, reeled backward. Anseth could see the lethargy in the man's eyes. The brute had no heart. Anseth could've laughed. Of course, he had no heart!

He drove Dariok to the cage wall, pressing him against femurs and scapulae and skulls. Anseth swung his cudgel again and again, quick as lightning, so quick he didn't even see the weapon, didn't see much of anything except the way Dariok's head threw itself this way and that, spurting blood and spit in every direction. The big Vaskultan teetered for a moment, then like a great tree he toppled over and smashed head-long to the ground. *Boom.* A ring of dust rose into the cold air.

Dariok lay still, staring senselessly up at the sky. Anseth stood over him, fingers squeezing around the blood-slick handle of the cudgel. "I *AM* the chieftain," he roared at Dariok. "*I AM the rightful CHIEF-TAAAAAIN.*" He shouted those words as his cudgel smashed down upon Dariok's face, again and again and again, until there was no face left but a lump of red pulp. Then he heaved to the sky a single, final cry, flinging the cudgel to clatter against the cage.

The crowd erupted into cheers. The sound was so sudden and so shocking to Anseth, who'd completely forgotten the spectators were even there. He staggered to where the Earthstone lay. He picked it up. The crowd cheered louder. He raised it skyward. They began chanting his name. "*LORD ANSETH! LORD ANSETH!*" No, wait, not *that* name. His Vaskultan name. "*LORD REVEK! LORD REVEK!*" Yes, that was the name they shouted. At least he thought it was. But by the gods he was too battered and bloody and half blind to know what the hell was going on. The cage opened. He tried to walk out but only got a few steps before his legs gave out. The ground rose up, not hard but soft and comforting, as if the Landforger were there to cradle his fall. He spread his arms out. He felt no pain, nothing at all, only a sense of peace, an immeasurably soothing peace, like the memory of his young mother's smile, or the embrace of his wife after returning home from an arduous campaign.

Anseth cracked a bloody smile. Dariok was dead. The Gray Plains were his. This was only the beginning.

EPILOGUE

Alarin was alone in the conservatory hall when Szathan Mordall came for him.

The giant man was a vision of colossal might as he stood by the entranceway, wearing his blackened steel armor and segmented spaulders and serrated hem general's cloak. And yet, for all his towering size, he seemed quite hesitant to approach, so Alarin got up and limped over to him. They met each other on the stone walkway where the main area of the hall branched off into the wide alcove. Szathan bowed his head but his eyes immediately wandered to the stone tiers of cloudfalls, all white and puffy like fresh dollops of flowery snow. Even as he spoke his eyes remained on them. "I do not seek forgiveness for what I did, but only for *how* I did it. I shouldn't have kept my secret heart to myself. I should've told you."

Alarin gave a soft shake of his head. "I blame myself, General, for thinking I could place an honorable man in an evil tyrant's host."

"I tried to run the bastard through," Szathan went on. "I tried but he got away. Raas Dragath always gets away from me."

"His time will yet come," Alarin told him. Szathan nodded but said nothing in reply. Behind him, a boy ambled along the walkway, gazing in wonderment at all the beautiful blossoms. Alarin gestured. "Is that . . .?"

Szathan glanced back. "Come here, Silas." The boy rushed over. He had a wooden practice sword in one hand, his pelletdrum in the other. When he saw Alarin his face broke into a smile. He looked bright and healthy, certainly better than the days in which he and Alarin and Demien were filthy and hungry and struggling across the cold snowscape. The memory of that ordeal still left a dull weight on Alarin's chest. "I've adopted him into my house," Szathan said. He mussed little Silas's hair, and the boy darted off. The big general spoke his next words slowly. "Demien would've wanted it."

Alarin could see the sorrow in his eyes. "The realm grieves for the loss of your brother."

"Some grieve, others condemn him as a traitor and a madman," he said. "What do you think?"

"I think he was an honorable man with a heavy burden."

Szathan seemed satisfied with that. "The garrisons outside the city, all are lightly manned. Where is Lord Merio?"

"On campaign with General Yuseth. He seeks revenge against the Redlands."

"Do you think he'll be enough . . .?"

Alarin told him yes, but in truth, he held little faith in his indecisive younger brother.

Thunk, thunk, thunk. The sound drew Alarin's eye. The boy was working his pelletdrum with one hand, while battling some imaginary opponent with the wooden sword in the other. Alarin observed him for a long moment, before focusing his gaze back on Szathan. "What will you do now?"

Szathan's oddly shaped head looked even odder when he frowned. "I've lost my brother, my officers, most of my soldiers. I still have my wife and sons, but I've no home to give them. You're the only one I could turn to. I'd like to settle here, unless Lord Merio won't have me."

Alarin shook his head and sighed. "I can't stay either. I'm no longer welcome in Stormhaven, not since Cathia . . ."

Szathan's tiny blackberry eyes dropped to the floor.

"I'm going north," Alarin went on, "to reunite with my brother Anseth. You are welcome to come."

His big, squarish head nodded at that. "North is where I will go."

Thunk, thunk, thunk. Silas darted past with the tireless energy that all young boys seemed to have. Szathan watched him before reaching down for something on the belt of his battledress, swiftly, as though he'd just remembered it. He untied a small satchel and handed it to Alarin. "I meant to give you this."

The satchel was of plain leather, but inside he found a box, and not just any box, but an ornate, raised-pattern box, one of imperial design. Alarin opened it. Five Sadralen stared up at him, twisted together and set in a circular inlay of silver and black jade. The Imperial Seal. "How did you get this?"

"Demien took it . . . the night the emperor was called to heaven. It's yours now, my lord. It belongs to you. I'm not meant to have it. You are."

Silas darted by. *Thunk, thunk, thunk.*

Alarin didn't know what to say. He didn't want it. He tried to tell the general that, but the big man didn't seem to be listening. "Are those cloudfalls?" Szathan asked.

"They are," Alarin said, without looking up. He used his thumb to wipe away a smear of dust from the seal's obverse. "The same flowers that shone for the First Emperor, the same that restored his vision and guided him toward the birth of the Anir dynasty and all that nonsense." He looked up. "You've read the annals, General, yes?"

"I've heard enough from storytellers. Do they really shine?"

Alarin laughed. "No."

"Might I have a closer look?"

"Yes, yes of course. I'll wait here." He watched Szathan move off, then decided to call after him. "If they do shine for you I'm giving back this seal, got that?"

Szathan held up a hand in reply. He moved down the alcove and stopped before the cloudfalls, his massive frame dwarfed by the tall tiers of stone. And fool that Alarin was, he actually looked to see if Szathan's presence might actually make the cloudfalls shine. But of course they didn't, and Alarin was left shaking his head and cursing himself. The stump of his missing leg began to throb, so he took a seat on a nearby bench. To his right, the conservatory's floor-to-ceiling open windows provided a generous view of the surrounding landscape. Spring had come quickly this year, as if eager to devour all traces of that nightmarish winter. The land now was a lush collection of verdant hills and broad trees and shimmering waterways. A magnificent sight . . . well, as magnificent as something could be when you have pain like a knife constantly stabbing you in the leg.

Silas ran by. *Thunk, thunk, thunk.* Alarin matched the sound of the boy's pelletdrum by rapping a knuckle on his wooden leg. Silas heard that and stopped, approaching shyly. *Thunk, thunk, thunk,* went his pelletdrum. *Thunk, thunk, thunk,* went Alarin's leg. They did this a few more times before the boy grinned and ran off to battle more imaginary monsters. Alarin couldn't help but smile. Something about the carefree nature of a child . . . truly, it could soften any man's heart, even this old goat's. And more, having Szathan back at his side meant he wouldn't have to search for his brother alone. Good news, because he had no idea how to find Anseth. It'd been months since he received any word, and the last incoming report of his scouts had told of a barbarian force defeating Seric Dyre at the banks of the Amber River. But then what? Where had Anseth gone from there?

Alarin looked down at the Imperial Seal. It felt good in his hand. Maybe it was meant to find him. Surely he couldn't deny the will of heaven. With the Imperial Seal he could steer this realm into the direction it was meant to go. He could stake his claim as the next emperor, and act according to the will of—

"*My lord!*"

The urgency of Szathan's shout made Alarin rise. He went over to the entrance of the alcove and saw the massive general rushing toward him. The man's tiny eyes were strangely wide, his open mouth displaying a row of gapped teeth. "My lord, I saw them—I saw them," he blurted.

Alarin tried to calm him. "What, General? What did you see?"

"The cloudfalls . . . they *moved*."

"What do you mean 'they moved'?"

"I don't know, it was only for a moment, but I saw them . . . come look."

Szathan spun and hastened back to the stone tiers, with Alarin limping behind, as fast as his cane and wooden leg could take him. Halfway down, Silas went zipping past. *Thunk, thunk, thunk.* Alarin hurried on. He reached the stone tiers. The cloudfalls were closed and motionless. Szathan kept pacing back and forth, but nothing was happening. Annoyed, Alarin said, "Does it amuse you to see an old cripple run?"

"No, my lord. I saw them. I saw them *move*." He kept pacing back and forth, back and forth, to no avail. Eventually he stopped, his great shoulders slumped, and he gave a dejected sigh.

Alarin turned and limped painfully back to the main hall. Again, Silas zipped past. *Thunk, thunk, thunk.* Alarin shook his head, irritated at the boy now, or maybe just jealous of his mobility. He cursed his stupid wooden leg, and his leg replied with a pang of lancing ache. He wanted nothing more than to sit back down on the bench, and, just as he was about to, believe it or not Szathan began shouting for him again. Alarin sighed. Normally he would've ignored it, but the pain also filled him with a deep sense of agitation, so deep that he marched back over to the entrance of the alcove and shouted, "Goddamn it, General, I'm not going over there agai—"

He stopped. All words vanished from his lips. Szathan was standing before the stone tiers, his giant frame outlined by the softest, most angelic light Alarin had ever seen. A light radiant enough to engulf the entire rear wall, but neither harsh nor blinding nor uncomfortable in any way. Just pure, white light. Like the glow of the moon, if perhaps the moon were as large as the sun.

Alarin didn't remember limping over to the cloudfalls—hell, a giant roc could've carried him there and he wouldn't have noticed. He saw only their petals now, so white and so pure, like the hands of an infant opening for the very first time. He couldn't believe what he was seeing. "How did you . . .?"

"It's not me," the general said. The light hid the expression on his face, but Alarin could see his outstretched hand pointing to his left.

Silas.

The boy stood unmoving before the cloudfalls. By the gods Alarin didn't even see him there, so small and insignificant he appeared. But the cloudfalls . . . the cloudfalls certainly saw him. The light from their opened petals bathed him, swathed him in a robe of ethereal light. Alarin called out his name. The boy turned. His mouth worked quickly, opening and closing. "I . . . can . . . speak," he said, touching his throat. It was a soft voice, mellifluous and youthful. "I . . . can speak. I can speak. My voice . . . can you hear it? Can you hear my voice?"

Alarin said, "We can." The boy smiled at that. Alarin thought of doing one thing and one thing alone. He limped closer to the boy. His leg groaned as he bent the knee. The Imperial Seal appeared in his hand. He held it up to the boy. Szathan must've seen what he was doing because he knelt as well.

"The realm is yours," Alarin said, "my lord and emperor."

THE END

ABOUT THE AUTHOR

Despite some missteps and failures, MA Liguori has always followed his passion for writing fantasy novels. He spent many years developing his craft, and his short fiction has appeared in *Heroic Fantasy Quarterly* and *New Realm Magazine*. He lives in North Carolina with his longtime partner. Aside from working as a writer, he's also a musician, a gamer, a cat lover, a college grad, and an Autism advocate.

www.ingramcontent.com/pod-product-compliance
Lightning Source LLC
Chambersburg PA
CBHW072332020726
47506CB00004B/861